NANNERL MOZART, AGE 34, 1785

Mozart's Sister

A NOVEL

NANCY MOSER

BETHANY HOUSE PUBLISHERS
Minneapolis, Minnesota

Published by Bethany House Publishers
11400 Hampshire Avenue South
Bloomington, Minnesota 55438

Bethany House Publishers is a division of
Baker Publishing Group, Grand Rapids, Michigan.

Printed in the United States of America

ISBN-13: 978-0-7642-0123-3
ISBN-10: 0-7642-0123-9

Library of Congress Cataloging-in-Publication Data

Moser, Nancy.
    Mozart's sister / Nancy Moser.
        p.   cm.
    ISBN-13: 978-0-7642-0123-3 (pbk.)
    ISBN-10: 0-7642-0123-9 (pbk.)
    1. Berchtold zu Sonnenburg, Maria Anna Mozart, Reichsfreiin von,
        1751–1829—Fiction. I. Title.
    PS3563.O88417M69   2006
    813'.54—dc22

To my husband, Mark.

The love of my life.

and

To all who live in this amazing age of opportunity,

Waste no chance to carry out your God-given purpose.

Too many have not had the luxury of *CHOICE*. . . .

～

NANCY MOSER is the bestselling author of fourteen novels, including *Crossroads,* the Christy-award winning *Time Lottery,* and the SISTER CIRCLE series coauthored with Campus Crusade cofounder, Vonette Bright.

Nancy has been married thirty-one years. She and her husband have three twenty-something children and live in the Midwest. She loves history, has traveled extensively in Europe, and has performed in various theaters, symphonies, and choirs.

To learn more about Nancy and her books, visit her Web site at *www.nancymoser.com.*

PRELUDE

*M*y brother was dead and I couldn't find his body.

I walked among the bleak mounds of the cemetery, pulling my cape close with one hand while clasping the hood tightly around my head with the other. It was too cold to be beyond the city gates of Vienna in this awful place, yet it was fitting that I was here under such conditions. To search a graveyard on a sunny day seemed wrong. Perhaps if I'd known where he lay and was bringing him a fresh spray of flowers, the sun would have been an appropriate prop. But not knowing his exact resting place, and fearing that I'd never know . . . cold air and skies that threatened rain were essential ingredients to my inner gloom. Mirroring my regret. Sustaining my sorrow. *Sostenuto. Espressivo.* An elegy for the dead.

I smiled at the terminology. My memory of the musical terms would have made our father proud. How many times had he drilled my brother and me about such things?

I walked on. There were no trees here. No tombstones. St. Marx wasn't a normal cemetery, where statues of angels and cherubs made the dead less dead. It was devoid of beauty. Yet I did not turn back but kept walking, hoping to discover some detail about my brother's final fate.

It was incomprehensible that the two most important men in my life were dead. Father and brother. Two musical impresarios, gone. It wasn't fair they'd left me such a musical legacy when there was nothing I could do to make it endure.

I could have—once. I had musical talent. I'd been a wonder-child along with my baby brother. He'd become interested in music by watching *me*. It wasn't my fault Papa had decided only one child could have center stage, only one child could be carefully sculpted for greatness. My brother. Not the girl-child who grew into a young woman too fast.

We'd started performing together in public thirty years earlier, in 1762. I was five years older than my brother, five years that accentuated his precocious talent and made mine less remarkable. If only we'd started touring when *I* was six years old and he still a baby. If only I'd had a few moments alone, basking in the glow of fame, letting the warmth of the accolades fall on me. Would Papa have pulled *me* onto his lap, looked into *my* eyes, and said, "You are an extraordinary child, Nannerl. With my help your talent will shine so kings and empresses will know your name and shake their heads in awe at your music"?

I tripped on a stone that had invaded the path. I righted my body—and my thoughts. Life wasn't fair. Otherwise, why was my brother dead at thirty-five, and me alive to . . . to do what?

The options were distressingly limited.

I was familiar with these thoughts and knew they would take me into dark corners where contentment was tightly bound and regrets had free rein. I knew I had to set them aside and get back to the task at hand.

Mound after mound of the dead.

I'd passed some nameplates on the outer wall. Perhaps . . .

"May I help you, *meine Dame*?"

I nudged the hood aside so I could see the speaker. The man was stooped, dressed poorly, and carried a shovel. "I'm searching for the grave of a relative."

"When did he die?"

"Three months ago. The mountain passes . . . I couldn't get through."

The man nodded. "There'll be no grave for him here. Not in this place. None you can visit."

"Why not?"

"You're not from Vienna, then?"

"I live in St. Gilgen."

"I don't know it."

Few did.

"It's a small town, east of Salzburg."

"Ah. It explains why you may not have heard about the law. Emperor Joseph decided people were spending too much on fancy funerals—going into debt they were, 'specially with churches over-charging. He didn't like timber being wasted on coffins neither, and seeing's how coffins slow the body going to dust . . . so a few years back he changed things. People didn't like it, and he took back some of the law, but still . . . this is the way we do it most of the time. A few blessings, the ring of a bell, then drop-drop, into a common grave they go. A few handfuls of lime and I cover 'em up." He made a sprinkling motion with his arm, then nodded around him. "These are them."

I shuddered. "So he's . . . with . . . others?"

"We can fit up to six in a hole depending on how many need burying. We been ordered to dig 'em up after seven years to make room for more."

The way his eyes sparkled . . . he clearly enjoyed my discomfort. I pointed toward the nameplates on the wall behind me. "There. May I find his name there?"

"He nobility?"

I hesitated. *He longed to be.* "No."

"Then you won't find his name."

This was unbearable. With no headstone and no marker, there could be no future flowers set in his memory, no hand on the grave-stone making the coldness of death real, no letting my gaze linger on the deeply carved letters of his name and dates.

No proof he was gone.

And I was still alive.

I spotted another mourner close by. Oddly, the man did not politely look away but kept his eyes on me. I lowered my head within the folds of the hood. I did not need an audience for my disappointment.

"Sorry to upset you," the grounds keeper said. "Even I admit it's a bad law. Maybe . . . what was your loved one's name so I can say a prayer for him?"

I hesitated, then decided it was not my place to halt any prayer for my brother's soul, even one from such a man as this. "Mozart," I said. "Wolfgang Amadeus Mozart. He was my brother. I am his sister." The last I added for vanity's sake—may God forgive me. . . .

There was the flicker of recognition on his face, but I didn't have time to study it, for suddenly the other mourner rushed toward me. His face screamed recognition.

"Mozart? You're Mozart's sister?"

I took a step back, as did the cemetery worker.

The man stopped his approach but not his query. "You're Nannerl?"

For God to reward me with recognition after I had so pridefully sought such attention just moments before . . . "Yes, I'm Nannerl," I said. I let the hood fall open so he could see my face, then pulled it tight again.

"I've been searching for his grave, his name," the man said. "I'm a writer and an admirer of his music. I have questions. So many questions."

I looked at the grounds keeper and nodded at him, giving him permission to go. He withdrew, leaving me alone with this stranger, this man in the middle of a cemetery. Yet I was not afraid nor concerned for my reputation. For who was there to see us but the dead and the grieving who were intent on their own private issues of character and situation?

The man gestured toward the exit, not twenty steps away. "Shall we, Fraulein Mozart?"

I accepted the idea of escape from this place and did not correct the name he'd connected with mine. He did not need to know that I was Frau Berchtold now: Baroness Maria Anna Walburga Ignatia Berchtold zu Sonnenburg, but simply Nannerl to all who knew me. I was the wife of a man twice widowed, the mother of six children, and far, far removed from my brother's fame.

Too far removed.

You're due the recognition. You're entitled.

But was I?

The man paused outside the cemetery walls, giving me no chance to ponder such intricacies of my worth.

"I have been remiss in not introducing myself. I'm Friedrich Schlichtegroll." He offered a tight bow.

I let the hood fall to my shoulders. The cold air took possession of the space around my head, nipping at my ears, expelling the warmth I'd so carefully hoarded. "You have questions, Herr. . . ?"

"Schlichtegroll. Your brother's music is well known, but I want to confirm some of the details of his personal life. Is his wife still living? How many children does he have? Are they well? Where do they live? Was he working on any piece of music when he died?"

Each question produced a weight, as if the gray clouds were descending downward, threatening to release my own private storm. I longed for the anonymity of the hood.

"Fraulein Mozart?"

I needed to be away. Immediately. I looked for my carriage and spotted it a short distance to the right. "If you'll excuse me." I walked quickly, praying he wouldn't follow.

I heard no other feet crunching gravel. When I glanced back, he still stood at the entrance. He raised a hand and called after me, "But, Fraulein Mozart . . . the questions are not difficult."

They shouldn't have been.

But they were.

~

I hugged the wall of the carriage, needing to feel substance around me, supporting me. If only the far wall were close enough to push against my free side to contain me completely, to put a limit to the breadth of my regret.

The jostling of the carriage on the cobblestone streets of Vienna prevented me from the oblivion of rest. *Apropos.* I did not look out the window as the world sped by. I did not deserve to be a part of it.

I heard rain against the carriage roof. It was inevitable the sky overflowed, letting the tears of God rain down on me. For surely the Almighty grieved at the distance that had developed between the brother and sister Mozart.

How could two siblings who had been bound as one, who thought as one, whose lives played out as if they were one being, lose contact like two appendages of the same body amputated so that neither could function fully?

Tears demanded escape and I let them come, for each one represented a wasted moment as Wolfgang and I had lived our lives apart.

The carriage came to a stop at an intersection. I leaned forward and saw two children rush by in the rain, urged on by their father—the older one a girl, the younger a boy. Both smiled and laughed while their father's face showed his opinion that rain was serious business. *Hurry, hurry, we have places to be.*

Two proud and happy children. Proud and happy for good reason.

Like the Mozart children.

Had been.

Once.

OVERTURE

~

Chapter One

A bow from Wolfie and a curtsy from me.

Applause. So much applause.

I glanced at my little brother and he winked at me. I wanted to stick my tongue out at him—and if we had been at home, that's exactly what I would have done. But we were not at home practicing. We were not even in our hometown of Salzburg. And though Papa and Mama were in the audience, there were even more important people to impress here in Vienna. Dukes and duchesses, counts and countesses by the dozens.

As Wolfie took another bow—he liked bowing; he liked sweeping his right arm to the side dramatically, as he'd seen grown-up courtiers do—I looked in the direction of Empress Maria Theresa and her husband, Emperor Francis. They were the rulers of the Holy Roman Empire, of all Austria, Hungary, and Bohemia. They sat in the front row, and it was their applause that mattered. They were a golden couple, dressed like heavenly angels in white brocade with gold trim. Yet they were not scary and stern as I'd imagined the rulers of an empire to be. Although their silk-covered chairs were a bit more grand than other chairs in the room, they were not massive thrones as I'd expected. And the empress and emperor were not giants in the land, as one would think. They were quite short— Papa was taller than both—and I'd noticed them fidgeting in their seats, and even scratching under their powdered wigs. Like real people. And though at first I'd found this disconcerting, it had also eased my nerves. As for Wolfie? He didn't have nerves and always played well. Actually, neither of us had made a single error while playing our sonatas on the clavier.

The applause began to fade, and the emperor leaned forward and rested his elbows on the carved arms of his chair. He pointed his finger at us. "Bravo, children. Yes indeed, bravo. But . . ." He surveyed the room with a smile, like a boy scheming mischief, and everyone gave him their attention. "It is no great art to play with all your fingers, but if you could play with only one and on a covered keyboard, that would be something worthy of admiration."

Papa had taught us such tricks, but before I had time to choose which trick to do first, Wolfie ran to the keyboard and began playing a Scarlatti sonata with one finger, just as His Majesty had requested. Wolfie's stubby little finger moved swiftly over the keyboard, more swiftly than I had ever seen him play. He did not miss a single note.

I glanced at Papa. He smiled at Wolfie.

I would do the next trick and earn my own smile. The worn leather satchel in which we carried our music held a length of cloth we could use to cover the keys. As my brother received his applause with another grand bow, I retrieved the cloth and stepped toward the keyboard. But Papa snatched the cloth from my hand like a magician pulling a scarf from his sleeve.

He made a great show of covering the keyboard, then adjusted the blue satin pillow Wolfie sat upon in order to reach the keys. With a sweep of his hand, Papa backed away and bowed to Emperor Francis.

"Your wish is our command, Your Majesty."

Through the cloth, Wolfie began to play Haydn's Sonata Number 5 in C. The lords and ladies gasped and clapped. We did this all the time at home, but I was not surprised they thought Wolfie clever. After all, he was only six. If Papa would let me play one of the *really* difficult songs, I'd let them see what five additional years of lessons had taught me.

Without warning, Wolfie stopping playing. He looked left, then right, as if in search of something. "Where is Herr Wagenseil? They said he would be here."

Silence enveloped the room as everyone stared at Wolfie, then glanced uneasily at one another. Mama looked horrified, and I could feel my own face growing warm. Wolfie hadn't learned when to speak and when to keep silent.

Papa stepped forward, his face and neck a deepening red against the white lace of his jabot. "Forgive him, Your Majes—"

The empress laughed and snapped her fingers. "Summon Herr Wagenseil at once!"

The room buzzed with low whispers as two footmen hurried out. Within minutes a man with a long, wavy wig entered and bowed grandly before the emperor and empress.

"Well, court composer," said the empress to Herr Wagenseil, "our young Mozart has requested your presence." She extended a hand toward Wolfie, who was sitting at the clavier.

Herr Wagenseil raised an eyebrow but, with a bow to Her Majesty, moved toward Wolfie—who scooted over on the bench, making room for him. The composer sat next to my brother, his smile uncertain, his eyes flitting across the audience. There was a hint of disapproval in his expression, as if he did not completely regard his summons with pleasure.

"Well, young Mozart," the man said, "what shall I play for you?"

"Oh no, sir," Wolfie replied. "I am going to play one of *your* concertos, and you must turn the pages for me."

The room was silent except for Herr Wagenseil's intake of breath. No one moved—until the empress laughed. "Indeed, Herr Wagenseil. Turn the pages for our young impresario."

Wolfie did justice to the court composer's piece, but I noticed that even though Papa was nodding and smiling, his eyes were angry. We would pay for making Papa angry.

After Wolfie finished and everyone applauded, he got so excited he jumped off the pillowed bench and ran toward the empress. *Don't run! Wolfie, don't run!* He hadn't taken a bow, had hardly acknowledged the applause at all.

Before he could reach Her Majesty, he tripped over the edge of a Persian rug and fell to the marble floor with an *oomph*. I moved to help him up, but the empress's daughter Marie Antonie—who was no older than he—was there first, taking his arm, pulling him to his feet.

Wolfie thanked the little girl, then added, "When I grow up I will marry you."

At first no one reacted. Then nervous laughter sped about the room. I wanted to slip away and hide. Why couldn't he behave?

But then, turning away from the archduchess, Wolfie seemed to remember why he was running in the first place, and ran up to the empress Maria Theresa herself and climbed into her lap. Then he put his arms around her neck and kissed her.

I couldn't move. Neither did anyone else. The man and woman behind me snickered and someone whispered, "The child presumes too much." Mama took hold of Papa's arm, and I saw his jaw twitch.

But then . . . to everyone's surprise, the empress hugged Wolfie back—and kissed him. The guests clapped, and my little brother was showered with praise and verbal tokens of affection. I would never cease to marvel at how Wolfie always ended up the darling.

That took talent.

~

Mama and Papa sat across from Wolfie and me in the carriage as we left Vienna's Schönbrunn Palace. With Mama's fancy dress and the bulk of my parents' cloaks, they didn't have much room, yet the one time I'd suggested Mama sit with Wolfie and I sit with Papa, my idea had received a stern dismissal. "You two squirm and fiddle too much. We would never have any peace."

It wasn't I who squirmed. I sat very still with my hands in my lap just like Mama. At eleven, my feet didn't touch the floor of the carriage as yet, and they sometimes skirted numbness from dangling. To escape their ache I might move, yet every time Papa flashed me a look, I was still.

Wolfie moved all the time. He constantly climbed onto his knees to see outside, played with the drapes at the window, or kicked the underside of the seat with his heels. Over and over Papa told him to be still.

When Papa sighed deeply and looked directly at us, I knew it was time for Wolfie to be punished for what he'd said to Herr Wagenseil, as well as for running and sitting on the lap of the empress. I reached for his hand, ready to comfort him.

"You did well today, children."

It took me a moment to realize Papa wasn't mad. His pleasure made me bold. "Papa, I wanted to do what Wolfie did," I said. "I wanted to play with one finger and with the cloth. Why didn't I get a turn?"

"Complaining does not become you, Nannerl," Mama said.

Papa's eyes held mine. "We . . ." He turned his gaze to Wolfie, but my brother had his feet on the seat and was playing with his shoe buckles. Papa waited for him to pay attention. When he didn't, I pushed Wolfie's feet to the floor and nodded toward Papa. Finally Wolfie looked at him.

Papa cleared his throat. "*We* must all work together to earn a living. That means adapting to each audience. Who does what is not important. We all must do our part."

"Part, sna-dart, pa-fart." Wolfie giggled.

Mama gave him a stern look to quiet him, then leaned forward and touched my knee. "You should be grateful for any opportunity to use your God-given gifts, Nannerl."

I was. If only Papa would let me use them more.

Mama and Papa started talking to each other about our schedule. Wolfie poked me in the side, then pulled his cheeks down and out. "Look, I'm Emperor Francis."

With a sideways glance at Papa, I giggled. Emperor Francis did have big jowls.

Then Wolfie hit his palm with his fist three times. He wanted to play rock-paper-scissors. I joined in, yet while Mama and Papa talked, I listened.

Mama touched Papa's arm. "Dear one, I noticed the empress called you the Kapellmeister of Salzburg. Since you are *not* the head conductor, you should have corrected her."

"I could not correct the empress!" Papa glanced in our direction, then lowered his voice. "Besides, that post *is* open. As is the post of Vice Kapellmeister, which I expect to obtain when Lolli gets promoted. It's only logical the archbishop will let me fill Lolli's place." He sighed and rubbed his hands against his thighs. "On that subject, I'm glad His Grace gave me a leave of absence to tour with the children, but I *am* afraid decisions are being made back home without me."

"You think the archbishop will make a decision on the positions before we return?"

Papa patted the pocket of his cape. "I'm urging our friend Hagenauer to pass round these letters I send him. Soon everyone will know of our success and know we are effective ambassadors for Salzburg. I still prefer Salzburg to all other places, but I must not be held back. I will not."

Mama took his hand and smiled. "*We* won't be, dear one."

He shook his head. "Time is against us. The children are growing. . . ." He sighed. "Ever growing."

"It will all work out." She leaned her head against his shoulder.

"For now," Papa said. "For now."

I'd stop growing if I could. For Papa.

~

I thought staying at an inn was fun. Papa . . . did not. One morning he stood near the window, adjusting the ruffles of his shirt under his waistcoat. "Have you ever noticed how this lodging is a thousand feet long and one foot wide?"

I hadn't paid much attention, but now that he'd made such a comment . . . it did seem strangely narrow compared to our Salzburg apartment.

He looked in the small mirror near the door, angling to see his cravat. Frustrated at not being able to see more than one portion of his torso at the same time, he sighed. "But at least we are in Vienna. That is something."

I liked Vienna. It was much larger than Salzburg. The streets were constantly alive with wagons and horses and people going by. There was a pub next door and I heard people singing—though not very well. And the guest in the room beside us liked to argue with his wife late at night. Mama said not to listen, but how could I not?

I tried to figure out what they were arguing about, but it was in French and was beyond what Mama had taught me.

It was never quiet here. Never.

His morning dressing complete, Papa arched his back and groaned. "A narrow room, and marginal beds."

I thought the beds were quite comfortable. Mama and I shared one, and Wolfie shared with Papa. That was part of the fun. We all shared a bedchamber at home too, though there I shared a bed with Wolfie. On the road I was glad to be rid of his fidgeting.

Papa pointed a finger at my brother, who was on his stomach retrieving a red top from under our bed. "You, young man, have sharp elbows. You throw me out of the bed with all your pushing."

I laughed. Mama touched the tip of my nose. "You are no better, Nannerl." She picked up the brush and patted our bed. I sat and she began to brush my hair. She shivered. "I do wish I'd brought along my fur cape. It's cold. Could we have it sent from Salzburg?"

"To send it by mail coach would be too costly. And it might get spoilt," Papa said. He moved toward us and kissed the top of her head. "But I shall have a new one made for you. Would you like that?"

A new fur for Mama when she had one at home? Papa didn't spend money on such things. Had someone paid us well for one of our concerts?

Mama raised her face for another kiss. I looked away, but in truth I liked seeing my parents in love. Back home, I didn't see many shows of such affection. But back home we weren't together as much. During the days Papa had his duties in the archbishop's orchestra playing the violin, and Mama had our household to run. On the road we were always together. Always.

I glanced at my brother, who lay on his back on the floor, his feet straight in the air, trying to balance the top on the bottom of his shoe. Wolfie was a handful. Being older, I tried to help with him as much as I—

There was a knock on the door of our room. Papa answered. It was the innkeeper. He nodded a greeting to Mama, then pointed downstairs excitedly. "You have a visitor, Herr Mozart. He says he's the privy paymaster?"

"I shall be down directly." When Papa looked back at us, his eyes gleamed. "Now we'll see how much the emperor and empress liked your playing." With one last look in the mirror, he left us.

Wolfie turned on his stomach and spun the top on the floor, where it hit the leg of a chair and rattled to a stop. He let it lie and hopped to his feet. "Do you think there are presents? I like presents best."

So did I, but I knew money was better for the family.

Mama finished tying a ribbon in my hair. She stood and held out her hands to us. "Come. We must pray for God's blessings."

And lots of money.

Although Mama moved her lips she prayed silently. I could tell Wolfie wasn't praying because he was staring at the door, waiting for Papa. I too found it hard to concentrate on my heavenly Father while waiting for my earthly one to return.

Footsteps sounded in the hall. Mama dropped our hands and we all turned to face the door. Papa came in, smiling broadly. He carried two huge boxes. "First, I present to you gifts for the children."

He set the boxes on the bed. Wolfie pulled the red ribbon without asking, but I looked up at Papa. "May I?"

"You may."

I carefully removed the emerald-colored ribbon on the second box and handed it to Mama for later use in my hair. Then I removed the lid. And pulled in a breath. Inside was a white dress so beautiful I was hesitant to touch it. Certainly, it was made for a princess, not an ordinary girl like me. It had pink lace and silver braid at the neck and at the bottom of the sleeves and hem, and tiny ruffles around the neck.

"Oh, Nannerl," Mama said. "It's magnificent. A broche taffeta. And look at all the fine trimmings."

Wolfie had his box open too. His was a coat, vest, and breeches. "Mine's purple!"

Although it was hard to pull my eyes away from my own present, I glanced at his—and corrected him. "It's lilac," I said. His suit had wide gold trim and satin cuffs. It was very beautiful, but not as beautiful as mine.

But as I took the dress out of the box, I was horrified to see it looked too small.

Mama held it up to me. "Oh dear," she said. "Last year this would have fit you, but not now." She looked up at Papa. "Perhaps we can exchange . . ."

I knew it was awkward. One did not exchange gifts from royalty.

Papa confirmed my fears. "The note says Wolfie's suit was made for the son of the empress, Archduke Maximilian," Papa said. "And yours, Nannerl, was from the wardrobe of one of her daughters."

The empress and emperor had eleven daughters. I wondered which one had worn the dress. The dress I would never get to wear. Mama touched my cheek. Her eyes were kind.

As if to rub it in, Wolfie proclaimed, "I will wear my suit forever!" He put on the coat and turned in a circle. It fit him perfectly.

Mama put a hand on his shoulder, quieting him. "You will wear it until you grow too big."

"Which, unfortunately, will be too soon," Papa said sternly. But then his face changed. He smiled and pulled out a small velvet pouch. "I have received something even better than beautiful costumes."

Money! The disappointment of the dress was forgotten.

Mama held out her hand, her voice breathy. "How much?"

He put the pouch behind his back. "First, you must know the best news. His Majesty the Emperor has requested we remain in Vienna a little longer."

"You said yes, of course," Mama said.

He made a little bow. "Of course. His Majesty will summon us soon. But until then . . ."

He emptied the pouch onto the bed. Mama knelt beside the mattress, staring at the coins. "So much!"

"One hundred ducats," Papa said. "Nearly two years of my violinist's salary back in Salzburg."

Wolfie ran his hands through the money, lifting it up, dropping it, making the coins clink and clatter. I reached out and took a coin I'd helped earn. I recognized the empress on its face, wearing a crown and standing with an orb-topped scepter and a sword. She looked prettier in person.

"In addition to your fur cape, I plan on buying us our own coach," Papa said. "With all our engagements, we've been needing a carriage two, three, even four times a day. Even when someone has been kind enough to provide the carriage, the tips to the driver and the footmen amount to the same expense as a hire."

"If you think it's necessary. . . ." Mama stood. "And toward that end, I could forgo the new fur."

"Nonsense." Papa turned to us. "But remember, you children must play well to continue to earn such generous payments."

I would. I would play very well indeed.

~

Mama sat on the edge of Wolfie's bed, stroking his hair, and blotting his forehead with a coarse towel. Papa stood in the doorway and I stood behind him in the hall, peeking around his arm. The doctor had told me to stay away or I would get sick too. Sickness was a shadow on our travels, always close, often distinct, but sometimes hiding in dark places.

"Well?" Papa said.

Mama put a finger to her lips and whispered. "He cannot go out, Leopold. The doctor says it's scarlet fever. Plus he's getting new teeth, so that pain, added to the other . . ."

Wolfie opened his eyes. "My back aches, Papa." It was hard to understand him because his tongue and cheeks were swollen. He had a rash on his neck and down his body. It was red like he had been in the sun too long, and Mama said it felt like Papa's cheek before he shaved.

"You look horrid," I said.

"That's not nice," Mama said.

But it was true.

"It's been nearly two weeks," Papa said. "This sickness has cost us fifty ducats at least."

While Wolfie had been sick, I'd seen Papa's worry and heard him making his excuses to people who wanted us to perform. I tugged on the sleeve of his coat. "I could go, Papa. I could perform."

"Sorry, Papa," Wolfie croaked.

"Shh," Mama told him. "Just get well, *liebchen*."

Wolfie closed his eyes and Mama tiptoed toward us, shooing us into the hallway. She closed the door. "Nannerl, go tell the innkeeper we need more towels."

I looked up at Papa. "I could perform, Papa. I'm very healthy."

Papa gave me a nudge. "Do as you're told, Nannerl."

I had no choice but to obey. I went down to the bend in the hall, but there I stopped and listened.

"You must not make the boy feel guilty for being sick, Leopold," Mama said quietly. "He is just a child."

"Which is one of the main reasons he has any musical venues at all."

He. Papa said "he". . . . .

Papa continued. "As soon as he's well enough, I plan to take him into public, for a stroll perhaps. The festival of St. Charles is coming up next week. If I take him out so people can see him, they'll know he's available for engagements."

"The doctor said his rash may last a long time—even when he seems well. People may think it's smallpox and will want nothing to do with him. Perhaps it would be better to wait until he is completely—"

"We cannot wait!" Papa's voice came out in a hiss. "Our time of favor is fleeting. We mustn't waste it."

I heard his footsteps coming toward me and I ran downstairs. Mama needed more towels.

Chapter Two

I didn't know the man and I didn't like him.

I was waiting to perform for the emperor and empress in Vienna one last time. Mama was busy straightening Wolfie's wig, and Papa was talking to an important-looking man I'd heard speak French— something about playing in Paris? Other people stood around the Mirror Room of Schönbrunn Palace, chatting as they waited to be seated. Standing amid the crowd, the man knocked my ear with an elbow as he stepped around me. He didn't turn around and ask for my pardon. He didn't even notice me.

For now. But as soon as I played . . . he'd notice me then, and know that I was not a normal child dressed like a miniature adult but an extraordinary girl with great talent. No one would ignore me after we played.

The man, who now stood in front of me, whispered to the man beside him. "Did you hear that the empress is not amused by the father's exploitation of his children? The boy's been sick, yet he was seen being paraded through town by his parents like a fine cut of meat for the market. Her Majesty calls it an 'aggressive hunt for ducats.'"

The second man raised a finger. "Those who cannot succeed according to their own attributes must find other ways of rising above their station, but . . . but . . ." He wagged his finger and made a *tsk-tsk* sound.

The first man snickered. "*But* they'd best be careful not to offend those with deep pockets at the risk of descending far below where they started."

"I hear Archbishop Schrattenbach in Salzburg is perturbed with the father for extending his leave of absence."

"Ah," said the first man again. "The archbishop is grumbling into the wind. The depth of *his* pockets can never compete with those of royalty."

"Ducats, O mighty ducats. How great is thy draw."

"And dangerous is thy temptation."

The crowd began to move and the men walked away.

But their words remained. They shouldn't talk about Papa that way.

~

Salzburg, home, sweet home! We came around the bend in the road and saw the Fortress Hohensalzburg sitting splendidly upon the precipice, embraced between the magnificent mountains and our city by the river.

I ran up the stairs into our third-floor apartment and was immediately met by smells I knew and loved: the smell of the wood polish Frau Hagenauer used on the banister, the sooty smell of the front room where the fireplace had never worked well, and the smell of warm cherries and fruit from the stollen bread Frau Hagenauer had made for us. We'd been gone three and a half months.

Papa directed the driver to bring in our luggage. We had a new carriage now, one of our very own. It was quite grand and Papa said it cost twenty-three ducats. He must have loved us very much to spend such money on us.

Mama held Wolfie's hand and led him right up to bed. Wolfie walked as if every step was an effort. After performing at the palace that last time, we'd accepted an invitation from some Hungarian nobility to perform in Pressburg. Although it was only a twenty-kilometer drive, the weather had been foul and fierce. Even the post-bags had trouble getting across the Danube, and the frozen road was bumpy and full of ruts. Wolfie and I could have had fun with all the jostling, but he hadn't felt well and had spent the whole trip home under Mama's arm, rubbing his fingers up and down the fur trim of her new cape. I worried about him. Papa said Wolfie's sickness had set us back four weeks.

Papa had also been sick for a short while. He'd had a toothache that made his face swell so much he called himself a trumpeting angel. Yet his illness hadn't held us back as much as the weather.

But now we were home!

Mama appeared at the top of the stairs. "We must send for the doctor."

"Is that necessary?" Papa asked.

She descended the stairs and flashed him a look I rarely saw. "In Vienna we took him out too soon, then undertook the journey to Hungary . . . he was not strong enough. It's cost him." She lowered her voice. "And us."

"But I must pay my respects to the archbishop."

"I wish you had not offered him so many excuses. His patience is surely tested."

"I needed to say *something* in order for us to take advantage of the opportunities offered us."

"He's a smart man, Leopold. He will see through the deceptions."

"Let's hope not. Our future depends on him."

Mama nodded toward me, then looked upstairs. "I know you want the promotion—I know it's a dream—but our future depends on other assets."

Papa angled his body so his back was to me, but I heard his words. "With a little skill and God's blessings, both assets can be intertwined. After all, they are what they are because of my instruction."

Mama turned to go upstairs. "The doctor, Leopold. Now."

~

Papa sighed with relief. "So it's not smallpox," he said to the doctor. "The Hagenauers had smallpox and I was afraid—"

"Not smallpox." The doctor patted Wolfie's forehead with a damp cloth.

"But his legs," Mama said. "He is swollen and paralyzed from his knees to his toes."

"That will pass," the doctor said.

As we watched, Wolfie thrashed his head back and forth and moaned. Oh, that it was I who was sick! I was stronger than he was. I would not have let myself be sick so long.

The doctor motioned Mama and Papa to the door where I was standing. I moved into the hall to give them room and was glad they did not shoo me away.

"He has rheumatic fever."

Mama put a hand to her mouth. "Will he recover?"

The doctor lifted his shoulders, then dropped them. "Unfortunately, the illness often produces a weakened heart that may permanently affect him . . . plus, he may be susceptible to this disease all his life."

All his life? I wanted my brother well; I wanted him pulling my hair, making me climb after him under the furniture. I wanted to play music with him. We were a team. The Wunderkinder—the miracle children. I was half without his whole.

The doctor gave Mama a paper packet of powder. "Give him this and keep him comfortable. I'll be back tomorrow."

Mama and Papa showed the doctor out, leaving me alone with my brother. Although they'd told me to stay away, I couldn't. Not when he looked so small in the bed. He was smaller than most six-year-olds—which was to our advantage while performing. But now, sick in bed . . . I wished him large and strong. I moved beside him and dipped the cloth in the water and wrung it out just as I'd seen Mama do. I placed it on his forehead.

He opened his eyes. He smiled. "Horseface . . ."

"I'm here, Wolfie. I'll always be here."

He managed a nod, then closed his eyes.

One thing would never change. He was my brother. Forever and always.

～

Papa was now the assistant conductor. The Vice Kapellmeister.

The table for our party was set with bread, cheese, meat, and cake. The apartment was crowded with guests, including my friend

Katherl. There were members from Papa's orchestra present, and some of Mama's friends from church. I wondered—but I did not ask—if Archbishop Schrattenbach himself would come. When we'd first returned from Vienna nearly eight weeks previous, he was peeved at Papa for being gone so long but seemed pleased with us now. When Wolfie and I played for him earlier that evening—February 28, which was his birthday—he patted our heads and called us special children who were bringing honor to Salzburg.

I didn't know about honor, but Papa and Mama were proud, and that was enough.

One of the musicians offered a toast. "To Vice Kapellmeister Mozart! May his direction be inspired, may our music transcend earthly bounds, and may his patience be bestowed by the very realms of heaven."

Everyone laughed and Katherl and I did too, even though we weren't sure about the joke. Katherl and I snuck food and whispered about whose dress we liked better (Frau Kraus wore my favorite: a pale blue satin with tiny bows like a ladder up the front.) Yet that sport soon paled and we escaped to the bedchamber. I had something important I wanted to tell her.

We sat on the window seat and I gave her an extra shawl against the draft. "So?" she asked. "What's the big secret?"

I glanced at the door one last time. "Papa is planning to take Wolfie and me on a Grand Tour."

"What's that?" Katherl asked.

"We're traveling to Paris, to London, then to Venice . . ." I took a fresh breath. "And maybe even to Rome."

"To play?"

I nodded. "We've been practicing very hard. Papa's even had Wolfie practice the violin."

"When did he start playing violin?"

"Just a few weeks ago. When Papa and his quartet were practicing here, Wolfie asked to play second violin. Papa told him no, he didn't want his chicken-scratching to interfere with their rehearsal. But Wolfie wept and had such a fit that the second violinist told Papa he didn't mind. So Papa gave his permission but told Wolfie to play quietly. Wolfie took up his tiny violin and proceeded to play with the group—well enough that the second violinist stopped his own playing in amazement. No one had taught Wolfie how to play. It was a miracle. I was watching from the hall and I saw Papa cry."

"Are you playing violin too?"

The instrument didn't interest me. But I thought of something else I could brag about. "I've been singing more."

Katherl drew her knees to her chest and tucked her dress around her shoes. "Those cities you mentioned . . . I can't imagine going to places like that."

"Papa is making arrangements for us to play at Versailles, before King Louis the Fifteenth."

"Who's he?"

I wasn't surprised she didn't know. If not for our travels and all the teaching Mama and Papa did while we were in the carriages, I might not have known. "He's like our empress, but he rules France. And we hope to play before royalty in London too. Papa and Mama have been working very hard to arrange it."

"But why is it a secret?"

I leaned toward her and whispered. "The archbishop would need to give us permission. And now, with Papa's new position . . ."

"Oh." Katherl put a hand to her mouth.

"Papa already fears the archbishop suspects. We've needed to get letters of introduction and . . ." I shrugged.

"But if he knows, why did he give your father the promotion?"

I'd never thought of that. "Maybe the archbishop wants Papa to have a title—'the Vice Kapellmeister of Salzburg'—so people will know we're from Salzburg, that we belong to him."

"Belong to him. That doesn't sound like a pretty position."

It didn't, but I was learning it was the way of the world. "We must have support, benefactors, money—"

"This is too odd. People of power coming to see you, to hear you . . ."

"And Wolfie."

Katherl shook her head. "Your little brat of a brother."

"He's very talented. People say so all the time."

"What do they say about you?"

I thought back to our trip to Vienna and Hungary. The applause, the smiles, the compliments. Wolfie had gotten most of the attention, yet I'd received my share.

"Nannerl? What do they say about you?"

"They say I'm greatly skilled at the keyboard and that my talent at accompanying is extraordinary." I was not lying. Such things had been said.

Katherl again drew up her knees. "But accompanying someone else . . . that's not very glamorous."

I resented her words. Katherl knew little about music, and for her to minimize the skill that I needed in order to accompany another musician . . . "There is much more to playing the clavier than playing written music. Do you realize with accompanying there is often nothing written out but the bass line—the left hand? There *might* be a few notations as to a suggested harmony, but it is up to me to fill in the music, at the proper volume, style, and harmony for the soloist—often instantly. I've heard it said that Bach questioned whether the soloist or the accompanist deserves the greatest glory. And Papa told me that women often play better than men because they are more sensitive to the needs of the music, and—"

Katherl laughed and held up her hands, stopping my words. "I give up. I give in. I was mistaken. Enough. Enough."

I felt my face redden. I hadn't meant to get so emotional. I was agreeable to Wolfie learning the violin *and* with the accolades he received. After all, Papa was taking both of us on the Grand Tour. He loved me just as much as he loved—

Suddenly the door opened. "Boo!" Wolfie jumped into the room, his hands curled into claws. His mouth was dirty with cake crumbs.

"You're a mess, brother."

He ran a finger along his lips, looked at it, then licked it clean. "I came to tell you someone brought a new cake. An apricot torte. If you don't hurry, I'm going to eat it all myself!"

And he was gone. I heard his feet pounding down the stairs.

I stood. "Shall we?"

Katherl and I went downstairs, our elbows intertwined like two ladies.

~

The daylight streamed through the window, and I angled my body so the paper on the worktable suffered no shadows. Papa had given me a music theory lesson, and I wanted to finish it before dinner.

Wolfie sat at the clavier in the corner, practicing. I didn't recognize the piece. Apparently, neither did Mama because she looked up from the pile of papers in her lap and said, "What song is that, Wolferl?"

He didn't stop playing. "My own." He tilted his head back and sang along with *fa-la-la*s, making his voice sound a harmony with his fingers.

"As I've told you before, you need to write it down," Papa said.

Wolfie continued to play. "I'll remember."

Papa's voice became stern. "Write it down."

Wolfie stopped playing. "It's not my tune. It's Haydn's. I just made it better."

"Don't be impertinent," Mama said.

"I thought I recognized the basic tune," Papa said. "And I agree. It is better." He pointed at me. "Nannerl, bring your brother some paper." Then to Wolfie he said, "You write it down. But remember, I want you to continue writing your own music. Original music."

I brought him a piece of staffed paper. He curled it over his head like a bonnet and giggled.

"Wolfgang!" Papa said.

Wolfie slipped off the bench and lay on his stomach on the floor. His legs were bent at the knee, in constant motion.

Papa pointed to my place by the window. "The table, young man. I will not have you using quill and ink on your mother's rug. Nannerl, make room."

I scooted over but didn't want to. I'd never be able to concentrate with him sharing the table. It was hard enough to work with Papa and Mama talking about the details of the Grand Tour. Letters of credit and introduction, lodging arrangements, discussions of which music and clothing to pack for all possible occasions. I wanted to help plan too.

Wolfie sat in the chair across from me, placing the sheet of staff paper directly on top of my work. I moved it. He moved it back.

I saw Papa hold a map between himself and Mama. He pointed to a city. "I would like to winter in Paris the first year."

The first year?

"Why Paris?" Mama asked.

"Because there will be plenty of money to be earned there. Travel is easier in the warm months, but during that time much of the nobility leave for their summer palaces, wreaking havoc on concert life. So we must plan to be in town when they are."

Mama lifted a list from her lap. "And I've made a listing of the special days of celebration at all the courts. Our patrons tend to be more generous at such times."

Papa smiled. "Especially if we can perform on their name day."

Mama pointed to the list. Apparently, she'd already noted such things. My name day was coming up soon. Actually, since Mama and I shared the given names Maria and Anna, we also shared the same day of celebration. St. Anne's day was July 26.

Papa sat back and perused the map with a sigh. "It's imperative we be organized."

Mama put a hand on his arm. "You are nothing if not that, dear one."

They were a good pair and worked together well. I wanted to have such a marriage someday. Perhaps after making a name for myself as a musician.

Wolfie kicked me under the table, then made a funny face.

Traveling with Mama and Papa would be fun, but traveling with my little brother—for over a year? I prayed God would give me patience. A double dose.

Chapter Three

I had little concept of the depth and breadth of the details for our trip, our Grand Tour of Europe. What I heard Papa and Mama say about lodging, horses, routes, and venues was noted but neatly discarded with a certainty that someone was handling what needed to be handled. Papa said adjustments would have to be made according to weather, opportunity, and the cooperation—or noncooperation—of our concert patrons. Yet how did one plan for a trip that would take years? Yes, years. For the "one year" I'd heard mentioned had been extended to many. To think I would start the journey as a child within a month of my twelfth birthday and wouldn't return until I was a young woman. . . . It scared me, but there wasn't anything I could do about it. Papa knew best.

Our Grand Tour began in June of 1763, with a trip to Munich.

The carriage was heavy with luggage. We had a servant along to help as a general domestic and hairdresser. His name was Sebastian Winter. The driver and coachman would trade off when we stopped for new horses and to rest, but Sebastian would stay with us for a while. I was glad. He was a nice man who did animal imitations. Wolfie liked his pig noises. I preferred Sebastian's rooster and could not rightly tell it from the feathered form.

When we began we were all in great spirits, and after a few hours of riding Mama started us singing songs. Wolfie sang very loudly and didn't care much about the right notes. He sang beyond the melody, making up harmony. At first it was annoying, but I eventually chose to like it, for it allowed me the melody. I found Papa smiling, even though he didn't join in.

Then suddenly, the coach dipped to the left, sending me into Wolfie's lap! Papa and Mama fell toward us, making our arms and legs bump and pinch.

"Whoa! Whoa!" the driver yelled.

There was a horrible sound of wood splintering and metal hitting rock. The carriage stopped but was tipped precariously.

"Oh no . . . Leopold?" Mama said.

"What happened?" I asked.

Papa helped Mama back in her seat and held on to the door of the carriage to keep himself in place. "This is *not* what we need. Not when we've only just begun."

"What broke?" Wolfie asked.

"The wheel. Obviously the wheel." Papa looked mad, but I knew he wasn't mad at us. He flung open the door on the low side and jumped out. Wolfie and I crowded together to look out the window.

"It's gone, completely broke to pieces," Sebastian said.

Papa rubbed the spot above his eyebrows. "One of my friends warned me the wheels were not in good shape, but since I'd just bought the carriage . . ." He sighed. "Expenses. Unforeseen expenses. This is not an auspicious beginning."

Sebastian and the driver looked down the road. "We passed a mill a ways back. Perhaps we can find help to—"

Papa waved them away. "Go. See what you can do."

I heard their footsteps on the road, running back the way we'd come. Papa looked at us and blinked, as if only now remembering we were there.

"Come. Come out." He helped Mama down first, then me, then Wolfie. Mama and I held our skirts above the dust of the road.

We looked at the wheel. All that was left were little pieces attached to the metal hub.

"What are we going to do?" Mama asked.

Papa knelt beside the carriage, looking underneath. "We wait."

"Yippee!" Wolfie ran off the road into the brush and picked up a stick. He pointed it like a sword. *"En garde!"*

I looked to Papa. "Can we play?"

He nodded and Mama said, "Don't get dirty, and stay close."

I found my own sword and defended myself.

～

What started out as an adventure wasn't fun at all. We had to wait by the side of the road for over an hour until Sebastian and the driver returned with help. Then the wheel they brought was too small and too long in the hub. Papa and Sebastian had to fell a small tree to bind in front of the wheel so it would not run away. They broke up the smashed wheel to take the metal with us to the next town of Wasserburg, where we could get it fixed properly, but even that they had to tie underneath. And Papa and Sebastian had to walk so as not to strain the carriage.

We didn't get into town until midnight. Papa left us at an inn while he and Sebastian went to find a smithy and a cartwright to forge the iron and form the new wooden wheel. Mama helped us out of our traveling clothes and we fell into bed. It smelled of perspiration—not my own.

The next morning at breakfast, Papa told us one of the other wheels was also in bad shape and would have to be replaced. As he drank his coffee, I noticed he was wearing the same shirt as yesterday. There were dark circles under his eyes and his hair was mussed. Hadn't he slept? He hadn't been there when Mama got us up.

Mama answered my unspoken question. "You must rest, Leopold."

"I will." He ran a hand over his hair, smoothing it. "Although this is a bad start, and having to board the horses and Sebastian during the delay is a bothersome expense, by heaven it is better to lose ten wheels than a foot or a few fingers."

Mama nodded. "When will it be ready?"

"We've been told tomorrow morning," Papa said. His voice echoed his unbelief.

Mama's shoulders dropped. "What are we going to do today?"

Papa pressed his fingers over his eyes and sighed. "There is a church here called St. James. I've heard it has a fine organ."

"Organ!" Wolfie said. "I want to try!"

Wolfie had played the organ for the first time on our last trip when we'd stopped at a small town near the Danube River. He'd played well then, even though no one had ever taught him. Perhaps this time I could try too. A keyboard was a keyboard, wasn't it?

"You may try, Wolferl." Papa smiled. "Actually, that is my intent."

Wolfie jumped out of his chair, nearly knocking it over. "Now! I want to go now!"

Mama righted the chair and pointed to it. "We will go when your father says it's time. Now, let him eat a proper breakfast. It's the least we can do considering his difficult night."

Mama was always looking after us.

~

"See, Wolfgang," Papa said. "These are the pedals. You played the keys before, but now it's time to play the pedals too."

Wolfie looked at Papa's feet and tried one of the pedals of the organ, though he had to slip off the stool to reach it with a toe. A deep bass sounded from the pipes above us.

Then suddenly, Wolfie pushed the stool away and played the pedals standing up, as if he were executing a complicated dance. He added his hands and, after just a few errors, was playing like he'd been practicing for months.

I heard applause from the sanctuary and peeked over the railing of the loft to see several priests and the choirmaster clapping and talking amongst themselves.

"Bravo!" Papa whispered in Wolfie's ear. "Indeed this is a fresh act of God's grace."

Mama beamed and kissed Wolfie's other cheek. I scooted over in the choir pew to the far end.

Into the shadows.

~

"Hurry, children. Now that we're in Munich, we must be seen." Papa glanced up at the windows of the Nymphenburg Palace, which was just west of the city, and moved us near some rosebushes along a path of the palace gardens.

"Don't push us, Leopold," Mama said. "We must look natural."

But Papa wasn't done placing us into a scene, creating the perfect picture. He leaned over us, smiling, though his words were stern. "Nannerl, you be on the garden side, and take your brother's hand so you both can be seen from the windows. Then the two of you walk in front of us." He pointed at Wolfie's nose. "Walk, don't run."

We did as we were told. We'd arrived in Munich the night before, and at breakfast that morning Papa had told us how things must work on our trip. As soon as we entered a new town, we had to make it known we were there. Sometimes Papa had letters of introduction—but most of those didn't refer to a specific date for us to perform, so we had to make that kind of arrangement after we arrived in town. And the only way to do that was to let those in charge know we were available. Papa said he wasn't too proud to knock on doors, but he preferred this subtler, more dignified approach.

Lucky for us, today was a gala day, the Feast of St. Antony, and many people were taking in the pretty gardens at Nymphenburg. Papa said the palace had been built in 1645 by an elector who was overjoyed by the birth of his son and heir. He'd had the palace built for his wife—or at least part of the palace. Since then it had grown enormous as other electors had added on. The grounds had all sorts of canals and pools with fountains. And flowers of every color and scent. It was like walking through sprays of summer perfume.

But we weren't interested in all that. We were interested in the promenades and staying close to the building in case anyone of importance happened to look outside—

"Herr Mozart!"

We looked at the windows. There, from the second floor, a man waved us over. He was about Papa's age.

"Who's that?" Wolfie asked, too loudly.

Mama pulled at his sleeve to quiet him while Papa herded us close to the stately white building. "Prince Frederick Michael, how wonderful to see you again," he said.

I stood straighter. From the way the man was dressed in a rumpled shirt and without a wig, I would not have known he was royalty. Perhaps he'd only now awakened—though it was midafternoon.

"You remember my family from our time in Vienna, don't you?" Papa asked the prince.

"Of course, of course," he said. "Greetings to you, Frau Mozart, and to you, children."

Mama and I curtsied, and after a poke to his back, Wolfie bowed.

"Are you here to perform for us?"

"That is our wish," Papa said.

The prince's eyebrows dipped. "Does the elector know you're here?"

"Not as yet."

Prince Frederick stood erect and called someone over from inside the room. We could overhear his instructions to the courtier. "Go inform the elector the Mozart family is here, and ask if he would like to hear the children perform."

The prince leaned on the windowsill again. "Why don't you stroll through the grounds and wait for a reply. I'm sure you'll be sent for shortly."

We said our good-byes, then walked away. Papa beamed. Wolfie walked backward in front of us. "Do we get to play, Papa? Do we?"

"Shh, child. And turn around!" He pulled Wolfie and me close, one beneath each arm. "It appears God *will* bless our efforts. But we must pray that what has been started ends in a desirable manner."

I looked at Mama. She nodded once and bowed her head a bit as we walked. Her lips moved and I knew she was already sending a request to the Almighty. I did the same.

God would hear us. He would help us make Papa happy.

Papa never did much praying. Back in Salzburg, Mama and I would join the other women in having masses said at particular altars in particular churches—depending on the nature of our prayers. We believed in miracles and fasting, and collected relics that were said to have power. And Mama was constantly looking for signs from God. We knew the Almighty was in charge and His will ruled over all.

Even over Papa.

~

"Eat, Nannerl," Mama said. "I know it's nearly midnight, but you must eat so we can get to bed. It's been a long day."

Too long.

Soon after we had talked with the prince, a footman had approached us with a message that we were to perform before Maximilian III Joseph, the elector of Bavaria, at eight that evening. I'd been so excited.

It turned out I could have stayed home.

I pushed the plate of food away, knowing it was rude, knowing the innkeeper's wife had made a special effort to get us something to eat at this late hour. But I didn't care. The chance to play for Maximilian in the palace was gone. For me. Gone for me.

I watched as Wolfie slathered butter on his bread and ate ravenously. He'd worked up an appetite performing tonight. For the entire concert had been his—except for two women who sang a few songs. The rest of the time my brother played the violin and clavier and created a constant stream of instant variations, making the audience gasp and clap. Over and over they gasped and clapped.

For him.

"I'm sorry they ran out of time," Mama said, patting my hand.

Papa reached across the table and chucked me under my chin. "No long faces. When a concert is going well, one does not change direction and risk the disfavor of the audience."

Wolfie put his feet up on his chair, his shins against the table. He pulled his bread apart, shoving the pieces into his mouth. "I played and played. . . ."

"Yes, you did," Mama said.

I pushed my plate away and stood. "May I go to bed now? I'm tired."

Mama glanced at Papa. He motioned me over to his side. "We are going to be in Munich awhile longer, Nannerl. Tomorrow night the two of you . . ." He looked at Wolfie, then noticing his feet on the chair, motioned for him to put them down. ". . . the *two* of you are to perform for Duke Clemons. And perhaps we can arrange another concert for the elector." He pulled my hand to his lips and kissed it. "I want all the world to hear the talent of my lovely daughter."

I nodded, kissed Papa good night, and let Mama take me up to our room. I believed what Papa said. He did want the world to hear my talent.

But he wanted them to hear my brother's more.

~

Papa and Mama had some papers on the table between them—bills. Papa tossed them into a mess and sat back with a groan.

"You knew we would have expenses, Leopold," Mama said. "We planned for expenses."

"But we also planned to be paid for our services. It's been five days since Wolfgang played before the elector, and there's been no payment, not even a present. Do they think we can sit around for days on end, building up expenses while we wait for them to remember the debt *they* owe?"

Mama straightened the bills. "I heard that your old violin student Tomasini performed twice for the elector, was in town for three weeks waiting for payment, and has only just been paid—and then, only seventy florins."

"Ah, but did he get the usual gold watch?" He sighed deeply. "Oh yes, this is such a charming custom, to keep people waiting for presents so that one has to be content if one makes what one spends."

"We *have* been invited to the gala dinner given by the elector tonight. Perhaps he will offer payment then, or request another concert."

"I do want to play for him," I said.

"And we want you to play for him." Papa sighed. "We must be patient."

His words sounded hollow—for *he* was rarely patient—but I held my tongue.

Suddenly Papa stood and called to Wolfie, who was playing with some blocks in a corner. "Wolfgang, come here."

Wolfie came close, banging two blocks together as he marched to an inner cadence. Papa took them away and got his attention. "Tonight at the dinner, if we have the elector's ear, I want you to tell him we are leaving tomorrow."

"But we aren't leav——"

Papa stopped Mama's words with a look. "If I nod to you and touch my cheek like this, I want you to say that aloud. Understand?"

"Yes, Papa," Wolfie said.

Mama straightened the pile of bills. "So you think he will invite us to stay if he believes we are leaving?"

"When we left the palace on the night Wolfgang performed, I heard the elector say that he regretted not hearing our little girl." He smiled at me. "See, liebchen? Papa will take care of everything. Just as I promised."

All would be well. *If* Wolfie remembered his line. . . .

~

We sat at a table with the elector, his sister Maria Antonia, and the prince-man from the window. My stomach was in knots wondering if everything would play out as Papa had planned. I kept watching Papa for the sign—the tap to his cheek. And I watched Wolfie, hoping if Papa *did* give the sign, he'd repeat the right words. But Wolfie was making his fork—and mine—march across the tablecloth like twin soldiers. If only Papa had asked me to say the line. He could trust me.

Suddenly I saw Papa's finger tap his cheek. I jerked my head toward Wolfie, ready to nudge him.

But I didn't need to. Wolfie set the forks down, smiled at the elector, and said, "We're leaving town tomorrow and I don't want to."

Those were more words than Papa had told him to say, but I didn't think they would hurt. I hoped they wouldn't hurt.

"Well, well," the elector said. "We can't have that." Then he smiled at me, right at me. "Not when I haven't heard the lovely Fraulein Mozart play. I should have liked to hear her."

I looked at Papa. The elector looked at Papa. Mama looked at Papa.

"Well indeed," Papa said. "I guess it would not matter if we stayed a few more days—if it would give you pleasure."

The elector hit the table with the palm of his hand. "Splendid."

Oh yes. It was splendid. I was going to play.

~

My chance to perform was delayed two days because the elector had a day of hunting planned, and then there was a French play he wanted to attend. But finally it was my night.

And I did well.

The applause!

I got off the bench and offered the audience my best curtsy. But it was Papa's eyes I sought. And there he was, to the side with Mama and Wolfie. He was clapping too.

I'd gotten my chance to perform. Papa was proud of me.

The world was good and right. I would hold on to this moment forever.

~

We got paid, and it was good pay too, Papa said. One hundred florins from the elector and seventy-five from the duke. Best of all, the money took care of our bills. The inn cost forty-seven florins. That left us a profit of one hundred twenty-eight florins—Papa made us do the math. I got it right first. Wolfie said "twelve." He was good at math, but when he didn't want to be bothered, he said "twelve."

Then we were on our way to Augsburg, the town where Papa grew up. Papa never said much about his childhood. An hour out of Munich I wondered about that.

"Papa?"

He sat across from me, making notations in his diary—he'd made me start a diary too, but I couldn't write in the jostling carriage like he could.

"Papa?" I asked again.

With a sigh he looked up. "I'm busy, Nannerl."

"I was just wondering if we are going to meet any of your family when we're in Augsburg. Do they know we're coming? Will they come hear—?"

He snapped his diary shut, and Mama leaned forward and put a hand on my knee. What had I said?

"We will not meet my family, and I'm sure *if* they find out about your concerts, they will purposely stay away."

There was so much anger in his voice. "But why?" I asked. "Isn't our grandmother still living? I'd like—"

"I don't care what you'd like, young lady. Children should not dig up what is better buried." He opened his diary. "Now, leave me be."

I wanted to cry. Why was he so angry at his own mother? I wanted to meet her. I wanted to meet all the Mozart family—especially since our own family was so small. We should have been a family of seven brothers and sisters, yet all but Wolfie and I had died.

Mama patted my knee. She nodded slightly to Papa beside her, put a finger to her lips, and mouthed, "Later."

Good. Mama would tell me. I'd hear the truth from Mama.

That night at the inn, while Papa worked with Wolfie on his violin, Mama asked me if I'd like to go for a walk. When she added "So we can talk" I hoped she would tell me about the Augsburg Mozarts.

We put on our bonnets and set out alone. It was a warm June evening and we didn't need a shawl. The sun was just beginning to set, so I knew our time was limited. Mama had taught me that women were not to be out walking unaccompanied in the dark.

As we moved past the edge of the inn, I didn't say anything. I wanted Mama to bring the subject forward.

And she did. "You asked about the Augsburg Mozarts. . . ."

"Papa was angry."

"He has a right to be."

We walked past a store selling books. Mama pointed to the sign.

"Your grandfather and his father were bookbinders."

I hadn't known that. "I love books."

She nodded but went on. "Your father could have joined them in the business, but . . . they wanted him to become a priest."

I started to laugh, then put a hand to my mouth. "Papa? A priest?"

"It was not what he wanted either." She smiled. "Nor what he was suited for."

"They're angry at one another for that?"

"They did not understand his passion for music."

I lifted my skirt and stepped over some horse-dirty in the street. "But if he had not become a musician, we would not . . ."

Mama put an arm around my shoulders. "He pursued what was in his heart. That . . . and me."

It took me a moment to understand. "They didn't approve of your marriage?"

She shook her head. "My family was poor. When your father and I fell in love, his father was dead, and his mother had remarried. And your father's siblings . . . they argued a lot."

"Wolfie and I argue sometimes."

"Not like they did." Mama withdrew her arm from my shoulders and I slipped my hand into the crook of her elbow. "I have never met them."

"Never?"

She shook her head. "What distresses your father the most was that your grandmother withheld money that was due him as the oldest son."

Money. Yes, that would upset Papa. "Was it a large sum?"

"Substantial. The other siblings received three hundred florins upon their marriage—that is equal to nearly a year's salary for your father. But we received nothing."

"Because he didn't become a priest?"

Mama shrugged. "Your father is a good man and did what needed to be done. That the family will not make amends brings me great sorrow."

I could not help but notice she'd said, "brings *me* great sorrow."

When Papa had gotten upset in the carriage, it had been out of anger, not grief.

Mama turned around and we started back. I had one more question to ask. "Why are we going to Augsburg if it brings him such pain?"

Mama leaned close. "Revenge can be sweet."

Ah. So that was it. His family would see that Papa was a success—and so were Wolfie and I. Maybe, if we played extremely well, his family would run toward us after the concert, take us into their arms, and say, "You are wonderful and it's been too long. Finally, we are together at last!"

I would have happy dreams tonight, imagining.

Chapter Four

Family was everything to Papa. Though, if offered this fact, he might have hedged and exclaimed that God was more important. But those of us who knew the truth would see his piety for what it was: a statement made for the Almighty's benefit.

We were not so easily fooled.

Yet, while in Augsburg, just weeks into our trip, amid the roots of my father's familial ties, I was confronted with a confusing fact: family was all-important—as long as it wasn't Papa's family.

"Keeping the proper people away from our concerts? It's the work of my brothers, I know it!"

"Shh, Leopold." Mama looked toward the door of our room at the inn, her hands pressing the air, trying to calm him. "You mustn't make such sweeping statements."

Papa purposely faced the door and spoke as if his extended family were directly on the other side. "I can—if it's the truth!"

Wolfie and I were behind the screen changing into our bedclothes, but we peeked through the slats. I wasn't sure how his family could keep people away. Or what people were "proper."

"And my mother . . ." Papa continued. "Though she remains my mother a thousand times over, she is wretched and has very little sense. She favors my siblings. She lets them take advantage. She always has."

Mama put a hand on his shoulder. "Dear one . . . the dowry is an old wound. We've been married for fourteen years now, and—"

Papa moved away from her touch. "It's an undressed wound!" His voice lowered. "And you know there are more issues at stake than that."

She moved close a second time and took his hand. "I know."

"I wanted them to *see*. I wanted them . . ."

She stroked his cheek. "I know . . ."

He grabbed her hand, stopping its comfort. "We played three public concerts here at the inn. Three. Yet they stayed away. They had to know we are here. It was in the papers. We are staying at this ridiculously expensive inn just so . . ."

I peeked at the carving on the ceiling and the velvet on the chair by the window. I'd noticed it was a better lodging than the others, and now I knew why.

He picked up a newspaper that was lying on one of the beds, opened it, and read, "'Leopold Mozart has afforded the inhabitants of his native city the pleasure of hearing the effect of the extraordinary gifts which the Great God has bestowed on these two dear little ones in such abundant measure; gifts of which the Herr Kapellmeister has, as a true father, taken care with such indefatigable zeal.'" He tossed the paper to the floor, then pointed to it. "*They* realize my accomplishments and my great success, which my family refuses to acknowledge."

Mama picked up the newspaper and folded it carefully. "Perhaps it is you who should call on them?"

"Never!" He began to pace in front of the door. "To do so would be submitting to their authority—a privilege they have never earned."

"To do so would be to follow God's directive to love one another."

He stopped pacing and glared at her. "Don't bring Him into this."

"Then don't exclude Him."

Suddenly Papa's shoulders dropped. He looked old. "I try . . . I try so hard."

Mama took him into her arms, and he dropped his head to her shoulder. She stroked his hair as she often stroked ours. "No one tries harder, dear one. You are a good man. A good husband. A good father. But I would like to meet your family. I would like the children to meet them."

Papa nodded into her shoulder.

Wolfie turned to me. "Is Papa crying?"

Papa immediately stood erect and faced the door, his hands busy at his face. Mama clapped her hands twice and moved toward the changing screen. We quickly returned to our dressing. "Come, come, children," she said. "It's time for bed. We leave tomorrow."

Good. I wanted away from here. I wanted Papa to be away from here too.

Papa put family first—our family. I hoped we would be enough for him. For it was clear he'd given up everything for us.

How could I offer him less?

~

Although Papa said we'd barely earned enough in Augsburg to cover our expenses, I was excited because it was in that city that he bought us a portable clavier from Johann Stein. The instrument would be handy for practicing during our travels.

Yet except for that one high point and seeing the beautiful scenery—from the left or right we saw an endless expanse of water, woods, fields, meadows, gardens, and vineyards, and all these mingled in the most charming fashion—our trip west during the next few days was tedious. We stopped in Ulm, where Papa spoke out against the Gothic architecture and the half-timbered houses. He said they were dreadful, old-fashioned, and tastelessly built. He much preferred symmetry. I didn't mind the fancy curlicues of the cathedrals. They reminded me of a land of fantasy. I didn't believe heaven would be symmetrical and ordered. Nature was too full of caprice to make heaven anything but.

I kept my views to myself.

We were heading to Stuttgart because we had a letter of introduction to Duke Karl Eugene, but at a station where we stopped to change horses, we discovered he was leaving Stuttgart for his palace at Ludwigsburg, and from there was going to travel to his hunting lodge fourteen hours away.

Papa had no choice but to change direction, and we headed to Ludwigsburg to try to catch him. But when we arrived, he had already moved on—and worse, had commandeered most of the horses. Papa spent hours combing the town for steeds.

The rest of us spent our time at the inn. While Mama rested in the bed behind us, Wolfie and I dragged two chairs to the window and marveled at the show being played out on the street below.

There were soldiers everywhere, marching, ever marching. Before going out to look for the horses, Papa had complained that when you spit, you spit into an officer's pocket or a soldier's cartridge box. We were told by the innkeeper that there were twelve to fifteen thousand soldiers in town, yet they really didn't have any reason for being there. Five months previous, the Seven Years' War had been declared over. France and our own Maria Theresa had fought Prussia and England over the eastern land of Silesia—with Frederick of Prussia getting to keep Silesia in the end. Yet Duke Karl Eugene didn't care that there wasn't a war going on. He liked having pretty soldiers around. Papa said they made him feel powerful. Most had been forced into service through raids of peasant villages and were hired out as soldiers to foreign states.

Wherever they came from or wherever they were going, all were grand.

Wolfie leaned out the window to see better—too far. I grabbed a handful of his shirt and pulled him back to safety.

"They look pretend," he said, totally oblivious to the fact he'd ever been in danger. "They look like they're about to take their places in an opera."

He was right. The soldiers were dressed exactly alike, even down to their hair, which was powdered white, combed back, and done up in curls. In contrast, their beards were greased coal black. It was an odd combination.

We listened to the officers yell out their commands: "Halt! Quick march! Right! Left!"

I leaned my elbows on the sill, amazed at the soldiers' straight lines as they marched. "I can't imagine them getting their pretty uniforms dirty in battle," I said.

Wolfie jumped off his chair and ran to an open travel trunk, where he retrieved the child-sized sword he often wore with his fanciest suits. He stood very straight and held it vertically, flat against his nose. "I will be a soldier. I will be very brave and fight for the empress!"

He spoke too loudly and I shushed him. I glanced at Mama, who was trying to nap, but too late. Mama sat erect. "You will not be a soldier, young man. Never!"

"Why not?" Wolfie asked. He thrust the sword at the trunk as if it were an enemy soldier.

Mama swung her feet over the side of the bed and tried to reach her shoes with a toe. I spotted one of the shoes under the bed and rushed to bring it close. She put them on and answered Wolfie with a sigh. "Because you are destined to be a great musician, that's why."

Wolfie caught the edge of a nightshirt with his sword and flung it across the room, where it caught the air and billowed to the floor. "I could do both," he said, running after it.

"You could not, and will not." She motioned him over. He complied, and Mama took control of the nightshirt and the sword and took his hands in hers. "You, dear Wolfgang, have a gift from God. Your father and I are doing our best to make sure the entire world knows about it. It is a gift that should be cherished and nurtured. *It* is your destiny."

I moved to her side. "What about me, Mama?"

But Mama wasn't done with Wolfie yet. She looked intently at his eyes. "Do you understand me, dear boy?"

Instead of answering, he kissed her cheek and went back to the window to watch the soldiers.

Finally finding myself with Mama's full attention, I asked the question again. "What is my destiny, Mama?" *To perform with your brother, becoming the greatest duo in all musical hist—*

Mama stroked my cheek. Her face lost its adamant edge and eased into a wistful smile. "You, my dear daughter, are destined to be a wife and mother. You will have many children and teach all of them to make music just as we have taught—"

I took a step back, shaking my head.

"You are upset?" Mama asked.

"I want to be a great musician like Wolfie. I want to compose and perform all over the world—with him."

"Even your brother will eventually need to find a paid position in a court. But paid musical positions are not available for women.

Now, if you were a great singer, you might be able to sing in an opera. . . ."

I felt the air go out of me. Finally I managed a fresh breath. "If I have no hopes of ever getting a position, then why am I doing this tour?"

"Because you can. Now you can."

"But later?"

Mama shrugged. She took my hand and kissed it. "Right now you are having experiences far beyond those of most girls—most women. Appreciate what you have now, what you are seeing and doing. Take it in and hold it close, here . . ." She touched the center of my forehead. "And here." She laid a gentle hand over my heart. "It's all you can do."

"But it's not fair. Just because he's a boy and I'm a girl . . ."

Mama stood and tugged at the corset that bound her torso. She looked past me toward the window. "Hopefully your father will be back soon. Help me get the brown trunk better organized so we will be ready to leave."

I looked toward Wolfie, who was once again hanging precariously out the window.

But this time I did not move to pull him safely inside.

~

The logistics of our journey kept my mind off the inequities of being female. For the most part.

Yet by the very nature of the different people, traditions, and lands we experienced along the way, I found myself gaining hope that somehow, in some place, life could be different. I *could* become a great woman of music. I could do what no woman had done before. I could challenge the system and change society for the better.

Couldn't I?

Perhaps. But first I had to learn all that I could on our travels and become the best musician I could be. So help me God.

~

Ludwigsburg had been unlike Augsburg, Heidelberg unlike Ludwigsburg, and Mannheim unlike Heidelberg. As the month of July passed, we discovered that every locale had its own unique flavor.

For one thing, the religious customs along the journey were very different to us. Catholics, Lutherans, Calvinists, and Jews, all living together. It was quite extraordinary. There were no fonts for holy water in our rooms. Nor crucifixes. We found this more interesting than distressing. Our own Salzburg had expelled all the Lutherans back in 1730, so we'd never known anything but what the archbishop decreed from his Residenz. To see that there were other ways of living, of thinking, of worshiping . . .

And dressing. In one inn we met a man from England whose trouser-waist was high under his arms with a coat that hung down to the middle of his calves. Add to this, old-fashioned narrow boot sleeves. The man bathed every other day in the Main River, just before the dining hour, coming to the table looking very much like a baptized mouse.

But in spite of our mocking in private about the odd fashion and customs, Papa bought a new pair of boots and I got a broad-brimmed English hat. How I loved walking the streets in it. I felt quite grown-up and worldly, as if I *could* be a new kind of woman. In Salzburg I would have received taunts. Oh, how large the world had become.

Although we missed the duke, we did get to play in a few towns along the way to Mannheim, where we heard the most luscious orchestra. There was a saying that "Prussian tactics and Mannheim music place the Germans in the van of all nations." We found that to be true. The people of Mannheim employed impeccable musicians, who looked upon their conductor as a musical emperor, yielding to his every wish.

The orchestra employed a new phenomenon called *crescendo* and *decrescendo,* where the music's volume swelled and faded, forcing the audience into alternating moments of ecstasy and straining to hear the music. Such interpretation made my heart swell and pound. If only I could attain such variations on the keyboard. But there I had little control. Once depressed, the key of a clavier pressed the string at one volume. Perhaps someday some brilliant inventor would create a way to monitor the loud and soft for keyboards too.

Unlike Ulm, Papa liked the look of Mannheim—especially at night. He found nothing more beautiful than one of Mannheim's illuminated prospects. And the terraces, waterways, and fountains . . . it was a lovely place, one that was difficult to leave.

And yet, we had no other choice.

We traveled next to Frankfurt, where Papa decided to advertise a public concert. He appealed to "all those who took pleasure in extraordinary things" and promised that I, a girl of twelve, and my brother, a boy of seven, would play concertos and sonatas, and that Wolfie would play both the violin and keyboard. But then Papa titillated the audience with our importance by adding, "Further, be it known that this will be the only concert inasmuch as immediately afterward they are to continue their journey to France and England."

Mama made a *tsk-tsk* sound when she saw the announcement, because we didn't have any pressing engagements in France and England and he made it sound as if people were waiting for us with bated breath.

But it worked. And after we'd done our first concert, Papa advertised that, because of the request of "several great connoisseurs and amateurs," we'd been convinced to stay on and do additional concerts. Through five public concerts, Papa had Wolfie do the note game, where he would name notes that people sounded—in singular, or in chords, on any instrument, or even clocks. Wolfie also did the covered-keys trick and improvised for extended lengths of time. He *was* very talented. I would never take anything away from my brother's prowess.

And I did well too—actually my very best toward my effort to become a musician who could not be ignored in spite of her gender. I heard Papa say, "Nannerl can be compared with the boy, for she plays in such a way that everyone speaks of her and admires her fluency." It was a victory that made me want to try even harder.

Wolfie's penchant for saying whatever came into his head nearly got him in trouble in Mainz. The violin virtuoso Karl Michael Esser played the clavier, and Wolfie told him that he did well, but he did *too much,* and it would be better to play just what was written. Actually, my brother was right. Esser wasn't that good at improvising and thus should not have attempted it. But for Wolfie to say so . . . we all hoped he would gain discretion with his years.

Along the way, Wolfie got the *Schnupfen,* the sniffles, and we had to slow down, taking an expensive riverboat up the Rhine because the roads were so drenched. The river towns were less than clean. Papa had feared we would have carriage trouble and opted to put the carriage on the boat and go that way. So many castles—on nearly every crest of every hill, on either side of the river, there was a castle looming down on us. Wolfie and I chose which ones we liked the best and claimed them as our own. I preferred the ones facing west, the ones that were bathed in the colors of the sunset. I would have a Castle Nannerl. I would share it with a husband and many children. But there would also be a grand music room with space for a large audience. And I would have my very own work-room in a parapet that would offer a glorious view of the Rhine, inspiring me to achieve great heights of music—music that would provide us with a good living. After all, I did need to be practical.

We all did. Money was always an issue: earning it and dealing with it. For even the smallest principality had its own coins, and Papa had trouble getting a good exchange rate for Bavarian money. He also received a few letters from Herr Hagenauer suggesting we not spend so much and not stay in such nice places. We'd already spent over a thousand gulden, but Papa said other people had paid for the expenditure. And we had to keep our health and our repu-tation in mind. We had to travel like nobles if we were to be asso-ciated with them. Every time I played I wondered how much we would receive—and when. The presents were very nice—we received a beautiful set of bottles valued at four ducats, a snuff box, a toothpick case, a ring, and a piece of embroidery (Papa said we would soon have enough items to rig out a stall). But money was always best. Money eased the wrinkles in Papa's brow.

Some places were profitable, and others were not. In one con-cert given to a small group of nobles, they were more interested in eating and drinking than in our music. But most audiences were very appreciative.

By the end of September we were in Cologne, but we found the cathedral there in a horrible state, like a stable. The pulpit that

Martin Luther had preached from was held up by a brick, and the furniture was in disrepair. We tried to go into the choir area, but it was closed to visitors. Yet what was worse was when we were met by a drunken priest, who greeted us and was eager to show off a display of the cathedral's treasures.

Papa wondered if it wouldn't be more edifying to get the house of God into a clean condition rather than to have jewels, gold, and silver—with which numerous saints' bones were thickly encased—lying in iron chests and shown for money. And the boys' choir shrieked more than sang. All this put Papa in a mood. I reminded Wolfie to be especially good.

Along the next leg of the journey, traveling west toward Brussels by way of Aachen, we met Princess Amalia, the sister of the king of Prussia. Yet even though she was a princess, she didn't have any money. Her traveling party was quite Spartan, not royal at all. Yet if the kisses she gave us could have been transferred to gulden, we would have been rich. But neither the innkeeper nor the postmaster was paid in kisses. She even tried to get us to *not* go to Paris but to Berlin instead. Papa thought this ridiculous, for Paris was to be the jewel in our tour.

And there was more that the princess offered Papa. . . . Although Papa spoke of it in hushed tones to Mama, there were implications that one of her proposals was of a more intimate kind. I thought less of her because of that. And yet, for her to be intrigued with Papa . . . he *was* a handsome man. So tall. So proud. He had a way of holding himself that made a person believe anything he said, that made a person want to be whatever he wanted them to be. Whatever kind of person *I* wanted myself to be.

How I strived to be that person as we continued on our Grand Tour.

Chapter Five

Oh, to be alone, to have five minutes to myself.

Cramped quarters, cramped carriages, being together every hour of every day . . .

One autumn afternoon in Brussels, while we were waiting for Prince Charles to summon us for a concert (weeks we waited), Mama needed some black headache powder from the apothecary, so I offered to go. Alone. At first Papa objected, worrying that I would feel uncomfortable venturing out on my own in such a strange place.

He was correct, of course, but my discomfort was eclipsed by my desire—alas, even my *need*—to be away from family. To walk among strangers, where nothing was expected of me except to stay on my side of the street, was akin to taking a cure. It was a refreshment, and as I walked I felt my nerves ease back beneath my skin. When my lungs filled with deep breaths of tranquility, I realized how short and constrained my breathing had become of late, mimicking the jerks of the carriage or the hurry-hurry as Papa herded us toward our next performance.

Since Brussels was such a large city, I blended in. I was interested in the wooden shoes. How awkward to walk on a surface that did not give way, and yet . . . the wood might have been a good buffer against the cobblestones. My leather shoes felt every stone, every juncture.

I walked past the shops and stalls selling lace and tapestries, and saw interesting vegetables called Brussels sprouts. So many vendors plied their trade and called out to me as I passed: coopers, fowlers, thatchers, bakers, smiths. The ships that took their wares to faraway places came up the canals in the center of the city on their way to the sea. The sea. I had never seen the sea. . . .

Or sea gulls. When I first saw the white birds diving and soaring I had no name for them, but Mama told me what they were. *Sea gulls.* Nannerl from landlocked Salzburg was seeing a bird of the sea!

A gothic cathedral loomed ahead. If Papa and Mama had been along, we would have gone inside. But I'd seen enough cathedrals, spent enough time in their cold halls. We'd already gone sightseeing at other churches and museums here. At one, Papa had stood transfixed in front of a Last Supper altarpiece by Dirk Bouts. His interest surprised me because I didn't like the piece. At all. The disciples were too lean and stilted, the perspective odd. I much preferred the movement of the Bruegel paintings we'd seen at museums that captured the life of the people around me, eating, laughing, playing games. They told a story that continued, while the Bouts work only captured a moment that seemed to have no future.

Papa would get after me for saying such a thing about a scene depicting Jesus, yet it's not the subject I objected to but the cold way it was portrayed. Even at age twelve I was quite full of opinions. Taking after Papa, I suppose.

I stopped a moment to check the address of the apothecary. A little dog sniffed at my feet and I bent down to pet him. I wanted a dog someday, someone to love me no matter what. The dog's owner came near, a woman wearing an apron and cloth headdress. She smiled at me and spoke, but I could not understand her words. *"Ich bin österreichisch,"* I said. *I am Austrian.*

Her face went blank a moment; then she nodded, smiled, said a long sentence I imagined to be something like "Have a lovely day," picked up the dog, and left me. I walked away with a spring to my step, which was odd because I hadn't successfully conversed with her. All we understood of each other was that we were not the same. And yet . . . we *had* shared a moment. We'd connected: two females with a cute pup between us.

NANCY MOSER

I wished the woman could come to our concert at the Palace Musée when Prince Charles summoned us. I would have liked to share my music with her as she had shared her dog with me. For music was the true ambassador between people. It needed no common language. I was so blessed to be a part of music.

Sometimes people asked if I was nervous performing before kings and queens. I didn't have time to be nervous. There were too many things to do, too many things to think about. I was more nervous for Papa to hear and approve than to worry about the opinion of any emperor or king. Papa was the one who held my future in his hands. Of course, if the royalty did not approve, they would not pay well . . . but that brought me back to pleasing Papa.

Sometimes I wondered why I cared so much. He was just a man. He would never do harm to me if he *did* disapprove. Yet it was his harsh or disappointed words I feared. Words. Just words. Absurd.

Ç'est la vie.

It was a new French phrase I'd learned. I also knew how to say hello, good-bye, thank you, please, and where is the water closet? Nannerl Mozart: girl of the world.

I successfully completed the task at the apothecary (the apothecary spoke German), and I meandered back to the inn, feeling rejuvenated. Wolfie met me at the door carrying his ball-catcher toy. "Look, Nannerl, I can do it fifteen times without missing." He proceeded to swing the ball on its string, catching it on the wooden spindle. It was his new favorite toy, and his wild gyrations as he attempted to catch the ball often made me want to rip it from his hands.

But not today. For I'd been out in the world today. I'd been free.

"Very good, Wolfie. I'm proud of you."

He stopped playing and looked at me, obviously suspicious.

I took off my hat and cloak and hung them on the back of the door. Mama was in bed trying to get over her headache. I handed Papa the apothecary's powder.

"Your errand was uneventful?" he asked.

"Completely," I said. It was a lie. I made plans to repeat the experience when we reached Paris in mid-November.

Walking alone in Paris. Could there be anything more exciting?

I imagined there was. But for now . . . I was only a girl. But almost a woman. Soon to be a woman.

~

Paris!

A city without a wall surrounding it. A city without fortified gates. Beautiful vistas of parks, and chateaux dotting the greens. The capital of all France. Papa said, "The city will be ours, children. Ours!"

He made me believe it. It was the stuff of fairy tales and dreams.

We had a very special place to stay in Paris due to friends of friends. My family knew Sallerl Joly, who was a servant in the household of Count Arco, whose son-in-law, Count van Eyck, was allowing us to stay at his townhouse at the Bavarian embassy. His wife, Countess Maria Anna Felicitas, had been a friend of our family for years and made us very welcome and even equipped our room with a harpsichord—a much superior instrument to our portable keyboard. It was such a luxury. Papa implied there was no cost involved, though I wasn't brave enough to ask him outright if our lodging was completely free. He was in a very good mood. . . . He was also especially pleased with the Paris Petite Poste, a citywide letter service that had deliveries four times a day. With its use we could find out if our patrons were at home without wasting the expense of a carriage ride.

But then, a hitch. Just five days after our arrival in Paris, Isabella, the grown granddaughter of King Louis XV of France, the wife of our Archduke Joseph, who would be the next emperor of Austria, died of smallpox, soon after giving birth. A baby daughter also died. The French court was thrown into mourning, and all entertainment was suspended for a month. Papa grumbled about that, and the expense of buying us mourning outfits.

But after a month, we were free to move forward—and Papa did so, quite quickly. Just one day after the mourning ended—on Christmas Eve—we were on our way to the palace of Versailles. It was thirty-two kilometers west of Paris and had once been a simple hunting lodge until the current king's grandfather had made it grander than grand. I'd heard stories about the gold and wealth. Now I was going to see for myself.

Even at first sight, Versailles made the palace at Schönbrunn seem small. We rode through golden gates into an immense court-yard surrounded on three sides by buildings that had their own wings going off in different directions. And the people. Everywhere people and animals. Some walking as if on a mission, and others meandering as if their only job was to be seen.

"What are they all doing here, Papa?" I asked.

"Seeking favor," he said.

"Like us?"

He glanced in my direction as if I'd said something wrong. "*We* have been invited. We have not come here on false hope, wanting something for nothing, as have most of these. We have something to give to the king and queen—your talent."

I sat straighter in the carriage. I had something to offer the king and queen. I was somebody.

Wolfie jumped onto his knees and pointed out the window of the carriage. "Look at that pig run!" He giggled, sat down, then pushed a finger against his nose, making a snout. "A pig digging in a wig." He oinked.

"Behave yourself," Mama said.

The carriage came to a halt. It was time to see our lodgings—we had secured a place to stay at the Au Cormier. However, unlike our room at the van Eycks', this lodging was not free.

Not free at all. We moved in and soon found everything to be very expensive. Food was pricey, and we were very glad the December days were warm as summer, for every log of wood cost five sous. In his next letter home, Papa even asked Herr Hagenauer to write smaller and on lighter-weight paper, as the recipient of each letter—as well as the sender—had to pay according to its weight and size and shape.

Papa's first words about Versailles never left me as I moved through the massive palace: most of the people here were seeking favor from the king. Did they seek a title? Land? A pardon for a family member? A job? Had some come because they'd been sum-moned for an indiscretion? Yet I imagined such negative matters were attended to more swiftly (and discreetly) than those of a more positive nature. How tiring it would be to be a king and spend your day granting audience to an endless line of people.

Yet I heard Papa tell Mama that the king was most concerned with hunting and liaisons. He glanced at me when he said this, and I pretended not to know what he meant, but I did. I'd heard such talk before. Many rulers had mistresses, and this king was no better. Papa implied Louis had more than one—and one particular mistress was even treated like a queen. Madame Pompadour. She'd been at Versailles for twenty years. I wished I could ask Mama about her, but that was awkward. So . . . I hoped to find a friend, one who might know the gossip.

I shouldn't have wanted to know about such things.

But I did.

We were presented at court more than once. Walking from one grand room to the next made my neck hurt from looking up at the painted ceilings and the crystal chandeliers. There was one room called the Hall of Mirrors that had seventeen (Wolfie and I counted them) huge mirrors that matched the arched windows across the room. There was so much gold in the statues and the candelabras—some taller than Papa—that it couldn't possibly be real, could it? Surely the riches of heaven couldn't match this palace. Yet Papa did a lot of shaking his head at the opulence. He said the bulk of France's wealth was divided amongst a hundred persons. That didn't sound very fair. If I were French, it would make me angry.

The extravagant appearance of the people who attended our concerts competed with the architecture. The women's dresses were made of yards and yards of silk and brocade and were very wide, forcing the women to walk sideways through many of the doorways. The dresses were edged with metal lace that glistened. There were three or four layers of lace at the elbow, and matching silk shoes with jeweled buckles. The men's fashions were just as lavish, with matching suits adorned by wide cuffs, vests heavy with trim, and shirts ruffled at both the neck and wrist.

Then there were the wigs. Why everyone wanted to have gray or white hair, I wasn't sure, but they did. Even Wolfie and I had wigs that had to be powdered. I liked the lavender-scented powder, but the whole process made quite a mess. Wolfie's and Papa's wigs had rows of curls on the side, and the ponytail was contained in a velvet bag tied with a bow. Some women had birds and flowers in their wigs, or a funny little hat. My wig wasn't as tall as some, but it did add to my height and forced me to hold my head erect. I wondered if the wig was wise. It made me look older, and the audiences seemed to like that we were so young. I was torn between wanting to look young to please them and wanting to look like a grown woman to please myself. I was nearly a woman. I was twelve and a half.

As for the outdoor clothes worn at Versailles? When the warm December days turned, the courtiers wore fur-trimmed garments with neckties of fur. Instead of flowers they put fur in their hair and had fur armlets . . . fur everywhere. But the most ridiculous sight was a type of sword scabbard which was bound with fur—an excellent idea, so the sword wouldn't catch cold?

And yet, even amid all this elegance, the place smelled horrible. There were not enough latrines, and I actually saw a stately man relieving himself in the corner of a fine hall. They called us Germans barbarians? And mixed with the horrid stench and the smell of nervous perspiration that was imbedded in the heavy clothes was the heady smell of perfume. I had a little pocket sewn into my corset for a sachet (I loved the smell of orange), but the perfumes in the court were so strong I often found my eyes watering—though I wasn't completely sure which odor was the culprit.

We played concerts before the king and queen and all their children. The queen, Marie Leszczinska, was Polish and spoke German with us, even translating for the king. She was very fat, and Mama heard a rumor that one time she consumed one hundred eighty oysters with two quarts of beer in one sitting. She smiled a lot, and Wolfie chattered with her for a long time. She passed delicious food to us from her plate as we stood with the other courtiers behind the king and queen's eating table.

The young princesses loved us and gave us many hugs and kisses, cooing at us in French we did not understand. Even the queen embraced us. People paused in galleries and apartments to greet us, and the English and the Russian ambassadors sought us out. Papa said Wolfie bewitched almost everyone when he played the organ in the chapel.

And the presents! Snuff boxes, writing cases, silver pens, and a toothpick case of solid gold. What were we to do with all the snuff boxes? And yet the gifts did make me feel special.

There was one very important difference in the women at Versailles compared to the Austrian women I knew: they wore paint on their faces—as did some of the men. Lots and lots of face paint. Papa said it made even a naturally beautiful woman unbearable to the eyes of an honest German. I found it less detestable. I would have liked to try it, but Papa would never have allowed it.

And then . . . we got invited by Madame Pompadour to play in her private apartments.

The king's mistress. Oh my.

By that time I'd heard more about her. She'd been married when she'd come to court twenty years previous and had met King Louis at a masquerade ball. They'd had an affair and she became his mistress. She left her husband for him.

But what if she hadn't wanted to leave her husband? What if the husband hadn't wanted her to go?

I suppose neither one had had much choice.

She was the king's mistress for five years, but since then had been his confidante, even directing him on political matters. Some say she pushed him to get involved in that Seven Years' War France and Austria had fought against England and Prussia—a war that had even carried over onto the soil of the Americas, where native Indians were involved. The whole thing had been resolved the previous February, but its effects were still seen. Yet it was odd . . . although we saw great poverty and hardship among the common people, the royalty at Versailles acted as if nothing had ever happened, as if extravagance was the key to their country's recovery. Did they act that way because they wanted to forget anything unruly or unseemly?

Papa said Madame Pompadour was a handsome woman, still

good-looking, even if she was forty-five—about Mama's age. She reminded him of our own empress Maria Theresa, especially in her eyes. She was tall and stately, stout, but very well proportioned. She was extremely dignified and very intelligent.

I thought it odd Papa would agree for us to perform in her chambers. He and Mama had made it clear (at least to us, in private) that they did not approve of spouses being unfaithful. Yet it was as though there were two courts at Versailles. One belonging to the queen and the royal children, and the other to this mistress. People lived how they wished here. Life was very sensual. Mama and Papa had the opinion that if God was not especially gracious, the French state would suffer the fate of the former Persian Empire, which had prospered with trade and art but was broken by weak rulers and decadence. I did not know much of empires, but I wondered something of a more personal nature—wouldn't the queen know of our performance before Madame and be offended?

Papa thought it wise to play both sides—at least at first. But he urged us to keep our ears open to what people were saying about us so we could parry to the other side if advantage was to be made.

"A paradise!" Papa whispered as we entered Madame's apartments. There was gold everywhere and painted furniture, heavy with carving. Her harpsichord was covered in gold leaf, lacquered, and painted in intricate detail. The rooms looked out on the gardens. On the wall were two life-sized portraits—one of herself and one of the king.

She was very gracious and lifted Wolfie onto the bench of the harpsichord. Then an odd thing happened. We'd been so used to hugs and kisses, and Wolfie—being of a demonstrative nature anyway—embraced her. But she repelled his affection, as if she wanted none of it. Wolfie pouted a bit and did not play his best. Afterward, when we were back in our room, he exclaimed, "Who does she think she is, not wanting to kiss me? Why, the empress herself kissed me!"

Mama consoled him, and Papa agreed it was rude. I remained quiet, for I never got as many hugs and kisses as my brother. Yet I did get praise. Just that day I'd heard Papa telling a gentleman, "My little girl plays the most difficult pieces with unbelievable precision and in such a manner that even fine musicians cannot conceal their jealousy." I hoped he wasn't just speaking as my father but out of true appreciation.

In regard to the choice between Madame Pompadour's court and the queen's? Even though we played for both, Papa chose the queen's. He cemented his choice by suggesting Wolfie dedicate two of the four sonatas he'd composed (and that we were having engraved) to the queen's court. One was to Madame Victoire, the most shy of the queen's daughters, and the second was dedicated to a lady-in-waiting who was the daughter of an influential duke. Papa also made sure the engravings noted that the composer was only seven years old. We looked forward to the furor that would cause.

All these women of influence . . . We came to see that it was women who made things happen in Paris. They were the people who could help us—or hurt us. It was odd to see women have such power, but it was the Parisian way. Being a woman of influence . . . Perhaps one day I would end up in this place, as a great woman musician.

If so, I needed to compose my own music, yet every time I mentioned it or got out a page of staff paper, Papa said, "No, Nannerl. Concentrate on your playing. Let your brother do the composing."

And Wolfie *was* good at it.

But couldn't I be good too?

Perhaps one day. We'd see. Perhaps when we got home and life was more normal.

～

We left Versailles and returned to the home of the Count and Countess van Eyck in Paris on the eighth of January, 1764. But our time of giving concerts was not over. We performed at many public concerts and Papa arranged posters. One afternoon, while we were practicing, they were delivered.

Papa unwrapped the brown paper to see them: *Come hear the incredible musical talent of the Salzburg Children! Hear Maria Anna Mozart, aged 11, and her brother, Wolfgang, 6. Be astounded by their musical prowess! Be humbled by their talent! Be amazed at their unparalleled ability!*

It was a nice poster. And yet . . . "Papa?" I asked. "It says I'm eleven and Wolfie six. I'm twelve now, and Wolfie is seven."

Wolfie raised his hand. "Almost eight! In a few weeks I'll be eight!"

Papa straightened the posters. "It was necessary. A necessity."

Mama shook her head but didn't say anything.

He removed one poster and handed it to Mama, then draped the rest over his arm. "Younger is better. Now I must go and arrange for these to be distributed. Get back to your practice."

He left with a *whoosh* of cold air. I looked at Mama, wondering how she really felt about this lie.

She ran a finger along the edge of the poster, as if reading it again. Then she looked at us. "Get back to your practice, children."

Younger. Papa said remaining young was a necessity.

How were we supposed to do that?

~

It was bright sunlight when I awoke. This was not usual. Mama always had us up before the sun.

I sat up in bed. Wolfie was still asleep, the covers twisted around his legs. But Mama and Papa were gone.

I heard voices and footsteps in the hall. People hurried up and down the stairs. Something was wrong.

I got out of bed and put a shawl around my shoulders. The fire in the grate was nearly out. Mama never let it go out. . . .

I cracked the door just as a maid walked by carrying a shallow pewter bowl. In it was blood.

Who was being bled?

As she started down the stairs, I called after her. "Who's sick?"

She paused halfway down. "The countess fell ill during the middle of the night and spit blood. The doctor has already bled her twice." She nodded toward the hall. "Your mother is with her." She continued downstairs.

The countess was sick enough to be bled? I'd heard that patients were only bled when whatever was harming them had to be given a means of exiting the body. So for the countess to have been bled twice already . . . I retreated into the room and quickly got dressed.

Wolfie stirred and opened one eye. "It's light. . . ."

I pulled on my stockings. "Go back to sleep," I said.

He nodded and snuggled into the pillow.

I put on my shoes and tied the back of my dress as best as I could without help, then hurried down the hall toward the family's quarters. When I came to the countess's bedchamber, the door was open, and the count stood in the doorway, his hand to his mouth. He looked in my direction.

"Sir?" I said. "Is she all right?"

His eyes returned to the room and he shook his head. "I don't know." When he looked back at me, I saw tears threatening to spill over. "Will you pray, Fraulein Nannerl? Will you pray?"

"Of course." I returned to our room and knelt at the side of my bed. "Father, almighty God, please heal the mistress of the house. Make her well. Make—"

"What's wrong?" Wolfie said from his bed.

I pointed to the place beside me. "We need to pray, Wolfie. Now."

"For what?"

I pointed again. "Now!"

He climbed out of bed and got on his knees beside me. "Is it Papa?" he asked. "Or Mama?"

I'd been too curt. He deserved to know our parents were safe. "It's the countess."

"She's pretty."

Pretty didn't matter right now. "Pray!" I commanded.

~

The Countess van Eyck was only twenty-three when she died on February 6, 1764. My entire family put on the mourning clothes we'd had to buy when the king's granddaughter had died the previous November. I didn't like wearing black, yet how could I possibly wear something gay when someone so young and dear had passed from us?

Through my tears of sorrow, I was angry at God for taking her. Weren't our prayers good enough? Perhaps if we'd prayed louder, longer, stronger . . . Yet Mama reminded me that God's ways are not our ways.

Indeed. *I* would have let her live.

Then, in addition to the veil of mourning that shrouded the house, Wolfie got sick. He got a sore throat, a cold, and a high fever, then developed such an inflammation of the throat that he was in danger of choking. The doctor stood over him, just as another doctor, in another country, had done before. Back then, it had been rheumatic fever. This time . . .

Dr. Herrnschwand was very gentle, stroked Wolfie's head and spoke softly to him, always smiling. The smile made me hopeful. . . . Plus the fact that this doctor had not ordered Wolfie to be bled. Since the death of the countess, there had been rumors around the house that the doctor had caused her death by too much bloodletting. So when Wolfie had gotten sick, and the count had offered the use of that same doctor, Papa had politely, but pointedly, declined. There would be no French doctor caring for *his* son. Dr. Herrnschwand was German. I too found that a comfort.

The doctor took a few steps away from the bed and motioned my parents close. "He should be inoculated for smallpox."

Papa shook his head vehemently.

"But the shot has been known to help—"

"No!" Papa glanced at Wolfie, then at me, then lowered his voice. "I have heard of children dying from the inoculation. I won't risk it. Not with my son. I would rather trust God to save him."

I did not know who was right, Papa or Dr. Herrnschwand. What I did know was that there was enough sorrow in this house. The count rarely left his room. His eyes were red and I could often hear his sobs. Repeatedly the maid returned down the hall with his food tray untouched.

Papa left to see the doctor to the door. Mama sat next to Wolfie. "What can we do, Mama?" I asked.

She shook her head and didn't answer at first. "This is all happening because we haven't been observing the fast days here in France." She looked up. "We tried, but the food was unavailable.

We have no kitchen in our room here, and the water is bad and needs to be boiled. We've missed many daily masses. And they do not even use rosaries in church."

I fingered the rosary I had in my pocket. It was never far from me. Everything Mama said was true. It was hard being a devout Catholic in France. Had our inability to exhibit our devotion caused God to be angry? Was the Almighty punishing us by afflicting the apple of our eye, little Wolfie?

With a pat to my brother's hand, Mama stood. "Come, Nannerl. We must make amends." She grabbed her cloak from the wall hook and handed me mine. "We must find a church and implore them to say a mass for our dear boy."

I tied the cloak at my neck. "Does Papa want to come with us?"

Mama gathered our gloves and was at the door. "He will stay with Wolferl. Besides, praying is women's work. We may not have influence and power in the here and now, but by our Lord, we have influence with heaven." She pointed a finger at my nose and leaned close. "And I dare any man to say different."

I could not argue. I would not. I liked the idea of having *some* influence.

~

The Lord be praised! After four trips to church, after countless prayers prayed, and after only two visits by Dr. Herrnschwand, Wolfie was up and about. In only four days.

Mama and I declared it a miracle. Papa pooh-poohed such a thing but could do nothing to change our minds.

Mama and I made Wolfie well—with God's help.

Chapter Six

After nearly five months in Paris, it was April, and I stood at the shore—the shore of an ocean! The feeling of adventure I'd experienced in Brussels when I'd seen oceangoing ships coming to port was multiplied tenfold by standing on the edge of the ocean myself. It was not ever-flowing in one direction like a river with somewhere to go, nor still and mirrored like an Alpine lake. This ocean, this sea, was alive. It ran away and advanced like a child with too much energy. Would it ever be satisfied and remain still?

Never.

That, in itself, stirred me. My family had a lot in common with the ocean. . . .

I walked to the edge of the tide, collecting shells. They were flat and many were broken. Had they come from the depths of the sea? The wet portion of the sand was worn smooth and glimmered in the sunlight. I teased the water, daring it to reach where it had not reached before. As if in answer to my challenge, a wave broke and sped over the wet sand until it nipped the toes of my shoes. *Tag! You're it!*

"Don't get your shoes wet, Nannerl," Papa said.

I retreated a step, even though the ocean beckoned me to do the unthinkable. How I longed to take off my shoes and stockings, lift my skirt and petticoats high, and walk in the water. Play in it.

"Come," Papa said, taking Wolfie's hand. "We must catch our boat to England."

I palmed the shells and took one last look across the water. Although warm, the day was overcast, and I found it hard to imagine there was land beyond the foggy horizon. I'd heard it said the earth was round, but looking over the expanse of ocean, I saw only endless flatness.

It made me afraid. What if we got out in the middle and began to sink? I had never tried to swim. And who would save us? Papa had chartered a boat, so we would not have the luxury of feeling safety in numbers.

We would not even have the security of all our belongings. We were leaving the carriage and some of the luggage behind with trusted friends. Choosing what to take and what to leave behind had been difficult, for who knew how long we would be in England? Papa had arranged letters of introduction to the court, but we could only hope we were as generously paid there as we had been during our stay in France.

I must say, I was not sorry to see France go. It was a confusing place, a land of contradictions, with opulence forever nudging the edge of poverty. And though we'd spent time in golden rooms that rivaled heaven itself, just streets away we'd seen legions of poor, many of whom were deformed in atrocious ways. Such suffering! And the suffering did not restrict itself to the poor. For in the Place de Grève there were many public executions. One day, a chambermaid, a cook, and a coachman had been hanged in company, side by side, for embezzling from their blind mistress. We had driven through the square quickly and Papa had said, "Avert your eyes!" But his warning did not come quickly enough, for I saw the bodies hanged by the neck, and I heard the crowd cheer.

"How can they cheer over death?" I asked.

Papa said, "However unfortunate, punishment must be carried out to ensure the safety of the masses." Out of the corner of his mouth he added, "Although this celebratory display is a bit uncouth."

I agreed. Shouldn't punishment for sins be a private matter?

Wasn't there enough shame in a person's heart to negate the need for public humiliation?

Besides confusing, daily living in France had also been stressful. The sanitary conditions were deplorable, with waste filling the street with nauseating smells. And we'd all suffered from a sickness of the innards that was embarrassing enough when we were at home, and much more so on the road.

As for the food . . . there was little cheese or fruit, and no good seafood. And the fish wasn't fresh. Oh, to eat fresh fish from a clear Austrian lake! Only wine was inexpensive, and though I didn't mind the taste, I could not drink much of it without feeling heady. So what alternative was there to thirst? Mama did not trust the milk, and since the water was taken from the Seine River, all of it had to be boiled before we drank. I left France thirsty. . . .

I left the French oceanside behind. Within the hour I would be riding upon its back.

May heaven help us.

~

"Look!"

I pointed over the side of the boat to some strange gray animals jumping out of the water around us. They had long noses and fins like a fish. But their size . . . They were as big as Wolfie.

Wolfie saw them too and scooted to my side of the boat. "Papa!"

Papa pulled him back on the bench. "Sit still or you'll capsize us all!" Papa said.

"What are they?" Mama asked.

A man who had paid Papa a fee to fill one of the four extra seats on our charter sailboat tipped his hat to her. In halting German he said, "Pardon, madame, but those are dolphins. They are a . . . a . . ." His German failed him. "A *mammifère*. They breathe . . ." He took a deep breath, demonstrating.

They breathed air? I looked back toward the animals—there were three of them now, swimming and jumping in unison as if they were playing and putting on a show just for us. Yet I'd seen them dive deep into the depths of the water. "How can they breathe?"

He struggled for the word but pointed to the top of his head. *"Trou."*

After a moment, Papa said, "Ah, *Bohrung*."

Hole? I saw that the dolphins did indeed have an air hole on the top of their heads. Periodically, they blew water from them.

One did so just then, and Wolfie exclaimed, "A fountain! He's making a fountain."

We all laughed. "They seem to be smiling," I said.

Papa nodded. "As they should." He put an arm around Mama and Wolfie, who sat on either side of him. "For they are happy the Mozart family is crossing the Channel to visit such a faraway place." He lowered his voice. "I am quite sure that not one other citizen of Salzburg has ever traveled so far."

I sat back in awe. To be the first . . .

Papa nodded. "In fact, I have decided to learn English myself. It will do no harm to have someone at the Salzburg court who speaks English; one never knows how handy it might be."

I looked again at the dolphins as they entertained us. So many new things. I was very blessed.

~

Perhaps being so enthralled with the dolphins' dance, watching their constant movement—combined with the pitch and yaw of the boat on the turbulent water—made us ill. The man who knew about dolphins said we were seasick.

Another new experience—one I could have done without. Papa suffered the most, but once we reached Dover . . .

The cliffs were bright and striking. Such a difference from the flat, sandy shores of Calais. It was as if England had created its own fortress against the sea.

To ease our entrance into this strange land of England, Papa hired two new servants. One was an Italian named Porta, who'd taken the France-to-London trip eight times. He knew some English and was very good at handling the porters—who, he warned, had a tendency to grab luggage and hurry it off to the inn of *their* choice, where they expected exorbitant payment for its return. He would surely save Papa money.

The other new servant, Jean Pierre, took the place of our dear friend and companion Sebastian Winter, who'd been with us since Salzburg. Sebastian left us to return to his hometown to take a position as a hairdresser to its prince, Joseph Wenzeslaus von Fürstenberg. Wolfie and I were distraught. Sebastian had spent a lot of time with us, playing, making animal noises, drawing maps of an imaginary land Wolfie had created—the Kingdom of Back. Wolfie often gave me a detailed account of this fantasy world where children reigned. I encouraged him *not* to let Mama and Papa hear of it, though, for occasionally his descriptions spoke too much of children being free to do as they wished.

Upon landing, we were immediately glad for Porta's presence as he took command of our arrival and arranged for a carriage to take us to London.

Mama and I noticed the difference in the clothing. It was less fussy than the clothes in France, with fewer adornments. And hats! It seemed no one could cross the street without wearing a hat. Plus parasols. We'd seen them in France but discovered the style had started in England—a necessity against the more frequent rain?

But as in France, fichus were worn about the neck, demurely covering the chest (as the necklines were low), and lace was the one common decoration. The fabrics seemed lighter in weight, and there were many hand-painted patterns on both silk and cotton. Painting on fabric? Who would have thought of such a thing? We were used to patterns being woven, yet we heard this new type of printed fabric was inspired by the English traders who'd been to the Orient and India. England had earned the title of being the master of colonization, having spread her dominance across the world from America to India and beyond. The entire country benefited from such trade.

Yet often, oddly, we found it difficult to tell upper-class from lower. There was less ostentation, less heralding one's position through dress and presence. The distinction between middle and high, ordinary and privileged, was blurred. Even beggars were elevated from the utter hopelessness we'd seen in Paris. In London they didn't just beg but offered something for the trouble—a quill toothpick, a flower, thread, ribbons, or even a song.

The immensity of London overwhelmed us. Looking down at the Thames River from London Bridge, I was amazed by a forest of ship masts. And at a zoo I saw an elephant and a horselike animal that had white and coffee brown stripes so evenly spaced that no one could paint them better. While I was interested in parks and animals, Papa was interested in business. He discovered there were 1,318 night watchmen, 166 public paupers' schools, and fifty squares in London. And the trade directory was the thickness of two fingers and was so commodious that it had to be arranged alphabetically. Certainly, London was beyond any Salzburger's imagination.

We immediately felt conspicuous in our French clothes—which we had purchased in order to fit in while living in France. In fact, we experienced prejudice because of them. Some street urchins yelled at us, crying out, "Down with the French!" Apparently, the animosity of the war was still alive. Papa took us shopping the very next day. He mumbled about the expense, but it was important we fit in, for if we elicited the ire of mere peasants with our dress, how could we hope to gain the favor of gentlemen and ladies?

Mama and I enjoyed our new wide-brimmed hats, and though he would not admit it, Papa looked proud in his new waistcoat and tricorn hat, with Wolfie strutting around in his smaller version. We were all quite dapper. It was an English word I enjoyed saying, the sound making me laugh aloud. *Dapper.*

Other things we had to attend to upon entering this new country involved obtaining proper coinage (they did not take French money) and delivering letters of introduction so we could begin to perform. Papa handled all this in his usual expert manner, even though language was continually a barrier. Papa's desire to learn the language was a good ambition—one he took to with aplomb.

But then the miracle—after only four days in London we were on our way to give our first concert for the king and queen at Buckingham House. Papa was excited that we'd been able to get started so quickly because our expenses had mounted. "I did not travel to England for the sake of a few thousand gulden."

I grew weary about the constant need for money. Although I knew the tour made my parents happy, although I knew we were seeing parts of the world that would be inaccessible if we did not give concerts, sometimes I longed for the simple days when we used to play in the Hagenauers' parlor. Yet as soon as I allowed myself such thoughts, I forced them away. Ungrateful girl. If I was going to be a great female musician, then I had to pay the piper. I took the whole thing very seriously. My brother did not.

On the way to the estate, Wolfie looked out the window of the carriage and saw a group of dogs run past. He began to make dog noises, whimpering, barking softly. I poked him in his side to get him to stop.

He accidentally kicked Papa.

"Enough!" Papa said. "We'll be there soon. Behave yourselves."

I was immediately still, but not Wolfie. He dropped something on the floor of the carriage. When he was retrieving it, I felt a tugging. He'd untied the ribbons on my shoes. I opened my mouth to tell on him, but he put a finger to his lips, daring me to be quiet.

In the seat across from us, Papa looked over his glasses. "What's going on?"

I'd get him back later.

"Who's going to be there, Papa?" Wolfie looked up at our father, the essence of innocence.

I leaned over and tied my shoes. In double knots.

"King George the Third and Queen Charlotte will be there. He is German," Papa said proudly.

"But I've heard he is also very English," Mama said. "He was the first Hanoverian king to be born on English soil. English is his first language."

"Oh." Papa sounded disappointed. "I'd hoped to converse with him."

"I'm sure he knows German," Mama said. She patted his knee. "I also heard that music is a large part of their lives. When he plays with his children, he often has the royal band perform."

"He plays with his children?" I asked. It was hard for me to imagine a king cavorting with his offspring—to music, no less.

"That's what I heard," Mama said. "The king plays the violin and flute, and the queen can sing and is quite talented on the harpsichord."

Papa snickered. "We've heard *that* before."

"She *could* be talented," Mama said. "Not all nobility exaggerate their gifts."

"Too many do."

He was right. It was often awkward—and even painful—to patiently listen to some gentleman or lady perform. And yet we'd all learned to smile and clap as if they had inspired us with their performance.

Except Wolfie. He still spoke the truth far too often.

The carriage slowed and pulled up in front of a redbrick mansion with white pilasters, doors, and window frames. Footmen came to open the door and helped us out.

"We are here," Papa said. "Make me proud, children."

~

The king had bought Buckingham House for his queen a few years earlier to give them a home near St. James' Palace, where most of the royal functions were held. It was not as large as Schönbrunn in Vienna, and seemed quite modest compared to the magnificence of Versailles, but I liked it immediately. If such a large place—with its wide, sweeping staircase and massive rooms—could seem homey, it was Buckingham House.

And the cozy feeling went beyond the ambiance of the building, for never had we received such a warm welcome. Walking through the house, people bowed to us and smiled widely, as if our very presence gave them pleasure. Papa even tried out his newest bit of English, "Good morrow," and they said it right back. I put my arm around Wolfie's shoulders, claiming him as my brother. They seemed especially charmed by this, and I heard many *ahh*'s as we passed by.

We were led to a great hall where we were met by a stately looking man and woman in their twenties. "Welcome, welcome!" they said, taking Wolfie's violin case from Papa and setting it aside so they could shake our parents' hands. The man turned to Wolfie and me, leaning toward us as adults often did. He spoke to us in German. "So these are the talented children. Are you ready to play for us?"

"Yes, sir," I said.

"We're here to play for the king and queen," Wolfie said.

The man stood erect and laughed. The other people standing around joined in—but looked nervous. Then the man took our hands and led us through the crowd toward the front of the room, where a beautifully carved clavier was stationed. I glanced back at Mama and Papa. They had just exchanged a comment with each other but smiled at us encouragingly. Yet Papa's brow was pulled. Something was wrong.

"Here you are," the man said, leading me to the bench. He turned to Wolfie. "Will you play violin while your sister accompanies?"

"I will," Wolfie said. But then he looked around. "But I need my instrument."

"Indeed you do," said the man. He turned to his right, then clapped his hands. "The boy's instrument!"

Two servants ran toward the back of the room. During all this commotion, I noticed the young woman taking a seat at the front of the room in one of two grand chairs. I pulled in a breath. No. It couldn't be. These two people couldn't be the—

The servants returned and one of them handed the case to the man, offering a bow of his head. "Your Majesty."

It was true! This couple were the king and the queen of all England! Yet it wasn't just their hospitable demeanor that had fooled us. They were not dressed as sumptuously as other royalty we'd met. In truth, my dress—and Mama's—was fancier than the attire of the king and queen.

While I was getting situated at the clavier, I'd been distracted by this revelation and had not heard what the king had last told us. Panicked, I looked to Papa for guidance, but he and Mama were being seated a short distance away in the front row. Others were also sitting now, ready to hear us play. But who was to play first? Had the king given a direction I'd missed?

Wolfie readied his violin under his chin, his bow arm in place. He was ready for me to play. But which piece? We usually started with my playing alone on the clavier. But because the king had asked for both of us to play . . .

Wolfie looked back at me. "Vivaldi," he whispered.

Ah. The sonata in G minor. I began, but it took me two full phrases to rid myself of the butterflies in my stomach. Yet once those were gone, the music took over and it didn't matter who was in the room, or where the room was located. I could have been in the Americas or playing in a field. The world consisted of only my brother and me. And the sound . . . oh, the sound. When I closed my eyes, I felt it weaving its way between us, wrapping around my torso like the embrace of God giving me comfort and lifting me to places divine.

Our fingers were not connected to our arms. Mere arms! Mere bodies! The sound came from our souls and merely borrowed our mortal bodies as a vehicle for release. For even without the playing, the music *was*. It existed. It was eternal, hanging in the cosmos, just waiting to be set free.

Then suddenly, my hands were still. The combined notes of violin and clavier hung a moment as if wistful at leaving the here and now, unwilling to travel to that place of waiting in the future where they might be set free once more.

Applause broke through the stillness. I opened my eyes, and for an instant was surprised to see we were not alone. I put a hand to my cheek and found tears there. Wolfie looked back at me, and though he seemed a bit surprised by my tears, he smiled. He understood. We were a trio: Wolfie, me, and the music. A team and, even more, a partnership. A holy bond, greater than life or even death.

The king rose. *"Bravissimo!"* He clapped as he walked toward us. But when he saw me up close, he started. "Oh my dear, Mistress Mozart. Tears?" He pulled a lace-trimmed handkerchief from his waistcoat and dabbed at my cheek. For my ears alone, he said, "The angels themselves were moved, my dear." He pressed the handkerchief into my palm, and I knew it would be a prized keepsake, not of worth for itself but for the moment it brought to mind.

In truth, the rest of the concert was a blur. I played well and did all that was expected of me, but for some reason, I did not recapture the glory of that first piece—nor did it leave me completely.

Even later, during the carriage ride home, Papa's happiness at being paid the equivalent of two hundred sixty-four florins did not touch my mood.

Mama reached across the carriage and put her hand on mine. "Nannerl? Are you ill?"

Papa's eyebrows lowered. "You're not getting sick, are you? We've been asked back to play again, and——"

I shook my head. I was far from ill.

Wolfie poked me and mimicked throwing up.

"No," I said, just wanting to be left alone. "I'm fine."

"You did very well," Papa said. "It was a great success. Nowhere have we experienced such a welcome. And the audience was not like those at Versailles, who often treated our performance as an intrusion into their true goal for the evening—their inane conversation. Tonight, the lords and ladies were attentive, and I could tell their interest spurred you to play your best." He leaned forward and put a hand on each of our knees. "I am very proud of you, children."

On any other night I would have soaked in his praise, but tonight I could only pretend to be pleased. For there was a sorrow in my heart that railed against the elation I had felt during the first piece. It perplexed me, and I took solace looking out the window at the dark night, at the candle-lit windows as we passed.

I'd experienced a good thing. A grand thing. So how could I feel sad?

Then I thought of Papa's words: *"I could tell that their interest spurred you to play your best."*

He was wrong.

It had not been the kind words or the applause that had spurred me to play well, but a near-desperate desire to recapture the ecstasy of that first piece. But no matter how hard I'd tried, no matter how much I'd willed myself to leave the reality of the moment in order to find the fleeting breadth and breath of the music, it had evaded me like mist running from captive arms. *Oh, dear music, come to me! Embrace me again!*

I felt Mama's eyes and looked in her direction. She gave me a pensive smile. She knew something was wrong, yet I couldn't share. She would think I was odd, or ungrateful, or even a bit mad. To have so much, yet long for an elusive something that held no definition—not in words, and certainly not in will.

But then, with an intake of breath and a hand pressed to my chest, I realized what was truly bothering me.

Fear. The fear that I might never find the moment again. I closed my eyes and offered a fervent prayer.

But even as I sought His comfort, my throat tightened with a horrible thought that He may not grant my wish. Ever.

Suddenly I was consumed with a terror that threatened to strangle me. "No!" I said. I reached for the handle of the carriage door, knowing, yet not caring, that we were moving through the London streets.

"Nannerl!" Papa yelled. He grabbed my hand roughly and pushed me back into my seat. "What are you doing?"

I couldn't explain; I couldn't put voice to it. My head shook back and forth, ineffectually speaking for me.

I saw Wolfie pressed against the other end of our seat, his shoulder against the wall of the carriage, his face confused.

"Wolferl. Change with me," Mama said.

They exchanged places, and within moments Mama's arms were holding me close, pressing away the fear with her soft arms and gentle words. "Shh, shh, Nannerl. What's upset you so?"

I'd recaptured my breath but could not share my fear.

"I'm fine," I said. "I'm sorry. I must have dozed and been dreaming."

Mama gave me an unbelieving look and rocked me close. I could hear her heart beating, beating, like a drum pounding the rhythm of a dirge. It was an appropriate accompaniment to the fear that was now a part of my being: *This will end. It will all end. Soon* . . .

I closed my eyes and let Mama do what mamas do.

~

"But I don't feel sick," Wolfie said. "I want to play."

Papa bustled about, smoothing his hair in a mirror. He'd told us he had an errand to do that had something to do with *not* playing at the benefit concert in London that Papa had arranged with the cellist Carlo Graziani. It had already been postponed once, from May seventeenth to the twenty-second—tomorrow—but today Papa had stormed into our room saying we would not be involved in the concert due to Wolfie's being ill. He was on his way to post that fact in the *Public Advertiser.*

He rushed out, the door slamming behind him. I turned to Mama. "I don't understand. Wolfie's not sick."

Wolfie slumped in a chair, his back curved, his chin to his chest. "I don't understand either."

Mama glanced at the door, then back at us. She sat in an armed chair that had become her favorite and extended her hands to us. "Children." She took a breath and offered a timid smile. "Your papa is very wise. He knows what's best for all of us. Yes?"

"Of course," I said.

"Right after God comes Papa," Wolfie said.

Mama stroked our upper arms and nodded. Then she said, "When we agreed to do the concert with Herr Graziani, we did not realize that nobody who has leisure or means remains in London at this time. They are all off to the country. We postponed once, but there are still no patrons in town." She sighed. "And it does little good to play before a small audience of ordinary folk. Our livelihood depends on the correct people hearing us."

"But I want to play!" Wolfie said.

"And you will, dear one," Mama said. "June fourth is the king's birthday, and all the nobility will have to be back in town. Your father has decided to promote a new, better concert for the day after. On June fifth you will have an audience worthy of your talent and our hard work." She took our hands and her smile was genuine. "Would you like to see the copy for the ad your papa wants to place?"

We did. Mama rose and retrieved a paper on which there were many cross-outs. She and Papa had obviously worked hard on this advertisement. It read: *Miss Mozart of eleven and Master Mozart of seven Year of Age, Prodigies of Nature; taking the opportunity of representing to the Public the greatest Prodigy that Europe or that Human Nature has to boast of. Every Body will be astonished to hear a Child of such tender*

Age playing the Harpsichord in such a Perfection—it surmounts all Fantastic and Imagination, and it is hard to express which is more astonishing, his Executing upon the Harpsichord playing at Sight, or his own Composition.

Wolfie clapped. "Bravo, Papa! Many people will come hear us."

I nodded, but was not as enthusiastic. Although Papa had mentioned me in the first line—again stating our ages as younger than we were—I was not mentioned again. The advertisement was all about Wolfie. He was the draw. I was—in all ways—the accompanist.

Wolfie took my hands and did a jig, wanting me to join him. "We get to play! We get to play."

I shook his hands away. I took up my hat and headed to the door.

"Where are you going, Nannerl?" Mama asked.

"I'm going to wait for Papa."

It was a lie.

I went outside and turned left. There was a church in the square just a block away. It was not Catholic—since the creation of the Church of England two centuries earlier, Catholic churches had been changed over, though we *had* found one at the French Embassy. But unfortunately, that church was not close and I needed one. Now. Just like Papa, when I got an idea, *now* was always preferable to *later*. Especially when it concerned my need to talk to God.

I entered the church with trepidation. Would I be welcome? Would God hear my prayers in such a place? Although I had heard Papa suggest that some points of Lutheranism might be valid (we even visited the church in Worms, where in 1521 Luther appeared before the council for his radical views), he had made it very clear that he wanted us to remain faithful to the Catholic faith. But surely he would not object to my seeking solace for my troubled soul?

I opened the massive doors and stepped inside onto the worn stone floor of the vestibule. It took my eyes a moment to adjust to the light. Straight ahead I could see a mighty altar with stained-glass windows behind. On either side were pews facing each other—which I thought odd.

Before entering the sanctuary I looked for a font of holy water but found none. I'd never entered a house of worship without partaking of holy water. But my need was greater than my apprehension. I genuflected and slipped inside, taking a seat in the nearest pew. I waited for God to smite me down.

He did not. In fact, I felt quite safe here. I even felt His presence.

I noticed there were some other worshipers sitting quietly by themselves. It took me a few minutes to calm my breathing, which had grown labored from the swift walk as well as my nervousness. But soon I was ready to pray.

But where to begin? I was not used to making up prayers: I said ones from my prayer book or those taught to me as a child. Occasionally I'd offered one to the Almighty, but I was not good at such things.

I sat forward and took hold of the pew in front of me. I rested my forehead on my hands. Perhaps I shouldn't be praying. My thoughts were far from pure.

"Miss?"

I sat back and saw an old man in a black coat standing in the aisle. He wore a white cravat like a priest, except there were two long bands hanging down upon his chest. Was he a pastor, a vicar, a preacher? I repeated the line I had learned here in England. "I speak no English."

He smiled. *"Deutsch?"*

Relief poured over me. *"Ja."*

"Was ist los?" he asked.

Much was the matter. But how much could I say to this man? He was not a priest. And yet his manner was kind, his eyes attentive.

He spread a hand toward the pew. "May I sit?"

I moved over, giving him room. He sank onto the pew with a groan as if his muscles complained. He spoke to me in German, his accent good enough to make me believe he had lived there once. "You come here with a problem?"

I nodded.

He smiled at me. "I listen well." He pointed upward. "And so does He."

I nodded again and let a sentence loose. "Thou shalt not covet."

It was his turn to nod. "Ah. What do you covet?"

This was harder to say. "My brother . . . I . . ." I drew in a fresh breath. "My brother receives more attention than I. We used to be equal, but now . . . he has risen above me."

"'Blessed are the meek: for they shall inherit the earth.'"

"But I am talented too."

His left eyebrow rose. He did not know who I was, and I was not about to tell him. He put a hand on mine. "It's hard seeing praise go to someone else. Make the Almighty proud, young miss. For 'Pride goeth before destruction, and an haughty spirit before a fall.'"

I had not heard these words before.

The pastor took a deep breath. "And perhaps it is also difficult seeing him take too much pride in himself? Perhaps your brother makes you feel unworthy?"

I shook my head vehemently. "But he doesn't! He's very gracious. He's my best friend."

"Then who?"

I stood. I did not want to delve further into my thoughts, even if they could be offered as prayer. "I must go," I said.

I fled the church and ran home to Mama, who loved me. To Wolfie, who encouraged me.

And to Papa.

Chapter Seven

Although we did not reschedule our concert with the cellist Carlo Graziani, Papa did follow through and arrange our public debut for the day after the king's birthday, on June fifth, when everyone would be back in town. If only the concert could have been in the winter, we might have gotten up to six hundred people, but as it was, there were over two hundred in attendance, and those, from the highest classes. Ambassadors and nobles. Papa arranged the whole thing, renting a hall down by St. James' Park, getting music stands, two harpsichords, candles, and even hiring extra musicians. We had two singers, a violinist, and a cellist. Papa charged half a guinea admission. Even with all the expenses, we made a profit of ninety guineas, receiving nearly four times as much as we'd received playing at Buckingham House—and that fee had been generous.

But even though I was glad about the income that caused Papa such happiness, what truly brought gladness to my heart was what he wrote to our dear friend Hagenauer. He read it aloud to all of us before sending it. "What it all amounts to is this, that my little girl, although she is only twelve years old, is one of the most skillful players in Europe, and that, in a word, my boy knows in this his eighth year what one would expect only from a man of forty." He lowered the letter and peered at us over his glasses. "See what pride I feel?"

I ran to his side and hugged him. Wolfie climbed onto his lap. "I love you, Papa," I said.

He cleared his throat and nodded. "Now, now. Away, children. It's bedtime."

As I let Mama herd us away, I looked back and caught Papa wiping his eyes.

~

Papa loved London and called England an exceptional nation.

We agreed with him and appreciated England for much more than its generosity. There was a sense of freedom here we had never experienced before, and a politeness between the few hundred Londoners who lived lavishly and those who did not.

One day, right from our window, we saw thousands of workers filing past, all wearing the green apron of a weaver. They brandished black flags and called out their protests against some French-import policy that was costing them employment. Their sheer numbers were intimidating.

Yet as we watched them Papa said, "How wonderful to see how these workers have the right to demonstrate and force a change for either better or worse. This is quite something, children. We would not see this back in Salzburg, where we are sometimes ruled according to whim, and certainly not in France, where mobs often rule. Freedom, children. Freedom should be cherished."

The reverence I heard in his voice . . . I rarely saw Papa in awe.

Wolfie grabbed my handkerchief and started marching around the room, pretending to wave a flag. He shouted, "No imports! No imports!" until Mama shushed him.

I would have liked to stay longer at the window. To watch what had touched my father so . . .

~

Things went along very well, but then, catastrophe. In July Papa became very ill. We were scheduled to play a six o'clock concert at the Earl of Thanet's home. Papa sent for a coach, but being a Sunday, there were none available, so he got a sedan chair and put

Mama, Wolfie, and me into it. He followed us to Grosvenor Square on foot. But he couldn't keep up, and it was a hot afternoon. When he arrived, he was sweating profusely. Then, when the evening air turned cool, he felt chilled and buttoned his cloth coat over his silk waistcoat. During the concert, with the windows open . . . By the time we were finished at eleven, Papa needed his own sedan chair to follow our own. Mama got him right to bed, and he tried to make light of it, saying it was likely a native complaint called a "cold."

But it wasn't. A few days later, after trying to cure himself by perspiring, his throat was sorely inflamed, and a doctor was called. Many remedies were tried: bleeding, purging, and even opium. But Papa only got sicker. Mama railed over the foreign doctor. She'd brought some home remedies with her from Salzburg, but English apothecaries didn't understand them, and so we were forced to use their remedies.

Which didn't work.

Papa got sicker and sicker, and experienced stomach pains and issues with his nerves. This was no simple "cold," or had at the very least become something worse through the treatments. The doctor had the audacity to say, "Mr. Mozart, it is obvious you are not a suitable subject to take such medicine." With that, he left.

Blaming Papa because the medicine didn't work? We all stood around Papa's bedside.

"What shall we do now, Leopold?" Mama asked.

With effort Papa swallowed. His voice was barely more than a whisper. "Get Herr Sipurtini. His cousin is a doctor."

"The cellist Sipurtini? The Dutch Jew who lives here in London?"

Papa said only one word: "Go."

Mama nodded. "Nannerl, take care of things here. I'll be back as soon as I can."

As the door closed, the silence was heavy. I was in charge? Wolfie looked at me expectantly. *Don't look at me, I don't know what to do!*

Papa moaned. His eyes were closed and his forehead furrowed with pain.

Wolfie carefully climbed onto the foot of the bed and curled up at Papa's feet, one hand near but not touching him. He looked ready to cry. And so, without truly making the decision, I knelt beside Papa's bed, leaned my head against the mattress, and prayed.

It was all I could do.

~

God hears prayers. And the new doctor was wise.

Three weeks after getting sick, Papa was well enough to be carried to St. James' Park for some fresh air. A week after that, we all moved to lodging an hour outside of London, to Chelsea, where the air was of better quality. Papa contacted Herr Hagenauer and had twenty-two masses said for us at five different churches.

Good came from the bad, for the view around Chelsea was beyond lovely. Wherever I turned I saw gardens and fine estates in the distance. It was calm there, and the air was fresh and invited me to take deep breaths that fueled me. And fueled Wolfie too. The place inspired Wolfie to compose his first symphony that included all the instruments, including trumpets and kettledrums. We were not allowed to touch the keyboard (so as not to disturb the quiet for Papa), so Wolfie and I sat side by side, and I would copy the symphony as he composed it. "Remind me to give the horn something worthwhile to do," he'd say. It was a special time between us.

Slowly Papa got better. But he was weak and didn't feel like eating. It was disconcerting to see mighty Papa as fragile as a child.

When we first moved to Chelsea, we'd had our food sent to us from an eating house, but it wasn't very good. Not that we ever enjoyed English food. Although we liked the meat, the cider was unhealthy, and Papa didn't like the taste of the alcoholic punch and rum. And we were in complete agreement about the horrid plum pudding. So, with Papa's sickness, Mama took matters into her own hands and began cooking for us. It was nice to eat familiar foods again: potato soup, liver dumplings, and sauerbraten. So nice that Mama decided she would continue cooking for us while we remained in England. We had all lost weight.

Papa despaired of how his sickness had impaired our concerts.

Two months with no income; having to spend our savings to survive. Yet Papa said that if God would grant us good health, we need not worry about the guineas. Papa always worried about guineas, so for him to say that . . .

Perhaps during his illness he and God had come to an agreement?

Did Papa fear dying? One time I heard him and Mama whispering with trepidation about dying in a strange land, saying how the pension Mama could expect from the Salzburg court would be pitifully small. We would endure a difficult fate if Papa succumbed. So I prayed even harder that he would get completely well. And stay that way.

One day, Papa declared himself well enough to start thinking of the future. He was ready to move back to London, where he promised to spare no effort to get us back into the concert scene. He vowed not to go back to Salzburg until he had hauled in a fine fish—a good catch of guineas. Several thousand were mentioned.

The question of our age loomed large. Although Papa fudged our ages, if we did not take advantage of the opportunities in this rich nation now, we would be fools. Yet I no longer looked like a child, and even Wolfie—always small for his age—did not look seven anymore. I, especially, felt time running by too quickly. For too soon I would be of marriageable age. If I did not establish myself as a great *artiste* by then . . .

If only time could stand still.

But alas, even God could not grant such a request.

~

After two months of sickness and silence, we were asked back to Buckingham House to play before the king and queen.

We were late leaving the inn. Papa, Wolfie, and I stood at the curb, the carriage ready, waiting for Mama. Papa pulled out his pocket watch for the third time and looked upward toward our room. "What is she doing up there?" he asked.

"I'll go get her." I ran upstairs, holding my heavy skirt and petticoat high. I found Mama trying to communicate with our

English maid, Amanda. She was pointing to her hair, then pulling her hands apart. She wanted her ribbons. Probably her blue ones.

Amanda skittered around nervously, holding up a comb, then a jeweled hair bauble.

"I can't make her understand!" Mama said. Amanda held up a hairpin. *"Nein! Blaue Bänder!"*

I stopped Amanda's frenzy with a hand on her arm. "Blue ribbon," I said.

Amanda's eyes widened with recognition, and she went to a box in the armoire and pulled out two.

Mama fell to sitting on the bed. *"Ja schlielich!"*

Amanda set to work weaving the ribbons into Mama's coif. I went to the window and called down to Papa. "We'll be right down." To expedite things, I handed Mama a mirror. "You really should learn English, Mama."

"I know English. 'Good morrow, sir,'" she said. "And I try to understand them, but the only Englishman I can understand is the night watchman calling the hours."

I was shocked. "Really?"

She turned her voice into a watchman's thick baritone: "Three o'clock and all is well!"

I had never heard her parody anyone, and I must have stared because she suddenly started laughing. Amanda stopped her work to look at me, and then we both looked at Mama.

"All is well!" Mama repeated, a baritone again.

Amanda and I began to laugh. Then I heard heavy footsteps on the stairs and remembered that all would not be well if Mama and I didn't get downstairs. Now.

Mama heard it too because she stood and did the last tucking of the ribbon on her own. She opened the door at the same time Papa did and sidled past him to the stairs. "Good morrow, sir," she said.

Papa looked perplexed. I held in my laughter and followed her down.

My mama, the wit.

~

While we performed at Buckingham House, Wolfie sat on the lap of Christian Bach—the son of the late Johannes Sebastian Bach. He was the reigning master of music for the royal family now, having taken Handel's place in their court. Such names were sovereign in the world of music, and there was my brother, sitting between Bach's knees, taking turns on the harpsichord, improvising new music for hours.

Although I enjoyed listening to the two of them, it was another evening of struggle for me. I started out standing near the instrument, the ever-attentive sister and compatriot, waiting for my turn. But as thirty minutes neared an hour, and as neither the audience's attention (nor my brother's or Master Bach's enthusiasm) showed signs of waning, I slowly edged away from the harpsichord, skimmed the aisle by the wall, nodded slightly to the lords and ladies, and pulled away from the scene. I ended up in the adjoining room.

Once there, I took a desperate breath. Had I been holding it as I'd made my escape?

Two footmen guarded the door, and I saw their eyes flicker in my direction. I moved toward the window, needing air. And though the October breeze made me shiver, I embraced it as I would an elixir taken to cure an illness.

For I *was* suffering. Yet my ailment was not something I cared to name. Only the Protestant reverend in the church knew of my despicable condition.

I looked down at my dress. Its color was appropriate, as it matched my heart.

Envy, thy color is green.

I heard a smattering of applause, accompanied by delighted laughter. But the music continued, unabated, fueled by the praise and by the joy the musicians found in the act of creation.

Horses neighed and fidgeted in the courtyard below as drivers conversed and smoked tobacco in their long pipes. What if I got into one of those carriages and had them drive me away? Anywhere. Just away.

"Nannerl?"

I glanced behind me to find Mama exiting the room. I realized I was crying and quickly wiped my tears before facing her. I managed a smile, but she would have none of it and came to me, her face concerned.

"I looked up and saw you were gone. Are you ill?"

"I'm fine." I linked my arm through hers, leading her back toward the room.

She stopped our progress. "Why did you leave?"

I tried to think of an acceptable excuse. I nodded toward the window and put a hand at my corset. "I needed air, but I'm better now."

She eyed me a moment. Obviously, I was a better actress than I thought, for after I endured a few seconds of her scrutiny, she continued our walk toward the door. "Your brother is doing well, don't you think?"

She didn't want to know what I thought. No one did.

⁓

As 1765 came upon us, the chances for us to perform became fewer. Knowing after we left England there would be no more guineas, Papa took action. He began to advertise that prospective customers might find the family at home—at the inn—every day from twelve to two o'clock. Many showed up, and Papa charged an admittance fee. I enjoyed giving these impromptu concerts because the attendees had obviously gone out of their way to come. These were people from all segments of society. Some were familiar with music, and others . . . I will admit that both Wolfie and I played best when we had a knowledgeable audience, as their expertise fueled ours. To those who came to hear trifles, we gave trifles.

In between visitors, Wolfie and I often played marbles. Once, when Wolfie was playing his violin, I saw a stray marble under someone's chair. When Wolfie saw me looking in that direction, he spotted it too and mouthed to me, "It's mine!" And sure enough, as soon as the audience moved to the door, he pounced on it and put it in his pocket. I truly think it was one of mine, but he was the swifter. Finders keepers.

Losers weepers.

Although Papa never said anything outright, as winter passed into the spring—in April we'd been in London a year—as he and Mama became engaged in many private talks (of which I heard snatches), and as he suffered many sleepless nights, I came to believe that he had been asked by the queen and king to take a permanent position in the English court. I had no proof, but where Papa had previously been complimentary and even envious of all things English, he suddenly saw only the negative. The weather was too variable and damp, the air too full of soot from thousands of chimneys, the houses too cold—oh, for the even warmth of a tile stove—and the diversity of its religions and the freedom of its classes now gave offense. It was as if he'd suddenly set his sights toward home and all things German.

If this were true, it helped explain why we were not asked to perform again at Buckingham House. Had Papa truly rejected a royal offer of employment and thus given offense? I hoped his decision wasn't because of Wolfie or me. For periodically we did whine about wanting to see our friends back in Salzburg, and we often egged each other on talking about the ecstasy of a good Austrian apricot torte. Surely Papa would not make such a significant decision because of our meager complaints?

Or . . . there might have been another reason we had not been invited back to Buckingham House. Had we done poorly? One Sunday as we walked to church, I took advantage of the fact that Mama and I were walking alone behind Wolfie and Papa.

"Mama?"

She adjusted her shawl. "Yes, Nannerl?"

"We haven't had many concerts lately. Did Wolfie and I do something wrong?"

With a glance to Papa up ahead, Mama put a hand on my shoulder and slowed our walk, ever so slightly. "It's not your fault. Nor your brother's. It is the fault of the nobility."

"How so?"

"The concerts we've been having for the ordinary people?"

"I like those. We make people happy. The other day a grand-mother cried after I played."

She nodded. "I also enjoy the experience of reaching common

folk, exposing them to a bit of the divine." Mama sighed heavily. "But the nobility don't like it."

It only took me a moment to understand. "They want us all to themselves?"

"Indeed."

"Then why don't they invite us to do more concerts—for them?"

"Your father thinks it's a conspiracy: retribution for us having the audacity to share you with the world instead of with just a privileged few. The haves are never eager to give up their advantage over the have-nots—not even in England." She sighed. "But unfortunately, the have-nots seem content to see you just once, while the nobility would ask to see you again and again. Would ask, but aren't."

A point entered my mind, but I wasn't sure I should share it.

Mama must have sensed my desire to say more, for she said, "Speak, Nannerl. Speak now and then we need never speak of it again."

Since she'd asked . . . "Papa is always worried about money, and since it *is* the nobility who can pay the good amounts . . . perhaps we shouldn't do the other concerts. They don't pay very well, and I've noticed Papa keeps lowering the price."

She squeezed my shoulder. "You mustn't worry so much about money, Nannerl. I know being in such close quarters you hear us talk of it, but . . . your papa has worked very hard to keep us here in London, where all in all, the receipts have been generous. Now that things have turned . . . a man's pride is delicate, especially when mixed with his necessity to provide for his family."

A man of the cloth who was walking in our direction suddenly slowed, then stopped beside us.

"Fraulein Mozart!"

His exuberant greeting caused Papa and Wolfie to stop and come back to join us. The man looked familiar, yet I did not—

But then I did. "Father. Reverend."

Papa had joined us, Wolfie in hand. His eyes were wary. "Sir?"

The reverend nodded with a little bow. "My apologies, sir. Madam. Let me introduce myself. I am Reverend Collins. I had the pleasure of meeting . . ." He hesitated and looked at me. I hoped he would not give away my secret—that I'd taken solace in a non-Catholic church. Finally he said to my parents, "I had the pleasure of hearing your children play at the Swan and Hoop."

Papa cleared his throat. "Yes, well . . ." I knew he thought our recent residence at the Swan was an indignity, so for this man to bring it up . . .

"The performance was glorious," Reverend Collins said. "I witnessed the children playing the covered keyboard, sitting side by side. The music was quite astonishing. And the four-handed duets were something these ears have never heard." He gave me a wink. "And then, of course, I especially enjoyed *your* prodigious playing, Fraulein Mozart."

I felt myself blush but gave him a quick curtsy. I looked at Papa.

Unfortunately, before Papa smiled at the compliment, I saw his left eyebrow rise. That one gesture disheartened me, but I maintained my smile and manners while Reverend Collins continued his chat, hearing him say that he had also purchased a copy of Wolfie's sonatas and a copy of the engraving the Parisian Carmontelle had made of me, Wolfie, and Papa performing. For some reason his litany of compliments embarrassed me. Finally he said his good-byes.

"What a nice man," Mama said as we resumed our walk.

"He liked *my* playing," I said softly.

Papa's eyes flashed. "Excuse me, young lady?"

Mama saved me by taking Papa's arm and leading him forward with chatter about our afternoon plans.

Wolfie kicked a pebble and it clattered ahead of us, coming to rest near a horse trough. "Your turn. Get it!" he said.

I ignored him and walked on.

~

Papa waved his hands in the air. "The very sight of all this luggage makes me perspire!"

I agreed. After living in London for fifteen months, we'd accumulated . . . too much. New clothes, housewares, souvenirs. Papa had spent a great deal of time picking out watches for his friends back in Salzburg—especially Herr Hagenauer. English watches were superior to German watches, but Papa worried whether, if they broke . . . could they be repaired in Salzburg? And Herr Hagenauer had requested some red cloth that had to be sent ahead because customs regulations in France were stringent about such things—though I had no idea why. There were many details to think about and plan for.

To ease our exit from London on August first, we looked forward to answering an amazing number of invitations: Holland, Copenhagen, Hamburg, and St. Petersburg. Yet even though I would have liked to see Denmark and Russia, none of us wanted to spend the winter in such places. Papa's plan was to return to Paris to spend the winter concert season there, and afterward, move on to sunny Italy.

But then Papa's choice of our next venue was decided for him. Holland.

I'd always wanted to see Holland with its canals and windmills, but Papa had been hesitant, fearing the people there would be crude and base as we had experienced in other lowland places. But the Dutch envoy to London had sweetened the invitation with promises of high pay if we would play at court for William V, the Prince of Orange. When the prince's sister, Caroline, insisted we come, the engagement was settled.

Unfortunately, with our carriage and many of our possessions stored in Calais, we had to return to the mainland via that route. Luckily, this time our Channel crossing was without queasy incident—the day lovely, and the seas calm. We even had a big lunch once we landed, then headed east to Holland via Dunkirk, Antwerp, and Rotterdam.

Both Papa and Wolfie suffered bad attacks of catarrh along the way, coughing horribly (was the variable weather to blame?), and we were delayed enough that it was six weeks before we entered The Hague in September. Once there, we were very glad to not have missed Holland, for its landscape and towns were unlike any we had ever seen: flat expanses of green, with tree-lined canals bisecting each plot of land. It was all so ordered and . . . perfect. To better see the land, we even left our carriage behind in Antwerp to utilize the horse-drawn barges on the water.

At The Hague we took lodging at an inn, and Papa sent word to the prince that we had arrived. The prince and princess arranged for us to give the first of many concerts two days after our arrival. They even supplied a carriage for us.

But then I got sick. At first I thought it was merely chest congestion as Papa and Wolfie had suffered. Yet on the night of September twelfth, when we were to present our first concert, I couldn't go. Mama stayed behind with me. Poor Mama. Always having to play the nurse for the rest of us. Mama never got sick. I admired her strength, and her patience and care. Every time I would wake from sleep, she was beside my bed, ready to help me sip water or broth, or stroke my head.

I tried to get well, I truly did, but each time I attempted to sit or stand, the illness demanded attention and I fell back to bed. After two weeks I realized it was serious, for on the twenty-sixth, a chill and fever took hold. Swallowing became an act of will as my throat was swollen and sore.

A doctor bled me, but I did not get better. He said the blood was very bad; it was inflamed and half of it was white slime and grease. I dared not look and make myself feel sicker still.

As the sickness took on a stronger grip I fell deeper and deeper into a place that had nothing to do with the inn at The Hague. My thoughts lived in places unreal and came in odd bursts that had no connection with one another. I even heard myself speaking in German, then French, then English. I would hear soft laughter then, and if I managed to open my eyes, often found Papa and Mama smiling at me. At something I said? One time Wolfie made a funny face and mimicked me in English, "I want more mutton, if you please!"

But then I'd slip away into a sleep where the odd dreams reigned. Dreams of standing before a massive door that led to a concert hall and having the music going on without me. Not being able to open the door . . . my fingers freezing on the keyboard, unable to play . . . watching from a window as Mama, then Papa, then Wolfie rode away.

Sometimes I heard Wolfie's music as I slept. It comforted me.

There were many doctors, and one blended into the next. I heard one say that he was going to stop up the cough with a milk cure, by driving the matter of the disease down into my lower body where it could be released. Honestly, I didn't care what they did, as long as I found comfort.

Death would have been welcome. Even Mama and Papa said so. But it was not allowed. Papa fumed, "I will not have one of us die on foreign soil. I will not!" And Mama lamented, "I have lost five children, I will not lose another! Take *me*, Father! Take *me*." I welcomed their fighting spirit, for I had little of my own.

For weeks they sat at my bedside. They often told me Bible stories: the story of Jesus healing the nobleman's son, and the young girl who was brought back from the dead.. At first these stories scared me, for it was apparent my parents found similarities between the dying children and myself.

Was I really dying?

I was really dying. I knew it even before the priest came to give me Holy Communion. Even before the date of October twenty-first, when the priest was so upset at my condition that he gave me Last Rites. Over and over Mama and Papa reminded me that the world was full of vanity and heaven was a good place. I would be happy there—and free from the pain that wracked my body.

I heard yet did not hear. I spoke but could not speak. I slept.

And then on that same day, another doctor came. I heard Mama say he was the retired doctor of the princess. One of the other doctors was there too, and Papa and the two men argued over me. The old doctor answered questions of the new one, but Papa argued and said, "What is this talk of boils and pocks? There are none present now, and never were!" I wished they would stop arguing as if I wasn't even there.

But then it was quiet and I opened my eyes to find the new doctor taking my pulse, then touching my forehead. He put on his glasses and examined my eyes and my tongue. He then proclaimed, "It is nothing more than extraordinarily thick mucus. Some good calves' soup with well-boiled rice will help."

And it did. For I began to recover. I was still weak, but slowly the world came back to me and took over the awful place of my dreams.

But just a week after I gained enough strength to get out of bed in early November, Wolfie became sick with the same illness. For four weeks he fought off death. Fever wracked him, and for a week he just lay there, barely breathing, unable to speak. And frighteningly, his lips turned black and hard, and peeled away.

As they had during my illness, Mama stayed with him from midnight to six in the morning, and Papa took the six-to-noon shift so Mama could sleep. They both stood watch during the day, rarely leaving the room. I tried to help as I could, but I was still weak, and they feared a reoccurrence if I remained too close. Wolfie was completely unrecognizable, nothing but tender skin and little bones.

For three months sickness held our family captive. What God sends must be endured, but as Christmas neared, Papa rejoiced that we had both risen from the dead. Wolfie walked a few steps on his own and received our applause as if he had run a race.

I knew Papa worried about the lost income, as well as the expense of doctors and medicines. But when I apologized for being sick, he said, "Expense must not be considered. The devil take the money, if one only gets off with one's skin!"

We had not planned to be in Holland so long and regretted having sent our furs and winter clothes on to Paris. How we could have used them in December! It was the people of Holland who made us warm. We made many friends during our stay, and Wolfie made a musical name for himself before he got sick. Alas, I did not have a chance to play there because I took sick the day after our arrival. But I wanted to. I was eager to prove to the Dutch that I was a viable part of this performing duo. It was not the Miracle Child but the Miracle Children.

God did not save me for nothing. I'd make sure of that.

⌒

Five months in Amsterdam, Antwerp, Brussels, then back to Paris for two months where we picked up the luggage we had left there. Did we really need these things we'd been without for over two years? Then on to Dijon for two weeks, Lyons for four, and Geneva, Switzerland, for three. Lausanne and Berne, Zurich, Ulm, and Munich. Places that had only appeared as a dot on a map became real in our memories. Before the trip I'd never imagined the vastness of the world. Afterward, I often thought about the people I'd met and imagined what they were doing while I floated on a canal in Holland or crossed a mountain pass in Switzerland. All these people living the same day, the same hours, seeing the same sun and moon and stars . . . yet so far apart they didn't even know of one another's existence.

I knew. Only lucky ones like my family knew. I sometimes wondered if even kings and queens had seen as much as we. And not just the places, not just buildings and rivers and hills. Not just paintings, museums, and statues. But people. I could never count the number of people we'd seen, and as amazing as that number was, even more so was the number who had seen *us* and heard us play. The multitude who'd talked to us, often in languages we did not understand. Kings and shopkeepers, ambassadors and farmers. We'd come into contact with them all. Who else could say as much? I didn't mean to sound proud, but . . . but who else? God was very gracious.

Along the way we added Wolfie's compositions to the concerts. Composition became his passion, and he spent many hours each day at work. Once a piece was completed, Papa arranged for it to be engraved (usually dedicating it to some royal personage), and soon after, we played it in public. In Amsterdam we repeatedly heard people humming one of Wolfie's melodies.

I tried to compose some too. Yet every time I started, Mama or Papa found something else for me to do, or shooed me away from Wolfie saying, "Move on, Nannerl. We must give your brother quiet."

After a while, I stopped trying.

~

We returned to Salzburg on November 29, 1766, filled with apprehension and exhaustion. Our trip home from London had taken sixteen months. Even as recognizable mountains graced our view, even as my stomach knotted with anticipation at seeing familiar people and places, Papa held Mama's hand, shaking his head, clearly worried.

"The archbishop will be angry we've been gone so long. Longer than we'd planned," he said. "Years more."

"But you've sent him music and presents. You've sent word through Hagenauer about our triumphs."

"Wherever we played, people knew our roots," I offered. "People always knew we were the children of the Kapellmeister of Salzburg."

"Vice Kapellmeister," Papa said.

Oh dear. I'd forgotten. On our trip, they'd always called Papa Kapellmeister—and he hadn't corrected them. But he wasn't Kapellmeister. Someone else was. I hoped nothing about that detail had gotten back to the archbishop. My own worry grew.

Papa adjusted the cuffs of his waistcoat. "Hagenauer told me there was talk of our going to Scandinavia next, then Russia. And even to China."

"We're going to China?" Wolfie asked.

"No, no. We're not," Papa said. "Though it *is* true we were asked to Russia and Denmark. But to have such talk spread . . ." He shook his head.

"How can it hurt if people think that well of us?" Mama asked. "Surely talk of such invitations—true or not—only strengthens our position."

"To the populace, yes," Papa said, raising a finger. "And I have no qualms about letting them think what they may. Our travels are a novelty to them, a dream, a fairy tale beyond their imaginings." He dropped his finger. "But in regard to the archbishop . . . if he believes we are leaving again . . ."

Mama pulled in a breath. "You don't think he'll take away your position, do you?"

"I don't know." He closed his eyes and rubbed the space between them. "And moreover, I'm not completely sure I care."

"Not care?" Mama asked.

"Oh . . . perhaps I'm just weary." He patted her hand; then their fingers intertwined and sat together on her knee. "As the miles between ourselves and Salzburg have diminished, the rumors and gossip have increased: which Salzburg musicians have composed what, who is controlling whom in His Grace's court . . . Life has very obviously gone on without us." He sighed and crossed himself. "For a few years—praise God—I was at peace and free from such idiocy, and I want to remain so. Truth tell, I'm not sure I'm capable of coming back from the grand courts of Europe to be a mere fiddler."

Mama drew his hand to her lips and kissed it. "You are much more than that, dear one."

Papa pulled his hand away and pointed angrily out the window. "Not to them I'm not!" He looked across the coach at Wolfie and me, and suddenly seemed embarrassed that we'd seen his outburst. He reached out and patted our knees. "I'm very proud of you, children. These years together have been precious and irreplaceable." He sat back and looked outside again, but this time his eyes were wistful. "Never to be replaced. . . ."

I appreciated his praise but had a question. "We *are* leaving again, aren't we, Papa?"

He looked at each of us in turn. "We do like to travel, yes?"

We all nodded. Although I was glad to be returning home, a part of me was a little afraid of staying put, of *not* hearing a multitude of languages, *not* seeing grand museums and concert halls, *not* being in exotic places beyond the ken of our neighbors. I had the awful fear if I remained at home, I would fall into the domestic destiny Mama had deemed mine. I was fifteen now, and the expectations that haunted my gender loomed distressingly close.

Then Papa eased my fears. "We still have many places to see, children. Many places that need to see and hear you. I would have liked to get to Italy, but the pull of the archbishop . . ." He sighed deeply. "Oh, who knows what is in store for us upon our return to Salzburg? Perhaps we will be greeted in such a distressful way that we will happily put our knapsacks over our backs and leave forever. I am bringing you back to the fatherland. If that isn't enough for them, if they don't appreciate you as others have . . ." He took a fresh breath. "They will not have you gratis."

"It *will* be good for the children to rest and recuperate," Mama said. She tucked a throw over Wolfie's legs. He was just getting over yet another illness.

Papa sighed. "I have promised to return home, and I am keeping my word." There was a hint of defiance in his voice.

Mama spoke to Wolfie and me. "Did you know your papa is trying to get us new lodging? For you are both larger than you were when we left. Nannerl, we realize you need your own sleeping area now, and we all need separate work areas."

"We're moving away from the Hagenauers'?" Wolfie looked worried.

"Eventually. But not until we find a place that's suitable," Papa said.

My own space. I would like that. Although I loved my family dearly, I was tired of sharing a bed with Mama on the road and sharing a bedchamber with my family at home. I had left Salzburg a child and returned a woman.

Suddenly Mama pointed out the window. "There's the Salzach River! It will lead us home."

"Mmm," Papa said.

~

I stood with my friend Katherl in front of the glass case. "Papa had Herr Hagenauer make it special. See? It has a lock." I opened the glass door and took out a gilded snuff box. "The queen of France gave this to me the second time we played at court." I held the intricate box in the palm of my hand. "Go ahead, you can touch it. It's real gold. Just be careful."

Katherl moved her fingers close but at the last minute withdrew them, clasping them behind her back. "What do you need with a snuff box?"

A good question. "It's not what it's used for that's important, but the fact it's gold, it's beautiful, and it's worth a lot of money. The queen wouldn't have had to give me anything. One does not question gifts—especially from royalty."

"I wouldn't know," Katherl said.

I put the snuff box away and picked up a cloisonné mirror a duchess in Holland had given me. "This used to have a matching brush, but Wolfie dropped it and it broke into a million—"

She looked toward the door. "I got a new kitty."

It took me a moment to move my thoughts from royalty to pets. "What's its name?" I asked.

"*Pfeffer.*"

I imagined a peppered calico. I turned back to the display case. My eyes focused on the figurine of a cat Baroness Solomon had given me when I'd played for her birthday.

"Want to see her?" Katherl asked. "And Otto Ferringer spent a week in Vienna with his parents and brought me back some chocolates. I saved one for you."

I glanced back at the case. How could she not be interested in these treasures and hearing the stories of how I came to have them, and who gave them to me? And so what if ferret-faced Otto Ferringer had been to Vienna for a week? My family had been gone three and a half years. I'd brought Katherl back some Belgium lace. Wasn't that better than any chocolates that were here today, gone tomorrow?

"Come on," Katherl said, taking my hand. "When I get her playing with yarn, Pfeffer will jump a foot off the floor."

I wanted to pull my hand away. What did I care of a house cat when I'd seen the world?

But I did not pull away, and I let Katherl lead me into the streets of ordinary Salzburg.

∼

Papa came into the kitchen for dinner and tossed his gloves on the chair. "Gossip! I despise gossip."

Mama looked up from setting the forks. "What gossip?"

Papa removed his coat and hung it on the hook near the door. "Beta Hübner has printed in his inane *Diarium* that . . ." He retrieved a page from his coat pocket and read, "I believe it certain that nobody in Europe is as famous as Herr Mozart with his two children."

"That's very complimentary," Mama said.

Papa shook his head, cleared his throat, and continued. "Indeed, after God, he has his children to thank for his fame and his great wealth. The now completed journey is said to have cost them something near twenty thousand florins; I can easily believe it; but how much money has he not presumably collected?" He turned the page over. "It also says our Nannerl is 'tolerably tall and almost marriageable already' but he worries over Wolfgang's small size." Papa wadded up the sheet and threw it into the fire. "I thought he was our friend. For him to speculate about our children's growth . . . and to even take a guess regarding our expenses and income is reprehensible. For us to have to come home to this . . . this . . . drivel . . ."

"The children *are* going to play for the archbishop next week," Mama said. "I've heard buzz regarding his pride in us."

Papa made two fists and held them close to his chin. "I am stifled here. They don't understand what we've done. They don't understand the importance of our work, our sacrifice in bringing the world this extraordinary talent." He looked around the room. His eyes skimmed past me, then landed back at Mama. "Where *is* Wolfie?"

I did not hear my mother's reply. Wolfie. He'd asked for my brother and only my brother.

I slipped from the room and hurried down the stairs to the street. The bite of the December air took advantage of my being without my cloak. But I could not go back for it. For anything.

I turned into an alley and walked until I was safely hidden in shadows. Only then did I let the wall of the building guide me to sitting. I tucked my dress around my legs and feet and leaned against my thighs for warmth. The cold was appropriate. For I'd felt very cold since returning to Salzburg. The warmth of our close family travels was slipping away. Every day forced us to deal with others beyond our small foursome.

And Papa was right in his subtle heralding of Wolfie as the talent. What did I have to show for our time away from Salzburg? Thousands of notes played and heard by the ear, but immediately gone as another note took its place? A glass case full of gifts from important people who cared little for me as anything other than an

oddity and a novelty? I had brought nothing substantial back to Salzburg except four extra inches in height—and width.

Marriageable age? How could people say such a thing? I was
one of the Miracle Children. And yet . . . Herr Hübner had also
commented on Wolfie's small stature. It was true my brother had
not grown much during our absence, as if knowing that looking
older would hurt our cause. Had he willed himself to stay small and
childlike? Had I somehow made a mistake because I had dismissed
God's ability to stop time and keep me a child forever?

As I huddled against the cold I felt my breasts against my legs. I
was a woman now. The novelty of two performing children, if not
gone, was waning.

And it was all my fault. No wonder Papa liked Wolfie best. My
brother, the eternal child.

And Nannerl, the girl of marriageable age.

It was over.

Chapter Eight

Smallpox and operas. I hoped to never again have anything to do with either.

One wouldn't think that a disease and a musical creation had anything in common, but they both loomed large. So much loomed large. . . .

After being home ten months, I was excited about our next journey to Vienna—at first. Spending time in Salzburg had proven tedious, and though I didn't want to come off as putting on airs— *de haut en bas*—in many ways it was a life too simple for my newly developed tastes. How spoiled we had become on our travels. For even beyond the places and people we'd met, there'd always been something of interest to do. But at home, as one day folded into the next, I felt in danger of being suffocated by the mediocrity of our normal routine. If I wasn't careful, would I wake up one morning and accept it all as my fate? Would I forget about my plans to be more than just a wife, more than just a mother, more than just a Salzburger?

So when Papa announced we were taking another concert excursion to Vienna, I was thrilled—and relieved. And when he spoke of his high hopes for our future, mentioning our destiny, I knew he was speaking from my heart as well as his: "Providence binds everything together in such a way that if we give ourselves up to it with complete trust, we cannot miss our destiny." Such lofty words, implying we would once again find our place in the world of music. I, Nannerl Mozart, would find *my* place.

The event that spurred the trip to Vienna was the wedding of Empress Maria Theresa's daughter, the Archduchess Maria Josepha, which was scheduled for October 14, 1767. We were not the only musicians of Salzburg to travel in hopes of being asked to play for the festivities that would take place over many weeks' time. Papa mentioned at least three others. But, he assured us, we would be the jewels in the royal crown.

However, once we reached Vienna in early September, protocol stated we could not play elsewhere until we had played for the empress. We were awaiting a summons from court when the first of our disasters struck.

Smallpox.

It had all started four months earlier in late May, when the second wife of the new emperor, Joseph II, contracted the disease and died, as had his first wife. Joseph was the new emperor because his father, Emperor Francis, for whom we'd played years before, had died while we were in France. Even Empress Maria Theresa succumbed to smallpox. She recovered, but in her recovery she only made things worse. . . .

The empress had a habit of visiting the tomb of her dear husband once a month. On one such visit in October, the soon-to-be bride Maria Josepha accompanied her and immediately fell ill with the pox. Rumor had it that the air of the tomb was infected because the body of the poor girl's sister-in-law was also present—in an unsealed casket.

Then, horror of horrors, the betrothed, Maria Josepha—who was just my age, only sixteen—died on the day after what should have been her wedding! The entire city roiled with shock and sadness. How could God allow such a thing? Papa said it was God's will, but if God is good, then how could He allow such a tragedy to happen? It's hard for me to wrap my mind around such mysteries.

Papa also moaned about how unfair it was that so many had come to Vienna with such high hopes of performing, only to be silenced by this turn of events. "Why did she have to die now?"

If he wished to speak of the inequities of life, I think Papa should have thought of poor Maria Josepha. . . .

But then the smallpox visited *us*. The son of the goldsmith with whom we had been living fell ill—but not before infecting two of his younger siblings. Papa went into a panic and sought new lodging. Yet he was unable to find any large enough for four, so two days after Maria Josepha's death, he left Mama and me behind at the goldsmith's and escaped with Wolfie to a safer part of town.

Left Mama and me behind in a house full of sickness.

Nine out of ten children who were dying in Vienna were dying of the pox.

Yet he left us there.

The next day, I did not get out of bed, and Mama wondered if I too had fallen ill. But my sickness was not caused by disease.

When I didn't get up on the second day, she sat at my bedside, feeling my forehead, asking if I wanted a doctor.

I shook my head and turned away from her.

"Then, what's wrong?" she asked.

Surely she knew. . . .

She smoothed my hair behind an ear. "Nannerl?"

Like poison from a body being bled, I let my accusation seep out. "Papa left us behind. He doesn't care if we live or die."

Mama removed her hand and sat back with a soft *whooph* of breath.

I pushed myself to sitting against the pillows. "Why didn't he take us with him to a safer place?"

Mama adjusted the coverlet under my arms. "He couldn't find lodging for four. Only for two."

"We could have made room. We've stayed in cramped quarters before. When something is life and death one makes do."

"When you were a child you had some pockmarks. We assume you are immune."

"Assume?" My voice rose and I waited for a reprimand.

I didn't get one. Mama stood, then stroked my cheek with the back of her hand. "He'll send for us soon." She left the room. Fled the room. Escaped more questions.

It didn't matter. I didn't need to ask more. Papa's actions spoke volumes. He'd made it clear whom he loved the most.

~

Papa finally sent for us, and we fled Vienna to Moravia. But there was something missing in our reunion. Upon seeing Papa, upon accepting his embrace, I held back enough for him to notice. "Is something wrong, Nannerl?" he asked.

"Nothing," I said.

It was a lie. For something between us had broken, and I wasn't sure it could ever be mended.

Then there, in Olmütz, in a smoky, damp room, in spite of all our precautions, Wolfie succumbed to the disease. His face grew red with fever while his hands felt cold. After a fitful night they carried him, wrapped in furs, to a better room. But his condition did not improve. The fever rose and he became delirious.

I felt bad for my complaints about being left behind. Yet what good had it done for Papa to move Wolfie when he'd still succumbed to the disease?

The innkeeper made it very clear we could not stay. Papa sought the help of a friend, Count Podstatsky, who made light of the fact that Wolfie had the pox and ordered rooms to be readied in his own home. He sent his private physician to the inn, from where Wolfie was dispatched to the count's home, again swathed in furs, his red swollen face nearly overwhelmed by the protective coverings.

At the count's we were waited on by his staff and treated with such kindness that we thought it was Christ himself showing us divine compassion. And though Wolfie suffered blindness for nine days, he did recover.

As did I. For I too got the smallpox. Obviously, the pockmarks of my youth had offered no immunity. Papa had risked my life, leaving me behind. . . .

I was not allowed such self-pity for long. After being away from home, away from Vienna for two months, enter the opera, *La finta semplice—The Pretend Simpleton,* and with it another testing of the familial ties.

After the smallpox epidemic had passed, we returned to Vienna, needing six horses to pull our carriage through the January snowdrifts. It was safe now, for once the imperial family accepted the miracle of inoculation, everyone else followed suit. In spite of the state of mourning at court, Papa still held on to the hope that we would be allowed to perform, that our trip to Vienna would find some profit. Yet people were wary of us because of the pox. It didn't help that Wolfie's pockmarks appeared redder in the cold. And I also heard talk that this time our musical "tricks" would not be so quickly accepted with pleasure. Had we become passé?

Yet, only nine days after we returned to the center of Vienna, three months after the death of the Archduchess Maria Josepha, we were presented at court in a private event attended by the imperial family. It went well—for others. Mama and the empress spoke passionately about childhood illnesses and our Grand Tour, and Wolfie and Papa chatted with the emperor Joseph about music.

I received no attention—other than one single time when the emperor commented on my blossoming beauty, which, of course, was pure flattery. It was clear I was of no consequence, any more than a nice vase or a finely upholstered chair. There was no attention given to me as a musician, or as an exceptional young woman of any kind. And we received no compensation, except a pretty medal that had no monetary value. Apparently, the empress had gotten into the habit of leaving issues of payment to her son, the emperor, who was very tight with his coins. Papa said, "The emperor enters it in his book of oblivion and believes that he has paid us by his most gracious conversations."

I would have liked to be a part of such conversations, but once again, Wolfie got the nod. In jest Emperor Joseph mentioned something to Wolfie and Papa about Wolfie composing an opera. It was nothing really, not a request, more of a comment made during small talk. Most certainly not a commission.

Yet Papa jumped on the idea as if our heavenly Father had requested an additional book to the Bible. Actually, I believe the idea was in his head all along, and he simply took the emperor's comment as vindication of his own will. A sign. An accomplishment that would lead us to the land of opera—Italy.

For the next seven months, the opera was *the* thing, the only thing. Oh yes, how it would increase Wolfie's notoriety to compose an opera at age twelve. Any other attempts to procure us concerts halted so Wolfie could concentrate on this great composition. "Shh, Nannerl! Your brother needs silence to work" rang through our rooms, forcing me to find solace on long walks where I'd often end up in the square, feeding pigeons. I began to name them. There was Alfons, Dieter, Klaus, and Henrietta. At least they liked me and took what I had to offer.

Snow yielded to green. And heat. And dust . . . We hadn't brought summer clothes with us, only furs and wools. Papa sent word to Herr Hagenauer to send some lighter garments.

Yet, in spite of the boredom and the endless days, I found that I could not stay angry at my brother. Poor Wolfie. Forget playing ball or tag or marbles—Papa had him holed up in the room for hours a day. And though I knew my brother enjoyed it, I wondered if he missed just being a boy and doing boyish things. Perhaps. Perhaps not.

Finally, in July, the opera was complete and I looked forward to a return to normalcy. Perhaps the focus could return to both of the Mozart children.

But the completion of the opera was only the start of new troubles. In trying to get it produced, negative talk surfaced—on both sides. As people spoke disparagingly about the opera, Papa talked badly about the nobility's taste for inconsequential music, and despaired over their tight pockets. Since Emperor Joseph was tight, so were they. Papa said, "If the chief is extravagant, everyone lets things rip. But if the chief economizes, everyone wants to have the most economical household." This philosophy was not good for our pocketbook.

Papa began to feel there was a jealousy-based conspiracy against us. He accused all the keyboard players and other composers in Vienna of talking ill against Wolfie's work. Papa even arranged to have one of those who spoke against Wolfie listen to him play. Afterward, the man agreed Wolfie's skill was unbelievable. But it didn't silence the gossip.

At that point Papa hoped to get the singers to support the work, as well as get some backing from the aristocracy. But toward this end, Papa miscalculated. The manager of the theater, Giuseppe Affligio, was having money troubles and only wanted to produce sure things. An opera by a mere boy, one that didn't have the complete support of other composers and musicians, was not what he had in mind. Plus, any support Papa might have had with nobility meant nothing to this businessman who was not beholden to the aristocracy (we'd heard that the imperial family did not even pay for their boxes). Paying seats had to be filled. Period.

Then, while dealing with the frustrations of getting Wolfie's opera produced in Vienna, near the end of December, Papa got a decree from the archbishop, ordering him to return to Salzburg. Now. Papa did not comply.

This threat was also made to other Salzburg musicians who'd traveled to Vienna and had not returned, so we were not solely persecuted. But to complicate matters further, we heard that Joseph Meissner, whose bass voice was greatly appreciated, reacted to the archbishop's request by moving on to Frankfurt. Papa didn't think he would ever return. This would not improve the archbishop's mood.

Yet doggedly Papa insisted we stay and get Wolfie's opera produced. "Never venture, never win," Papa said. And though I did not tell him my opinion, I thought it was a mistake to stay. Especially when the rumors we heard about the opera were so daunting. Boring or not, I longed for the stability of Salzburg.

But Papa said, "Should I sit back in Salzburg with the empty hope of some better fortune, let Wolfgang grow up, and allow all of us to be made the fool until I'm too old to travel and until Wolfgang looks too old to be the prodigy? Was this opera for nothing? Should Wolfgang not continue along this current road that is so easy to follow?"

Easy to follow? The road seemed arduous and even dangerous in my eyes, like trying to walk on the icy Danube, fearful that any moment the ice might break and topple us into its freezing currents. I, for one, did not want to be swept away.

Was Papa brave or reckless? I rarely questioned his decisions, but this time . . . since the singers said they couldn't sing the parts (amazingly, many couldn't read music and had to learn their parts by ear) and the musicians didn't like the idea of being conducted by a boy, continuing on this road seemed foolhardy. Plus, there were complaints that the rhythm combined with the Italian lyrics was slightly off. Were these complaints valid? Without hearing all the portions played together, I couldn't be sure. Although my brother was talented, was he *this* talented? At age twelve?

And then to add salt to our wound, people started saying Papa wrote the music, not Wolfie. Papa said, "If a man has no talents, he is unhappy enough; but if he has talents, envy pursues him in proportion to his ability."

To dispel the rumors, Papa arranged for another test. He had people bring in librettos and made Wolfie compose music for the words on the spot. Wolfie did well, and people believed in his talent. Once again Papa pressed the idea that Wolfie was God's gift to music, and anyone who didn't agree was not allowing God the honor He deserved.

Perhaps Papa pressed too much?

One evening, when we were at a performance of someone else's opera, I stood near two local composers during intermission. What I heard chilled me. They were talking about Wolfie's opera, as well as Papa and Wolfie. "If I hear that father say the boy is a gift from God one more time . . ."

"I know. Enough, I say."

"So *my* talent is not from God? I beg to differ."

"Ah, but you are not eleven."

The first man laughed. "And neither is he. I've heard the father lies about his age."

"Oh, really?" The man looked across the room where Papa was introducing Wolfie to a group of adults. "The boy *is* small in stature. . . ."

"But large in ego. Or soon will be with a father like that. Vienna does not need an upstart barging into our territory, trying to take over."

"The boy *or* the father," the man said, laughing.

"The father is worse than the boy. For now."

"I've heard the father is on the verge of being fired by the archbishop back in Salzburg."

"As he should be. And if he thinks he can obtain the patronage of another member of the aristocracy . . . no one around here would hire Leopold for their court. He is not worth the trouble. In spite of the son's talents."

"And the daughter's."

"Is she still around?"

"I assume. Although I haven't heard of her of late. Perhaps she's back in Salzburg."

"Getting married and having babies, no doubt."

They moved away. But I could not move. Their words were like a smothering blanket. To hear my family disparaged, and my own talent dismissed.

Rumors. Just rumors.

And yet . . . I felt they held more truth than falsehood. For I agreed with the sentiment of "enough" regarding Papa's deification of my brother.

Mama walked toward me, the swish of her blue taffeta gown adding to her gentle rhythm. "Come, Nannerl. The opera is resuming."

I did my duty and sat in my place. But I did not listen to the notes; I did not appreciate the phrasing nor marvel at the talent. I could not. For my soul was too distressed.

~

It was only after I received an odd look from the man selling hazelnuts in front of St. Stephen's cathedral that I realized I'd walked around the church—and in front of him—three times. Even as I started on trip number four, I vowed not to pass him again. I had to get past my anger. I had to let it go.

To do so, I needed to throw the offending letter away, banish it from my mind.

But I could not.

I slowed my pace and read the letter from my friend Katherl one more time, my eyes finding the offending passage like a flagellating monk suffering for a cause: *I spoke with Frau Hagenauer the other day and asked for news of you. She responded by saying that your father's letters to their family have not even mentioned you. Are you all right? Are you even there?*

I lowered the letter. Was I all right?

I stopped at the back side of the cathedral, wadded up the letter, and tossed it to the ground. It blew in front of a woman begging for coins at the foot of the spires. She picked it up and, with a glance in my direction, unfolded the angry creases. She smoothed it against her thigh, muttering to herself in a way that made me question the stability of her mind. Then she held up the page, adjusting the reading distance. And though I doubted she could read, the thought that anyone else would read of my humiliation and my father's disregard incensed me beyond reason. I rushed toward her and grabbed the letter out of her hands. "That's mine!"

Two other women begging close by rose to their feet. "You give that back to her!"

"It's my letter," I said.

The first woman looked to her allies. "She took it from me! A letter from my husband it is, a letter from beyond the grave."

The other two beggars moved forward, obviously unable—or unwilling to recognize the lack of logic in her explanation. To them a possession was a possession, no matter how great or small in value.

But this was my letter, and I would not let her keep it.

I clutched the letter to my chest and started to walk away, but the youngest of the women rushed in front of me. Her teeth were cracked and brown, her face streaked with dirt. She held out a hand. "Give it back!"

"It's mine," I said.

She shook her head. "We saw you toss it away. It's Frieda's now. Give it to her."

I shook my head and realized what an inane conversation it was. Common sense was not in play. I also realized the only sure way out. With one hand I slipped the letter into a pocket and with the other found a few coins. I tossed them toward Frieda and the third woman. One clattered off the wall of the church. The youngest ran to get her share.

I—the girl who was not "even there"—ran away.

❧

Happy birthday to me.

Mama and Papa invited some of our Viennese friends over to celebrate my seventeenth birthday on July 30, 1768. But even amid their laughter, their gifts, and the toasts to my health and happiness, I felt the need to slip away from the party to our rooms upstairs.

But the rooms weren't far enough. I wanted to go home. Home home. Salzburg. Even if that place held few promises beyond the domestic norm, it seemed better than this limbo I currently lived in. In Salzburg, I was a seventeen-year-old woman with friends and prospects. Here in Vienna, I was extraneous, a pesky fly buzzing in and out of a room, only noticed when I flew too close or droned too loudly.

I closed the door behind me and fell onto my bed. The rigid stays in my corset didn't appreciate the new position, and I tugged at them until I could breathe and resume feeling sorry for myself.

I closed my eyes and remembered other birthday celebrations with the Hagenauers in their summer house outside Salzburg. With their children. With Katherl. Celebrations very similar to the one being held downstairs. So why should I long for that instead of this?

It wasn't as if I hadn't celebrated other birthdays on the road. Many birthdays. My twelfth had been near Heidelberg, my thirteenth in London. I turned fourteen in Canterbury, and fifteen in Lyons, France. My last birthday *was* in Salzburg, so who was I to complain that this one was in Vienna? I'd celebrated birthdays in four countries. How many young women could make such a boast?

I pulled a pillow close, burying my face into its down. I was an ungrateful, churlish girl who needed to count her blessings.

And yet . . .

I adjusted the pillow to give myself air. What was I doing here? In regard to Vienna specifically, and life in general. Wolfie and I weren't playing concerts. We weren't bringing in income. I'd heard Papa despair of the expense of staying here, and him with no salary coming in from the archbishop since last April. . . .

Opera. It was all about the opera.

And honor. We stayed to prove the naysayers wrong. I understood the theory that if we left Vienna many would think it was because Wolfie couldn't compose the opera, or that it was of such poor quality that it could not be performed. They would deem him a failure—and the rest of us, by association, would also suffer. So we stayed. And so Papa pushed Wolfie to create, pushed the musicians to accept him, and pushed the public to believe in the miracle of the boy composer.

I was not a part of that miracle anymore. I was merely an appendage, an annoying burr on the smooth skin of perfection, an extra expense.

Happy birthday to me.

~

The opera that never was.

That should have been the title of our folly. It was September again. We'd been in Vienna a year when we'd only planned to be gone three months. There'd been countless hours of work done by Wolfie, and countless arguments between detractors and Papa, which led to the opera *not* being produced. At all. The theater manager Affligio was to blame. He was a master of excuses. He'd even reneged on the one hundred ducats he had finally, personally, promised us for the opera. Had he promised the money to keep the peace, never believing the opera would come about at all?

If so, he got his wish.

Papa was incensed. He paced even more than usual, shook his head so constantly I feared his neck would snap, and muttered his frustrations to himself—when not voicing them aloud for all to hear. I'm sure our neighbors knew a great many details that should have been private. And Mama's pleading for Papa to talk more softly only led him to higher volumes. "Why should I be quiet? The whole of Vienna should know of this injustice, this inequity, this betrayal!"

And they did. I could not go anywhere but that I'd hear murmurings and conversations regarding the opera that never was, and the reasons—both true and false—why.

One evening, after having a particularly nasty bout with Signor Affligio, Papa sat at the table until the candle was but a stub, writing out his complaints in a petition to present to the imperial family, beseeching them to take up our cause either to see the opera produced or at least offer us compensation for our act of good faith. I overheard Papa read part of it to Mama. "I beseech you to investigate the shamefully envious and dishonoring calumniators who attempted to suppress and cause unhappiness in the capital of his German fatherland to an innocent creature whom God has endowed with an extraordinary talent, a boy whom other nations have admired and encouraged." It seemed to be strong language to use toward the emperor, and Papa was obviously more hopeful than I that anyone would listen. Or care about the plight of one family.

Papa had gotten Herr Hagenauer to send more money, and insisted that heaven would repay everything—both bills and slights. But I wasn't so sure. Even the day before, when I'd wanted to buy a new bonnet, Mama had been forced to say, "Not now, dear girl. It would not be prudent."

A wasted year—in so many ways.

~

I raised my head off the pillow, held my breath, and listened.

There it was again. A sniff. A small moan.

I sat up in bed. "Wolfie? Are you crying?"

Another sniff.

I slipped out of bed and glanced toward the door. Papa and Mama were downstairs talking with some friends. I hoped they stayed busy awhile longer. If Wolfie was crying . . . Papa did not react well to tears.

The floorboards were cold on my feet and I grabbed a shawl before going to my brother's bedside. As soon as I sat, he turned in my direction. By the moonlight I could see his cheeks were red and wet. I wiped them with the edge of my shawl. "Why are you crying?"

"No one likes me."

I felt my eyebrows rise. "Everyone likes you. Just tonight the landlady said you were her favorite person in the whole world."

He shook his head. "They don't like my music. My opera."

Oh. That.

He scooted over to make room for me under the covers. His

feet were cold. His feet were always cold.

We lay on our sides facing each other. Even in the moonlight I could see that his complexion still showed evidence of the smallpox. He looked so small amid the covers. I adjusted the goose-down coverlet over his shoulder. "It's not your fault, Wolfie," I said. "Haven't you heard Papa talk about the problems with the theater manager, the singers, and the musicians?"

He nodded against the pillow. "They don't like me."

"It has nothing to do with you." I wasn't sure this was completely true because I *had* heard talk about how many professionals weren't keen on working under a boy or being conducted by a child seated at the harpsichord. In truth, I could see their view. But Wolfie's age was not his fault.

He sighed deeply and his eyes closed. Then opened. "They don't like my music."

To this I could respond with my whole heart. "That is not true!" I sat up. "That is never true. Your music . . . there is none like it. You *are* the music. You set it free."

"Really?"

I was taken aback by his doubt. Papa always went on and on about his music. Everyone did. Hadn't he been listening?

I had.

Shame overwhelmed me. Oh yes, I'd listened to every compliment and had found them chiding, as if saying nice things about my brother had been an affront to me. What was wrong with me? How had I let jealousy and envy cloud what should have been happiness and support? Why had I not rejoiced at every glorious note? Why had I focused on the fact they were his notes and not mine? What kind of sister was—?

"I try so hard," Wolfie said, interrupting my disgrace.

"I know you do." I put my arm beneath his head and pulled him close. He snuggled against my shoulder. "No one tries harder than you, Wolfie. No one."

"Then why—?"

I put a finger to his lips, stopping his uncertainty. "Shhh. No more. Don't worry about them. Don't worry about anyone. Just write the music."

He nodded against my arm. "It just comes out, Nan. I can't help it."

And there it was. So simple. So plain. The essence of my brother's talent, his gift from God. Who was I to want more attention from Papa or the world? I had not created music like Wolfie. I played other people's music—brilliantly, it was true. And I *had* tried my hand at composing a few times. But it was not necessarily a need in my soul as it was in my brother's.

"I love you, Nan," Wolfie said. "I'm so glad you're here with me."

His tears were gone now, and I kissed the top of his head. After all the recent turmoil, after all the jealousies, frustration, and anger, I was glad I was here too. Here, with this boy who couldn't stop the music from pouring out—sweet, delicious music the world could not help but savor. Music the world needed to hear.

I also needed music. But the question was: did the music need me?

～

Finally, in January 1769, we arrived home. We'd been gone sixteen months and had little to show for it. Wolfie had managed to compose a few pieces beyond the opera while we were away, but it was not enough to balance the great scales of Papa's expectations—both professional and financial. Besides, Papa had always planned to move on from Vienna to Italy, playing on the success of a Mozart opera.

It was not to be.

And so, on this return home, we did not approach Salzburg with the same exuberance we'd rendered on our last return two years previous. For then we'd come back as triumphant world travelers who'd conquered the courts of Europe. We'd gone where few Salzburgers had ever gone—or could hope to go.

But this time, returning from Vienna . . . we had conquered nothing and were far from triumphant. And though I'd privately ached to return home for many months, my stomach tightened as the white Hohensalzburg Fortress on the hill came into view. Did the entire town know of our failures? Had the gossip so prevalent in Vienna reached this town too?

And did Papa even have a job? He'd not received his salary for ten months, and though the archbishop had finally agreed that he could stay away as long as he wanted, there was no guarantee Papa would be accepted back with open arms. I imagined some groveling at the archbishop's satin-clad feet might be necessary. Yet proud as he was, Papa would grovel. For us.

I turned to Mama as I heard her sigh. "Home," she said.

"For a short while," Papa said.

She turned toward him. "We are not staying?"

Papa suffered his own sigh, wiping his palms on his thighs. "You are." He looked at me. "And Nannerl is."

"What?" Mama's question was explosive.

Papa began to pat her hand, but she pulled it away. "We both sense what little future awaits me here. And as for Wolfgang?" He looked at my brother. "It will only be a few years before this miracle of ours will fade away into something natural. We cannot wait."

"But, Papa," I said. "What about me? I want to perform too."

He reached across the carriage to take my hand, and unlike Mama, I let him do it. "Our finances are strained, Nannerl. To travel with an entire family is a luxury we can no longer afford. If it is just your brother and me, we can stay in monasteries along the way."

"So it's merely a matter of money?" I asked. *Not my talent?*

When he withdrew his hand and looked out the window at the buildings of Salzburg, I knew my father was going to lie.

"It's just the money," he said. He still did not meet my eyes. "Just the money."

January 5, 1769. No matter when my body would eventually die, this would be the true date of my death.

INTERLUDE

Chapter Nine

To move from the archbishop's disfavor to favor is an art my father mastered. For ten months he'd received no salary, yet when we returned from Vienna in January 1769, Papa's salary was restored—as was his position as Vice Kapellmeister. All was forgiven.

I was pleased, of course, but a part of me wondered if it should have been so. Should Papa have been reinstated to the position he'd misused? The position he'd ignored for years?

It was traitorous for me to have such ungenerous thoughts of my father. He'd traveled extensively for the family. He hadn't sought glory for himself. Not much glory. And if the archbishop chose to restore him to his previous position, I should embrace it as a blessing to the Mozart family. I should not question it.

But I did.

I wished Papa and Wolfie had left on their trip right away. It was bad enough knowing I wouldn't be joining them on their Italian journeys, but for them to linger from January until the end of the year, planning a trip I would *not* be taking, talking about it excitedly and incessantly . . . It was torture.

What was especially difficult was explaining to Katherl and our other friends—and yes, even to our dressmaker and the butcher, for everyone knew—why I was staying behind.

These truths could not be shared easily, and so after a few clumsy answers, I came up with an excuse that was just as embarrassing but less personal: traveling with a family of four was too expensive. Let the reason fall on practical matters, not emotional ones. Even Mama agreed it wasn't fair. "But life is not fair, Nannerl. Especially for women."

It was a fact I was learning firsthand.

However, during the spring after our return from Vienna, I did everything in my power to convince Papa that I *should* go along. I practiced with extra fervor, listened intently to all his direction, watched my spending, and even practiced my singing. Since Papa was so enraptured with opera, I wanted to become good enough to sing the arias Wolfie was composing.

But alas, I wasn't good. Even before Wolfie came into the room the day I was singing—his fingers in his ears, his face pulled into a painful grimace—I knew singing was not my forte. I yelled at him for being rude and chased him out, but I also let go of any aspirations of being a great soloist. One can learn to play the clavier or violin with practice, as those instruments possess their own lofty tone and inbred potential, but if the human voice does not own a lovely timbre . . . the extent of its improvement is limited.

By God, I suppose, if one wants to think of it that way.

And yet . . . hadn't God given me the gift of my other music? I'd been given much talent and God expected me to use it.

But Wolfie had been given more.

I tried not to think that way. It was not right weighing brother against sister, creating a competition. Yet wasn't that exactly what Papa was doing by pulling us apart and forcing distance—both earthly and emotional—between us?

During the months spent waiting for them to leave, Wolfie and I did have occasion to play together a few times. Our last concert was in October for about fifty people gathered at the Hagenauers' country home to honor Father Dominicus. I, of course, did not understand it would be our last concert for years. . . .

What I did come to understand was that I had absolutely *no* understanding of why people acted the way they did. Logic seemed to decree that the archbishop would not be happy about Wolfie and Papa leaving again. Yet in November, just a few weeks before they departed, the archbishop gave them a royal sendoff, including a gift of six hundred florins. Plus, he bestowed upon Wolfie the title of Konzertmeister and the promise of a job once he returned. The title was unpaid, but the prestige for a thirteen-year-old boy . . .

I could only shake my head in awe. And sorrow. For it was clear that time had run out on our partnership and collaboration. I found a poem by Thomas Gray I'd learned while in England. A poem that spoke of my thoughts:

Yet ah! why should they know their fate,
Since sorrow never comes too late,
And happiness too swiftly flies?
Thought would destroy their paradise.
No more; where ignorance is bliss,
'Tis folly to be wise.

Was ignorance bliss? Was it folly to be wise? Although sometimes I longed for God to tell me what was in store, I knew it best that He kept it from me. There was enough pain in the present. Why borrow it from the future?

And yet what future did I have in Salzburg? Papa said I should continue to practice, and he lined up four students for me to teach. And I was instructed to help Mama with the household duties.

My excitement was nonexistent.

∼

I received a wave as their carriage pulled away on that cold December day. I received my mother's arm through mine as we walked back to the house. I received the sound of the front door closing with a click. And I received the silence of that day, which would certainly run into the silence of the next day, and the next.

"Would you like some hot chocolate?" Mama asked as she removed her cloak.

I shook my head and went to the bedchamber. Wise mother that she was, she let me go. Although Papa had promised us a larger apartment, in the nearly twelve months we'd been home he'd been too preoccupied with their travel plans to search for something suitable. Besides, what did Mama and I need with more room?

Once inside the chamber I sat at the window seat in the place that had become my haven in recent months. Take the rest of the house away; make it disappear into fire, wind, or mist; this was my place to *be*.

Be what?

I covered my face in my hands, ready to cry. But the tears did not come. Nothing came. I was tired of feeling, thinking, being angry and bitter. More than anything, I was tired of feeling sorry for myself. It was exhausting.

I moved my hands to my lap, smoothing my dress against my legs. I took a cleansing breath and looked beyond the room, out the window at the world below. Frau Kraus was sweeping the cobblestones in front of her candle shop. She'd been making candles with her husband ever since we'd lived here. That was her lot. That was her life.

Did she enjoy it? Did she have regrets? Did she have buried talents she'd set aside?

Sensing my eyes, she looked up, smiled, and waved. I returned her greeting. And by offering my own smile, I felt some of the bitterness fall away.

Yet surely it couldn't be that simple.

My gaze left the street and returned to the bedchamber we'd all shared. It fell upon a collection of inlaid boxes I'd received as presents on our Grand Tour. The blue one was from the queen of England, the gold filigree was from the king of France. How pretty they were.

How pretty they were?

I gasped at the absurdity of the thought. When had I reduced these gifts from the crowned heads of Europe into mere baubles? I moved to the bed stand and picked one up, cupping it in my palm like an injured bird. I remembered the moment when Queen Charlotte had given it to me. Her smile. The way her dangling earrings had bobbed with her laughter.

I curtsied as if she were in the room with me now. "Thank you, Your Majesty," I said aloud.

I set the box down with a renewed reverence and moved to the wardrobe that held my dresses. I pulled out the dress I'd worn the first night I'd performed for her and held it against my simple wool garment. The skirt stopped inches above the floor. I pressed a sleeve against an arm. It was far too small.

Holding the dress at arm's length, it was evident it was made for a girl many years younger than I. It was made for a girl who no longer existed, but who *had* existed. I had experienced many grand things on our travels. I had done things Frau Kraus had never dreamed of. Could never dream of.

"How ungrateful I am!"

I had not meant to say the words out loud, but they hung in the room like a public condemnation. I must not think about what I didn't have now but what I'd been lucky enough to experience before. Blessed enough to experience. *Forgive my indifference, dear Lord.*

I heard Mama in the hall, the soft *swish-swish* of her skirts as she moved through our tiny three-room apartment made larger now by the exit of half its inhabitants.

How dare I not think about her pain? For she was losing something too—her husband. She had been left to deal with the household on her own. Her partner, her companion, and yes, even her lover, was gone for an indeterminate time. She was alone.

No, she wasn't.

I tossed the too-small dress on the bed. I found Mama seated in the workroom in her favorite blue chair with the light of the window behind her. It was a good chair for reading or embroidery. She looked up as I came in and managed a smile. But then I saw what she was holding in her lap—a pair of Papa's leather gloves.

My heart cried. I knelt beside her chair and we looked into each other's eyes but a second, as if fearful tears would intrude.

I lowered my head to her lap. There I smelled the bite of the old leather as Papa's gloves caressed my cheek.

Chapter Ten

As the months of Wolfie and Papa's absence marched on, Mama encouraged me to get out, indulge in the pastimes of normal eighteen-year-old girls. She even encouraged me to accept the intentions of a certain Franz von Mölk. He was the son of the court chancellor and was quite in love with me, making eyes, constantly smiling and bowing. Although it was nice to have his attention—and the small gifts he sent to the house—I was stubbornly uninterested in marriage on principle. I would not succumb to a female's fate. Not without a fight. I resented being propelled in that direction so quickly. I was not a wife yet. I was a performer.

With a jolt I realized the full truth of that statement.

I *was* a performer.

Once.

With effort I prevented my thoughts from turning in that direction. Actually, it was another attentive young man that made me forget my bitterness. Joseph. Joseph Ferdinand von Schiedenhofen. He came from a very nice family we'd known for years. That they were well off and had two estates was a fact I could not ignore.

One Saturday afternoon, Joseph stopped by and we talked and took turns playing the clavier. It was a lovely afternoon, and Mama kept poking her head in the room, asking if we wanted some cake or coffee. *No, Mama, we haven't eaten what you brought earlier.* The way she winked at me . . . it made me blush.

But then it turned awkward when Franz von Mölk came to call—Franz with the cow-eyes. He asked if I would like to go for a sleigh ride. I didn't want to hurt him by saying no and immediately realized then how little experience I had regarding the etiquette of such matters. But Joseph took advantage of that particular moment and slid in behind me as I stood in the doorway so Franz could see him.

"Hello, Mölk," he said. "Isn't it a bit cold for a sleigh ride? It's plenty cozy in here."

I must say Franz's expression was rather humorous—his dropped jaw, his blinking eyes, and his stammer as he bowed and made his apologies, saying he'd come back another day.

Joseph had a good laugh over that as he and I returned to the clavier. "He who comes first eats first." With a gallant bow, he took my hand and kissed it, then grinned up at me. "Do you agree, my dear Nannerl?"

Yes. At least in this instance. For I was spending the afternoon with the suitor of my choice. Yet having two men interested . . .

Perhaps there were a few advantages to being left behind.

~

"Come now, Berta," I said to my pupil. "Play your G scale again, more evenly this time. You're getting uneven sounds because your fingers are flat. When you round your fingers and don't let the first knuckle collapse, your sound will be more controlled and even."

Little Berta tried a second time.

"There now," I said. "See what a difference that makes? One more time."

Berta banged her fingers on the keyboard. "I don't want to do another scale. I want to play a song. A real song."

Well, then. I took Berta's hands and placed them gently in her lap, prepared to give her a lecture on the importance of scales and technique. But when I looked into her face and saw her ten-year-old brows dipped with frustration, I relented. I didn't like playing scales either. The joy of music was not experienced through a scale.

I patted her arm. "All right. Get out the sonatina I gave you last time."

The little girl's face lit up. She slid off the bench and retrieved the sonatina I'd copied for her use. She brought it to the clavier reverently, as if to say *this is real music*.

She returned to her place on the bench and set her hands in place. I noticed how she corrected her fingers' position, offering a better curve. She looked up at me, as if for permission.

"Remember, Berta, in this piece, you must look and listen for the melody. When your left hand plays the accompaniment too loudly, the melody is obscured. Let the melody soar."

As she played, I had to admit she had little talent. Not that she couldn't practice and get every note correct, but I—perhaps more than most—knew there was more to music than correct notes.

"Even," I said. "Keep the left hand accompaniment even."

The next measure was improved, but the next fell back into a jerky rhythm. I remembered practicing this very piece with Papa by my side. *"Do it again, Nannerl. The music deserves more of you than you're giving it."* If it had not been for Papa's patience—and even his impatience, and his insistence I practice more than I desired—I would not have become a true musician.

"Aach!" Berta said as she fumbled a note.

Absently, I pressed the correct key, and she continued playing while I continued my musings. If I was such a great musician, why was I giving lessons to children who would never become true musicians, who had no desire to become true musicians and were only taking lessons because proper society believed it was wise for every child to learn to play?

More of Papa's words intruded, along with the image of him dressed to leave for Italy with snow skimming the edges of his cloak and hat. . . . Just before getting in the carriage he'd taken my face in his hands and said, "Take care of your mother while we're gone, Nannerl. Accept as many pupils as you can and also work on your voice. Perhaps there will be some occasions for you to sing. Bring in whatever money you can, and we will do the same."

Money. It was always about money. Kreuzer, gulden, ducat, franc, or shilling. It was the same wherever one went. Nothing in life was free. Everyone must do their part.

And so I gave lessons.

"Fraulein Mozart?"

How long had my pupil been sitting there, not playing, just looking at me?

I put a hand on her back. "You are getting better, Berta. I'm very proud of you."

The little girl beamed. At least one of us was satisfied with the situation.

~

We waited for the dance to begin. Joseph took my hand, leaned close, and whispered in my ear, "Are you ready?"

"Shh!" I told him. But I nodded just the same. As we danced, the plan was for me to remember the first and second phrase of Haydn's minuet, and he would remember the third and fourth. Then, as soon as it was intermission, we would rush outside into Joseph's waiting carriage and write it down. We'd planted ink, quill, and paper inside the carriage, ready for our conspiracy.

The plan was for me to take the melody—melodies, for we planned to do this again, after intermission—and compose a complete work on the clavier from it. Or a derivation of the melody. For I would change it slightly. Although it was not unusual for minuet melodies to be used by many composers, it was best not to be blatant about it, whether in the stealing or in the metamorphosis from melody to complete piece.

It was done in fun. I would not dream of making profit from such a game. But I did enjoy the process. The camaraderie with Joseph regarding the scheme, the way we'd sit shoulder to shoulder in the immobile carriage, arguing and laughing as we tried to recreate the melody without benefit of any instrument but our minds.

I'd written to Wolfie about our exploits and had even sent him a copy of my compositions. The last one he'd enjoyed immensely, telling me that I'd composed the bass incomparably well and without the slightest mistake. He'd even begged me to try this kind of thing more often.

I intended to.

In return, he sent Joseph and me copies of the latest Italian dance music. At the last ball we'd attended, Joseph had given the quartet copies. We danced and danced. . . . I so loved to dance, to look into the eyes of my partner as we slid past each other into our respective lines, our shoulders and arms skimming. Then palm to palm as we passed in our *danses à deux*. Plus the swish of the gowns as they moved to the rhythm, and the elegant pointed toes of the men as they showed that they too could exhibit grace.

The musical introduction began, and the dancers stepped into place. My memory prepared to grab hold of the notes as my body employed the correct moves. As we bowed and curtsied to begin, Joseph made a face, trying to distract me.

With a lift of my chin, I looked away. I would not be distracted by his handsome smile.

That would come later. In due time.

~

I untied my cloak and carefully put it on the hook near the door. I slipped off my shoes and tiptoed toward the bedchamber I shared with Mama, carrying a candle in my free hand. I walked in an angled manner so my wide skirt would not skim the walls of the narrow hall. I did not want to wake—

Mama was not in bed. She sat in the dark, on the window seat, her green shawl over her nightdress. Her night cap was squarely in place. And she wore slippers. She had not been to bed. "You are late, Nannerl. Very, very late."

I set the candle on the cabinet holding the wash basin. I knew she was right. The last time Joseph had checked his pocket watch it was nearly one. In the morning.

"I'm sorry, Mama. Surely, you didn't wait—?"

"Surely, I did." She pulled the shawl tighter around her shoulders. "You are my one and only daughter. There are no men here to protect us and take care of us and . . ." Her words broke off and she put a hand to her mouth, dipping her head.

Was she crying?

"I just want you to be safe."

I set my shoes on the floor and hugged her. "I was perfectly safe," I said. "I was with Joseph and other friends. After the ball we went to have coffee and kugelhopf cakes. I didn't mean to make you worry."

Mama pulled away, wiping her eyes with the corner of her shawl. I retrieved a handkerchief from my waist and gave it to her. "I am alone here, Nannerl," she said. "I want you to have fun. You are young, you must be out with others in order to find a husband. But be mindful that I do get lonely sometimes."

The guilt fell upon me. I honestly had not thought of Mama, alone and lonely. She had her women friends. She seemed content to stay at home and manage the household.

She sniffed. "I enjoyed balls once too."

Ah. That was it. "You could come with us."

Mama shook her head vehemently. "Not without your father. Never without him."

"But it's already been six months. He may be away for a long . . ." I did not finish the sentence. I could not. For no one knew when they would be back. And both of us knew that all plans were variable as new opportunities presented themselves.

Mama took a deep breath and managed a smile. "I'm just being a needy old woman."

"You're not old." Too late I realized I should have added "or needy."

She kissed my cheek. "Get to bed now, Nannerl. We both have a busy day tomorrow."

I knew I did. I had two pupils coming for lessons. But as far as Mama's busy day? I wasn't sure what that entailed. But as I began to undress, I promised myself and God above that, from now on, I would make a point to be a part of it.

~

Three months later, as summer started its descent into autumn, I ran into the kitchen. "Mama! Letters!"

Mama stopped cutting the turnips and wiped her hands on her apron. "Four letters?"

I held three toward her and held the other against my chest. "Three from Papa to you, and one from Wolfie to me." This was the way it was; as if the two men had been assigned our names as their partners of the quill. Occasionally Papa put a line in his letters specifically for me, but it was clear they were mostly meant for Mama's eyes. In his defense I recognized there were a lot of household issues that needed to be addressed, ones that Mama was not used to handling. It wasn't easy for her, and I noticed she periodically asked Herr Hagenauer for help.

She took the letters and sat at a stool near the light and breeze of the window. I leaned against the sill and did the same. This was our usual custom—we read the letters to ourselves first, then shared by reading them aloud. It was a wise habit because Wolfie could get quite crude in his choice of words, and though I didn't mind—for I understood his odd humor better than anyone—I felt some responsibility to edit them for our mother's ears.

Wolfie wrote: *I have no time to write much. My pen is not worth a fig, nor is he who is holding it. Immediately after lunch we play boccia. That is a game which I have learnt in Rome. When I come home, I shall teach it to you. When I have finished this letter I shall finish a symphony which I have begun. The aria is finished. A symphony is being copied (Papa is the copyist, for we do not wish to give it out to be copied, as it would be stolen.) In Milan we saw four rascals hanged. They hang them just as they do in Lyons. We also saw a ballet in Cremona. There was a woman dancer there who did not dance badly and, what is very remarkable, was not bad-looking on the stage and off it. The others were quite ordinary. A grotesco was there too—whenever he jumped he let off a fart. As you know I have never been shy about telling other musicians their weaknesses. But Papa is trying to make me change. "Don't be so candid! Play the Englishman, Wolferl." But I like being candid. The pride of some of these musicians is legion, as if they truly know what they're doing. Thanks for sending me that arithmetical business, and if you ever want to have a headache, please send me a few more of these feats. I am simply panting from the heat! So I am tearing open my waistcoat. I send a thousand kisses to Mama and one pockmark of a kiss to you. I remain the same old . . . old . . . what? . . . the same old buffoon.*

It was signed: *Wolfgang in Germany, Amadeus in Italy.*

I'd finished reading mine first. As usual, Papa's letters were multiple pages, and Mama was still on the first one. She noticed I was finished, but instead of asking me what Wolfie had said, she pointed to the letter she held. "Papa reminds us again to save all his letters."

Yes, yes. I glanced toward the cabinet in the corner of our workroom. "Soon we're going to need a separate room for them all."

Mama gave me a chastising look. "They're important, Nannerl. They chronicle many things."

"But who will ever want to read them?"

Mama did not answer at first, then said, "Someone. Someday. We must do as your father says."

I shrugged, knowing she was right, yet also slightly bothered by the instruction. I doubted Papa and Wolfie were keeping our letters.

Mama began to reiterate what was in Papa's letter, passing on tales of mountain roads that prevented him from sleeping and Italian audiences that crowded Wolfie so he had trouble reaching his instrument. The audiences in Naples accused Wolfie of having a magical ring that made him able to play so well—so he'd taken it off to prove them wrong. The two of them had seen the volcano Vesuvius smoking, the ruins of Pompeii, and had ridden in a gondola in Venice so long they continued to feel the movement when in bed. They'd even attended the carnival.

I was glad that most of the time they didn't go into much detail but told Mama and me to look the places up in the three-volume guidebook Papa had bought for us. Though I hadn't done that much of late. . . . My rebellion was childish, but it was my way of handling what I was *not* seeing.

Mama laughed. "Apparently your brother has deemed the Mediterranean the Muckyterranean Sea. That sounds so like—" Suddenly Mama stopped her reading and gasped. "Oh no, Papa was injured in an accident!"

My bitterness left me. "What does he say?"

Mama read the letter aloud. Apparently, in the act of leaving Naples for a second trip to Rome, Papa had hired a *sedia,* a two-wheeled carriage pulled by one horse that had a groom riding to the left with another horse yoked to the frame. By using such a light and fast rig, it was possible to take only twenty-four hours to make the trip.

But one of the horses reared and stumbled, pulling the carriage down. Papa had extended a hand in front of Wolfie, trying to keep him safe, but in the process they fell, and Papa split his shin on an iron bar. The injury was the width of a finger. They'd finally gotten to Rome, and Wolfie had been so tired he'd fallen asleep in a chair and Papa had undressed him without waking him.

"I don't care about Wolfie's sleep—I want to know about Papa," I said.

"He says he's fine . . . yet that was over a week ago." She set the letter aside and tore open the next. She skimmed it. But the news was far different than I expected. "They had an audience with Pope Clement! And Wolfgang has received the papal Order of the Golden Spur! He is a knight."

I glanced back at Wolfie's letter. "He doesn't mention that here."

Mama put a hand to her chest, her face proud. "He can now legitimately take the title of cavalier."

"I can't imagine Wolfie using a title like that." *But what of Papa's injury? And what of . . .* I thought of something that had happened during their first trip to Rome. "I'm surprised the pope gave Wolfie that honor after he got in trouble for writing down the *Miserere* after hearing it played in the Sistine Chapel. It's forbidden to take away even a single part of it, to copy it, or to give it to anyone. He could have been excommunicated for that, yet they give him this honor?"

Mama looked perplexed. "Papa must have made it right."

That seemed to be the only explanation, yet did Papa really wield such power?

This question didn't seem to bother Mama, as she went back to reading the letter. "Papa wants us to make sure the archbishop knows about the honor. And they got new suits too." She referred to the letter and read, " 'Our Wolfie's is a rose-colored moiré trimmed with silver lace and lined with sky blue silk. While mine is the color of cinnamon and is made of piqued Florentine cloth with silver lace, lined with apple green silk. I'm going to have Wolfie's portrait painted in his, with the sash of the order across his chest.' " Mama sighed. "How beautiful."

And how expensive. Papa constantly reminded us to be frugal, yet he and Wolfie were indulging themselves in extravagant new clothes?

"They are meeting with royalty, Nannerl," Mama said, guessing my thoughts. "They need to look their best."

I nodded, understanding. In theory.

"Perhaps when you receive payment for your Tuesday lesson, you can use a bit of it to buy a new hat. We could go without meat on Sunday if need be."

I got a hat at the expense of meat, and Wolfie and Papa got silk and silver lace? Yet there was no point arguing.

Mama turned to the second page of the letter. "Here. Finally mention of the leg . . . He says it's worse. His leg has swollen so much that he's hobbling around Rome. But he assures us he'll be fine." She turned the page over. "That's not enough!" she said. "I need more information!"

"The last letter, Mama."

She hurriedly opened the final post. Her lips moved frantically as she read Papa's words. "The wound opened . . . his ankle is swollen to the size of his calf. And now he's getting pain in his other ankle!"

"Has he seen a doctor?"

Mama scanned more of the letter, then nodded. "They've been offered housing by the field marshal Pallavicini at his estate not far from Bologna." She read in silence a few moments. "It's very palatial, and they are waited on like royalty." She smiled and finished reading. "They provide a comfortable chair for him in every room, with a stool for his foot, and he is not required to stand even when his host comes into the room."

I let out the breath I'd been saving. "So they're all right, then."

Mama nodded, her face clearly relieved. "They are fine. They plan to stay there many weeks, until his leg is completely healed." She folded the letter carefully. "It also says that Wolfie has ridden a donkey and loves the variety of fruit there."

Donkeys and fruit? What did that matter? Papa had been injured, and we hadn't been there to nurse him back to health.

Mama finished folding all the letters. "My son, Cavalier Wolfgang Amadeus Mozart, Knight of the Golden Spur. . . ." She put the letters in the cabinet and went back to the turnips. "By the way, Papa sends a thousand kisses."

The feelings of envy I thought I'd set aside returned. During the past nine months, I'd managed to deal with a myriad of letters regarding the sites they'd seen, the important people they'd met. But for them to stay in a palatial home and be waited on, while we lived in the three rooms Mama and Papa had lived in since they were married, the same house they'd birthed seven children in. The same house they'd lived in since before Papa was Vice Kapellmeister. And then for Papa and Wolfie to have an audience with the pope and receive an honor from him . . .

"I have a pupil coming," I said, moving toward the door.

Mama looked up. "But Wolfie's letter? What did he have to say?"

"Nothing important. But he also sends a thousand kisses."

Mama actually smiled. As if a *million* kisses would be enough.

~

Some piano teacher I was. Once again I'd subjected a pupil to only an ounce of my attention as I dealt with my own problems.

Or was it the same problem, come round and round in different form?

The day after yet another half-hearted lesson I took action to quench the issue once and for all. I packed a lunch of hard-cooked eggs, bread, and ham, put on my oldest dress and sturdiest shoes, and headed up the mountain.

"To think" had been my excuse to Mama. And in her moment of hesitation, I saw a glimmer of sympathy in her eyes. Although she was more resigned to our fate than I, she did seem to understand my torment.

But did I? I could only hope. . . .

I remembered a path where Papa had taken us one Sunday afternoon. It had been years earlier, before we'd started our travels. I remembered it to be peaceful and lovely, two commodities that would be helpful in my situation.

I walked down the streets to the east edge of town. There were many paths that led up the hills that cradled Salzburg. There were even craggy mountains close by. Yet hills were enough for me. It was not the exercise I craved but the need for solace and solitude.

Although I planned to think while I walked, I found my mind consumed with watching my step on the path that was covered with dirt and small stones. I'd tied my lunch in a towel. As I carried it with one hand, my other hand held my dress and petticoat out of the way so I could see the path. Oh, to be a man and wear breeches.

Suddenly I turned an ankle. I grabbed the branch of a tree that lined the path to steady myself, only to trip again and end up with scratches. I searched for a rock on which to rest, but there was none. Maybe I should go back?

I shook my head against the thought. It was then I realized I had not even begun to think through my problems. I *had* to go farther. I could not return home until things had been resolved.

I remembered a clearing where we'd sat to eat our lunch. Wolfie—he must have been only three—had chased a butterfly there. I needed to reach that clearing. Ankle or no ankle.

I leaned against a tree and gave my ankle a look and a rub, though neither did it any good or harm. Then I tested it out. If I was careful how I placed it on the path . . .

I had no choice. I had to work through my pain.

Work through my pain. I snickered. Yes indeed, that was exactly what I needed to do.

I headed up the hill.

~

The clearing matched my faded memory. Low grass mixed with edelweiss and other wild flowers. I stopped to take deep breaths and look over the city. The church spires poked their way above the rooftops as if they had a head start to heaven. The Salzach River meandered through the town while the Hohensalzburg Fortress loomed large from the top of its precipice, our protector for seven hundred years. Salzburg was a lovely city, as lovely as any I'd visited, and it made my heart race to be able to be here, above it all—

Above it all? Surely I didn't think of myself in that way? Surely

I didn't feel that somehow I was better than the rest of Salzburg? Because of my travel, because of my talent, and even because of my family?

My legs felt weak—and not merely from the hike. I sat on the grass and pondered the notion of such pride.

But I *had* been places most Salzburg residents had never visited. And I did have talent, and so did my family. After all, my brother had just been honored by the pope himself.

But you weren't.

I shielded my eyes with a hand, blocking the truth as well as the sun. But no matter how I hid my eyes, my mind and heart had seen the truth. Knew it intimately.

I was jealous of my brother.

There. I'd admitted it. I wanted an award too. I wanted to meet the pope. I wanted to travel with Papa and see volcanoes and oceans and visit Italian churches, eat Italian food, and speak Italian to Italians. I wanted things to be like they used to be when I was important too.

You are important to Me.

I started at the thought. Me who? God? Had God put a thought in my head? How absurd. Speaking of being prideful . . .

A sparrow lit on the ground beside me, turning its head so we looked eye to eye. It was probably just interested in the bread wrapped in the towel.

Yet it didn't move toward the towel, didn't peck at it. It just stood on the grass and looked at me. At *me.*

So small. So unimportant.

And yet it too was there in the meadow. Thriving. Carefree. Living with an assurance that food would be found and the wind would keep it aloft. If God took care of this little sparrow, then surely . . .

Wasn't I of more value than this lowly bird?

"Of course I am," I said aloud.

I remembered my previous thought: *You are important to Me.* I knew it *was* a message from God, and I knew He meant it, and I knew I was loved.

The bird was still beside me. But at this point he stopped his stare-down and hopped over to the towel. He pecked at it, as if asking for his share now that his work was complete.

I was happy to oblige. I unknotted the towel and tore off a piece of bread for him. I tossed it close by and tore off another piece for myself. Nourishment for two creatures loved by God.

What did I care for honors or fancy sashes or portraits or the praise and attention of any man? I had worth in my own right. Up here on the edge of magnificent mountains, above the city I called home. I belonged here.

Until God moved me on.

Until then, I would enjoy my lunch—and fine company.

~

On the way down the mountain my footfalls found a cadence that reminded me of a marching soldier.

Marching soldiers . . .

A slice of time returned to my thoughts. Wolfie and I watching the soldiers marching at Ludwigsburg, and Wolfie's childish proclamation that he wanted to be a soldier when he grew up.

And Mama's adamant response that his destiny was to make great music.

And my question to her about my own destiny.

And her response that my fate lay in having a husband and children. *Not* in making great music.

My breathing turned heavy—though not from physical exertion. I stopped on the path and remembered my reaction to Mama's horrible words. I would be different from other women of my time. I would become a renowned performer in spite of my gender. I would reach the world with my music. I would not succumb to what was expected *of* me, ordained *for* me, against my will.

I put a hand to my eyes, trying to block the memory of that ambitious twelve-year-old. In the seven years that had passed, much had changed. Too much. I was not touring anymore. I was not a part of the Wunderkind phenomenon. I had been left behind to wallow in the mediocrity of the mundane. I should have lived in the fortress on the hill for all the walls that held me captive.

"There's no way out," I said aloud. "I'm no one. I'm unimportant."

At the sound of my voice I opened my eyes—and saw another sparrow light on the path in front of me. And with the sight of him, I remembered the words I'd heard on the mountain. *You are important to Me.*

But the words did not have the same calming effect they'd had earlier. Once aroused, memory of my ambition could not be so easily appeased. Yet what choice did I have? I possessed little control over my own life, much less over the whims, opportunities, and reactions of others. I could not force my talent on the world. If I could, it would fail and fall on deaf ears. Only the Almighty could make it happen.

Or not.

Papa could help. But Papa was not here. And even if he were, his focus and attentions were set elsewhere.

There was one fact I could not deny: I had no choice but to accept the limitations of my future. If God wanted to make a miracle, He would do it. But if He did not . . .

I wrapped my shawl closer around me and walked toward home. The sparrow wisely flew away.

≈

I finished playing the measure, then looked up at Joseph lounging on the chair by the window. His eyes were closed.

"You don't have to stay while I practice," I said. "You must have better things to do."

He opened one eye. "Can't think of a one."

"Are you trying to flatter me?"

He sat up straight. "Is it working?"

I began the piece again, preferring to have the safety of musical notes in the air between us. "You need not resort to flattery, Joseph. I'm your friend and will continue to be your friend." I heard him get up but dared not look at him.

He leaned on the clavier. "Do you miss it?"

"Miss what?"

"Performing." His arms swept through the air expansively. "Traveling the world and performing for gilded royalty in gilded halls."

It took me a moment to change the direction of my thoughts from romance to performance. It was a disappointing transition. "No, I don't miss it."

He flicked a hand against my music, forcing me to stop. "Nan . . ."

I put my hands in my lap. "Yes, I miss it. But I don't miss the too hot and too cold of the travel, the bumpy roads, the bad food, and the sooty rooms."

Joseph moved beside me and put a hand on my shoulder. "You're very talented, and Salzburg is lucky to have you here."

Though I didn't want to stir the envy or bitter-tinged thoughts that were never far from the surface, I couldn't help but snicker. "A lot of good I do here. Playing at dinner parties and weddings."

"Ah yes. Meager Salzburg. It must be a disappointment after playing at royal dinner parties and weddings for kings, queens, and empresses."

"Royalty are just people." It sounded snobbish.

He laughed. "Very rich, powerful people."

"Who put their knickers on the same way we do."

"They jump into them?"

I loved how he made me smile. "Did you know that the palace at Versailles doesn't have decent plumbing? I saw many a lord relieving himself in the hall."

"No."

I raised my right hand. "I did."

Joseph leaned on the keyboard case, cupping his chin in his hand. "Ooooh. Gossip. Tell me more."

I moved to the display case where Papa had placed our royal gifts. The locked display case. I put my fingers on the glass that prevented me from touching these tokens from my past, from truly owning them. My jovial mood left me. "I don't remember anything else," I said. "I'm sorry."

He came close, and my spine tingled with the thought of him touching my shoulder or back, but instead he took my hand and swung me under his arm in dance. Then he bowed and said, "To cheer you up and to show you just how appreciated you are in Salzburg, my mother has invited you and your dear mama to our country home at Triebenbach."

"Your mother has invited us?" I wanted more than that.

"At my request."

I smiled. "I've heard it's very lovely."

He took my hand as if to kiss it. "Loveliness is a requirement of any lodging that will be blessed with the presence of the lovely Mozart ladies." He bit the tip of my finger.

I pulled my hand away. "I'll have to ask Mama."

He winked. "Beg her if necessary."

I didn't have to. Mama was as thrilled as I.

~

It was very satisfying writing to Wolfie to tell him about something wonderful *I* was doing. And Mama, of course. Although I wouldn't have minded going to Joseph's Triebenbach estate on my own—at nineteen I was old enough, after all—I was glad Mama got to go too. While on the carriage ride there she'd been practically giddy, wondering aloud what amusements the Schiedenhofens would have planned, and giving me advice as to which dress to wear first.

"He's not my beau, Mama," I told her.

Her smile was full of conspiracy. "He could be. And perhaps he will be—after his mother and I are through."

The thought of them plotting . . . it's not that I objected to the end result, for beyond my unrealistic desire to be a great musician, I did want to marry, but I did not want them embarrassing us with their scheming.

Triebenbach was just outside Salzburg, but it could have been worlds away. Even though Salzburg was not a large city, compared to the silence and serenity of Joseph's family estate, it was blaring and chaotic. The estate consisted of buildings of yellow and white stucco, with interesting turrets and red-tiled roofs that were striking against the fall colors of the hillside. We passed gardens that led to trails through the woods. Snow-topped mountains were its neighbors, protecting the grounds from the rest of the world. We felt very blessed.

"I could live here," I said.

Mama chuckled. "I'm sure you could."

I felt my face redden. I had not meant it so literally. Or had I? Since my time on the mountain—and my disconcerting journey home—I'd let my thoughts turn toward romance and home and nonmusical destinies. It was either that or face a constant inner battle between what was and what could never be.

As the footman opened the door for us, Joseph rushed out of the house to take our hands and help us down. "Welcome! Welcome!" He kissed both of us on our cheeks. "Come inside. Mother is waiting."

Frau Schiedenhofen was a short woman who only came up to her son's shoulders. I could see where Joseph got his curly brown hair and his plump cheeks—though Frau Schiedenhofen's plumpness extended beyond her face.

The next few minutes were a glimmer of greetings and niceties. One would have thought our mothers had known each other for years the way they dipped their heads close as they talked, and took each other's arms as they walked into the parlor for some coffee and cake. Surely they weren't conspiring already.

Joseph took my arm. "After we've done our duty and performed the required chitchat, I want to take you outside and show you our shooting range. Some other guests are coming in two days, and—"

"Shooting?" I asked.

"Air guns. At a target. Unless, of course, you'd rather go after live game?"

"Targets are fine," I said.

I looked again toward Mama and Frau Schiedenhofen. But by the way they smiled and looked in our direction, I wondered if *we* were the targets.

～

Having my own bedchamber was a luxury. Although we'd stayed at the homes of nobility many times on our travels, I had always shared a room. Even if more rooms were offered, Papa had never wanted to press the hospitality of our hosts.

Actually, sharing had not been an imposition. Wolfie and I had fun staying up too late, talking and giggling out of earshot of Mama and Papa. It was far better than the *one* room we were used to sharing at an inn and at home. We were not used to large spaces, and the luxury of being able to spread out . . .

Here at Triebenbach, my room had a bed covered with a yellow spread, and windows flanked by full-length sashed draperies. There was a writing desk stocked with paper and quill, a mirrored dressing table, and a fireplace the servants kept stoked. I felt like a lady in a manor. Once in bed for the night, I made a point of moving from far left to far right on my bed. It was silly because, once I was asleep, what did it matter how much room I had? But I enjoyed the feeling of spaciousness just the same.

In the morning I looked in the mirror as Katrina, the lady's maid, stood behind me and fixed my hair. She pulled the sides back into pinned curls, letting the back hang long. Joseph had said he liked my hair. . . . I handed Katrina a tortoiseshell comb.

"Your hair is so much easier to fix than Fraulein Daubrawa's. This morning she had me come in very early to help her dress for a special breakfast."

I sought Katrina's eyes in the mirror. "Breakfast? Have I missed breakfast?"

"Oh no, Fraulein. The breakfast for most of the guests will not be served for half an hour. This was a special breakfast between Fraulein Daubrawa and Master Joseph." She lowered her voice and leaned into my ear confidentially. "I think a match is being made."

I nearly gasped. A match? But Joseph and I were . . . were . . . Were what?

Friends.

There was a knock on the door. It was Mama. I expected to see her looking refreshed and relaxed, but her mouth was drawn, her forehead tight. Before I could even say good morning, Mama's eyes flitted from mine to Katrina's. "I'll finish up here, Katrina. Thank you."

Katrina handed over the comb and hairpins, gave a little curtsy, and left. Mama did not take the position behind me but moved to face me. "He's not available," she said.

I could have played ignorant, but what was the point? "It's that Anna Daubrawa, isn't it?"

"You heard?"

"Katrina told me they had a special breakfast this morning."

Mama picked up the brush, fingering the shell inlay on the back. "She's rich, you know."

"Money? This is all for money?"

"It's always for money, Nannerl. You know that."

Unable to sit in the midst of my humiliation, I walked to the window. "But Joseph's already rich. Certainly he doesn't need more."

Mama came up behind me, resting her chin on my shoulder. *"Das Geld findet eben immer zum Gelde."* She sighed. "The money finds the money and the rich get richer. It's a fact of our lives, Nannerl."

"But we aren't poor."

"But we aren't rich. And no matter how we hold your father and his abilities in high esteem, he is still *just* the Vice Kapellmeister."

I turned to face her. "But Wolfie and I have played before kings and queens. Wolfie is composing—"

Mama shook her head. "It's not necessarily what you've done as much as what title you possess. Name a member of nobility who's *done* anything of consequence. That's why your father's trip to Italy is so important to all of us. If he can secure a position for Wolfie *and* himself, our future will be assured."

"Or if I marry well." I looked down. "If I marry at all."

Mama lifted my chin. "You are a lovely, talented girl. You will marry and you'll have many children. That will be your blessing."

Or my lot. I moved back to the bench of the dressing table. It was nearly time for breakfast. "I like Joseph," I said as Mama took the comb to finish my hair. "I could have married him."

"Suitors will come and go, but one husband . . . just one husband is all you need."

155

I knew what she meant, but down deep I also knew a husband was not *all* that I needed.

~

I must admit after my outing to Triebenbach, I was so consumed with disappointment at hearing that Joseph had been matched with another that I did not pay much attention to Papa's and Wolfie's letters about his opera in Milan. What had previously happened with his opera in Vienna was happening again. Frankly, all Papa's talk of conspiracies wore on me. Surely the whole world wasn't against him. Wolfie. The music.

But then a letter arrived right after Christmas that said the opera, *Mitriadate rè di Ponto—Mithridates, the king of Pontus,* was a huge success. It was the first opera of Milan's season, and though generally those drew weak houses, Wolfie's had not. The performance—with ballets added in between acts, and with encores—lasted six hours. Although Papa intimated that Wolfie needed to work on his interpretation of the dramatic aspects of opera in general—perhaps he was too young to grasp the emotional intricacies of the story—Wolfie did enough right to receive the praise: *"Viva il maestrino."*

I was happy for him. Really I was.

Then why wasn't I out with Mama, spreading the news to all of Salzburg? Why wasn't I right this minute writing a letter in response, sharing my joy and congratulating him on his victory?

Perhaps I needed another trip up the mountain. Many trips.

Chapter Eleven

I blamed the sound of snoring for my early rising, but that wasn't the truth. I got up early and slipped out of the house because of resentment. Papa and Wolfie were home. And not for the first time. They'd already been home from their first Italian trip—home for over four months after being gone fifteen—before taking off for Italy a second time. Now, after being gone four more months in Milan, they were home again. And even last night, as we sat around the fire and heard about their last trip, Papa talked about a third trip to Italy, perhaps next fall.

"Can we go too?" I'd asked for Mama and me.

"We'll see," Papa said.

Which meant no.

I put on my cloak and slipped out of the house. The December air was bitter, and I held the hood tightly around my face. The leather soles of my shoes slipped on the patches of snow that were barely lit by the first of the day's winter sun. I had the streets to myself. No one else was foolish enough to venture out on such a cold morning without good reason.

I had a reason. Whether it was a good one . . .

My eyes focused on the street, trying to tiptoe my way through the snow and ice, when I heard a door open up ahead. It was Frau Hensler, the baker's wife. She stepped outside and shook the dust and crumbs from a rug onto the street.

She looked up and saw me. "*Grüsse Gott,* Nannerl. What are you doing out so early? In the cold?"

Brooding.

I glanced back toward home and offered the core of the truth. "Papa and Wolfie are home again, and—"

Her eyes brightened. "And you're wanting some special bread for their first breakfast at home." She opened the door and led me inside the shop.

The aroma of baking bread elicited feelings of warmth and home. Good feelings that made my pettiness seem absurd.

She spread the rug in front of the door. "The bread won't be ready for another ten minutes." Frau Hensler patted a bench, then held out her hands to take my cloak.

"I'll leave it on," I said.

"As you wish." She took a seat beside me, taking up two-thirds of the bench with her ample frame. "So. How go the traveling musicians?"

"They're well."

She waited, clearly expecting more. Although Papa and Wolfie had regaled us with many stories, my mind was blank.

She patted my arm. "You and your mother have done a fine job while they've been gone. The whole neighborhood speaks of it. Not many women have to fend for themselves as you've had to do off and on these two years—at least not voluntarily."

At least someone understood. "It's hard having them gone, but . . ."

She looked at me a long moment, then nodded. "It's hard having them return?"

I added my own nod.

Frau Hensler bumped her shoulder into mine. "Men can be difficult," she said. "Although I *have* enjoyed the letters your mother has shared. What an honor it was for our little Wolfgang to compose a *serenata* for the marriage of one of our empress's sons."

"Papa hopes they're pleased enough to offer Wolfie a position in their court." I leaned forward with my own bit of confidence. "They stayed in Milan until the bridal couple got back from their wedding trip, hoping . . . And then they *did* have an audience with Archduke

Ferdinand but . . ." I shrugged. I didn't tell her that Papa had feigned illness in his letters—coding them to tell Mama he was all right, but with full knowledge that illness was one of the few acceptable reasons for their extended delay home. When Mama had shared the letters speaking of intestinal problems, vertigo, and rheumatism, all of Salzburg sympathized. Or so we thought.

"Nothing was offered?"

"Papa is still hopeful."

Frau Hensler looked in the direction of the oven and sniffed the air. She did not get up. "I heard the archbishop stopped your father's pay while he was gone. Again."

I couldn't imagine Mama sharing that bit of information, but I was not totally surprised it was known. Little remained unknown in Salzburg. "He hopes to be reimbursed. And we hope Wolfie will soon start receiving a salary to go along with his title of Konzertmeister."

"He hasn't received any pay for that?"

"None."

She spit on her finger and rubbed at a stain on her skirt. " 'Tis logical, I suppose. After all, the men in your family haven't exactly been around to do the work."

"But they *are* promoting the archbishop and Salzburg on their travels. Everyone knows of their roots—and the archbishop's patronage."

Frau Hensler shook her head. "Perhaps daily work means more than a few good words said in faraway places."

It was a point I'd thought of myself. But just as I began to answer, Herr Hensler came in the door with a load of wood. "Hilda! There's—" He saw me and nodded. "Grüsse Gott, Nannerl."

"What's got you huffing and puffing so?" his wife asked.

"There's news! Archbishop Schrattenbach is dead!"

I put a hand to my chest, feeling as if my heart had stopped. "But Papa just arrived home."

Herr Hensler looked confused. I did not feel inclined to explain but stood and made my good-byes.

"But the bread for your father . . ." Frau Hensler said.

Upheaval and chaos. Those were the conditions that reigned upon our family for the three months after Archbishop Schrattenbach's death on December 16, 1771. Papa had trouble forgiving His Grace for waiting until he and Wolfie had returned home. "If only he'd had the courtesy to die while we were away, we might have stayed longer in Milan and secured a position."

Mama chastised him for saying such a thing, but we all knew it to be the truth. Yet Papa did concede—in an attitude more private—that it was good they were home because all of Salzburg was in an uproar over who would be our next prince archbishop, and beyond that was the underlying question of what the new ruler would do about his court musicians. Would Papa finally get the promotion to full Kapellmeister?

While Wolfie worked on two commissioned operas that Papa had arranged for him to write (one for Milan and one for Venice), Papa bustled about town, smiling the smile, talking the talk, bowing the bow. Though he was charming to everyone else, at home he was testy, always after me to practice. "Your fingers have grown stiff, Nannerl."

He was right, of course. I had slacked off during their second trip to Italy. For what was the point of honing my skills when no one of import would ever hear them? And yet . . . I had not given up the music. I could never do that. It was as much a part of me as was air, drawn in and let out. Over and over. . . .

Actually, practicing did provide solace. If I played loudly enough I could overlay the music upon my parents' discussions about the future. It's not that I wasn't interested—for until I married, Papa's future impacted my future—but their talk drained me and made me long for the simpler times when Mama and I had the house to ourselves and led less dramatic lives.

Hmm. What a hypocrite I was. Complaining of the mediocrity of life when the men were away, yet complaining of the commotion they brought with them when they were home.

In truth, most of the time, even my practice had to be postponed because Wolfie needed the keyboard for his composing. And so I found it best to make myself scarce by spending time with Katherl and my other friends. I also tried to make new friends—new male friends. I was twenty now, and though Joseph Schiedenhofen had not married as yet, I had backed away from any hint of flirting with him as a defense against a broken heart.

One day in mid-March, I had plans to go shooting and was just gathering my air gun when Mama came back from the market, her face flushed.

"They've chosen!" she said. "The name is going to be announced from the palace balcony at noon."

The shooting was forgotten—as was Wolfie's opera, as was all else.

This, *this,* could change everything.

~

A crowd gathered in the square in front of the Residenz Palace. Papa pushed our way toward the front. Some people looked peeved at him, but others let us through. Once settled, he placed Wolfie in front of him, his hands on his shoulders. At sixteen, Wolfie was still short in stature and looked years younger. The crowd was abuzz with conjecture. There were many possibilities, some good for our family, some bad.

Finally the door opened and an official came onto the balcony. The crowd quieted. "I am pleased to announce that the new prince archbishop of Salzburg, assuming the sacred throne of St. Rupert, is . . . Count Hieronymus Franz de Paula Joseph Colloredo, canon of Salzburg and prince-bishop of Gurk."

No. This couldn't be!

I wasn't the only one who felt this way. The entire crowd stood in stunned silence. Why would they choose Colloredo, who only graced us with his presence every couple of years, who held himself up as better than Salzburg, who was cold, aloof, and often rude?

The official's face was perplexed. He had obviously expected cheering and applause instead of this low murmuring.

The street-level doors opened and the archbishop's attendants appeared, all dressed in their finest robes. They were going to lead him in a procession to the cathedral for the celebration of the *Te Deum*.

The crowd parted, making way, but as the new archbishop emerged and began his short walk to the church, they still did not cheer. And even worse, their murmuring had turned to silence.

At first the archbishop waved to his constituents, but when they did not respond with adulation, he set his chin and walked through the crowd, his eyes straight ahead.

As soon as he and his attendants passed, the people filled in and began their chatter. I was eager to hear what Papa had to say.

"Is this a good thing or bad?" Wolfie asked him.

"He is definitely an arrogant one," Papa said, moving us toward home. "But he does have an appreciation for music. He plays the violin quite well."

Wolfie scrambled to keep up with Papa's long gait. "But will we benefit?"

Papa put a hand on the back of Wolfie's neck. "We will break through his haughtiness and find the favor we need. I promise."

I felt a little better. Papa never broke his promises.

~

"But I was promised!" Papa banged his fist on the table, making his spoon jump out of his bowl, splattering soup.

Mama dabbed at the soup with a towel. "Promised, Leopold?"

He waved her comment away. "It was implied. As Vice Kapell-meister, it was logical when Lolli retired or died that I move up. Even mere children can understand the logic in that." He spread an open hand across the table in our direction. Even at ages sixteen and just months away from twenty-one, it was clear we were "mere chil-dren."

Yet Papa was right. His promotion was assumed because he'd been waiting so long. Lolli was a good Kapellmeister, so the only way Papa could attain his position was from Lolli's death or retire-ment. And now that Lolli was seventy and his health was tenu-ous . . .

"Perhaps His Grace wants new blood?" Mama passed Papa a roll, which he tore in half, causing flakes of the outer crust to crumble to the table.

He let them lie. "At nearly twice the pay?"

We'd heard that the newly appointed Kapellmeister, Domenico Fischietti—who had the gall to be an Italian, *and* from Naples, a place Papa had found particularly dirty and distasteful—was going to be paid eight hundred florins for his services. Lolli had received 456—plus perks and free lodging. And poor Papa was paid only 354 florins—with no perks. At least now that he was home again, he *was* getting paid. But to know his chances of promotion had faded, that perhaps he had achieved his pinnacle in Salzburg . . .

Papa tossed the bread in his soup and pushed the bowl away. "I'm fifty-two years old. I gave my life to our son and to further the glory of Salzburg throughout all of Europe, and this is the thanks I get?"

"I'll get a position somewhere, Papa," Wolfie said. "Then I'll support all of us."

He looked so proud when he said it, I suddenly wondered if Papa would take offense.

Yet when Papa looked across the table at Wolfie, his eyes weren't stern at all; in fact, his brow dipped a bit, and I sensed that only through great effort did he keep his expression under control. "You are a good son. You work very hard to bring this family honor and income."

Mama extended her hand to both of the men of the family and gave me a nod too. "We have many blessings. I pray that someday both of you will find a patron who appreciates who you are and what you do."

After a moment of hesitation, Papa nodded. He slapped the table again, but this time his palm was flat. "In fact, enough with this tiresome intrigue. If they do not appreciate us here, we shall go elsewhere."

Oh no. Not again.

"We've already been to Italy twice, Papa," Wolfie said. "They don't want—"

"Nonsense! Archduke Ferdinand did not tell us no."

"But he did not offer us a position."

Papa's voice turned stern. "He did not tell us undefiably, undeniably no."

I looked to Wolfie. He was the only one other than Papa who'd been a witness to what was truly said. He glanced at Mama, then at me. "No . . . I suppose not."

Papa pulled his soup bowl close, retrieved a soggy piece of bread, and took a big bite. "Exactly! When we go to Milan in the fall for the production of your opera *Lucio Silla*—which will bring us even more favor—we will ask again. Surely, after the production of two operas in his fair city, he cannot refuse."

But he could refuse. If I'd learned anything, it was that no one could force royalty to do anything they didn't want to do.

Not even Papa.

Papa and Mama were out for the evening having dinner with friends, leaving Wolfie and me alone. It was a rare occasion when we had our apartment to ourselves, and I planned to make the best of it. I went to the kitchen and took up two pieces of stollen and some wine. An evening spent talking and enjoying each other's company sounded perfect.

I walked into the workroom, my arms full. "Food for the prodigy! Refreshment for the—"

I stopped. Wolfie sat at the clavier, his head in his arms.

"What's. . . ?"

He lifted his head to look at me. "Don't call me that."

I tried to remember my words. "Prodigy?"

"I'm sixteen. I'm not a prodigy anymore. I'm no one special."

I set the food on a table, catching the bottle of wine as it rolled toward the edge. "You *are* special. Just because you aren't six doesn't negate your talent."

"But if I were six they would notice me, smile at me, love me." He got up from the bench and began to pace. "As it is now, I'm just a short, ugly man with pox scars on my face."

It was true he was not terribly handsome. Stunning looks were not my lot either. Our noses were too large and our eyes too wide set. I changed the subject. "I could wager that no one on the face of this earth has had multiple operas produced by age sixteen." I pointed to the work on the desk and the clavier. "With two more in progress."

Wolfie stopped at the edge of the instrument and fingered the top page, making it come into line with the one behind it. "To produce on demand . . ." He looked at me. "Sometimes it's difficult."

I went to his side, linking my arm with his. "But you do it. Somehow this miracle happens and you do it. I often wonder where you get your ideas, one upon another."

He strolled to the table, unstopped the wine, and poured two glasses. "When Papa and I were in Venice we stayed at a lodging that housed a lot of musicians. Above and below us were violinists, next to us was a singing teacher who gave lessons, and in the room opposite ours was an oboist. It was exhilarating to compose in such a place. I picked up many ideas." He downed the wine, then poured some more. "But here in Salzburg . . ."

He didn't have to elaborate.

"Papa is right," he continued. "We can't stay here. I must go elsewhere to get a position. One for myself and one for Papa."

And none for me.

I was hesitant to bring this up, but . . . "Papa is old. To find two positions will be difficult."

He set the glass down hard. "Which means that the financial future of this family falls on me!" He strode back to the keyboard and picked up some papers lying nearby. "This is the libretto for the opera—or part of it. The writer gets it to me in bits and pieces, and I am supposed to compose music for it. How can there be any consistency in that? And then we go to the town of the opera's production to start rehearsal, and the violists don't like their part, or the soprano complains that the runs are too difficult or not difficult enough to show off her voice." He threw the pages into the air, letting them float to the floor. "It's all about them. It's never about the music." His face was stricken. "It should be about the music!" He fell into my arms and rested his head against my shoulder. "I'm so tired, Nan. So many depend on me. How I wish Papa would have let you compose too. Then we could have worked together." He pulled back to look at my face. "Wouldn't that have been grand?"

What I really wanted to say was overpowered by what he needed to hear. "I would have liked that."

Wolfie returned to the table and took a huge bite of stollen. Raisins and nuts fell to the floor. "I asked Papa why he didn't let you compose."

My mouth went dry. "What did he say?"

"He said, 'What would be the use? She's a girl. It's hard enough for a man to get his music noticed, much less a woman.'"

I sucked in a breath.

Wolfie was quick to my side. "Did I offend you? I didn't mean—"

"No, no," I said. "You have not said anything I didn't know." I picked up my glass, wanting a diversion from my impending tears.

It didn't work. I began to cry.

It was Wolfie's turn to comfort me. "Shh. There, there, Horse-face. Sometimes I envy you being female."

I swiped the tears with a finger and snickered. "Why would you ever do that?"

"Because you don't have to worry about finances every waking moment. You can go to parties, and go shooting, and—"

"And have absolutely no way to earn decent money on our own, making us totally dependent on men. Women have to marry in order to survive. Have to. And not just anyone will do. Our spouses must have *means*. It's not fair."

Wolfie scrunched up his nose. "I guess it's tit for tat." His eyes brightened and he took my hands, turning me in circles about the room. "I know a smashing solution to all our troubles! We'll run away and you can wear breeches under your petticoats, and I'll wear a corset under my waistcoat, and we'll shave our hair and go live in the Kingdom of Back. Remember that?"

I did. When we were little, on our travels, he'd created an imaginary Kingdom of Back where there were no adults and we could do what we wanted. Our servant Sebastian had even made maps of it.

In our circling, my hip bumped into the table, making the pewter goblets tip over. So much for our kingdom.

Wolfie headed to the kitchen. "I'll get a towel."

I righted the goblet and waited for him. Our frivolity had been fleeting—as were the games and wishes of our youth.. They had no place in the here and now. God had created us, male and female.

It was my unlucky fate to have been created the latter.

~

The music made Wolfie sick.

That was too strong a statement, yet essentially true. The pressure to create the music was the knife that Papa wielded. It may have been sheathed in love, but it still wielded a sharp edge that scraped away at my brother's fortitude until he ended up in bed, completely drained.

One morning after Mama and the doctor left and I was on my way out of the room, Wolfie grabbed my arm. "Stay," he whispered.

Mama paused at the door, "Nannerl? Come now. Leave your brother to rest."

"In a minute, Mama."

She eyed me, then Wolfie and, apparently satisfied it was a mutual choice, nodded and left us.

I took a seat beside the bed, managed a smile, and tugged at a lock of his hair. "So . . ." I'd let him fill in the silence.

He took a deep breath, though it was evident it took effort. "I can't do it, Nan. Papa has had to tell Venice that I cannot give them an opera for carnival, the appointment with Archduke Ferd-face has never materialized, and even the job Papa tried to get me with a music publisher has come to nothing."

I knew of all these disappointments. "He's asked too much of you."

Wolfie nodded, and I was relieved he made the admission. "Papa thinks the music comes from some magic place."

I gasped in mock shock. "Are you saying it doesn't?"

He didn't smile but looked away, his head shaking back and forth. "I do have talent, but . . ." He sighed deeply.

I offered him a laugh. "Yes, I think you have a *bit* of that."

He turned on his side, his arm under his pillow. His eyes were glazed and rheumy, his skin yellow. "I have talent, but the composing takes work. I am learning, Nan. All the time learning from those who've composed before: Haydn, Gluck, Handel, Gassman . . . even Papa. I'm influenced by their work, learning from their mistakes, taking their successes and molding them to what's in my head."

"We know that."

He suddenly grabbed my wrist roughly, his eyes wild. "No, no you don't! I may have been a prodigy once, but even the majority of that involved being a performing monkey, rehashing what others had done."

"But you used to improvise before an audience for hours."

He looked at his hand on my wrist and suddenly let go as if he hadn't realized the extent of his aggression. He laid his ink-stained fingers on my arm, making amends. "That was a game. A glamorous game I thought could continue. But this reality is far different from appeasing the ears of a few royals." He leaned back on the pillow. "As is said, I do have talent. Perhaps great talent. Perhaps I even tap into moments of the divine. But it's work, Nan. Hard, hard work." His eyes filled with tears as he rested his forearm across his forehead.

His vulnerability encased him in a vessel of delicate glass. Too easily cracked, too easily broken. I smoothed the edge of the bed-covers. "I was a monkey too."

He was still a moment; then he moved his arm, peeking out from beneath it. "You and I were partners once."

"Indeed we were. The Wunderkinder."

He covered his eyes again and sighed deeply. "I miss that."

"Me too. Remember the time in Paris when we—?"

He turned on his side and snuggled into his pillow. "I need to sleep, Nan. We'll talk more later."

～

A change in plans!

Soon, it would be time to leave on *our* journey to Italy, to start production of Wolfie's opera *Lucia Silla* in Milan. Papa had always said Mama and I would see Italy one day. Oh, to see it *this* way, for this special event. To witness Wolfie's opera come to life, to see the sets and the costumes, to hear the applause. Seeing him attain what I could not offered some consolation. It was such a blessing that my jealousy had finally been transformed into pride in my brother. Had I, at age twenty-one, finally attained a laudable measure of maturity? Or was I merely resigned? Either way, it was an acceptable place to be.

We were scheduled to leave in one week's time. In preparation I looked through my armoire, trying to choose a dress to wear opening night. Wolfie came in the room, one foot bare, carrying a stocking. "Can you darn this? I just poked a hole clean through."

I swung around with a red crepe in front of me. "What do you think?" I asked.

"That is too open a question, sister dear."

I ignored his barb. "What do you think of the dress, silly. For opening night."

He tossed the stocking in my direction. It landed on the bed nearby. He moved to a drawer. "Where are the rest of my stockings? When was the last time you did laundry?"

"What?"

He shut the drawer with a slam. "Laundry. Stockings? I have none."

It was hard for me to focus on his question. "There are some hanging in the kitchen."

"Fine." He moved to leave.

"Wolfie? Answer my question about the dress."

He turned around, gave the dress the once-over, then shrugged. "It doesn't much matter what dress you pick. You're not going."

"Not going?"

"To Milan. Only Papa and I are going."

My arms were too heavy to hold the dress in place. "Not going?"

"Papa says it's too expensive and the mountain passes in late October can be snowy and treacherous. Papa can't even sleep on such trips because he has to be continually watchful. He still remembers the accident when he hurt his leg so badly. And it will surely be cold."

"On your first trip to Italy Papa said we couldn't go because we would have never been able to handle the cold, on the second, the heat . . . now we're back to cold again?"

"That's not the only reason," Wolfie said. "Once we're there I'll be consumed with work. Although I've mapped out my basic plan and worked on some of the recitatives, I haven't even begun to compose most of the arias, and the opening is set for late December, just two months away. And who knows how many adjustments I'll have to make for this reason or that."

I tossed the dress at his face and he raised his arms in defense of it. "Mama and I can find things to do. You've gone on and on about how beautiful Milan is. Isn't it time we see it?"

"It's not up to me, Nan. You know that. It's not my fault."

But it was.

I ran at him, pushing him over. He fell hard on the wooden floor.

Within moments Papa came in. "What's going on here?"

"I tripped," Wolfie said.

Although I was surprised at his cover-up, I did not want his effort. It was time for all of this to come out. "I pushed him down."

"Why?" Papa asked.

"I—"

Wolfie stood and brushed off the back of his breeches. "She's mad because she can't go to Milan with us."

Papa leveled me with a look. "I've decided—as I was forced to do before—that it's too expensive for four of us to travel, Nannerl. Besides, the mountain passes are difficult and—"

I didn't need to hear the same excuses twice. "But I need to go!"

Papa gave me a condescending smile. "Now, now. Need and want are two very different things, and it's best to realize—"

I shook my head and stomped a foot on the floor. "This isn't fair! Not fair at all!"

Papa's eyebrows rose. He took a step toward me and it took all my effort to hold fast. When he was close enough for me to smell the bratwurst on his breath, he said, "Is it fair that I was passed over for the Kapellmeister position after over three decades in service? Is it fair your brother works his fingers to the bone and is still not offered a salaried position? Is it fair he and I have to constantly be on the road—rough, dusty, and dangerous roads—staying in inns with far fewer amenities than home, eating bad food, dealing with the stress and nerve-wracking tension of never knowing how things will turn out in spite of our best intentions? Is it fair your mother and I are forced to live out our marriage apart more than we are together? Is it fair that the livelihood and utter future of this family—of you, my dear ungrateful Nannerl—is on our shoulders? Is it fair you get to spend time with friends, playing cards, shooting air guns, taking leisurely strolls through the Mirabel Gardens, while we—your brother and I—barely have time to breathe?"

He took a new breath. He needed it. His chest heaved.

He lowered his voice, but his final words were thick with intensity. "Do not talk to me about what's fair, nor about *need*."

What could I say? I had no defense, no counter to any of his points, each of which had been a lead weight, weighing down my arguments. I stood there, torn between anger and shame.

"I would think you would be more grateful. I've given everything to—"

Shame won out. I lunged toward him, wrapping my arms around his torso. "I'm sorry, Papa. I didn't mean it."

He hugged me close and kissed the top of my head. "There's a good girl, Nannerl. For what I *need* you to do is keep your mother safe and our house a home so Wolfie and I have something wonderful to think about on our journeys."

I nodded, rubbing my cheek against the rough wool of his waistcoat. "I will, Papa. I will."

It was the least—and the most—I could do.

~

They left me. Again. And then again. First Milan for the opera, then Vienna, where Papa desperately continued his quest to find a post for the two of them. Although they were home a few months in between, it didn't really count. They were not *here*. They lived in the future of their minds, in the next commission, the next concert, the next opportunity for a position that was anywhere but home in Salzburg.

When I allowed myself to be understanding, I knew they were being stifled by the new archbishop Colloredo—whom Papa often discredited in private by reminding us that he had been elected on the forty-ninth ballot. Colloredo was completely reshaping the music program that was under his tutelage, and his new Kapellmeister, Fischietti, was loving every minute of it. The only satisfaction Papa gained was that the archbishop was peeved at Fischietti when he found out the man was married. Wives created expense and expected pensions. . . . Plus, Fischietti showed his true greedy colors by coveting the retired Lolli's living quarters *and* holding out for more money.

Not that any of Fischietti's actions counted against him. For the archbishop still gave him a three-year contract at a ridiculous salary and retained the old-fashioned rococo style of music that Papa had longed to change. Papa would rather have died than be held musically stagnant. So I understood their burning need to go elsewhere. Yet the archbishop had made it clear there would be no pay in their absence.

It was an extremely delicate situation because the more they made it known they were looking for a position, the greater the risk the archbishop would find out and cut Papa's ties completely. Plus, I'd heard rumblings from the parent of a piano student that the empress herself was not pleased with Papa and Wolfie putting themselves out there, like itinerant musicians, like beggars. Apparently, they cheapened themselves in her eyes. I wondered if her opinion was the reason her son Ferdinand had not hired them and that so many doors were closed.

Dealing with royalty required a careful balance—being confident could work for or against you. Of course, the empress had more important things on her mind besides the Mozart men. Poland, for one. She was in the midst of a tug-of-war over that country with Empress Catherine of Russia. . . . The politics were beyond my ken. The empress had her concerns and I had mine.

Which were focused on my father and brother's continued absence from home. They missed all our birthdays, Christmas, and even Mama and Papa's twenty-fifth wedding anniversary. For that momentous event all Papa sent Mama was a note in a letter: *Today is the anniversary of our wedding day. It was twenty-five years ago, I think, that we had the sensible idea of getting married, one which we had cherished, it is true, for many years. All good things take time!*

"It was twenty-five years ago—I think?" I think? Mama had been distraught on the anniversary day and stayed in bed. Her mood was not improved days later when she received the letter. The least Papa could have done was send it ahead of time, to try to have his greeting—bland though it was—arrive on the actual day. And he forgot St. Anne's day, Mama's and my name day, then chastised me for forgetting to send a greeting for his name day—after I *did* send it.

Yet I'm sure he was too busy to think much of us—except to give us directions about life in Salzburg and to ask for Mama's hand-cream recipe. And all the letters from Wolfie, complaining about having to sleep in the same bed with Papa and not getting any sleep, or being together all day, every day, and his intense longing for his favorite liver dumplings and sauerkraut, fell on my deaf ears. Papa even presented the news that some grandstands in Milan had collapsed just across the street from where they were sitting—killing some people—as another reason we should not have been along on that trip.

Even their difficulties with the opera performance in Milan made me roll my eyes. So what if Archduke Ferdinand held up the start of the first performance two hours because he was home writing a New Year's letter (obviously not being adept at such things). So what if the packed house grew antsy. Singers who overacted, or got sick and had to be replaced? It was trivial to me. Worthless information. An annoyance in my day.

During their months of further travel, I came to believe that what Papa really wanted was to have his son all to himself. How could I think otherwise? For what man would so eagerly give up house and home, along with the companionship of a daughter who loved him?

And a wife. As an adult I was also aware that the long months of abstinence would wear on most men. Yet he chose to repeatedly extend the separation. I'd thought my parents' marriage strong, yet the very fact they were willing to remain apart so long made me wonder.

It was not something I could talk to Mama about. And on her part, I did not see any hint of true longing. At least, not for . . . that.

Once, my friend Katherl brought up the subject when we were sitting in the garden doing petit point. "Do you think your father has a mistress?"

It had come forth just that bluntly. I was taken aback, of course—not because I hadn't asked such a question within my own mind but because Katherl had spoken the words out loud.

"I don't think so," I said. "No." I shook my head. "No, I'm sure he doesn't."

"How can you be sure?"

"Because Papa is Papa." I'd gone back to the leaf of my petit-point rose. "Besides, German men don't do such things. Just the French." I remembered the court at Versailles, where even as a child I was privy to men flaunting their mistresses and women bragging about their lovers. I hadn't fully realized what it meant back then, but now . . .

"I bet Italian men do it too," she said.

"I wouldn't know." And I wouldn't, for I had never seen Italy. Which led me back to the issue at hand. . . .

It wasn't as if I sat idle while they were gone. I found things to do and was very capable of amusing myself with activities and friendships. It was the principle that rankled my pride. The injustice. Getting invited back to Joseph's Triebenbach estate was a highlight in our time without Papa and Wolfie. And oh, how Papa went on and on about how happy he was for us! I believe he *was* happy— that we were gaining pleasure and it didn't cost him anything. He even told us we could have some new dresses made. As if a few dresses could ever take the place of what we were missing in Italy. I told Mama it was bribery, and other than saying, "Oh, Nannerl," she did not argue with me. And we did get the dresses. I admit to having expensive tastes when allowed.

And then we received a bribe that was probably worth staying home for.

We got a new home. Gone was the three-room cramped quarters we'd rented from the Hagenauers my entire life as we moved across the Salzach River to the Hannibalplatz, to a house called affectionately the Dancing-Master's House. It had eight rooms on the first floor, one of them a huge room that had been used for dance lessons. The doorways were arched, the floors were covered with a patterned wood parquet, and the windows were large and airy. Best of all, I had my own room from which I could look upon the busy square and people-watch. As a bonus, out back we had a large garden where we could entertain, shoot targets, and rest in real beauty.

It was grand compared to our worn-down, cramped third-story quarters on the Getreidegasse, and I wondered how Papa afforded it. It was hard to know how we were doing financially. Most of the time Papa was frantic about it, and yet, with this move . . . Wolfie's commission work must have made the difference. Mama and I were even able to hire a cook and occasionally hire someone to come in and do our hair.

I hated the boring hairstyles of most Salzburg women—shoving their hair back in a hood—and liked mine piled high as I'd seen as a child. Papa and Wolfie made fun of me for my *geshchopfte* and teased me about the amount of time I told them I spent creating it. But what should they care? They were not here.

Actually, in many ways, neither was Mama. Although Papa sent her detailed instructions regarding how to handle things while they were gone, it was not something Mama enjoyed doing—nor something she was particularly good at doing. She did it because she had no choice. But those responsibilities, combined with the usual household duties, plus the absence of her husband and son, wore on her emotions and mental state so, I began to fear for her health. She faded. She pulled inward.

It took effort not to follow her.

For all my complaints, it was hard to see Papa and Wolfie return home from Milan disheartened about not getting a position. They'd even had an audience with Empress Maria Theresa herself—to no avail. Papa had delayed their return as long as possible—feigning rheumatism so the archbishop would think he couldn't travel—in hopes of hearing from the courts of Lombardy and Tuscany. Considering both places (as well as Milan) were ruled by children of the empress . . . it seemed obvious she influenced them. I would imagine the children of an empress would bow to her wishes from two fronts: to please her as a mother, out of loyalty and love, but also to please her as their ruler, out of duty. It was a detail we might never confirm, though I, as much as anyone, knew the influence of a parent on a child.

Yet for Papa and Wolfie, coming back to staid and stodgy Salzburg, with its smothering atmosphere, was like wearing a fur cloak on a summer's day. Papa had written as much in his final letter from Milan: *You cannot think into what confusion our departure has thrown me. Indeed I find it hard to leave Italy.*

What remained unspoken was the subtext: *I find it hard to come home.*

In March, after they had been home a few days, I passed the kitchen and heard Mama and Papa talking. The serious tone of the discussion made me hold back and keep my presence unknown.

"So all is lost?" Mama asked.

"No! Never."

"But if all avenues in Italy are closed . . ." Mama sighed. "What of the Kapellmeister position in Vienna?"

"He's recovered from his illness. There is no position. If only the archbishop had not been in Vienna on the same day as our audience with the empress . . ."

"So you think they talked?"

"I'm sure of it."

I heard Wolfie behind me. I put my finger to my lips, and he joined me in the eavesdropping.

"I'm feeling very old, Anna. I'm afraid the job prospects for an old man and a boy are slim."

"You can't give up," she said.

Wolfie pulled me away, into the music room. As soon as we were there, he let go and began pacing. "I'm going to end up like Papa, I know it!"

The statement took me aback. "But Papa's a good man. A talented—"

He swung toward me, his eyes blazing. "None of which matters!" His eyes skimmed the doorway and he lowered his voice. "Papa is stuck here. He's too old to be named Kapellmeister; he gave up his own composing to travel around Europe chasing fireflies. The archbishop pats him on the head and says, 'Yes, yes, how nice. Now, get to work.'"

"Papa gave up his own ambitions for us, Wolfie. For you."

He began pacing again. "A lot of good it's done me. I'm a great composer. I'm a great musician. Yet I'm made to feel like a peon who's peddling some carved knickknack or painted teacup. Why can't people realize who I am? Why can't they treat me with the respect I deserve?"

Because you have to earn it.

Although I truly thought my brother was God's gift to music, I didn't like his new attitude. There was a fine line between pompous and possessing a proper pride in a gift God had bestowed upon—

Wolfie suddenly stopped his pacing, his eyes blinking with a new thought. "I must get away. On my own. Papa's right; together we're an old man and a young boy. Two undesirable ends of the spectrum. But alone, I could make them see . . ."

"People know how young you are."

He laughed sarcastically. "Of course they do. Papa's made sure of that. And bragging about my youth and even shaving off years was fine then, but now . . . I must be seen as a man. An independent, vital, mature man of the world."

To look at him, there was no way people would think of him as being even as old as he was—which was nearly eighteen. He looked fourteen, perhaps fifteen. And his habit of flailing his arms when he talked, of bouncing on the balls of his feet when excited, of showing every emotion on his face like a child . . .

He took two steps toward the doorway, then stopped. "I will tell Papa that the time has come for me to go off by myself." He looked at the doorway, then back at me. "Yes?"

His indecision and need for approval made him seem younger still.

Papa's voice sounded from another room. "Wolfgang? Where are you, boy? We have work to do."

Like a breath taken in, then released, he was gone to Papa. I did not doubt his desire to be free. I too felt the lure of independence. I was twenty-two. I should have been married. I should have had my own household, my own husband, my own life. To feel the draw to be elsewhere was one thing. But actually doing—

Papa's voice resounded again. "Nannerl?"

"Coming, Papa."

Chapter Twelve

I set down Papa's letter with a sigh.

Mama looked up from her darning. "Are the opera rehearsals going badly?"

"They are going better than expected."

"Then why the sigh, Nannerl?"

I brought her the offending letter. "Papa offers yet another excuse why we can't go to Munich to see the opera's premiere. He says if we *all* leave Salzburg, it might appear as if we are thinking of moving away, perhaps seeking a position with the elector. The archbishop would not—"

"The archbishop, the archbishop," Mama said. "I grow weary of speculating on his reaction or action regarding our family's business."

I was surprised by her tone. Mama was the one family member who encouraged peace at all costs. Yet we'd both looked forward to seeing Wolfie's latest opera, *La finta giardiniera—The Pretend Garden Girl*. The premiere was tentatively set for the Munich pre-Lenten carnival season. Munich was only a two-day journey, and many of our Salzburg friends attended carnival there. We'd been left behind on the Italian journeys, as well as Papa and Wolfie's trip to Vienna. This time . . . we were determined to go.

But Papa continued to offer excuses for us to remain at home, the main one being that he and Wolfie had needed to go to Munich ahead of time, in December 1774, so Wolfie could write the arias to fit the singers' voices. How would Mama and I get there at a later date? And since the men's lodging was too small for our inclusion, where would we find lodging during this busiest time of Munich's season?

I didn't know. I didn't care. Just so it happened.

Mama finished reading the letter on her own. Her hand fell to her lap. "I'll stay here."

"What?"

"If I stay behind, Colloredo cannot imagine our defection from Salzburg."

"I can't let you do that, Mama."

She set her darning aside and moved to the desk. She took up quill and paper.

"What are you doing?" I asked.

"I'm writing to your father telling him of my decision."

"But, Mama . . ."

"Go watch for the postman. I'll write as quickly as I can."

I wrapped a cloak around my shoulders and stepped outside onto the square, feeling guilty for her sacrifice.

And elated.

~

I was set free on the third of January, 1775. And though I knew a cage awaited my return, I took advantage of the time away from Salzburg and relished each moment. For myself. And for Mama, who'd sacrificed her own joy for the sake of the archbishop's suspicions and Papa's fears.

Arrangements had been made for me to travel—free of charge—with our family friend Frau von Robinig. Once in Munich, I stayed at a respectable boardinghouse, and brought with me some music Papa needed, many clothes for parties and sightseeing, and the costume of an Amazon for the masquerade ball. Papa had wanted me to wear the Salzburg national dress. But at age twenty-three, I made my own decision—at least in this. Actually, it worked out fine because Papa did not see the costume until the night of the ball, and by then it was too late for him to argue. It was a small victory that was enhanced by Wolfie's whispered comment, "You look amazing, Horseface."

But in spite of the wonderful times of merriment in Munich, first and foremost, we were there for the opera. At home I'd read the libretto—which was a bit farfetched, with more disguises, mistaken identities, and deceptions than were easily grasped. I'd urged Wolfie to make changes, but at this stage in his operatic career, he'd thought it best to use what he'd been given. Would he not be given additional praise for making the mediocre great?

And he did make it great. The entire theater was so crowded that many were turned away. After each aria there was a terrific noise: the clapping of hands and cries of *"Viva Maestro!"* I was so proud of him. Her Highness the electress and the dowager electress, who were sitting across from us, even called out "Bravo!" And afterward, Wolfie went to a room where the whole court passed by, and where he kissed the hand of the elector.

The opera was performed a second time a week later, and then a third, but alas, that was all. There was much competition during the season. Over twenty operas were performed, so one could not be greedy—though Wolfie certainly deserved to be. An additional disappointment was that the archbishop did not time his visit to Munich to avail himself of the performance, though we received some consolation by knowing that others told him about the opera's success. How the praise must have galled him. . . .

At first Papa had only planned for me to be in town twelve days, but as my ride back to Salzburg did not materialize (I had secretly hoped and even suspected it would not), I was allowed to stay and return with Papa and Wolfie on the sixth of March, two months after my arrival. Although I missed Mama's presence during this extended visit, it was the first time since our Grand Tour that I'd truly felt a part of things again. Wolfie and I even performed together a few times. The applause was a soothing elixir and fuel to my dormant dream of being a performer. After all, nothing was happening on the husband-family front, so could God have been opening a door to a career?

Yet all good things must come to an end. As did my season of freedom. Salzburg beckoned because the current Kapellmeister,

Fischietti, was on the outs with the archbishop, and the larger question loomed: Would he be let go? Would there soon be an opening for Papa to move up?

We sped home to place ourselves close to the action, Papa, full of hope, and Wolfie and I, full of deep reluctance. For we had both enjoyed our time in Munich, breathing free.

The emotions were so strong that as our carriage neared the town of our birth I found my throat constricted and my chest heavy. And as the view of the road from Munich was swallowed up by familiar streets and buildings, I heard the door of my cage slam shut.

~

Why do things never work out as we plan? I'd returned from Munich with hopes that the performing Mozart siblings would find life again. A voice. A European audience.

It did not happen.

Although we performed around Salzburg, we never managed to travel elsewhere, to get away, to breathe the air of freedom. The same people who'd always heard us play heard us again. And again. Until we were seen as talented but nothing that special.

We'd also returned from Munich with hopes Papa would be promoted. When Kapellmeister Fischietti left to pursue his own composing (ahead of the end of his three-year contract), the archbishop asked Papa to assume some of the Kapellmeister duties until he made a decision about who would officially take the position. It was a good sign, and so Papa did as he was asked—for no additional pay.

But then two years passed. . . .

Papa came in the house, slamming the door so hard the crucifix on the wall fell to the ground.

We all came running. "What's wrong?" Mama asked.

"He hired another Italian!"

We all understood who "he" was. The archbishop Colloredo. Cocky, cantankerous, callous Colloredo.

Mama and I led Papa to a chair, but he popped right out of it, his anger demanding movement.

"Who, Papa? Who?" Wolfie asked.

Papa's lips curled back in a snarl. "Giacomo Rust." He returned to the chair, closed his eyes, and perched his fingertips on his forehead. "I've been duped! Two years I've worked with no additional pay. Two years I've stayed here, afraid to leave and seek positions elsewhere. I formed myself into the most pliable, acquiescent employee, assuming His Grace would see and appreciate . . ." He leaned his head back against the chair's cushion.

Wolfie pointed toward the window, in the direction of the archbishop's Residenz. "He should at least pay you the difference in salary. He owes you an additional five hundred florins—per year. He needs to make things right." Wolfie had become much more forceful in his opinions since turning twenty-one and suffering his own employment inequities. For since Munich, there had been no job offers. A few commissions, much composition and growth in that regard, but no salaried position.

Papa opened his eyes and smiled sarcastically. "Ah, but the new Kapellmeister gets paid even more than Fischietti. He gets a thousand florins a year."

We all gasped. Compared to Papa's salary of three hundred fifty florins, it was a fortune.

Mama moved beside his chair, her hand touching its back as if wanting to touch Papa in consolation but not sure if she should.

Wolfie grabbed the sill of a window and leaned heavily upon it, his head shaking back and forth. "An Italian again. I find snobbery against one's own kind unconscionable. Why can't Germans appreciate Germans?"

"We must take solace in the fact that even Christ was not appreciated in His hometown," Mama said.

Papa flipped a hand, "Oh, that's just Jesus, don't mind Him! Oh, that's just Leopold, don't mind him either. He's just a native son who's spent thirty-six years in service, a great portion to an ungrateful, unscrupulous, demanding, arrogant, ignorant—"

Mama glanced toward the open windows. "Shh, dear one."

"Let him say it, Mama," Wolfie said. He opened the window wider and leaned out to yell, "It's not fair, I tell you! Not fair at all!"

Mama stood between Papa and Wolfie, her mouth open but

unspeaking, her arms extended toward both, as if she wanted to calm them but didn't know how.

I was of no help. For I was angry too and would have liked to open a second window to do my own yelling. How Papa was treated reflected on all of us. Wolfie was still on only half pay as the concertmaster but was at least getting commissions for his compositions. I was helping out as I could with Wolfie's music and by giving lessons, but our main source of income continued to be Papa.

His deep sigh broke through my thoughts. "I'm done," he said. "I know of no more I can do."

Wolfie left the window and stood before him. "I can do more, Papa. I can leave this horrible place and try for another post. Years have passed since we last ventured out to look. We've been two good boys, at the court's beck and call, bowing and accepting their scraps as dutiful peons. But now that they've humiliated you so . . . it's time I leave. I can find a post, a great post that will support us all."

Papa leaned forward in his chair. "Perhaps it is time to leave again. We've been home for over two years. I shall petition for travel, and we can—"

"No, Papa. Not us. Just me."

We all stared at Wolfie, though I'm sure the source of our dismay was different. Mama and Papa saw his declaration as the boast of a whippersnapper. I saw it as the boast of a brave brother—a boast I'd heard in private many times over the past years. I was proud of him for finally being bold.

Papa pushed himself out of the chair. "Don't be ridiculous. You, pack? You, handle money exchanges? You, handle transportation and lodging?"

"I could. I've seen you—"

"Seeing me do it all *for* you is not the same as you doing it for yourself."

"But if I never get to go by myself, how can I—?"

Papa took the ends of Wolfie's cravat and tied it correctly. "Look. You can't even dress yourself."

"I am at home, Papa. I was composing. It doesn't matter if my cravat isn't—"

Papa snapped his fingers at Mama. "Get me some clean paper and a fresh quill. I have to write a petition for travel."

During this exchange, my mind had hovered over Papa's use of the word *we* in regard to travel. He hadn't said to Wolfie "You and I," he'd said "we." I wanted to ask Papa to clarify, yet I was afraid to do so. I didn't want to hear another no.

Blessedly, Mama did it for me. "We are all going, then?" she asked from the doorway.

Papa blinked twice, as if the question surprised him. "Of course not. The expense. No, no. You and Nannerl will stay here."

I looked at Mama. She looked at me. I silently begged her to stand fast, insist we travel as a family. For though I *had* been allowed to hear Wolfie's opera performed in Munich, that had been over two years ago. We'd all been home since then, Papa tied to his work as the interim Kapellmeister, and the rest of us stuck in Salzburg because *he* was stuck.

Yet in spite of my wishes, Mama only nodded at Papa's words and left the room. She accepted her fate. If there was going to be any rebellion, it would have to come from me.

Papa was at his desk, mumbling to himself, verbally creating the words he would soon put on paper. I moved beside the desk, facing him. He was so mentally entrenched in his words that he did not even look up.

"Papa?"

His head whipped in my direction, his brow tight. "Not now, Nannerl. I have important work to do."

"I know, but I would like to reaffirm what Mama asked. I would like to go along. I've been helping Wolfie, and I can give lessons anywhere, and Mama could help with the packing and the lodging and—"

He put a hand on mine. "My answer now is the answer I gave when you both wanted to leave before. If we all leave, the archbishop will guess that we are searching for a position. If just the two of us go, we can mask the travel by saying it's in regard to a commission. Besides, I can't afford to pay for our home here as well as the on-the-road lodging for four people. It's not feasible, Nannerl. Not at all. You and Mama must remain here."

Like good little girls who had no say in anything.

The archbishop might have been unfair, but so was Papa.

~

Six months later I found Wolfie bent over a paper, writing with a painstaking hand instead of his usual vibrant flourish.

"What are you doing?" I asked.

He finished the word and sat back, taking with him the breath he had been holding. "I am copying a very important letter to the archbishop."

"*You're* writing a letter to him?"

He pointed at the sheet beside him. "Papa wrote it. I'm just copying it and will sign it as my own." He lifted the paper, studying it as if it were a piece of art. "Papa is intent on getting the archbishop to let me leave so I can pursue another position."

"But Papa's already asked," I said. "He petitioned the archbishop for an increase in your salary and for leave." During the past months our household had been consumed with petitions. Unsuccessful petitions.

"You know Papa. He won't stop asking until he gets the answer he wants. At one point the archbishop said I could go, but he quickly reneged." He pointed the quill at me. "But since he said it once, Papa is hoping with a little cajoling from me . . ." He gave me his most charming smile, "Me, His Grace's most faithful composer and clavier player extraordinaire."

Wolfie seemed confident, but I wasn't so sure. I knew how angry Papa got when Wolfie or I pressed him with the same question over and over. Our actions often brought punishment.

"Read it for me," Wolfie said, handing it to me. "Make sure I didn't spell anything wrong."

The paper read: *Most Gracious Sovereign Prince and Lord! Parents take pains to enable their children to earn their own bread, and this they owe both to their own interest and to that of the State. The more talent that children have received from God, the greater is the obligation to make use thereof in order to ameliorate their own and their parents' circumstances, to assist their parents, and to take care of their own advancement and fortune.*

The Gospel teaches us to use our talents in this way. May Your Serene Highness graciously permit me, therefore, to beg most submissively to be released from service.

I looked up. "Released from service? You're quitting?"

Wolfie shrugged, but the way he looked away spoke of his uncertainty. "Papa says there is no other way. The archbishop will not release us, so I must ask to be released. My income of one hundred twenty-five florins can surely be found elsewhere." His eyes met mine. "It must be found elsewhere."

I looked back at the petition and wondered about the tone. I wasn't sure His Grace would take the biblical lesson kindly. It was almost as if Papa was admonishing him. "But perhaps this is a bit . . ."

"Arrogant? Overstepping our bounds?"

"You see it too?"

"I do."

"Then maybe we should bring it to Papa and—"

Wolfie laughed. "Would you like to bring it to Papa?"

I handed him the page. He angled it to finish and dipped his quill. "We have to trust Papa, Nannerl. He's taken care of everything so far, yes?"

So far. Yes.

~

During the time between presenting Wolfie's petition and receiving an answer, a strained hopefulness hovered over our home, as if by the sheer act of our wills everything would turn out fine. If all went well, the archbishop would release Wolfie from his position and give his blessings. Wolfie was giddy about the idea of traveling alone, but I found it hard to believe Papa would let him go. Yet what choice would we have? There needed to be *some* regular money coming in, and that meant Papa had to stay. Yet I still suspected Papa had an alternate plan, that somehow he would find a way to also get travel leave. Papa had ways. Amazing ways.

~

Papa stormed in the door, shaking a piece of paper. In the past few months, his emotional entrances were becoming far too familiar. "Anna! Children!"

We gathered round as we always did, and Wolfie squeezed my hand. "Is it from——?"

"Yes, it's from . . ." Papa said. "You can bet your knickers it's from . . ." He raised the letter and read, "Father and son have permission to seek their fortune elsewhere—according to the Gospel."

I didn't know which part of the declaration to react to first: my father and brother's dismissal, or the fact His Grace had flung the Gospel back at them.

"You're dismissed?" Mama asked. Her voice was small.

"I'm dismissed! We're both dismissed!" He looked at the letter again, smacking it with the back of his fingers. "But the way he's said it . . . so smug, so arrogant. We can seek our fortune elsewhere . . ." Suddenly Papa wadded up the page and threw it across the room, where it bounced off a windowpane. "Pack our bags!" he said. "Since he wants us to leave, that's exactly what we're going to do."

Mama stepped toward him, her hands grappling. "But, Leopold. You can't. You can't leave us without income."

He stopped in the hall leading to the bedchambers, which allowed her to catch up to him. Touch him. Yet now, with her husband within reach, Mama withdrew her hands.

"I can't leave," he said simply.

He looked at Mama, then at me, and I hated the pain in his eyes. We were a burden on his back, holding him down, preventing him from flying free. I'd wanted my own freedom, but at this moment, for the first time, I realized Papa wasn't free either. In fact, perhaps he was the most imprisoned of us all.

Wolfie was the one to break the moment. "I can go alone, Papa. I can. I know I can."

Papa looked toward him, but I could tell his eyes were full of other sights, other thoughts beyond this slice of time. He changed direction and strode to the front door.

"Where are you going?" Mama asked.

"To grovel," he said.

He left us alone in an aching silence.

Mama took our hands. "We must pray, children. Pray for your Papa, pray for us all."

~

In gracious confidence that the petitioner will conduct himself calmly and peaceably with the Kapellmeister and other persons appointed to the court orchestra, His Grace retains him in his employment and graciously commands him to endeavor to render good service both to the Church and to His Grace's person.

So wrote the archbishop. So ended Papa's hope of ever being free. Yes, he had his job back—but with the contingency he behave himself. It was a humiliation. It was an affront. It was a blessing.

It was not just Papa's life that changed with the letter. The world as I knew it stopped. I didn't much care whether the world was flat, round, or shaped like a snuff box when Papa declared that Wolfie and Mama were going to travel in search of a position, leaving me behind with *him*. Such a scenario had never entered my thoughts.

The idea filled me with excitement *and* trepidation. Over the past few years, Papa hadn't shown much interest in me. Wolfie had been his focus. His life. I was *just* his daughter. He loved me, I knew he did, but I was not special to him. I didn't make his ambitions and creativity soar like Wolfie did. Wolfie stirred something deep inside him, touching an unreachable place. But with Wolfie gone, with Mama gone with him . . . would Papa see me differently? Would he let me in? Or would we live separate lives, together, yet apart?

Mama walked past me, carrying linens into their bedchamber. Her brow was drawn. I hurried after her, taking some of her load. "Are you excited, Mama?" I asked. "You get to *go*." There was much implied in that one word.

She faced me, the linens a barrier. "I have to go."

I didn't understand. "You don't want to?"

"Your father and brother are the travelers."

"As am I," I said. "I love to travel."

She raised her chin. "But I do not." Her eyes scanned the bedchamber. "I like it here."

"I agree this house is lovely. It's so much better than the last—"

She shook her head. "I liked it there too. The house is not the home in my heart, Nannerl. Salzburg is. I know *here*."

"But Wolfie will be with you."

She gave me the look I deserved. "I am going along to help *him,* not the reverse. I will have to handle all the arrangements your father managed in the past. I will have to deal with the constant packing and unpacking, I will have to cope with the different monies, plus curtail your brother and his undisciplined ways." She shook her head. "Your father has indulged him. It is not to my advantage. Nor his."

I knew this to be true. Although Wolfie lived with great responsibility and pressure in regard to his music, he had not been held accountable for daily tasks. To my brother, food magically appeared without cost or effort, living quarters cleaned themselves, and carriages emerged at just the right moment to whisk him away. In this, I was as culpable as my parents. I'd always doted on him, and somehow he'd made me feel it was worth it.

While he'd been away with Papa there was little need for Mama or me to worry about such logistics. In Papa's presence, the world—whether it be Milan, Paris, or Rome—was suitably controlled. Curtailed. Cushioned for the rest of us. But without that cushion . . .

"I have to go now, Nannerl. I have much to do."

Mama went into the bedchamber and I hesitated to go after her. In the many months and even years we'd been left behind, we'd come to recognize each other's moods and knew when space was required. As it was now.

Wolfie popped his head out of his bedchamber. "Psst!" He motioned me inside and closed the door.

"I can't have Mama go! I won't allow it!"

I was taken aback. His juvenile declaration proved he was not capable of going alone. "Allow, Wolfie? You won't allow it?"

He sat on his bed and fell backward, his arms wide. "I know, I know. What I want is not considered." He pushed himself up to his elbows. "That's the problem. What am I going to do, Nan? I don't want to be saddled with Mama for months and months."

I felt my eyebrows rise. "Saddled?"

He slid off the bed, moved to his wardrobe, and began plucking out shirts and breeches, discarding them on the floor. "Don't act all huffy. If I can't be honest with *you* . . ."

I retrieved a pair of silver blue breeches and folded them. "Why do you say that about her?"

He wrapped a neck scarf around his hand, over and over, staring past me. "She's so . . . dull. She isn't bold like Papa or vibrant like you. She's just *there,* like a table or a pretty settee." He cocked his head. "In fact, forget the pretty part."

I grabbed the scarf away from him. "That was rude!"

"So be it. I have absolutely nothing to say to Mama. Nothing."

"But she's your mother."

He shrugged. "I know the woman who collects the refuse from the cistern better than I know her."

Although I was appalled by his coldness, inwardly, I knew it might be true. Mama was not demonstrative nor outgoing (or pretty). Even when we had company, she was content to serve the food and let the others fill the evening with lively chatter and jokes. And though *I* knew her well, Wolfie had been away for most of his growing-up years. . . .

I could not imagine their trip being filled with lively chatter. Pairing the two of them would be like pairing a swan with a squirrel. The impression intensified as I imagined them in a cramped carriage, the swan sitting erect and regal, while the squirrel chattered and scattered, never able to be still.

It would never work.

Wolfie took the scarf back and tossed it on the bed. "I wish *you* could come with me, Nan. We'd have such a grand time." He took my hands in his and danced me around the room. "The two Wunderkinder, off to conquer the world!"

I pulled my hands away, stopping the dance—but not because I didn't enjoy it. The shock of Wolfie's suggestion forced me to concentrate on the thoughts swirling in my head. Me? Go with Wolfie?

He smirked at me. "You like the idea, don't you?"

I put a hand to my chest, trying to calm its beating. "I do." I laughed. "I really do! I never thought of such a thing. Why didn't I think of such a thing?"

"Because you're the good child, the obedient child who always does as she's told, and once Papa said Mama was—"

"Yes, yes. That's it." And it was. I was so used to being left behind that I'd never truly believed there was an alternative.

Wolfie took my hand and pulled me out of the room. "Let's go tell Papa."

I pulled him to a stop. "We don't tell Papa anything. We ask."

He flicked the end of my nose. "We ask with confidence, with force if necessary. This is the best way, Nan. We both know it."

We knew it. But could we convince Papa?

～

Papa was in the music room, going through scores. He looked up as we entered and spoke to Wolfie. "You'll need to get copies made along the way, as needed. It would be much too bulky to bring all of them. . . ." He stopped talking and looked at each of us in turn. "What's going on?"

Wolfie bounced on his toes. "I want Nannerl to go with me on the trip."

Inwardly, I cringed. I would not have stated it so plainly.

Papa looked directly at me. "Surely, this is not your idea, daughter?"

"No, but I think it's a good one." I looked to Wolfie for support. "We could be the Wunderkinder again—performing, making money to pay our way, and—" I saw Mama come in the room.

Papa pointed in her direction. "Maria, the children have informed me *they* want to travel together."

"Leaving me here?" There was a hint of hope in her voice.

"Exactly. It's an absurd idea. Two children—"

"I'm twenty-six, Papa," I said.

Wolfie hopped beside me. "And I'm twenty-one. We're plenty old to—"

"To get into trouble."

"We wouldn't, Papa," I said. "I'd make sure."

Papa took my face in his hands and kissed my forehead. "Ah, youth. You are not your brother's parent, Nannerl. You do not have the authority needed to keep him in line."

Wolfie put his hands on his hips. "I don't need a nanny. I'm a grown man."

Papa snickered. "Neither one of you has ever handled money—much less carefully budgeted money. And where do you hire honest coachmen? And what is a reasonable price for a room? And what if one of you gets sick?" He turned to his wife. "Mama and I are the ones who know the remedies, who know what to ask a doctor and why."

I looked to Mama, wishing she'd say something. But she just stood there, her eyes down, her hands busy with the edge of her lace neckerchief.

I took a breath and let the truth spill forth. "Mama doesn't want to go either."

While Mama looked aghast that I'd betrayed this confidence, Wolfie pounced. "See? Mama wants to stay here with you. The two of you could have a lovely time of it without your grown children in the way, and—"

Papa cleared his throat. "No. In lieu of myself, your mother must be the one to go. Her maturity and business knowledge will be to our advantage."

I knew Papa was referring to the various business instructions he'd sent to Mama while he and Wolfie had been gone, instructions about getting music copied, obtaining good prices on loans, of distributing Papa's book on violin technique. . . .

What he didn't know was that I had been the one to make sure most of his instructions were carried out. Mama said they gave her a headache. We'd both agreed not to let Papa know that it was I carrying out his orders, but now, when the truth would have been to my advantage . . . to break that confidence along with the other . . . I wasn't sure I could do it. Mama looked so forlorn, and there was no way I could tell whether her distress was caused by having Papa know she'd rather stay home, or the fact that he still seemed adamant in making her go.

Papa put his arm around his wife, offering her a smile. "Your mother and I are used to being apart. And you children are every-thing to us. We will make every sacrifice necessary to ensure you receive only the best life has to offer. Right, Anna?"

Her eyebrows touched, then parted. He squeezed her shoulders, forcing an answer. "Yes, dear one," she finally said. "You know best."

"Of course I do. So there will be no more talk of two youngsters venturing out into the world. Discipline and maturity. That's what is needed on such excursions. Not frivolity and youthful notions."

"But, Papa. Nan and I—"

"Will do as I say." He pointed at each of us.

And that was that.

As if by mutual decision, the four of us kept our distance that evening and went to bed without the usual banter. It took me a long time to get to sleep as the thoughts and images of what might have been refused to retire peaceably.

If only Wolfie hadn't reawakened them in the first place. . . .

~

The evening before Mama and Wolfie were to leave, Papa called a meeting around the kitchen table, his instructions laid before us. He smoothed a map of Germany and pointed to Munich. "See here? First you go to Munich. If you get offered a position there, your trip is short and you return to us triumphant."

"If not?" Wolfie asked.

"Then you head toward Mannheim." His finger traced a route. "You go through Augsburg, Dischingen—where Prince Carl Anselm is staying—stop at the Cistercian Abbey of Kaisheim, then on to Wallerstein or Hohen-Altheim. You'll have to find out at which location Prince Kraft Ernst is staying. . . ."

On and on Papa talked, giving distinct directions on where to go, how to get there, when, and whom to see. That last was the most important ingredient. This trip was all about making contacts, providing those contacts with music that suited their needs (making Wolfie appear indispensable), and then obtaining a paid position—a highly paid position that would help support us all. A position of honor too. For Papa had stressed how important it was that the archbishop be made to feel intense regret at Wolfie's absence.

Finally Papa sat back. "Well? Do you understand?"

Mama stared at the maps. "I think so."

Wolfie slapped the table. "It will be glorious! We will take Germany by storm."

"No storms. You will take the journey one step at a time," Papa said. "One carefully planned step."

Wolfie sprang from his chair. "I want to go now. I don't want to wait until tomorrow."

Papa shook his head. "There is still much to do." He suffered a fit of coughing. He had a chest cold and shouldn't have been out of bed.

Mama carefully folded the maps and instructions, looking at them as if they were in Greek. She spoke to Wolfie. "Did you get your music packed? And your violin?"

"I'm not bringing my violin. I hate the violin. I don't want to be one of many; I want to be one of a kind."

Papa's coughing grew worse, so he left the room. Yet something about the way his shoulders slumped made me follow him. I caught up with him in the dark, standing at a front window, his arms wrapped tightly around himself. He barely glanced at me when I moved beside him.

"It will be all right, Papa. They will be all right."

He shook his head slowly, his eyes gazing over the square below. "This journey is going to be disastrous. I know it. I feel it."

The serious tone of his voice scared me. "No, Papa. It will be—" His cough began again, wracking his entire torso. "You must get to bed. They're leaving at six in the morning. You need to rest and be well to see them off."

He shucked my hands away. "I have packing to do."

"I'll help."

"No, *this* I can do. This I must do."

His footsteps fell away, leaving me in silence except for the clop of a horse's hooves against the cobblestones outside.

~

I'd expected a teary good-bye, but as Mama and Wolfie's departure played out, there wasn't time. The carriage was late, Wolfie had *not* gone through the music as he'd been instructed, Mama couldn't find her extra embroidery needles, and Wolfie tore the seam in his sleeve, and I had to mend it while the horses grew restless outside.

Papa yelled instructions at the coachmen, telling them which trunks needed to go where, coughing and wheezing through his words. He'd stayed up until two in the morning packing, and I was fairly sure he hadn't slept well in the few hours since then.

I hadn't. Although I wasn't going away, my mind swam with lists—so much so that, in the middle of the night, I brought a piece of paper and quill to my bedside. By morning, the paper was full. But even my list didn't stave off the chaos. I'm sure we woke every-one on the entire square with our calls to one another for this and that.

But finally the carriage was packed, and with a quick hug and a kiss, we sent them on their way—as if they were only going across town and not across steep mountain passes.

As the carriage turned the corner by the river, Papa suddenly left my side and ran after it with one arm raised. "Wait!" There was a plaintiveness in his voice that tore at my heart.

He stopped a few houses away, consumed by a fit of coughing. His upraised hand, which had been open, closed, then fell to his side. By the time I reached him, the coughing had subsided, but his shoulders were slumped. His eyes were locked on the road where they had gone.

This was not like Papa to show his emotions so blatantly. Of all people, Papa had the ability to be calm in the midst of whatever feelings claimed his heart.

Gingerly, I touched his shoulder. "Papa?"

"I should never have let them go."

"You had no choice."

He shook his head. "This will not end well. Will not. Will not."

Before I could ask what he meant, he did an about-face and strode toward the house, ignoring the neighbors watching in the square. I hurried after him, nodding a greeting to friends, offering a smile that hopefully implied everything was all right.

But it was not. Once we were both safely inside, with Papa still shivering from the late September air, I found it hard to look at him, to acknowledge the vulnerable and pathetic image he'd created with his run down the road. And so I was relieved when he walked past me and said, "I need to lie down."

I helped him to his bed and tucked him in, then returned to my own. Sleep seemed the only acceptable alternative to a quiet, empty house.

"This will not end well."

What had we done?

~

I found my way toward accepting our situation before Papa did. For though I missed Mama and Wolfie, I began to bask in the knowledge that finally, after a lifetime of sharing my father's attentions—or being ignored—I now had him all to myself. Wolfie had had his turn. Years of his turn. Now it was mine.

And yet it proved awkward to be just the two of us. Mama and Wolfie had always been a shield between Papa and me, like two fences keeping father and daughter apart while still allowing us to see and speak to each other when needed. Now, with the fence dismantled, knowing there was no one else in the house to hear us when we spoke—except Therese, our cook, and she wasn't much for talking *or* listening—the pressure to not disappoint each other was palpable.

At least on my end. I'm not sure Papa felt any pressure in that regard. He was never one to pay much notice to his effect on others. To a lesser extent, Wolfie was the same. Once either man positioned a goal in their minds, the blinders rose and they saw only what they wanted to see, and did only what they determined needed to be done. Hang the world.

I asked forgiveness for the sentiment. Not that I hadn't heard such emotions repeated with even stronger language throughout my life. Our family was not one to mince words. And in truth, I wished I could have been more like Papa and Wolfie. I spent far too many moments analyzing my words and actions. *What will happen if I. . . ?* sped through my thoughts many times daily. To my credit, I usually guessed correctly. But to my dismay, the question meant too much to me. Why could some people care little about their effect while I cared too much?

Because God said so. It was the only answer that offered comfort. I'd heard it said God delighted in variety, so how could I argue with the Almighty if I didn't find such variety easy to tolerate? Or understand?

What I did find in the weeks that followed Mama and Wolfie's departure was a father who sank into a deep melancholy. Although he was not confined to bed and got up every morning to make his way to work, as soon as he came home in the evening, it was all he could do to make polite conversation. On my side, it was exhausting trying to be merry in a desperate attempt to pull him out of it. Occasionally I even resented him for forcing me to be the strong one. I didn't want to be strong. I wanted to wallow too—at least a little.

But every time I worked myself up to tell him so, I'd catch sight of him staring out the window with a piece of Wolfie's music on his lap like a second-best companion, and I remained silent, unable to add to his distress in order to share a bit of my own.

On one evening, two weeks after Mama and Wolfie left, I couldn't find him. I'd just finished mending the velvet in his favorite slippers and wanted to bring them to him as a surprise. But Papa was not in his bedchamber, nor in the music room. I carried a candle through the rest of the house, calling for him. Nothing. Therese had not seen him leave. Nor had I. I even checked the garden, though the evening air was full of bite and, considering his recent chest cold, I hoped beyond hope he was not there.

He wasn't. But where was he?

Then, in passing the door to Wolfie's room a second time, I heard a soft cough. The door was ajar, but the room was dark. I pushed the door open slowly and let the candle lead my way inside. Papa sat at Wolfie's desk, his head in his arms, asleep. He stirred, perhaps awakened by the light. He looked over his shoulder at me. "Nannerl?"

I held up his slippers. "I brought these for you. Your favorite, all mended." My words seemed pathetic, needy, wrong. But they were all I had.

He scooted the chair back and turned it to face me. He held out his hand to receive the slippers, but I said, "Let me do it."

I knelt before him, removed his shoes, and put them on. Right foot first. . . .

When I'd finished, he touched my cheek. I looked up at him and he smiled, and by the way the smile touched his eyes, I felt as if he was really seeing me for the first time since they'd left. "Don't worry, dear girl. I'll be the complacent, calm, and peaceable man that's required. As the archbishop has instructed, I will endeavor to render good service to both the church, His Grace, and . . ." He sighed deeply. "And my family. And you, dear Nannerl. Mark my words, I will render good service to you too. I will do what I have to do."

His words were pitiful and full of sorrow. Not knowing what to say, I held my hand in place against his cheek. He leaned his forehead against mine.

We held this position, skin to skin, mind to mind, until the candle snuffed itself out and left us in darkness.

~

I loved petticoats, as did Mama. Just two months previous, we'd each had a new one made. But mine had not held up well, the lace tearing away easily, the seams ripping. I brought it back to Marta, the seamstress who'd made it, in order to complain of its lack of longevity and ask for repairs—free repairs, as per Papa's direction.

Marta pulled at the lace that had ripped from its ruffle. "You must have caught it on something."

"I assure you, I did not. I fear the stitches were not close enough together to hold it." I showed her stitches that were too few per inch.

She raised an eyebrow and moved her fingers along the ruffle to another torn area. "I hear your brother has left to seek his fortune." She glanced at me, her smile sarcastic. "With your dear mama this time? How old is he now, fifteen?"

She knew very well how old he was. She'd made him a new waistcoat for his twenty-first birthday, the previous January. I ignored the jab. "My brother's experience has far exceeded the needs of our humble town."

"Such is his oft-voiced opinion." Another glance. "Or so I've heard."

I felt my face redden. I knew Wolfie and Papa had an awful habit of disparaging the musical opportunities of working for the archbishop's court. They'd made it known they believed Salzburg would never be a city of high culture such as Vienna, Paris, or Milan. It was an opinion I shared—in private.

Marta continued. "All those years when your family traveled and the old archbishop paid your father's salary in his absence . . ." She shook her head. "His Grace was so patient. So kind."

In comparison to the current archbishop, Colloredo, I agreed that his predecessor, Schrattenbach, had been a gem. I pointed to the lace in her hands. "I'd like the lace replaced. The quality . . . it didn't last."

"It's the quality you paid for."

"I'd like it repaired and replaced." I positioned a rent seam in front of her. "Here too."

She shrugged and pretended to study the tear. "I heard that the archbishop instructed your brother to go to Italy and enroll in one of its conservatories—to get a real education."

This was a direct slap to our father. "He said no such thing."

Marta did not apologize but merely offered me another shrug. "Then for your brother to ask to be released from his position so he could travel some more . . ."

"He did not ask to be released." *Not exactly.* "He simply asked for a leave in order to travel. It's the archbishop who took it too far and let him go. Wolfie was quite willing to stay and—"

Marta removed her glasses and looked at me. "I suppose I will repair it. Though I do think it's received hard wear, *I* am a woman of my word and good reputation."

The way she looked at me was as if she would like to add "Unlike some."

My thoughts reeled. Some of the things she said went against what Papa had told me about the break with the archbishop. But surely Papa wouldn't have lied to me. To Mama.

As Marta wadded up the petticoat, I grabbed it away from her and shoved it in my satchel. "I'll fix it myself," I said. I strode toward the door and offered her one parting barb. "My stitches are quite fine and I take pride in my work."

"Pride." She snickered. "That's something your family is familiar with. Suit yourself. After all, I'm sure you can do it better than anyone else."

I strode home in double time, intent on confronting Papa, asking him to deny everything Marta had said. But once I reached the square in front of our house and saw him sitting on a bench alone, I could not. By the stoop of his shoulders, I could see he was still not himself. There was no vibrancy and power in his manner, just awkward surrender and brokenness as he meekly read a book, his glasses perched on the tip of his nose. Did knowing the whole truth really matter? If Papa thought it necessary to pad a few details to make himself feel better or to shield Mama and me from worry, so be it. My loyalty was not to the rumormongers of Salzburg but to my family.

Sometimes I envied Wolfie's escape.

~

We lived for the letters. There were fewer than we would have liked, and the ones we did get were void of the details we craved. The truth was, Papa was the one who had the talent to write letters with detail. The rest of us got by with as few lines as possible. Yet, every day Papa looked forward to the post, and if there was nothing for us, he would brood and sulk.

When we did get letters, beyond the lack of detail, there was a notable tone of frivolity and irresponsibility on Wolfie's part. He spoke of going to the theater and sitting with the nobles in their boxes while Mama either sat in the general audience or remained back at the inn, alone. Although Mama *was* a homebody, considering she wasn't at *home,* and the rooms they were staying in to conserve money were probably small, dank, and dark . . . it was not a pleasant image. She'd written that in order to save money, she only had the fire lit in the morning and evening when she was dressing.

The thought of Mama cold and huddled . . . I wished Wolfie would have included her in more of his excursions. If he were traveling with Papa, the two of them would rarely have been apart.

I remembered Wolfie's opinion of Mama before they left. How he'd called her dull as a chair, and how he had nothing to say to her. Obviously this trait was not stopping *him* from socializing or making friends. But I feared for dear Mama. How lonely she must be. And what did she do in the room all day and evening? Mend clothes? Read? Look out the window? Worry about how Wolfie was behaving beyond her sight? After all, he was a vibrant, virile young man, and had revealed to me a burgeoning appetite for copious quantities of wine as well as the company of young ladies. Mama had enjoyed many friends here in Salzburg but did not take to strangers easily. When Papa and Wolfie had been traveling, they were of equal status and could divide up to make contacts. Not so with poor Mama.

The news we'd received after they'd been gone only a little over two weeks was that Munich had proved unfruitful. Though Wolfie *had* been offered a position, Papa had told him it did not possess enough status and would not let him take it. "The archbishop will mock him if this is all he gets," Papa said. A step down was not acceptable. The world must appreciate him for the genius he was.

After Munich, Mama and Wolfie moved on to Augsburg, where Wolfie performed. Papa was disappointed there wasn't a newspaper story about the performance that he could fling in the archbishop's face. I was glad there wasn't.

They didn't stay in Augsburg long and arrived in Mannheim just four days later. Along the way they did *not* stop at Dischingen or the abbey or Wallerstein—which incensed Papa. "Why don't they follow the route I laid out for them? They have missed many opportunities!"

"Perhaps the people you wanted them to visit weren't home?" I suggested.

Papa turned on me, his finger pointing. "Don't defend them! They are acting without logic. I paved their way. I made the best choices for them. I borrowed money so they could go. I swallowed my pride to return to a job I hate. I've given up everything. . . ." He withdrew his finger and turned away. "The least they could do is follow my directions and give us some proper details." He moved to his desk. "Get me some paper. I have some things to tell our pitiful travelers."

I brought him paper and quill and started to edge out of the room to return to my ironing. But Papa called me back. "Stay. Listen to my words and learn from them." He dipped the quill in the ink and began. "First," he said after quickly writing the salutation, "it grieves me that you have chosen to ignore my directions regarding lucrative stops along your journey from Munich to Mannheim. Only you know what would cause you to be so thoughtless and unwise. But since you are now in Mannheim, please be quiet about your intentions so you do not make the other musicians jealous. Also, since the costs in Mannheim are notably higher than Munich, I assume you have found a private lodging. You must do whatever it takes to be frugal. The money I procured for your excursion must last until you have been victorious and must be supplemented with income from concerts given." He glanced up at me. "I expect to have my investment repaid—with interest."

I found it hard to swallow. I would not have liked to be under such pressure. . . .

He went back to writing. "Make sure you practice your Latin so no fault can be found with your sacred pieces, and continue your compositions, for they may prove to be the most lucrative way to cover your expenses. If you cannot find a proper copyist in Mannheim, send them home and Nannerl will do it for you. Do not let poachers get ahold of the copies and sell them for their own gain. The cost of a reliable copyist is an acceptable expense. If needed, we will find you the name of one with good reputation." He nodded at me, and I nodded back. He had added to my to-do list.

"Nannerl goes to mass every morning to pray for the state of your souls and for your safe journey. Wolfie, please behave and make your mother and me proud. Restraint, dear boy . . ." He took a fresh breath. "Above all, treasure each other, and keep safe."

"And write more often and with greater detail," I added.

Papa nodded, added the words, then said, "We send you a thousand kisses."

And a thousand and one admonitions.

I prayed Wolfie would heed them.

SERENADE

Chapter Thirteen

My fingers amazed me. The way they sped across the keys so swiftly, as if they had a life of their own. And the miracle of it all. My eyes saw the notes on the page, and somehow my fingers lived out what the eyes saw. I'm sure my mind was involved, yet I never consciously thought, "That is a D flat. That is an F. That is a trill." The music seemed to bypass my mind and rush to a greedy partnership between eye and hand—for the ear's pleasure.

Odder still were the pieces I knew by heart. It was not as if my mind had copied a picture of the page. I did not *see* the notes in order to play them. In fact, I usually played best with my eyes—and my mind's eye—closed. I dared not *think* much at all about the music and could even let my mind think of other things, like the food I wanted Therese to make that night for our company or what I should wear. At such times my fingers were alive and in charge. They were the part of my anatomy that knew the music, that remembered. This was profoundly evident when a mistake was made and the fingers came to a halt. At such times they weren't sure what to do or how to begin again, for they had no page, no measure, no beat as reference. They only had a feeling, the indefinable, pulsing lifeblood that made the notes flow one to another. How could they recapture that life and flow again?

Often, they climbed back to the top of the mountain from whence they could see their path. They started at the beginning, and tentatively gathered speed and confidence as they traveled down the music's slope to a safe landing at the bot—

"You are progressing well, Nannerl. The runs are even in their execution."

I reached the bottom of the run with a flat where there should have been a natural. My fingers pulled away from the keys as if embarrassed for being caught.

"Continue," Papa said.

It had been years since he'd asked me to play. "On that piece?"

He strode to the stack of music on the table and fingered through. "No. This one. I heard you play it last week, and you executed the trills incorrectly." He brought me the music, a sonata by Haydn. He pointed to a measure containing a trill marking. "Play this for me."

I was oddly nervous but played it the way I had always played it.

"No, no, you go on too long." He nudged me over on the bench so he could demonstrate. "See? If the composer wants a trill, he will write it this way. But an embellishment is merely that." He played two notes, the first barely there. "It should be a flip to the ear, like the vibrato of a voice, so the listener is pleased but isn't sure why. You are making the notes bright red when they should be palest pink."

I nodded, truly understanding. I played it again.

"Bravo!" Papa said with a clap. "You are a good student."

We sat there, shoulder to shoulder, looking at each other. "I used to be *your* student, Papa."

His eyes held mine for a long moment before looking away. "We must go back to that. I have been preoccupied too long. It's time you benefit from my knowledge. After all, you are *here*." He chuckled and smiled at me. "You are here and so am I. I have the time and you have the talent. It's the perfect situation, yes?"

Oh yes.

~

After work one day, Papa sought me out as I painted some targets for our air-gun shooting. I was painting the trees for a mountain scene when he found me and said we were going out to dinner.

"But why?"

He kissed my cheek. "Can't I take my favorite daughter to dinner?"

"But Therese has made—"

He took the paintbrush out of my hand and dropped it in the glass of water with a soft *phlop*. "We can have it for lunch tomorrow. Come, Nannerl. We have something to celebrate."

In spite of my prying, he would not say more. Yet just the fact he was in a good mood was reason to celebrate. Working for Archbishop Colloredo day after day had generally made grumpiness and melancholy our evening's companion.

We walked arm in arm to the Boar's Head, where Papa ordered breaded veal and gnocchi for both of us, with kirsch cake for dessert. He joked with the proprietor and with the other patrons. He was his old self again: confident, outgoing, gregarious. I did not press for the good news. Knowing he had felt out of control so long, I was willing to let him be *in* control now.

Finally he was ready to share. He placed his arms on the table and leaned toward me confidentially. "The news is . . ." He drew it out, smiling at me.

"Yes, Papa, yes?"

His eyes glanced furtively around the room, making sure no one was listening. "The archbishop has been humiliated."

That was it? I sat back, disappointed.

He pulled my hand, wanting me close again. "I heard that Count Firmian had a conversation with the archbishop about our Wolfgang."

"And. . . ?"

Papa looked practically gleeful. "The archbishop started by saying, 'Now we have one man less in the orchestra,' to which the count replied, 'Your Grace has lost a great virtuoso.' To which His Grace replied, 'Why so?'" Papa straightened his back, grinning. "The good count replied, 'Mozart is the greatest clavier player I have ever heard in my life; on the violin he rendered very good service to Your Grace, and he is a first-rate composer.' The archbishop was silent, for he had nothing to say!"

"That's good," I said.

It was his turn to sit back. "That's the extent of your reaction?"

"That's very good." It was all I could manage.

"You don't care that your brother is missed? That his talents are being requested? That the very person who has shamed our family with such deplorable treatment is held accountable and is told he is wrong?"

I knew I should be happy, even giddy with vindication. I knew that's what Papa expected.

And so I gave it to him. Pulling from a place beyond the emotions of here and now, I pasted on a smile, leaned toward my father, took his hand, and willed there to be a gleam in my eyes. "The archbishop is getting what he deserves. Vengeance is ours, Papa."

He raised a finger. "Saith the Lord!"

He'd made the proclamation too loudly, and other patrons looked in his direction. Which made us break into laughter.

He lowered his voice. "The point is, our dear Wolfie is loved. His talent is acknowledged. And His Grace's actions have been brought to bear at last. His humiliation is frosting to our cake."

This last fact made me a bit nervous, for humiliation was not an emotion most people took lightly. Especially men in power.

~

It is a sad fact that one never appreciates a person until they are gone.

So it was with Mama. When it had been the two of us alone at home, I'd done my share of the chores and had never given too much thought to what *she* did. But now that she was gone two months and I was left with her chores as well as my own . . . *Oh, Mama. I'm so sorry for taking you for granted.*

Papa gave me a compliment. He said he was proud of me, and called me industrious and steadfast. I appreciated his kind words, and yet, as I stood in the kitchen, ironing his shirts with the sweat pouring off my brow making the curl in my hair rebel, I found them less than appealing. For the same traits could be said of Therese, our maid and cook, or of Roth, the man who handled our mail, or even

Dren, whose job it was to scoop horse muck from the square in front of our house.

I caught my reflection in the mirror that hung above the hooks that held the bed warmers. It wasn't as though I hadn't looked at myself that very morning, but seeing myself in this glance, without benefit of adjusting a smile or a stray hair, was shocking. Was this old woman in the mirror me?

I left the heavy iron on the stove and moved closer to the mirror to study this person I didn't know. My fingers ran over my cheeks, my neck, my lips. I was not pretty. My nose was too large, my eyelids too pronounced, my forehead too high. My eyes were brown but devoid of the yellow and hazel flecks that graced Wolfie's. I had a dimple in my chin, and my mouth was small when compared to my other features, my lips far from voluptuous like some women I knew. My eyebrows were expressive, as if they made up for the blandness of the rest of my face. I had no pronounced cheekbones; the outline of my face was simply drawn, with few variations as points of interest. And my skin . . . Though without blemish, it was pale to the point of pallor. The slight blush to my cheeks on this day came from the heat of my chore rather than health or happiness. And the lustrous hair of my youth was gone. It had turned a nondescript dark blond, nearly brown, and was without sheen. My hair was the color of a dusty bird's nest. I leaned closer. Was that one gray? I plucked it and stood back.

I looked old.

I was old. I was twenty-six and unmarried. My merits were few. As a young girl I'd seen the world and had entertained princes and queens with my talent. But except for a few trinkets kept in a locked case, my memories of that time were so faded that sometimes I wondered if any of it had been real or if they were merely a pleasant dream. How I wished I'd been an artist, able to sketch the places I'd been . . . to capture the moments with a picture.

My adolescent ambition to become a great musician was ailing, if not dead and buried. My European performing career, which was cut short because I'd become of marriageable age, seemed ironically wasted, considering I was *not* married and had no eager prospects.

My career had been sacrificed for a domestic ideal that was . . . less than ideal.

I was not only old. I was an old maid.

A pitiful vocation, all in all.

No wonder I didn't have a beau.

Apparently being industrious and steadfast wasn't an enticement.

~

The music room was a godsend. When we'd lived in the small apartment, we'd had no room to entertain a large group of friends, but here in our larger quarters, with this wonderful room that stretched across the street-side of the house . . . we could entertain well, giving everyone plenty of room to perform and mingle.

That evening there was a roomful, including some visiting musicians from the theater whom we'd met after their performance. There was an oboist, a flautist, a cellist, and two violinists. All had brought their instruments. And to my delight Francesco Ceccarelli, the famed castrato, was also present. I had been so impressed with his voice at the performance. Clearer than any woman's.

Papa had splurged for this assembly. He often did so with traveling musicians because he hoped they would spread the word about the Mozart name and household along their travels. Word of mouth was so important. In return we often received free tickets. If only Wolfie were here to perform with us. Now, *that* would have been of even greater benefit. And pleasure.

Papa clapped his hands to get everyone's attention, then took up his violin with one hand and pointed to the music on the keyboard with the other. "Gather up, gentlemen. My daughter and I have just completed copying portions of the latest opera by my son, Wolfgang, who is currently off on tour."

I inwardly shook my head at Papa's exaggeration. Tour, indeed . . .

The musicians gathered close, finding their parts. "Herr Mozart, we are not a full orchestra. There are parts that will not be played," the oboist said.

Papa extended his bow toward me. "That is where our lovely

Nannerl comes in. She will cover those parts on the keyboard."

"All of them?" the cellist asked.

He winked at me. "She is very talented."

I felt my face flush, and my mind flitted back to the kitchen that very afternoon, where my pallor had been broken only by the heat of my chores. How much better to gain beauty through the compliments of one's father.

As the musicians got settled with their music stands and chairs, Signor Ceccarelli took his place to my right. "I will read off your music and turn pages, *sì, mia cara?*"

Blushing proved rampant that evening.

~

Signor Ceccarelli completed his solo. The musicians voiced their approval. "Bravissimo!"

Ceccarelli bowed but extended an arm to include me and the others in the movement's success. Therese scurried about with a pitcher, making sure goblets were full as the musicians chatted about the music and lauded their own abilities.

The oboist, a handsome man with a stunning smile, walked in my direction. I stayed on the bench and waited for him.

"Well, Frau Mozart. I never dreamed I'd discover such playing in little Salzburg."

I ignored the compliment and corrected him on his choice of title. "It's Fraulein Mozart."

He looked confused.

I pointed to Papa. "He's my father."

The man put a hand to his chest. "Oh my. Forgive me. I thought you were his wife—his younger wife to be sure, but—"

Papa's wife? My stomach clenched. I rose, feeling the need to escape. "If you'll excuse me."

I edged my way out of the music room and slipped into the room down the hall that Papa used as a study. I stood behind the door in the dark. My chest heaved and my tears surprised me. *The man assumed I—*

Suddenly Papa came in the room, looked around, found me, and said, "I saw you run out. What did that man say to upset you so?"

"I . . ." I wished I could draw deeper into the shadows where Papa could not see my pain.

He pulled me fully into the light of the doorway, his eyes scanning my face. He intercepted a tear on its journey down my cheek, then pointed in the direction of the main room. "If that man's offended you, I'll kick him out and—"

I pulled his arm down. "No, Papa. He didn't offend. At least not on purpose."

His shoulders relaxed a bit. "Then why are you here in the dark, crying?"

My reason would sound absurd. Papa would never understand.

"Nannerl, I am not leaving until I know the reason."

I took a fresh breath. "He thought I was your wife."

"My. . . ?" He shook his head. "Why would he think that?"

I moved away from him, deeper into the darkened room. "Because I'm twenty-six years old and unmarried. Because I still live with my father. Because I look . . . old."

"You do not look old."

It was the only point he could even try to dispute.

"I should be married, Papa. The years fly by. Most of my friends are married or betrothed. Some have children. And though I have male friends, I don't have a suitor. Sometimes I feel like sitting in the square and choosing the first man who walks by. The results wouldn't be any worse than doing as I have been doing."

He took my hands in his, pulling the two of us close enough to see each other's faces, even in the dark. "Never settle, dear daughter. You are far too precious and far too prized to settle."

I had to laugh. "Prized?" I pulled my hands away and took a step back. "Papa, I'm an old maid, a spinster. It's not natural for me to be unmarried. I've heard people talk."

"Who's talked?"

I shook my head and pointed to the music room, where laughter and exuberant talk overflowed. "The nonexistence of suitors makes me look at even Signor Ceccarelli with interest."

Papa shook his head vehemently. "The purpose of marriage is to have children. Don't even think such a—"

I sighed. "The point is, my prospects are minimal. I don't have much to offer, Papa."

"Nonsense! You are a talented girl, handsome and true. You are . . . you are industrious and steadfast and . . . and would make any man happy."

Industrious and steadfast. The words haunted me.

"I don't want you settling, Nannerl. I won't—"

I slipped past him into the hall. "We need to get back to our guests."

~

Sleep did not come easily that night—though it was much needed. I had avoided Papa's company by helping Therese with the kitchen cleanup rather than helping him straighten the music room. I lingered over the dishes until Papa came into the kitchen and announced he was going to bed. Only then did I leave my drying towel behind and escape to my own room.

I undressed, sat at the window seat in my smock, and removed the ivory pins from my hair. My mood had not improved after talking to Papa about my marriage prospects—or lack thereof—and it had taken a great deal of effort to return to our guests and assume the happy face of a hostess. I'd managed to avoid the oboist and had given considerable attention to the cellist, a certain Hans Kraubner from Linz.

I'm sure the man thought my interest was more than I intended, for he asked if he might come calling when next they were in town. I did not even have the strength to create a probable excuse to tell him no. And who knew? Perhaps becoming the wife of an itinerant musician would be my just fate—appropriate or not.

What other choices did I have?

It's not that I didn't have male friends. Beyond the gatherings at our home, I spent many an evening at concerts or at the homes of friends for dinner. I might have been an old maid, but I was not a hermit. I was well practiced in flirtation and thereby enjoyed the attention of many young men of Salzburg.

But so far there had been none that truly piqued my interest.

My girlfriends and I often discussed the lack of eligibles in our fair city. For one did not marry a coachman, a cooper, or a baker's son— even if he was handsome and made us smile. A woman's immediate happiness was not to be considered. Nor romance. The future loomed large and must be addressed. *How could this man provide?* was *the* question.

And the truth was, though I should not marry *down,* the chances of my marrying *up* were slim. Papa was the Vice Kapellmeister. I was proud of him. But we were not nobility. And though Papa sometimes acted as though the position of paid musician was akin to sitting at Jesus' right hand, it was a position of servitude. He was certainly higher in rank than a cook or maid, but the people he worked for were his superiors—no matter how hard he pretended otherwise.

And so, the unspeakable part of my situation, the one Papa would never hear from my lips, was that I did not have much chance of marrying a man who could offer me the financial security that obsessed Papa's waking moments. Oh, how I prayed Wolfie would be successful and find a good position. For all our sakes.

As for the sake of my heart? I pulled my knees close and bowed my head against them.

～

As soon as Papa left for work, I took our fox terrier, Bimperl, for a longer walk than usual. The November morning was not intolerable, though I could see the effort of my exertion in the bursts of breath that slipped into the folds of my hood. On such days people walked briskly with heads lowered, as if they were thieves in the night trying to make an escape.

I enjoyed the bite to my cheeks as well as the need to increase my pace. My dog took advantage and pulled her leash out of my hands.

"Bimperl! Come back—"

"Whoa there, little one." A soldier coming from the opposite direction scooped her up with one hand. He nestled her in the crook of his arm, and she tilted her head back, exposing her neck for more attention.

I hurried toward them. "Thank you," I said. "If I walk faster than usual, she gets excited and the terrier in her takes over."

"Ready for the hunt, yes?"

"I'm glad you were there to stop her or I may have ended up searching the hills. She likes to chase mice."

"As all good terriers do." He gave me a smart bow, tipping his hat. "Captain Franz d'Ippold, at your service."

I curtsied. "Maria Anna Mozart, but friends call me Nannerl."

His right eyebrow rose. "Mozart?"

I was surprised to find I felt some trepidation at the fact he knew our name. "My father is—"

"You are a skilled musician, yes?"

For a moment I was taken aback. "I play. I give lessons."

"I heard you and your brother play a duet for the archbishop last summer. I was quite impressed. Your fingers fairly flew over the keys."

"My brother composed that piece especially for us."

"Composed it very well, I think." Bimperl squirmed in his arms, so he handed her back to me. "Would you care to join me for some coffee or hot chocolate?"

I could think of nothing better. "We would be delighted."

⁓

By the way my stomach danced, you would have thought I'd never had a conversation with a handsome man. I tried to mentally couch my excitement by reminding myself that I was in a vulnerable state after the previous evening's awkward exchange with the oboist. But if I were honest, I had to admit that the pleasure I received in talking with Captain d'Ippold far exceeded the pleasure gained from *any* conversation in the recent past. With anyone. Male or female.

Of course, it was made doubly easy because he was extremely handsome. Where the noses of the Mozart family were prominent, the captain's was small, allowing his blue eyes and wide smile to command the attention. His blond hair was tied with a red bow that matched the red in his uniform. The only detriment to his looks was the accumulation of lines about his eyes and forehead, indicating he was probably at least forty. Yet what difference did age really make?

Upon acknowledging his maturity, I noted there was no ring on his finger. Although not all men wore wedding bands, the lack of a ring, plus his invitation to join him for hot chocolate, were two vital clues to his marital status.

I must have been staring at his hand, for he said, "I come here most mornings for a coffee and roll. You'd think with being single so long I would have learned to cook something, but I have surrendered to the fact my talents are not meant for the kitchen."

I felt myself blush. But in spite of my pleasure that my deduction was right, I tried to deflect my true interest in his hand by mentioning the scar that bisected its top. "Was that received in battle?"

He held his hand close, as if long ago forgetting the scar was there. He ran a finger across it. "I should say yes, shouldn't I? Then I could regale you with some laudable story of bravery and saber fights where I appear the hero."

"But that would not be the truth?"

He sipped his coffee. "The scar is further proof of my ineptitude in the kitchen. It's a burn. I was stoking the stove and burned it on the top of the opening." He stroked it again, tenderly. "It did hurt terribly," he said, smiling.

"Poor Captain d'Ippold. But since you speak of sabers and scars . . . have you been in battle? Are you going to battle?"

"I have not, and hope I never need to." He ran his hand down the row of buttons on the front of his uniform. "I usually do not dress like this, but later today I have a meeting with my unit."

"So what do you do day to day?"

He grinned. "Think about meeting a beautiful lady like yourself."

It was too blatant a ploy for me to even blush. I rolled my eyes. "Has such an answer worked in the past?"

He blushed—then ignored my most recent question and answered the original query. "I am the director of the Virgilianum. I live in a wing of Holy Trinity when I am not teaching the boys."

"Holy Trinity is in our square," I said. "We are practically neighbors."

"I know." He sipped his coffee.

I thought of the unspoken implications.

"You go to mass every morning, you walk your dog multiple times a day, and I hear lovely music coming from the windows of your home—day and night."

I was pleased. "You have the advantage, Captain."

He winked above his coffee cup. "As intended, Fraulein Mozart. As intended."

~

Getting ready for bed that night, I took pause at the mirror and found myself smiling. And present with the smile was a look of youthfulness. I was not old yet. Nor done. The world had revealed new promise.

And his name was Captain Franz d'Ippold.

~

I hated being the bearer of bad tidings.

Papa looked up from his work, his eyes expectant.

"No," I said. "No mail."

Papa slammed his hand on the table, making the inkwell surrender some of its contents. "Why can't that boy write? How can I give him advice if I don't hear from him?"

"It's hard to give advice anyway, Papa. The mail to Mannheim is so slow—six days. By the time a letter gets here and you respond to it—"

He pushed away from the table and began to pace. "Last we heard he'd only been paid with a gold watch instead of cash. And his offer to write a German opera to break through Europe's insipid fascination with all things Italian caused interest but no real commission. I could have pushed it through. I know it."

"But there's the Kapellmeister position opening up there," I said. "The man is old and Wolfie was hoping—"

"Apparently the Kapellmeister is not doing the polite thing by dying so Wolfgang can take his place. And then there's your brother's habit of leaving your mother in her room while he goes gallivanting about town." Papa pointed a finger at me. "It's not healthy for her. If she gets sick . . ." He shook his head and I filled in the rest of the threat on my own.

So much rode on the shoulders of my little brother. I wasn't sure they were strong enough. And though I was always Wolfie's advocate, he was testing even my patience. His handling of money, for instance. Papa had arranged for letters of credit to be available in Munich and Augsburg. When Mama and Wolfie moved on to Mannheim, Wolfie should have thought ahead to the money he would need there and arranged with our contact in Augsburg to have the letter transferred. But in Augsburg they'd had enough money, so Wolfie hadn't thought of it until it was too late and they were in dire need. Papa had been forced to step in, but with the slow mail . . .

Wolfie's flippant attitude was also a concern. He made a joke of every situation, as if his pockets were lined with gold and all he had to do to get his way was play a few notes on a keyboard. I'd seen a change in my brother I didn't like. Where he used to affect some level of humility, now, on his own and away from Papa, he was getting as cocky as a rooster strutting his colors. *They seem to think that because of my small size and youth I possess no importance or maturity. They will soon learn.* Though I wasn't sure if people reacted badly to his attitude or simply because they did not know him, Wolfie seemed to believe *Genius* was stamped on his brow.

Of all people, we believed in his talent, but the rest of the world had their own concerns. England was at war with America, which had declared its independence; a future czar had just been born to the Russian Czarina Catherine II; Spain and Portugal were having issues about their colonies in South America; and the daughter of our beloved Maria Theresa, Marie Antoinette—who'd been called Marie Antonie when she was just a young archduchess who'd helped my brother up when he tripped after playing at Schönbrunn—was the reigning queen of France, having married the man who became Louis XVI. The world was a busy place. So in spite of what my brother would have liked to believe, he was not the center of the universe.

Papa continued his ranting. "I owe three hundred florins to Bullinger, two hundred to Weiser, forty to Kerschbaumer, some more to Hagenauer, and another hundred and fifty to the lenders on the road. Plus, we have bills of our own to be paid." He stopped in front of me, his hand to his chest. "Good God! Solely on his account I am in debt, and he thinks he can coax me into good humor with a hundred stupid jokes? I owe over a year's salary! Doesn't your brother realize that? Doesn't he care?"

I moved to calm him, but he stepped away from my reach. "He's trying, Papa. It's just that he's never had to deal with practical issues before, and—"

"Which proves I was right in not wanting him to travel alone."

Or with me. "But Mama's with him. . . ."

"And *she* should know how to handle these details. After all, while Wolfgang and I were gone, she handled the business side of life here just fine."

With my help she may have handled it, but she had not enjoyed it. Too many times I'd found Mama anxious about such issues.

There was a knock on the door. I moved to answer it, leaving Papa to mumble further complaints without me. But when I found that our visitor was the postman, I ran back to Papa, waving the letter. "News! We have news!"

Papa grabbed it away and started to read. But then he scanned the pages faster and faster, his head shaking.

"What's wrong?" I asked.

He tossed the letter at me and the pages floated to the floor. "Your brother sends greetings to all his friends in Salzburg—listing one for each letter of the alphabet. Useless! He's useless."

I retrieved the pages and saw the evidence for myself. How I wished I would have read the letter first and kept it from Papa's eyes. No letter was better than a frivolous one. Yet near the end I noted something that *was* of interest. "Wolfie says he and Mama have moved into rooms at the elector's residence, where he is giving lessons. Mama is happy because she is included for all meals and has companionship throughout the day."

Papa stood still, his breath going in, then out. "At least there is *some* income."

"At least there is free lodging," I added.

With a flip of his hand, he asked for the letter back. I pointed to where I had left off. After reading, he offered an exaggerated sigh. "Wolfie has been told he is getting a two-hundred-florin commission for a flute quartet. He also states that he and three other musicians are planning to go to Paris before Lent."

"See, Papa? Surely shared expenses will be reduced expenses. All is going well."

"Better. It's going better, not well." He folded the letter and put it on the desk. "I don't suppose your brother has received an advance on the commission. I don't suppose he's thought to ask for that."

Probably not. "But Paris . . . I never dreamed he would have to go so far."

"It's too far for your mother. When Wolfgang leaves for Paris, we will arrange to have Mama come home."

I touched his arm. "Do you miss her, Papa?"

His eyes met mine for but a second. "It's the prudent thing to do." He sat back at his desk. "Now go. Practice. Your improvement is evident, but it must continue. Two hours a day, Nannerl. At least

two hours a day."

I took my leave and did as I was told. At least one of us could please Papa.

~

Another month passed. Papa and I endured Christmas alone as Mama and I had done multiple times. We'd had so many holidays apart from one another. Yet in a way, the Christmas of 1777 was easier to tolerate because Papa and I both knew that Mama would be coming home in the spring. We both missed her for our own reasons. I, because she was my mother but also because I was more than ready to let her share some of the housekeeping duties. Papa wanted Mama back for other reasons—and I wasn't sure if any of them were directly related to love. Yes, he loved her, but Papa needed her for more than that. In the months since she'd left, I'd seen a deterioration in his entire being.

It didn't help that some of his friends had died. The main organist at the cathedral, Aldgasser—a mere forty-eight years old—had suffered a seizure while playing the organ during Vespers. I'd been there that day listening to the concert when I'd heard the organ part falter. At first, Papa and I thought the man was drunk, as was his occasional habit, but when the music decayed even more and began to sound as though a dog were running over the organ, we ran to the box and found him trying to play the psalm melodies with his right hand, while his left was clenched in a fist. Papa lifted his left hand out of the way, and a tenor, Spitzeder, played the bass line while Aldgasser continued to play with his right hand.

Aldgasser's eyes rolled back, he vomited, and it was quite horrible, because in his cramped quarters above the nave we could barely move to help him. The service somehow managed to go on, and we got him home. But he died the next day.

With Aldgasser's death, and the death of a few other friends, Papa was never the same. It was as if his own mortality had come calling, and he realized the futility of fighting it. Added to that was the stress about what Wolfie was doing (or not doing) and his concern for Mama's well-being. Mama had written about not feeling well, asking for more of the black powder we usually used for fever, and Papa had reminded her of the importance of being bled. These worries caused my father to become an old man who simply wanted his wife close for comfort. He continued to fall into times of deep melancholy, and it took all my energy to pull him out of it.

And then, just eight days after Aldgasser's death, the elector of Bavaria, Maximilian III Joseph, died in Mannheim. The man in whose house Wolfie and Mama had been staying, the man for whom Wolfie and I had played at the Nymphenburg Palace a lifetime ago, the man whose children Wolfie had been teaching, the man whom Wolfie had been trying to woo into offering him a position, was gone. Without an heir. Within hours his successor was announced—his cousin, the elector palatine, Karl Theodor—thus uniting two branches of the family that had been separate for centuries. Yet this choice was not looked upon with complete joy. The new elector was not friendly with the old elector's people, and he added insult by closing up the court in Mannheim and moving it to Munich. So instead of having two courts that had musical positions available, now there was one. What were we going to do?

There were, of course, repercussions beyond our family. The threat of war loomed large over all of Germany because the emperor (being German in descent) had always been rather annoyed at the independent Munich in Bavaria and now saw an opening to move in. He promised the new elector, Karl Theodor, that if he agreed to bow to his control, the emperor would make all of Karl Theodor's children legitimate heirs of the larger empire. To our surprise, Karl agreed. But then King Frederick of Prussia decided Bavaria would look nice on his plate too, and he came in pretending he was the champion of the Bavarian people and would fight for their independence. It was very confusing, and we all wished everything could go back to the way it had been.

Especially since my new beau, Captain d'Ippold—for he had become my beau, even though we'd kept it discreet so Papa wouldn't know—was appointed the court war counselor by the archbishop. Although Salzburg was independent and not directly involved, being on the edge of the conflict, with soldiers at the borders of its neighbors, meant there was tension. Soldiers were seen in the streets more often, and the anxiety of all-out war added to the distress of having our loved ones gone. Mama was worried that she'd never be able to find a safe passage back to Salzburg. Surely she would die of fright if she came upon soldiers on the road.

Yet in spite of everything, we were determined Mama *would* come home soon—as soon as Wolfie left for Paris with his music partners.

But it was not to be—and it had nothing to do with the wrangling of kings and emperors. Suddenly, without warning, we started getting letters from Wolfie decrying the morals of the very partners he had previously commended to us, indicating he would not enter into any job opportunities with them. Surely, Papa would not want him to be involved with such people.

It did not make sense. How could he be so completely enmeshed and enraptured with these three men, writing glowing accounts of their character, talent, and hopes for a future in Paris, and next call them unfit to be his friends and totally without religion?

Then Wolfie's letters changed from woe at losing three friends to glee at gaining others: the Weber family. To my astonishment—and Papa's horror—Wolfie stated he was in love with Aloysia Weber, an opera singer with four siblings. My brother's plan to find himself a position to support *our* family suddenly expanded into a grand scheme with himself as Aloysia's manager, seeking out venues throughout Europe for her voice based on the Mozart name so *he* could help support the Webers! He wanted to take her to Holland or Switzerland—and stop by in Salzburg so we could meet her.

He was totally smitten. And totally off task. We worried he was spending money on her—and on her family—that he should have been spending on our own concerns. And on Mama.

Unfortunately, there was little insight to the situation via Mama's notes, which were added at the end of Wolfie's letters. Her words seemed guarded, as if Wolfie was her censor, her literary captor. This had been illustrated to its fullest extent the previous day in the latest notation we received in her hand: *In greatest secrecy and haste while he is at table so that I am not caught . . . in a word, he prefers being with others to being with me. I take exception to one and another thing not to my taste, and that annoys him. This family has bewitched him. For such a person he is ready to give his life and all he holds dear. You yourself must ponder what is to be done.*

Papa exploded when he read that and went into Wolfie's room and tore through it, upsetting the bed, pulling out the old clothes, tossing them every which way. If Wolfie would have been in his presence, there might have been bruises. Before this time Papa had not been a violent person. But Wolfie was pushing him beyond his limits.

And I understood all of it. If it would have helped matters, I would have joined Papa in his tirade.

The next morning I found Papa packing. "Where are you going?" I asked.

"To Mannheim. To retrieve your mother. To save her from our ungrateful son. To salvage something from this horrid situation."

I put a calming hand on his arm. "But, Papa, you can't leave. The archbishop's concert is tomorrow. . . ."

He stopped all movement, staring at the satchel on the bed.

There was no sound at all, as if he too had stopped breathing—for I certainly had.

Then he turned his head and looked at me. "I can't leave. I can't save her."

His face was so drawn, so lined with the stress of the past few months. "She can still come home, Papa. Even if Wolfie doesn't go to Paris, even if he marries this—"

"Marries? He can't marry. He has God's work to do!" Papa tossed the shirt on the bed. "He's too hotheaded and rash. Somehow I have to save him from himself." He touched the shirt with the tip of his fingers. "The greatest reserve and highest acumen are needed with women. Nature herself is the enemy, and a man who does not call upon his entire and keenest judgment will have to extricate himself from a labyrinth, a misfortune that often ends in death."

"Death?"

Papa looked directly at me. "Disease, dear girl. He's playing with fire. He's already given this girl his heart and his common sense. If he hasn't already, he'll give her . . . more. And then all will be lost."

Suddenly everything became clear. I knew my brother. I knew how easily—and totally—he could let his entire self become consumed, especially by someone who offered him the love and adoration he craved as much as air. Getting involved with this Aloysia, traveling about Europe for her sake instead of his own . . . our own. And now with Papa so incensed with my brother's love life, there would be little hope he would be open to my own.

"Don't cry, girl. We will find a way."

I hadn't realized I was crying and wiped the tears away. Who was I crying for? Wolfie? Papa? Mama? Or myself?

The packing forgotten, Papa strode toward the door. "Tears benefit no one. Action must be taken; your brother must be stopped. The Mozart name is at stake. If you'll excuse me, I have a letter to write. Wolfgang *must* complete the task and find his destiny. He wanted to go to Paris? He will go to Paris—and your mother will go with him as his chaperone. We will get him away from this siren of a woman, one way or the other."

I sank onto the bed exhausted. What horrible irony that the

person with whom we'd planted our hopes seemed oblivious to all but himself.

~

My life became consumed with the sagas of Mama and Wolfie's moving on to Paris and getting settled, of dealing with Papa's tirades against the inadequacies of Wolfie's life choices, and his ranting against how little the two travelers wrote, as well as their method (they often didn't answer questions he'd asked in his letters). In addition, Papa reviled the way the post often brought letters out of order.

Yet in spite of all this, I did have joy in my life.

Franz. I enjoyed his company immensely, and could actually thank the distraction of Wolfie's misbehavior for keeping Papa occupied.

Not that I misbehaved. It was not my nature. But with Papa's attention consumed elsewhere, I attained a certain freedom to see Franz—to take walks in the Mirabel Gardens, include him in our shooting forays, and even invite him to our musical evenings.

The other highlight of my life was the music. The castrato Ceccarelli was present at our home many evenings, and his voice and ability on the violin inspired me to expand my own talent. I wrote a bass part to one of his solos that prompted Papa to an effusive compliment that ended with him encouraging me to write more.

Papa encouraging me to compose? The world was indeed upside down.

But it was another musical venture that piqued my interest. Count Czernin, who was a nephew of the archbishop, decided to start an amateur orchestra. Participants were from every social class, age, and walk of life. There were students, nobility, tradesmen, and some professional musicians (Papa among them). But there was only one woman considered good enough to be included.

Me. I accompanied all the music on the keyboard. My talent was the glue that held them together. It was the first time in my adult life that I felt fully appreciated. And I had Papa to thank. For it had been his attention and his lessons that had spurred me to move beyond the level of playing that I'd been lolling in for years into this advanced level where Papa could brag, "She plays as well as any Kapellmeister."

Occasionally there would be women soloists who would sing or play a keyboard solo, but I was the only female member of the orchestra.

However, we were not a great orchestra. Some of the nobility who pushed their way onto the solo lineup were far from good, and Papa declared that new time signatures were often created. But I didn't care. It was the first chance for me to show Salzburg my newly honed accompanying skills. If Wolfie failed in his quest to find a position good enough to support us, I was hopeful I could at least support myself. Added to this was the fact that some of our music pupils received a chance to perform, thus in a backhand way showcasing the skills of me and Papa as educators. At the moment, Papa was teaching Countess Lodron's two older children, and I was teaching the two younger ones. Last week the countess commented on how improved her children were since we'd taken over their instruction from Aldgasser (since his death). The importance of such compliments could not be taken lightly.

So I didn't. In fact, they sustained me.

~

Papa picked up his quill. "Would you like to add anything for your mother? The post will be here any minute."

"Did you tell her I am sending her something for her name day?"

"I did." We both looked toward the street as the sounds of the post announced its presence. "Oh dear. I suppose I will finish it tomorrow. Go see if we have a letter."

There was one, and I brought it to Papa. He opened it and began reading aloud. But suddenly his words slowed. " 'I have very sad and stressing news to give you. My dear mother is very ill. She has been—' "

"Ill?"

He held up a hand and continued. "'She has been bled as in the past; a necessity. She felt quite well afterward, but a few days later she complained of shivering and feverishness, accompanied by diarrhea and headache. At first we only used our home remedies—antispasmodic powders. We would gladly have tried a black powder too, but we had none and could not get it here in Paris, where it is not known even by the name of *Pulvis epilipticus*.'"

"We should have sent her some of the powder, Papa. We should—"

"Let me finish!" He adjusted his glasses. "'As she got worse and worse—she could hardly speak and lost her hearing, so that I had to shout to make myself understood. Baron Grimm sent us his doctor, but she is still very weak and is feverish and delirious. They give me some hope—but I do not have much.'"

"Do not have much? What is he—?"

"Shh, Nannerl." He read some more. "'For a long time now I have been hovering day and night between hope and fear. I have resigned myself wholly to the will of God and trust that you and my dear sister will do the same.'"

Papa stopped reading aloud, his eyes devouring the rest of the first page, then the next. "This is absurd. He goes on to talk about the symphony he's writing."

"He what?" I took the letter from him. "There has to be more about Mama. He has to give us more details!"

But there was only Wolfie talking about rehearsals for some symphony and how upset he was at the orchestra's progress.

As if orchestras mattered. As if music mattered.

Papa grabbed the letter back from me, poring over the words. "She can't hear. She's delirious. And the doctor . . . How long did Wolfgang wait to send for him? Is he German or some French quack? I remember when you nearly died at the hands of a French doctor. Do they even have proper doctors in France? I should have fetched her from Mannheim. If I would have been with her, she would not be sick. She would not!"

I began to cry, the tears turning into sobs that made me fall to my knees.

"Stop that!" Papa said, pulling at my arm, trying to get me to stand.

But I did not want to stand. I wanted to fall even farther to the floor and lie upon it, prostrate before God as an offering to Him. *Save Mama, dear Lord. Save Mama.*

Papa stopped his pulling and pressed his hands into his eyes. "No, no, no, this can't be happening. No. This cannot happen without me there. This cannot. I won't allow it. Our fate cannot be in the inept hands of my son, a son who hasn't had the decency to make sure his mother has a fire to warm her, who abandons her so he can go out and have fun, who—"

His words sounded like evidence presented in a trial. I couldn't hear any more. "Papa, stop, please stop." Why had we ever let the two of them go away? Mama, the homebody who was ill at ease in the world, and Wolfie, the lover of fun who needed someone to pick up his clothes and tell him what to eat. A new bout of sobbing consumed me. Unable to get enough air, I pulled at my corset but ended up coughing, which made it worse. My head began to ache and I felt as if I might vomit.

Papa called for help. "Therese! Come here!"

Therese appeared in the doorway, her eyes darting, then landing on me. She came to my side.

"Take her to her room. Get her to lie down, calm down."

"What's wrong?" Therese asked.

Papa started laughing, a horrible hysterical laughter. "Oh, nothing, nothing at all. Except our darling Wolfgang may have just killed us all."

I did not want to go to any shooting party that afternoon, but Papa insisted. Since we had agreed to host it, he said we had a responsibility to provide the prizes, the painted targets, and refreshments.

I wasn't in the mood to hear about responsibility. Wasn't it Wolfie's responsibility to take care of Mama? She'd certainly done her best to take care of him. *He* seemed to be thriving. While she was dying.

Was she dying? Wolfie's letter had been written nine days previous. Before the shooting party I went to mass and prayed that the days since then had made Mama strong. Drat my brother for not telling us earlier. And drat the post for taking eons to connect us to our family. How I wished I could fly to Paris like a bird over the mountains and land on Mama's windowsill, where I could see her, talk to her, comfort her, and nurse her to fine health. I would not leave her side until she was well. Then I would hire the finest carriage and wrap her in a silky robe and bring her home. I would cater to her and continue to do the household chores. She wouldn't need to do anything but lie around and accept the attention of visiting friends. I would help Therese make her favorite strudel and bring her piece upon piece until she begged us to stop. I would bring Bimperl to her room and let the dear puppy sleep at her side, keeping her company during all the times I could not. I would make the memories of her difficult time away from home fade and be replaced with new memories of happy times and blissful days.

I would make her happy.

"Come, Nannerl," Papa said from the door. "Our guests await."

The targets could have been as big as a house and I would not have been able to hit them. But instead of making fun of me—as my friends were wont to do—they either said little or sympathized. Yet I knew their sympathy was not for bad aim but for Mama's bad health.

I was glad Papa had told them from the start. His honesty had allowed me to move forward with the day. If Papa had insisted no one know, I would have expired from the effort required in pretending to be happy.

Our friends' commiseration also allowed the afternoon to end early. And none too soon. Yet as I took Papa's arm to head back home from the park, I noticed that Herr Bullinger had stayed behind while the others had quickly scattered . . . eager to be free from the tension of our worry? Joseph Bullinger was the friend responsible for loaning us the original three hundred florins that had made Wolfie's present trip possible.

"Sorry the afternoon was cut short, Joseph. But we cannot keep our minds on the target. They keep straying to Paris."

"Ah yes," Joseph said. "Paris."

There was an odd tone to his voice that made us stop our walking to look at him. Obviously uncomfortable, he cleared his throat. "Your letter from Wolfgang was . . ."

"Was a shock," Papa said. "I pray the post tomorrow has more news. Better news."

With a sigh Joseph looked at the ground. The toes of his shoes were dusty.

"Joseph?"

Joseph looked at Papa, then away. "I've been trying to think of a way to tell . . ." He took a breath. "I received a letter too. From Wolfgang."

"There's more news?" I asked. "Is she better? Is—?"

Papa's head started shaking. "No, Joseph. No."

Joseph put his hand on Papa's shoulder. "I'm sorry, Leopold. She's gone."

Papa's face turned white and he fell to his knees. I suffered disbelief at the sight of him, as well as with Joseph's words. But even as my mind said, *This cannot be,* my body accepted the truth. My knees gave way and I followed Papa to the ground, where my arms wrapped around his torso, clinging to him, needing him to cling to me.

It was then his wail began, slicing through my very soul.

My voice responded in kind, and together we created a horrific duet beyond reason.

Beyond sensibility.

Beyond bearing.

Chapter Fourteen

On a sunny day, if I asked my brother the color of the sky, I would get an evasive answer as if his primary consideration was what I wanted to hear.

What I wanted to hear—what Papa demanded to hear in the months following Mama's death on July 3, 1778—was the truth.

It was slow in coming. Upon receiving the latest letter, Papa crumpled the paper into a ball before I could even read it. "Will of God? Will of God, he says! It is not the will of God my darling wife died; it is the negligence of her son!"

With difficulty, I left the letter on the floor—I'd retrieve it later. "Papa, you yourself have said it was God's will, and—"

Papa swung toward me, his index finger raised. "The Almighty is in control—on that point we agree—but God expects us to do our part. I fear that when your mother became ill, Wolfgang sat back and said, 'Let God's will be done.'"

"He called a doctor."

"Too late." He sank into a chair, his huff turning to weariness. "I am partly to blame. I always did too much for Wolfgang, while emphasizing a certainty of God's will being accomplished." He held out his hands, as if studying them. "Yet God gave us hands to act, to achieve His will through hard work." He made fists and dropped his hands to his knees. "We are not to ignore logic or shun labor, confusing laziness for the blessed assurance that comes with knowing one has done all one can humanly do." He pressed his hands to his eyes. "Even your mother relied too much on prayer alone, thinking it was a magic potion to all our woes."

I didn't like him speaking badly of the dead. "Mama had a very strong faith."

He sighed. "Yes, yes she did." He held out his hand to me. "And thank you for listening to the rantings of an old man. It's just that I have so many regrets. My mind keeps returning to the memories of the day your mother and brother left us, when I was so consumed with packing and my own health issues that I never had a chance to say a proper good-bye." He kissed the top of my hand. "If only I'd known it was the last time I'd see her. And now, to have her buried so far away . . . Saint-Eustache in Paris is not our St. Sebastian." He gripped my hand to stand. "At least your brother is sending her things home to us." He hesitated and glanced at the letter on the floor. "Unfortunately, he used your mother's watch to pay the doctor, and gave her ruby ring to pay the nurse."

"Papa, no!"

He put an arm around me. "I know you would have liked to have those possessions, but Wolfgang implied if he hadn't paid the nurse with the ruby ring, she would have taken your mother's wedding ring."

My head shook back and forth. "Couldn't he have found money somewhere else? Did he sell any of his own possessions? Why Mama's, when she had so little? Couldn't he collect on the compositions he's been writing for people? Or have all those commissions been a lie?"

Papa's eyebrows rose. "It's not like you to be bitter, Nannerl."

No, it wasn't.

Until now.

∼

How I missed her. With Mama gone, I was alone. With men. Dealing repeatedly and incessantly with men.

Wolfie was still in Paris driving Papa to distraction; Papa was here at home, consumed with his own sorrow and the politics of his work for the archbishop, and with his constant struggle to find work for Wolfie.

And then there were the suitors. Plural. Where there had been none, now there were three. For in addition to my dear captain Franz d'Ippold, I had Franz Mölk's renewed interest, as well as that of a widower named Johann Adam. The latter was persistent, proclaiming his love for me for all to hear, causing me to find excuses to *not* be home when I knew he was coming to call, to *not* attend functions he said he would attend. He forced me to be rude. But he was not for me, and the sooner he accepted that, the better.

So who was for me?

It was no contest.

I pulled the lace curtains aside and looked out the window toward the Virgilianum where my dear captain lived and worked. He'd said he was coming over this Saturday afternoon.

But this was not a normal visit amongst a group of friends where Franz and I could parry and flirt behind the backs of a crowd. No indeed, on this day Franz was coming over to speak to Papa about *us,* about his love for me and my love for him. About our future.

We had not let Papa be privy to our connection. With other suitors I had never been hesitant to let Papa know of my flirtations. Why had I been so hesitant to let him know about Franz?

Because Franz was different. I loved him. And I desperately wanted Papa to love him too and accept him as a prospective son-in-law.

I spotted Franz coming around the corner of the church. He looked toward our house and our eyes met. I waved. He waved back. My stomach flipped at the sight of him—and at the magnitude of the upcoming meeting.

I hurried toward the front door, not wanting Therese to answer it, wanting Franz and I to have a moment alone before we talked with Papa.

I opened the door to find his knuckle ready to knock. Startled, he stepped back, then smiled. "Eager, are we?"

I put a hand to my corseted midsection. "Petrified."

He took my hand and, with a glance at the street, pulled me close for a swift kiss in the doorway. I, in turn, pulled him inside, closing the door behind him. He looked into the music room, then whispered, "Where is he?"

"In his study." I tried to catch a breath. "I'm nervous."

Franz stroked the curve of my cheek with a finger. "We are united in this. That's all that matters."

It was a nice sentiment—even if the latter declaration was wishful thinking.

He took my hand and patted our connection. "So. Let's proceed with the meeting so we can proceed with our life together, yes?"

My vote was yes.

~

Although we approached the door to Papa's study hand in hand, once there, I let go. I knocked on the doorjamb. Papa looked up from his desk, his glasses perched on his nose. His eyes moved from me to Franz.

He removed his glasses and stood, extending a hand in greeting. "Captain d'Ippold. You are just the man I want to see."

Franz looked at me, but I had no idea what Papa was referring to.

Papa pulled a chair close. "Sit, sit. Nannerl, go ask Therese to bring us some wine."

Franz raised a hand. "No thank you, sir. I have a pupil coming later this afternoon, and—"

"Yes, yes, another time, then." Papa nodded at me. "You may leave us, Nannerl. Don't you also have a pupil arriving soon?"

My head shook back and forth. This was not going as I'd planned. Or hoped.

"Actually, Herr Mozart, Nannerl is the reason I have come here today."

Papa's right eyebrow rose and he sat back in his chair. Franz extended a hand in my direction and I took my place beside him, our hands clasped.

Papa's eyes seemed locked on our hands, yet with the appearance of a deep furrow between his brows. I wished he would look elsewhere. Unfortunately, although I would have liked to burst forth to declare my love for Franz, it was up to Franz to speak of his intentions first. At this moment, I was but a minor character in this scene.

"Sir . . . as you know I am a teacher at the Virgilianum and am also a captain in the imperial army and have been assigned to the archbishop's war council, where—"

Papa's eyes lit up. "I'd forgotten that. It appears you work for the archbishop in many capacities, don't you?"

Franz looked confused—as was I. Papa had little regard for Archbishop Colloredo, so if anything, I'd expected Franz's multiple associations with that man to be a detriment in Papa's eyes. Yet Papa was acting pleased? It didn't make sense.

Papa leaned forward in his chair. "You know that our Wolfgang is currently in Paris."

"Of course." Franz glanced at me, then back at Papa. "And let me extend my condolences on the tragic death of your—"

Papa flipped his concern away. "Yes, yes. Thank you." He extended a pointing finger. "The issue now is Wolfgang, and getting him back home to Salzburg."

Franz squeezed my hand and gave me a smile. "I know that would please our Nannerl very much. She misses him so—"

"Perhaps you can be of help to us. I have been negotiating with the archbishop, trying to secure a position for Wolfgang as the organist, in Aldgasser's position, with hopes of his being Kapellmeister someday."

Franz's face showed his surprise. "Nannerl has mentioned you wanted him to come home, but—"

"It's more than a *want*. Wolfgang needs to come home and assume a salaried position. According to my calculations, it will take two years to pay off the debts he's incurred on his travels. And Paris has proven to be a disaster—though there *was* talk of a position at Versailles." Papa sighed. "At this point, Salzburg offers many advantages over any German city in that ours is a cathedral court rather than a political one. Being an employee of the court here means we are better protected in the event of the death of our ruler. It's not like the debacle caused by the death of the elector Maximilian, wreaking havoc to the point of war." Papa cocked his head. "Speaking of . . . what is the current talk of war?"

I was shocked into deafness as Franz answered. How had a discussion about romance turned to talk about Wolfie's job prospects—and now war?

Franz fidgeted beside me, bringing my thoughts back to the conversation. Papa stood. "So as you see, we would really appreciate anything you could do to procure a good position for our Wolfgang." He glanced at me. "Nothing can go forward until then."

I was taken aback. So he'd guessed why we'd come?

Papa showed us out, saying he had work to do.

Apparently, so did we. I led Franz to the front door. "I'm so sorry," I said. "Papa tends to focus on one thing, and one thing alone. My brother is everything to him."

Franz pulled my hands to his lips. "I assure you, that is not true. He loves you very much. He is rightfully concerned about your future."

I pulled my hands away. "Then why wouldn't he listen to our plans—our plans to be together?"

"Because he is a father and has bigger concerns than his daughter's immediate happiness."

I snickered. "As you say."

He fingered the lace at my shoulder. "He is your provider, Nannerl. Your protector. And you know—as does he—that my salary is not worthy of excitement."

I leaned my forehead against his chin. "I don't need riches, Franz. I just need you."

He cupped the back of my head with a hand and kissed my hair. "We will work this out, my love. We will."

He sounded so certain.

~

The rest of the day was full of lessons, chores, and a trip to the theater in the evening to see a traveling troupe. As usual Papa invited some of the lead players to our home afterward, and though I was the good hostess, my heart wasn't in it. After the failed discussion about my future that afternoon, I'd wanted to talk with Papa alone, to somehow explain to him how being married—even to a man who wasn't rich—would ease his own financial burden.

But all day Papa was unavailable to me—whether by busyness or design. I'd regrettably resigned myself to having our discussion another day, when on my way to bed, I passed his room and saw that a candle was still lit. I hesitated, not sure—even after the anticipation I'd experienced all day—that I was up to the task of this confrontation.

He must have sensed my presence, for he said, "Nannerl?"

I took a fresh breath and opened the door the rest of the way. He was propped in bed against some pillows, reading by the flickering candle on the bed stand. "Did you and Therese get things put to right?"

"Yes, Papa." My mind locked on the trivial. "To let you know, Therese has asked for a new flour container. The one we have is letting in all types of bugs. She's tired of picking them out."

"Just last week she broke the hourglass and asked for a new one. And now this?"

"We need it, Papa."

He sighed deeply. "There is always something."

Money. Again. My courage was doused. I turned toward the door. "Good night, then."

"You love this man?"

I was stopped in my tracks and turned to face him. "I do."

"Are you wanting to marry this man?"

I nearly laughed at the way this entire subject had been brought into the open. "I do."

Papa shook his head. "We need more, Nannerl. He is not enough."

My laughter died. "We, Papa? We would not be getting married. I would be getting married."

He lowered his chin and looked at me through his lashes. "Surely you are not that naïve."

I crossed to the safe shadows near the wardrobe. "I know my marriage affects the family. I know that. But Franz makes enough to support me. And you still have a fine job as the Vice Kapellmeister and—"

"So I am to work the rest of my life?"

I felt the air go out of me. The rest of his life? Now *I* was the provider? My thoughts moved to Wolfie. "But when Wolfie comes home from France and gets a position . . ."

Papa shut his book with a snap. "If. If. And yet that *is* the only solution. That boy has no idea of the debts that hang over our heads, that prevent you or me from having a good night's sleep, that prevent us from having the life we would like to have. We all must make sacrifices, Nannerl."

My legs buckled. All energy was gone. I turned toward the door, needing the comfort of my bed to enfold me.

"Nannerl." Papa held out his hand, wanting me close. Somehow, I managed to go to his bedside. "I'm not saying no—not yet. But there are obstacles. First and foremost, our debts."

"Franz doesn't care about our debts."

"He would have to. They are a part of us until we find a way to get them paid. He is not a rich man. You cannot saddle him with our financial burdens. It would not be fair to him."

Put that way . . .

"Besides, the archbishop will never approve of the marriage."

"Why not?"

"Because he hates us, Nannerl. And your d'Ippold is in his employ on multiple accounts, as a teacher and as a member of his war council."

"I agree we've had our problems with the archbishop," I said, "and Wolfie has tested him sorely. But right now you're negotiating with him for Wolfie's return. That doesn't sound as if he's against us. He wants Wolfie back. He doesn't hate us."

Papa shrugged. "I'm just stating that these are obstacles you must address. It will not be easy."

My heart jumped. "So you don't disapprove—not completely?"

He shrugged again. "Obstacles must be overcome. With that . . . we'll see."

I leaned over the bed and wrapped my arms around him. "Oh, thank you, Papa. Thank you."

"Yes, yes, enough of that. To bed now. To bed."

Dallying. That's what Wolfie did best. He dallied in every city he was in—anything to keep from coming home. The autumn after Mama's death we expected Wolfie home many times, but he always found a reason to stay away—some lead or some great opportunity. Some near-miss that never materialized.

The truth was, Wolfie didn't want to come home and work for Archbishop Colloredo. I knew that. Everyone who knew Wolfie knew that.

Except Papa—who knew it but refused to acknowledge it. To Papa, getting Wolfie back in Salzburg, safely ensconced in a salaried position, would save our family's finances. I couldn't see that he was wrong in this, but I knew keeping Wolfie in such a position would be like trying to cage a hummingbird. I'd nearly come to believe that the reason God had not allowed my brother to obtain a position *anywhere* was because the Almighty knew it would kill him.

Money. A necessary evil. If only Wolfie didn't have to think about money but could concentrate on creating and performing for the sheer joy of it.

If only we all could do what we wanted to do.

In mid-January 1779, after months of taking his time heading home, Wolfie finally showed up in Salzburg. It was evening and he fell into bed without giving us a chance to talk. The next morning Papa slipped away to work with instructions to let Wolfie sleep. But when it turned twelve noon . . .

We were morning people. I'd already been to mass at seven, taken care of the household chores, done some ironing, gone to the home of one of my pupils for a lesson, and had walked Bimperl—twice. Papa would be home for lunch soon, and even though he'd pretended to be lenient about Wolfie's first day home, I knew if Wolfie wasn't up and about, Papa's nerves would pay. As would the peace of our home.

After Mama's death, peace became my goal. Keep the peace, create peace, nurture peace. Perhaps it was the cowardly path, but as grief continued to hover close, peace became more than a desire. It was a lifeline to survival.

Toward that end I carried a tray of rolls and coffee to my brother's room. I'd awaken him, take the edge off his morning hunger, and cajole him into getting dressed and presentable before Papa showed up for lunch.

I tapped on the door but did not wait for an answer before entering. I found Wolfie sprawled on the bed diagonally. He was on his back with his head hanging precariously close to the edge. The covers were in disarray and were wrapped around his limbs as if binding him down. Only the deep timbre of his snores indicated he was a twenty-two-year-old man, not a boy.

I set the tray on a table and yanked open the drapes, letting in the midday sun. "Up!" I said. "The day is wasting."

He put his forearm over his eyes and moaned. "Leave me alone."

"I can't do that, brother dear. It's nearly noon and—"

He sat erect, the covers falling away. "Papa will be home."

He scrambled out of bed, his nightshirt tangled around his torso. I handed him the coffee. "Last night Papa let you go to bed because you were weary from traveling, but today he'll want some answers about—"

"About Mama. I know."

I was going to say "About the position he's trying to arrange for you with the archbishop." Yet Wolfie was right. Papa would want to know about Mama too.

As would I.

He handed me the coffee and started getting dressed. I sat at the foot of the bed.

"It wasn't my fault, Nan. I did what I could."

But could you have done it sooner? I let that point go, as I knew Papa would cover it. What concerned me even more than the medical aspects of the situation were the social ones. "Why did you leave her alone so much, Wolfie? When she did write to us, she sounded terribly sad."

He tucked his shirt into his breeches. "She didn't fit in. You know that. Our mother had the personality of a chair. And when her time came . . . she simply burned out like a candle."

"That's a horrible thing to say."

He shrugged and dug some stockings out of a travel trunk. "You want to know the truth of things?"

"Of course I do."

He sat on the bed beside me and pulled on a stocking. "I didn't like her. I loved her, but I didn't like her. And she knew it." Suddenly his composure crumbled and he put a hand to his eyes. "She knew it."

"I'm sure it wasn't that bad."

"It was. She cried a lot. . . ."

The thought of Mama crying alone in her room pained me more than mental images of her being sick.

"I wanted to like her. I wanted to include her. And I would have, if she'd shown the least spark, the least hint that she approved of the company I was keeping, that she understood what needed to be done so I could obtain a position that would be satisfactory to . . . to . . ."

"Papa."

Wolfie moved to a mirror and ran his fingers through his hair. As usual, it did not behave. I retrieved a black ribbon from the floor and helped him tie it back. Only then did he turn to me and answer. "I'm beginning to believe there is no pleasing Papa."

"That's not true."

"It is true." He sighed deeply. "But I'm home now. That should count for something. Though how sad it is, and what a loss, to waste my youthful years vegetating in such a beggarly place as this."

"Wolfie!"

He shrugged. "Be happy I'm here, Nan, but don't expect me to feel the same."

I heard the front door open and Papa's voice. "Children?"

Wolfie looked at me and rolled his eyes. "We will always be children to him, Nan."

I didn't know what to say.

Wolfie offered me his arm, and we went to greet Papa together.

～

Wolfie burst through the front door, ripped off his waistcoat, and threw it on a chair. "That man! He's a liar! A man of God, full of lies!"

I ran to quiet him, but with his pacing, I couldn't get in front of him. "Who are you talking about?" I asked. Though I knew, I knew.

Wolfie's arms waved wildly as he moved. "His Gracelessness. The archenemy of everything good in life. The man who makes me consider breaking each and every one of the Ten Commandments!"

Therese appeared in the doorway, her face clouded with concern. I waved her away. She'd already heard more than her share of imprudent ranting. Although she'd proven herself loyal, with Wolfie home these eight months, I was sure the temptation to tell others even a small bit about the vociferous complaints my brother had regarding the archbishop and his new position had been increased a hundredfold. Salzburg was a city that thrived on gossip, and Wolfie walked on one side of a very precarious line that once crossed could destroy our family's reputation beyond repair. For him to feel these things in private was one thing, but to shout them from the rooftops—or in a street-side room with the windows open to the spring breezes—was dangerous.

I moved his waistcoat and patted the back of a chair. "Please, Wolfie. Sit. Then tell me what happened."

He dove into the chair, twisting his body until he finally sat in some semblance of normal. "My position as organist and Konzertmeister is not what I was promised. They're making me do the most mundane tasks—tasks Papa assured me others would do. I don't want to spend time with the other musicians—though they certainly want to spend time with me. And the people I do want to associate with—the nobility—will have nothing to do with me."

It distressed me that Wolfie only wanted to associate with the elite. Had Paris done that to him?

He continued. "No one appreciates my music. Colloredo treats me as he would a tramp pulled in off the street who tinkers with music between picking at his lice and getting drunk. The other musicians are mediocre at best. The woodwinds are atrocious and squeak and squawk like caged birds." He took a fresh breath. "My best years are being wasted here. I feel as if I've returned to serfdom in Salzburg."

"I'm sorry things aren't going well," I said, folding his waistcoat over my arm. "But you're being paid better than any other musician of your level has ever been paid in Salz—"

"And that's supposed to make me feel good about things? Just because Papa allowed himself to be treated like chattel his entire life doesn't mean I should do the same."

"Wolfie!"

He rose from the chair. "Oh, don't defend him. You know I'm right. Colloredo's court may be all there is for Papa, but the world is out there waiting for *me*." He pointed toward the windows. "The world, Nan. You and I both had it in our hands, but then it slipped away. Now you're here and I'm here and . . ." He took hold of my upper arms and looked at me eye to eye, for we were of the same height. "You seem to like it here, Nan. But I don't. I hate it."

Did I like it here? It wasn't something I'd thought about much. Salzburg was home. Salzburg, I knew. And yet . . . "I would like to travel and perform, Wolfie. But I wasn't given that option."

He actually looked shocked. "Other than our impromptu plan to travel, the plan Papa laughed at because he said we weren't old enough, weren't able enough . . . you've never said anything. You've never asked . . ."

I threw the coat at his face. "How could I ask? What could I say to anyone? Should I moan about being a woman? Groan about having to stay home and take care of the household tasks? Should I resent every letter you send that tells of concerts and dinners and chances to create music—music that I love every bit as much as you do? Should I be angry because up until the last few years when he was stuck here with me, Papa focused all his attention on you, on your talent, on your education, on your potential? Should I let envy eat me up because you're seeing the world that I only remember in childish snatches of memory? Should I hate you because you've been given a thousand chances that haven't materialized, complaining all the way?"

During my tirade he'd retreated to the chair and I ended up standing over him, my finger pointing in his face. I touched the tip of his nose. "I should hate you, brother. But I don't. God help me, I don't."

I took a step back, my chest heaving. I'd never blown up like that. Ever. Yet in spite of the embarrassment that tinged the edges of my feelings, my strongest emotion was pleasure in this unexpected surge of power.

Wolfie was only temporarily cowed. He recovered quickly and applauded. "Bravo, sister! Who knew you had *that* in you?"

Now he was teasing. I swatted at his hands. "Don't make fun of me. I'm serious."

"I know. And though your presentation is surprising, the content of what you said is valid and correct."

I had trouble remembering all that I had said. "It is?"

He took my hands and pulled them to his chest. "I am a vain, arrogant, stubborn human being. And I'm blind too. For me to not see your suffering . . ."

"I haven't been *suffering*. I've accepted my lot. I know how little can be done to change it. I am just one woman. I can't change the world."

"Oh, but *we* can!" Suddenly he swung me in a circle, dancing the length of the music room. My skirt trailed behind me, knocking over a music stand, moving a chair . . .

"Stop!" I said. "We're going to break something!"

He pulled me close and we spun to a halt, out of breath. "We *could* change the world, Nan. You and I could leave this horrid city together and venture off on our own Grand Tour without Papa's interference."

I smoothed my hair, hooking a loose tendril behind my ear. "We're not the Wunderkinder anymore."

"No, we're not. We're better than that. We are the Magnificent Mozarts with a lifetime of experience and practice behind us, and with an overabundance of God's gracious gifts fueling us on." He tucked in his shirt as he talked. "We could make a hundred thousand florins and become more famous than Handel or any one of the Bachs." He tugged at the ruffle of my sleeve. The lace was ripped at the edge. "We could get ourselves luscious, matching clothes and have powdered wigs so tall they'd nip the ceiling. Your neck would be heavy with jewels, and I would have gold and diamond buckles on my shoes."

"Don't be silly," I said—though I was laughing. "We could never afford all that."

"Why not? If the ex love-of-my-life, Aloysia Weber, can get an appointment in Munich that earns her one thousand a year when she's just a singer, then—"

"One thousand? She makes that much?"

"She *is* very talented. But so are we, sister. And our talents are far more diverse than hers. I would compose music for the two of us that would showcase our talents and make audiences swoon."

I giggled. "I've never seen an audience swoon."

He pinched my cheek. "Then you have not lived, dear Nan. You truly have not lived." Wolfie looked at the clock on the mantel. "When will Papa be home? We must tell him our plans, and we won't take no for an answer. Not this time."

The lofty door to the world that had just opened to me snapped shut. "Papa will never allow—"

Wolfie swung toward me. "Allow? I've had enough of people *allowing* me to do things! We are both adults. It is time we created our own life instead of allowing Papa to create one of *his* making."

My mind swam with logistics. "But with Mama gone, he has no one, and he has a tendency toward melancholy. He often sulks and barely smiles. He worries about everything and—"

"So that's *it?*" He snapped his fingers. "With just the mere thought of him, you abandon our plans?"

"We have to think of reality, Wolfie. You couldn't find a position in Paris, or Mannheim, or Munich. Why should we think that two of us could do better?"

"We don't need a position; we just need an audience. I want to write operas, Nan. I can't do that here. And you could play the keyboard for all of them, and help me direct. You could even help me compose. We could be a team in every musical sense."

It sounded wonderful.

It sounded impossible. A fantasy.

A knock on the door surprised me. I went to get it. It was Franz. After kissing my cheek, he saw Wolfie. "Am I interrupting something?"

Wolfie looked at me, then Franz, then me again. He was not smiling. "Aha. I see how things are. You've made your choice, and it has nothing to do with Papa, or opportunities, or lost chances to use your talent. Seeing what I see . . . you have no right to give me a hard time about wanting to use my chances, Nan. To each his own. To each his own."

He grabbed his coat and pushed past Franz on the way out the door.

"What is he so upset about?" Franz asked.

"Life." *Lost dreams. Dashed hopes.*

Franz pulled me close, smiling. "I have news. News about *our* life."

I pushed away, needing more distance to fully capture what he was going to say. What I hoped he was going to say. "Meaning?"

"I spoke with the archbishop again."

"About us?"

He nodded and pulled me close again.

Once again, I pushed away. "Did he give us permission to marry?"

"Not yet," Franz said. "But he assured me he's giving it the highest consideration."

It was something, yet not enough.

"You look disappointed."

I was overreacting. I needed to show my appreciation, offer encouragement, think positively.

I put my hands on his shoulders and traced the curved braid on his waistcoat. "I'm sorry. I just want a decision now. I want to marry now."

"As do I, dear lady. But we must be patient. These things take time."

His kiss made me forget about the inequities of being a woman.

~

Life went on, and Archbishop Colloredo controlled us all. Franz and I waited for his permission to marry. Wolfie continued to complain about Colloredo, and Colloredo continued to complain about him—with poor Papa in the middle.

A reprieve was received when Wolfie obtained a commission from Elector Karl Theodor to write an opera for Munich's carnival—an opera called *Idomeneo,* about the king of Crete, sea monsters, and sacrifice. Both he and Papa were so excited about it that they agreed he should charge less than the normal rate. The librettist, Giambattista Varesco, visited our home in August 1780, and the work began. The archbishop reluctantly granted Wolfie a six-week leave to go to Munich to work on the composition and supervise the rehearsals. It seemed a generous offer but wasn't because the work wasn't scheduled to be performed until late January 1781, and with Wolfie leaving on November fourth . . . I left the discrepancy in time for Papa and my brother to work out.

Papa showed his support by taking over some of Wolfie's duties under the archbishop and by acting as go-between with Wolfie and Varesco. Changes in the libretto were many, and Papa had to use great tact and grace to make the project come to satisfactory fruition.

Even after Wolfie arrived in Munich, the work did not progress smoothly. The lead character—Idomeneo—was to be played by Wolfie's friend Anton Raaff. But Raaff was getting old and was not a good actor, and the castrato playing the other lead part wasn't particularly good at acting *or* singing and seemed incapable of memorizing. As usual, Wolfie had to adapt the music to the limitations and egos of the singers, which was both frustrating and time-consuming. Rehearsals commenced in early December, before Wolfie was even done with the composition. It was hard for me to understand why Wolfie loved writing operas so much. The stress and politics involved made the composition of a sonata or flute solo far preferable. At least in my eyes.

But not in Wolfie's. Although his letters were full of complaints about the process, I could also sense that *these* types of complications fueled him. Having no musical challenge—as was the case in Salzburg—sapped his life breath and made him suffocate for lack of creative air.

And though I never mentioned such thoughts to Papa, the idea of Wolfie coming home again . . . I wanted better for him. Despite wanting his company, I knew that the best thing for my brother would be liberation from this place we called home.

Little did I know Papa agreed with me. One night over his

mushroom soup, Papa said, "When the opera is complete, Wolfgang needs to make his way to Vienna."

I choked on a bite of bread, and Papa had to slap my back until I was breathing normally again.

"Eat slowly, Nannerl."

My choking had nothing to do with the speed of my eating. "What would he do in Vienna?" I asked.

"With the success of *Idomeneo*—and I do believe it will be a success—your brother's worth will increase in the eyes of the world. He's been very open to the changes I've suggested to him, and the work is progressing nicely. It may even be his best to date. That's why Vienna is the logical choice. There he will earn new operatic commissions, perhaps even a few in Prague. Plus I'm hoping to get the publisher Breitkopf to print some of his music. We do have other options beyond the archbishop, Nannerl."

If only it were true. "But his position here . . . We need the two salaries to survive."

"Ah." Papa dabbed a napkin at his mouth. "We needed the two salaries to pay off Wolfgang's traveling debts. But now, since those are paid . . ."

"They're paid?"

He shrugged slightly. "They will be soon—but don't let Wolfgang know."

"But the pressure of our finances on him . . ."

"Needs to remain in place in order to keep him focused. You know your brother. If I give him ten florins he will spend twenty. If I tell him to save ten he will save five." Papa reached for my hand across the table. "I believe the time has come where the security of two salaries isn't worth the drain on our Wolfgang's talents." He let go and nodded once. "Your brother's right. He's being wasted here."

There. He'd finally said it plain. I could do nothing more than gape at him.

"What?" Papa asked. "You do not agree?"

I managed to hold in a laugh. "I agree completely. Although I'll hate to see him go. I know the restraints set by Colloredo are—"

Papa tossed his napkin on the table. "If I could leave with Wolfgang, I would. I am a prisoner here when I long to be in

Munich to help with the opera. The archbishop is being incredibly stingy with leave."

"But you did say the two of us were going to Munich to see the final performance."

"That is the plan, dear girl. But, in truth, I'd prefer to go earlier." He leaned closer and lowered his voice. "Actually, that could come about. The father of His Grace is sick and there is talk he will visit him in Vienna. Let me tell you, if that happens I will not be the only Salzburg musician to slip out of town during his absence." He suddenly sat back, his face clouded. "Unless Colloredo's father dies and he cancels the visit. Or . . . or what if the opera itself is post-poned because of the mourning for the death our dear Maria Theresa?"

This time I could not stifle a laugh. "Your compassion for the sick and dead is moving, Papa."

He raised his chin defiantly. "I am a pragmatic man."

Of that, there was no question.

～

When Wolfie was little he had a saying, "Next to God comes Papa." Every night before bed he used to stand on a chair and sing to Papa, kissing him on the tip of his nose, telling him that when he grew old Wolfie would put him in a glass case and protect him from every breath of air, so that he might always give Papa honor and have him close.

Although Wolfie still loved Papa, during our time with him in Munich, seeing his opera come to life before our eyes . . . I saw my brother in a new light. He was no longer the dependent boy, eager to please. He was a man of twenty-five whose inner essence showed forth with a strength that surpassed even the love of a son for a father. Seeing him direct the orchestra, direct the singers and actors with the knowledge that every movement, every note, and every sound that filled my heart and soul were from his annoying but bril-liant mind made me accept that he was not ours anymore. Not entirely ours.

Sitting in the audience as they clapped and shouted, "Bravo!" I realized I *could* let him go. But glancing at Papa standing beside me, seeing the way his spine was erect and his chin held high . . . seeing how he perused the room, nodding and smiling as if he too were responsible . . .

I wasn't sure Papa could let him go, and I sensed—and feared— the battles yet to come as Mozart the younger fought for independence.

~

Papa got his wish about Wolfie going to Vienna. Archbishop Colloredo *had* gone to that city to see his sick father, taking with him an extensive retinue of his court. Weeks later, after the opera performances were over, he sent word to Wolfie that Wolfie's presence was required in Vienna. The archbishop was putting together a musical group there (no doubt to show off the musicians as his possessions) and wanted Wolfie to join them.

Papa had wanted Wolfie to go to Vienna, yet for Colloredo to be the one to summon him there was advantageous, but odd. His Grace also made insinuations that Papa needed to get back to Salzburg immediately. The two Mozart men were being purposely separated. None of us was sure how this would play out. Wolfie had wanted to leave Salzburg to escape the thumb of the archbishop. But to be summoned to his city of choice *by* the archbishop? And what about the question of my marriage to Franz? Would Colloredo ever make a decision? I hated that so many of the major options of our life were in the hands of this one man.

Wolfie agreed to go to Vienna, but of course he had ulterior motives. He would use the time—while under salary—to peruse other alternatives on the sly. Leaving Papa and me, he played out one of his character's lines: *"Andrò ramingo, e solo"*—he would "wander forth alone."

Though we parted in Munich as though his trip were temporary, I had a feeling even then that my brother had no intention of ever returning to us. I'd witnessed a different Wolfgang in Munich. Gone was the bitter anger of my Salzburg brother. In its place was a confident, exuberant, significant man who knew exactly what he wanted and was not beyond plucking a few strings to the point of breaking in order to get it.

In truth, I could not imagine this new Wolfie back home with Papa and me. As he'd hinted at before, I'd actually witnessed audiences swoon to his music, and had far too many memories of Salzburg audiences offering no more response than an audience of tables and chairs. How could I deny him the one while condemning him to the latter?

And so I said good-bye to my dear Wolfie with an extra hug and two extra kisses as he headed from Munich to one city and we to another.

Godspeed, brother.

~

I opened my eyes from sleep, froze, and held my breath.

What sound had taken me from dreams to awake?

I turned my head so both ears were free of the muffling effects of the pillow.

Pluck, pluck.

Strings being plucked on a violin? I got out of bed and pulled a dressing gown over my smock. I glanced out the window at the street below. All was quiet. All was dark. It was the middle of the night, nowhere near morning.

Pluck, pluck.

I ignored the need for slippers or light and ventured out in the hall. The door to Papa's bedchamber was open. I looked inside. The bedding was rumpled, but he was not there.

If he had his violin, he was probably in the music room. But why in the middle of the night?

The plucking sounds drew me closer. And there I found him, sitting in the dark on the bench of the clavier, a violin in his hand— and not just any violin but the miniature instrument Wolfie had played as a young child. Papa wore only his nightshirt and cap, the moonlight cutting a swath across his figure, revealing a furrowed brow and eyes that stared absently into air. He cradled the violin in the crook of his arm, strumming it as one would a mandolin. He

253

seemed unaware of his action, or its result.

I was about to enter the room when he sighed loudly and changed positions, holding the violin erect in his lap, resting his forehead against its tiny scroll, closing his eyes as if in pain.

I could not stay in the shadows any longer. I stepped into the room. "Papa?"

With a start, he sat erect. "Nannerl. What are you doing up?"

I pointed to the instrument. "I heard . . ."

He looked at the violin as if only then realizing it was in his possession. "I apologize. I took it up . . . I needed . . ."

Comfort? From what? I drew a chair close and sat. "What's bothering you?"

He hooked a finger in a corner of his nightshirt and polished the back of the violin. "Nothing you should worry about."

I extended a hand across the space between us, touching his knee. "Papa, what affects one of us affects all."

He put his hand on top of mine and smiled wistfully. " 'Tis only too true, dear daughter. Unfortunately, too true."

His tone frightened me. I pulled my hand away. "What's happened?"

"The end has begun."

"Papa?"

His hand stopped its polishing. "Your brother has decided he doesn't need us; it is we who need him."

I could not argue, because I saw the truth in the statement. We *were* depending on him to do well in Vienna. And so far, he had. Beyond fulfilling the requirements of the archbishop, he'd managed to take in a few students and often played in private homes to paying patrons. Between that pay and his salary—which was sent directly to Papa—we were getting by quite well.

Papa interrupted my musings. "Your brother has forced the archbishop's hand."

I didn't understand. "Wolfie is in Vienna *with* the archbishop, at his request. He was chosen to go. Not every—" I stopped the sentence, for to finish it would hurt Papa's feelings. For he, as a musician, had not been invited. Lately it seemed as though Papa's duties had decayed from those of a valued musician to those of a teacher and manager.

By the way his eyes cast downward, I knew he'd finished the sentence for me.

"I'm sorry, I didn't mean . . ."

He shook his head and turned the violin over, running a finger up and down the strings on its neck. "I don't know what to do with Wolfgang. He's been given special lodging in Vienna, a stipend for meals, opportunities to serve the archbishop, yet his letters are full of venom, complaining about everything. And he doesn't even have the restraint to use code."

I'd considered my brother's rantings about having to eat with the staff and having to parade into concerts with other musicians en masse as typical complaints regarding his perceived position versus reality. Papa had always told us we were unlike other musicians in every respect, and though I wanted to believe it, I had also seen signs that Papa's opinion differed from the opinions of others in authority. But instead of accepting the signs—as I did—it was apparent Wolfie fought against them. Apparently, at one concert, he'd even refused to gather with the other musicians and had made his own solo entrance, walking straight up to Prince Golicyn, conversing with him while other musicians like Ceccarelli and Brunetti stood against the wall, appalled. Of course, Wolfie's rendition of this event was told with glee, but I saw beyond the pride in his own boldness, to recognize how it must look to others.

"So you've heard that the archbishop is upset with him?"

Papa snickered. "Upset, disgusted, tried beyond bearing."

"Oh dear."

Papa stood and returned the violin to its case with the care of a father putting his child to bed. He closed the lid and snapped the latches. He came back to the bench but did not face the keyboard. He showed me his profile and hung his hands between his knees, causing his nightshirt to pull taut against his legs. He looked straight ahead and offered another sigh. "The archbishop has cast him out."

"What?"

"I've heard firsthand accounts of an awful row. The archbishop screamed at Wolfgang—and Wolfgang screamed back."

My heart pulled and I pushed a hand against it. "I cannot imagine such a thing. Are you sure?"

Papa's smile was eerie. "Apparently when His Grace's father recovered and he decided to come home to Salzburg, he gave his employees permission to follow. One at a time they left Vienna."

"But Wolfie hasn't said anything about being given leave to return."

"Everyone has been given their instructions to come home—except Wolfgang."

I had trouble swallowing. "But perhaps . . . Wolfie had always planned on asking for an extended leave so he could stay in Vienna and—"

"He never got a chance to ask for it, because the archbishop found a way to make sure he *had* to come back here. He told Wolfgang he had a very important package he needed him to bring back to Salzburg."

"Wolfie wouldn't like being treated as a messenger."

"Your brother doesn't like a lot of things. And apparently he made a string of excuses why he couldn't leave Vienna, the strongest being that he needed to stay in order to collect fees for lessons and concerts he'd given, suggesting that surely His Grace would not insist upon doing him financial injury. . . ."

"Was this the truth or—?"

Papa rose, as did his voice. "Of course not. It always comes down to Wolfgang only wanting to do what Wolfgang wants to do."

I could not argue, for more and more I'd noticed that his rebellious streak had widened.

"As it played out, Wolfie took the advice of the archbishop's valet, who suggested he show himself cooperative by meeting face-to-face with the archbishop, to explain how he couldn't take the package because there were no available seats on the coaches." Papa shook his head. "It was a trap. He was lured into a trap by a valet loyal to His Grace. In fact, I don't believe there ever was a package."

"What happened?"

Papa stood at the window. The moonlight cast the front of him in light, leaving his back in darkness. "The archbishop greeted him by saying, 'Well, boy, when are you going?' To which Wolfgang offered the valet's excuse of there being no seats. Others took the opportunity to come forward and accuse him of lying—which he was. Which gave fuel to the archbishop's listing all of Wolfgang's indiscretions, such as not waiting outside his antechamber for instructions every day like the other musicians did. He called him the most negligent knave he knew, and complained about how badly Wolfgang had served his court." Papa took a breath and looked in my direction. "The archbishop was ranting, red in the face, in a terrible rage."

"What did Wolfie do?"

Papa shook his head and snickered. "He yelled back. 'So Your Grace is not satisfied with me?' To which the archbishop replied . . ." Papa looked to the ceiling. "Let me make sure I get this correct . . . 'What? You dare threaten me? You miserable fool! Oh, you miserable fool! Look, there is the door. I will have nothing more to do with such a rogue.' "

"Oh no."

"To which your brother answered, 'Nor I any longer with you.' He was shown the door." Papa looked back to the street. "Everything we've worked for is over. Ruined. *Finis*."

I went to his side, put my hands on his shoulders, and leaned my cheek against his back. "Oh, Papa . . ." I wanted to say everything would be all right, but I wasn't sure it was the truth.

Had Wolfie gone too far?

~

It was over an hour before Papa and I returned to bed—but not to sleep.

Archbishop Colloredo had fired my brother. My brother had yelled at the archbishop and further strained the already faltering relationship between His Grace and the Mozart family. The hate he'd previously shown had surely been fed to the point of satiation.

Yet in our favor was the fact that Papa had been a good employee of late. He'd done whatever the archbishop had asked of him. So perhaps the court would accept Wolfie's indiscretions as those of an immature individual and not those of the Mozart family as a whole.

My own words spoken earlier interrupted my wishful thinking: "What affects one of us affects all."

Then, with a bolt as swift as lightning, my thoughts sped to dear Franz, who'd asked the archbishop for permission to marry.

No, no, no, no, no . . .

No matter how many times I repeated my mantra, *willing* the answer to be otherwise, I knew the archbishop would refuse our request.

There would be no marriage. All our waiting had been for nothing.

I slapped my hands against my mouth, my head still shaking in a feeble attempt to stop the inevitable. Tears came, tears of frustration, sadness, and . . . and . . .

Even hate.

How could Wolfie do this to me?

I tore off the covers and started to dress. I would go see Franz and share the horrible news. Surely he'd say I was overreacting, calm me, and take me in his arms, where all things were possible.

But as I saw the deepness of the night through the lace curtains, I knew I could not go out. Although Franz lived just across the square in the school in which he taught, I could not risk disturbing others simply because my worries loomed large and frightening.

I forced myself to sit on the bed, to pause amid my panic.

My heart thundered against my chest and my breathing was audible. The worry pressed around me, threatening to smother me and crush my bones to dust.

I shook my head, fighting against its presence. I'd always lived a life of hope; I could not let this worry break me. The fact the whole situation was out of my control was nothing new. I'd lived with such limitations every day of my life. I'd survived. And I'd held on to hope.

As I had to do now.

I forced a deep breath into my chest and pressed a hand against the beat of my heart. Calm. Calm. Things might work out. Perhaps by some miracle of God, the archbishop would look upon Franz and me with mercy and grant our request, allowing two of his subjects to marry out of love.

Perhaps it would snow in June.

~

I opened the door and felt a wave of dread enter with the summer heat.

Franz stood before me, his eyes holding mine for but a moment before seeking the floor.

"The archbishop said no, didn't he?" I said.

He came inside and shut the door behind him. He took my hands. He nodded.

I shook his touch away. "Did he give his reason?"

Franz gave me a look. "His Grace did not say why—he did not have to, either by protocol or common sense. We all know why."

Wolfie.

"Did you remind him that my father and I are very loyal? That my father has served the court for over thirty years?"

"One does not argue with His Grace."

Wolfie did.

And look where it got him.

Franz pulled me into his arms until my cheek rested against the rough wool of his waistcoat. "I am not brave enough for you, Nan. I should resign my teaching position, resign my position on the archbishop's war council, and run away with you to a far-off land where no one knows us, where we can begin again."

I closed my eyes, letting his words ring with possibilities. But then I thought of Wolfie—truly a man of extraordinary talent— who'd been unable to find positions in countless cities, even with the unrelenting force of our father working to make it happen.

Although I loved Franz deeply, he was a quiet man. Unassuming. Unremarkable to all who did not love him. It was not prudent to discard any position and venture out without capital—especially at his age of fifty. And without the archbishop's blessing, there would be no monetary wedding gift, which was key to helping any couple start their new life together.

Papa always said, "Marriage is irresponsible without an adequate financial basis."

Unfortunately, in spite of our desire to be otherwise, neither Franz nor myself were irresponsible sorts. Our lives hinged on duty, loyalty, and doing what was expected of us. Holding on to the *status in quo*.

Only Wolfie had managed to break free of this burden to act as was expected, and to fear disturbing the peace over any desire to obtain something new—no matter how enticing. Although Wolfie frustrated me, sometimes I admired his courage to just *be*.

I held Franz tighter and he put a hand on the back of my head, holding me close. We stood like that for a long time. There were no further words required.

Or available.

~

My dear friend, Katherl, stopped by one day soon after Franz and I abandoned our hope to marry. I was glad for her presence. I hadn't been able to openly display my grief and anger with Papa, and a stew of emotions welled within me to the point of overflow. With Katherl, I would find blessed release.

I was mistaken.

After I'd aired my feelings, Katherl took a sip of coffee and set her cup against the saucer. She put a hand on her burgeoning mid-section, very much with child—her third child in four years. "You must move on, Nan. It does no good to think about could-have-beens."

I was momentarily stunned into silence. "But you managed to marry the man you loved. Surely, you understand how I also want—"

She shrugged. "Even if a woman gets what she thinks she wants, it doesn't mean she wants what she gets."

I felt my eyebrows rise. "You're not happy with Heinz?"

Another shrug. "Is anyone happy with anyone?" She pressed a finger against her plate, getting the last of the cake crumbs. "Sometimes I envy you, Nan."

"Envy? Me?"

"You get to stay in a familiar home that offers comfort, your thoughts are your own, and your life is not disrupted by the constant needs of children—and a husband."

"I thought you loved Heinz."

"And I love my children. But that doesn't mean I'm happy." She sighed deeply. "I look back at the days before my marriage when I had time to go shooting and to the theater. When I could spend an entire afternoon walking the Gardens, having a picnic, being jolly with friends. Now . . ."

I was shocked. I had no idea how to respond.

Katherl tried to get comfortable on the chair that was now too small. "You still have that life, Nan. Instead of being sad or angry about what you think you lost by not being able to be with Franz, I suggest you count your blessings."

~

I looked back at my bedchamber one final time. I grieved not being able to fit more of my clothes into my satchel, but for that I would need a trunk. And a trunk of clothing was an impossible encumbrance when one was running away. Perhaps after Franz and I were settled somewhere I would send Papa a letter asking him— begging him—to have my things sent to me.

Whether he would comply. . . ?

It was not the time to think of petty items like dresses or favorite music. I would have to live with the clothes on my back and the music in my head. Yet as long as I was side by side with the man I loved, nothing else would matter.

When I'd gotten up that morning, if someone had told me by midafternoon I would be leaving forever, I would have laughed aloud. If such a thing had been suggested while I was serving Katherl her third cup of coffee, I would have said, "Don't be absurd." Such a decision was unfathomable even in the half hour after our visit ended.

But in the half hour after that . . . as Katherl's ridiculous statement that she envied *me* sank in . . .

How dare she negate what she had accomplished by marrying the man she loved? How dare she toss aside that privilege and honor as if it were an annoyance to her day? How dare she choose the frivolities of an unencumbered afternoon over the love and devotion of a husband and children? How dare she misuse her blessings?

As my anger grew, so did my resolve. I would not allow others to determine my future. I would grab hold of it with my own two hands and yank it to submission. I would take the happiness that could be mine and make it happen.

I picked up the satchel and adjusted the note on the dresser so Papa would be sure to see it. *I'm sorry, Papa, but I could not discard my love because of the vindictive decision of the archbishop. I am not my brother. I have done nothing wrong and do not deserve to be punished. I will write to you as soon as Franz and I are married and settled. Be happy for me, Papa. Be happy for my happiness. A thousand kisses, your Nannerl.*

I knew the note would not be enough. I knew Papa would be furious. I knew he might come after us. But I did not care. I could not care. My future had to override my past, enrich my present, and . . .

And cause Papa sorrow?

I shook the thought away and hurried toward the kitchen, where I slipped out the back door. If I allowed myself to entertain such thoughts of guilt and loyalty, my habit of being the good girl would envelop me and kill the independence that had been sparked that afternoon.

As I walked across the square, I kept the satchel low against my skirts, hoping it would not be seen by neighbors and friends who would wonder about the trip it represented. If only it were night and the darkness could cover my escape.

But I dared not wait until dark. I had to go immediately, while the fire within me burned brightest.

I entered the Virgilianum, the school Franz directed, and deposited my satchel in a corner behind a coatrack. In the classrooms around me I heard boys reading aloud and teachers giving lessons. Doubt suddenly assailed me. How could I interrupt Franz with this most serious of all decisions while he was in the middle of his work?

How could I not?

I turned down the hall toward the classrooms and was immediately fueled by the sound of his voice. I paused outside a door and basked in the knowledge that he was near. I waited for a pause in his teaching. Taking him away was bad enough. I didn't have to be rude and interrupt.

Then suddenly I heard a bit of commotion from the room, and before I knew what was happening, I heard Franz say, "Master Dieter, come outside with me a moment, please?"

I slid behind the opened door just as Franz came into the hall with a boy. I held my skirts close against my body and peeked around the edge of the door. There a boy of seven or eight stood with his arms crossed defiantly. Franz had one hand on the boy's shoulder. "Now, Dieter. Why did you shove Markus out of his seat?"

"He made fun of me for doing poorly on the test."

"You *can* do better."

The little boy shrugged. Franz took the boy's chin in his hand and lifted it, looking directly in his eyes. "You are a smart boy, Dieter Schultz. You can get the best mark of any boy in that room."

"I can't—"

"You can." Franz tousled the boy's hair. "And you will. You stay after class today and I will help make you the best in the class." He leaned close. "Markus will be very jealous."

The boy smiled and nodded.

"Good. Now, let's go back inside, and no more shoving. Impress them with your knowledge, Dieter. Knowledge is something not even time can take away from you."

They returned to the classroom, leaving me behind the door. As I heard Franz claim control of his charges once more, as I heard him continue the lesson, I knew that I could not take him away from this world of knowledge he loved. I could not force him into an uncertain life in a new place where he would lose all that he had gained through decades of hard work. Would he find another job as the director of a school? Or even as a teacher? Perhaps. But perhaps in our effort to survive and start again, he'd have to take a job as a smithy's assistant or earn a living as a farmhand or by chopping wood.

Such mental pictures were alarming. I could not imagine this gentle man doing manual labor. He was not a man of muscle but of mind.

Yet . . . I could help earn a living. I would give lessons and offer my music-copying abilities to various churches and—

I sucked in a breath. Give lessons? On what? I would not have a clavier, nor even be guaranteed access to one. As we would be starting with nothing, a clavier would be an unaffordable luxury.

"This will not work," I whispered to the empty hall. "It can never work."

A moment passed. Then another. No new, enlightened thought overrode my conclusion.

So with this final truth reverberating in my soul, I retreated down the hall, picked up my satchel, crossed the square, and re-entered the home of my father. I did not pause. I did not look left or right. I went straight to my room and set the satchel on the bed.

Then I picked up the note I'd written to Papa and took it to the fireplace. The coals were smoldering and nearly cold. Did they still possess enough spark to do this final job?

I held the corner of the note against them, hoping, praying . . .

Blessedly, a flame burst to life.

My declaration of independence was quickly consumed.

Ashes to ashes . . .

~

What affects one of us affects all.

In the months after I resigned myself to life without Franz as my husband, in the months after Wolfie severed his ties with the arch-bishop and remained in Vienna, life continued. Yet it was forever changed.

First off, Papa changed. He grew fat and talked too much about who'd died and what aches and pains visited his body. He stopped speaking of the future. Gone were detailed plans and grand schemes. Nor did he reminisce about the golden years of our family, when we traveled through Europe playing before royalty. The future and the past became dead to him as he immersed himself in the here and now.

His decision to avoid two-thirds of his life—whether made unintentionally or with dogged determination—caused a part of him to die. Instead of living, he existed. Instead of breathing deeply, he settled for short snippets of air. Instead of immersing himself in all things musical, he was content to sit in his chair and doze. Doze? Leopold Mozart doze?

He acted like an old man. And though he *was* sixty-two, up until this time he had seemed much younger. His surrender to life's inequities aged him.

As they aged me. For in my own way, I too was old. I was nearly thirty, unmarried, and living in the house of my father. And though I did not succumb to letting my health deteriorate as Papa did, I found it increasingly difficult to look at myself in the mirror. I had never been a beauty, but now there were lines at my eyes and forehead, and the glow of youth was only falsely achieved by pinching my cheeks.

Although I allowed myself the smallest glimmer of hope that someday I would marry, it was a hope born out of desperation and self-preservation. I'd already given up hope of being a noted musician, impressing the world with my prowess and talent. So to let this final hope of home and family die would be to risk succumbing to my own desire to doze the rest of my life away in a favorite chair.

I still thought of Franz often and knew he would never completely leave my consciousness. Initially Papa had offered his condolences at our situation—though I never did tell him how close I'd come to running away—but he soon became so consumed with the world of his own melancholy that I was forced to deal with my plethora of feelings alone.

Franz tried to make things easier, and we still saw each other—though less often because the angst of what could have been was too painful.

And so while Papa surrendered, I became resigned. The distinction may have been slight, but it kept me going. My prayers—though they had not been answered as I had wished—continued. Surely God had some plan for my life beyond this?

Surely there was more. . . .

Chapter Fifteen

I could not stay angry at my brother for breaking his ties with the archbishop so dramatically. I could not stay angry at the archbishop for denying my application to marry his loyal employee Franz. I could not stay angry at Franz for not being the kind of man who could shun the known for the difficult life of the unknown.

If only I could.

Time moved on for Papa and me in Salzburg, and for Wolfie in Vienna. Alone.

But not alone. Oh no, not at all alone.

For after leaving the archbishop's employ (how delicately said, Nannerl!), Wolfie moved into a boardinghouse owned by the Webers, the very same Weber family he'd stayed with back in Mannheim. After the Weber father died, they'd moved to Vienna. Wolfie's old love, Aloysia, had married (she'd been with child at the wedding), leaving the mother and three other daughters to fend for themselves by opening their home to boarders.

From what Wolfie implied in his letters, the oldest sister, Josepha, at twenty-one, was too old for his twenty-seven-year-old tastes, and the youngest, Sophie, at eighteen, was too young. Which left the middle girl, Constanze, aged nineteen. Papa and I noticed in his correspondence that unlike his letters describing Aloysia, lauding her beauty and talent, his letters describing Constanze heralded her tender care and solicitude, and her two little black eyes and pretty figure. Not that being a beauty or having great talent was a necessity in a mate, but in many ways it seemed that Wolfie was settling.

And then we began to hear rumors regarding unsavory behavior within the Weber household in regard to two unmarried young people being in such close quarters. . . . Wolfie had to move out or risk having Constanze's mother call the police. Once that was accomplished, he complained about his new lodging arrangements, saying that the household was too set in their ways. Apparently at the Webers' he'd been allowed to compose until all hours, delaying meals as long as he wished. They'd coddled him and let him keep the eccentric habits that were his preference.

Over and over he asked Papa's permission to marry Constanze. And over and over Papa said no. *"What does Wolfgang not understand about the word* no*?"* Beyond Papa's obvious hesitations regarding the reputation of the Weber family—her mother was said to be a drunk, and a Salzburg friend had declared Constanze a trollop—Papa stated that, in order to marry, Wolfie was still in need of a permanent position. One did not become man and wife and enter a time of life where the added expense of children would surely follow without a good job. It was common sense.

Something Wolfie sorely lacked.

In his defense, Wolfie *was* earning some money through teaching (which he abhorred), giving concerts in the homes of nobility, and getting an operatic commission for *The Abduction from the Seraglio*. Yet his greatest dream of being hired by Emperor Joseph II remained elusive.

Papa and I weren't sure whom to blame. Although a family friend (the one who'd called Constanze a trollop) had also brought word from Vienna that Wolfie was despised by the Viennese court and nobility for the whole Weber affair, we also knew from other sources that salaried positions were scarce under Emperor Joseph, which had the consequence of sending more and more musicians into the freelance market. Times were indeed tight.

And Wolfie was not.

Wolfie seemed incapable of adjusting his lifestyle to his income. When he had a windfall, he spent as though he were aristocracy, but when he fell on hard times, he had trouble pulling in the purse strings. It was my opinion that if Mama and Papa would have made him aware of the financial side of life instead of always doing for him, he would have been better off.

Not that I ever told Papa that.

Yet in my brother's defense, the money situation was often unfair. For *Abduction,* Wolfie received a one-time payment of 426 florins. It incensed him that even though the opera played to packed houses, even though the theater owners were said to have brought in 1706 florins in two weeks, Wolfie did not receive another coin. The lot of a composer was difficult—no matter how talented.

I also empathized with Wolfie's desire to be married. Luckily for Wolfie, since he didn't live in Salzburg anymore, he didn't need to play by the archbishop's rules. Once he received Papa's consent— "Your brother wore me down, Nannerl. Better to have them marry than to create further scandal"—Wolfie and Constanze were man and wife.

As I congratulated them, I hated them.

Some sister I was.

~

With their wedding vows still fresh, Wolfie and Constanze started talking about coming to Salzburg for a visit. After all, we had yet to meet his bride. And though Papa and I were not thrilled about the union, we looked forward to seeing Wolfie again. It had been over two years since we'd parted in Munich with Wolfie traveling to Vienna and us heading home.

Yet during the postmarriage months we received two things from Wolfie in abundance: excuses and delays.

Papa read his latest excuse, allowing his hand to fall into his lap with a familiar sigh of exasperation. "It's the weather, the concert season, Constanze has a headache, she's pregnant, his students won't let him leave. . . . Why doesn't he just admit that we are no longer important to him?"

I brought Papa a cup of coffee. "That's not true, Papa. His letters flow with their longing to see us."

Papa snickered. "Purple prose." He rolled his eyes. "A distraught

Constanze is forcibly restrained from running after a friend's carriage that's leaving for Salzburg. Constanze walking around an entire day, holding my portrait to her chest, kissing it over and over." He made a face. "The image is not pleasant. Nor the sentiment real."

I had to agree with him. I sat nearby with my own coffee and biscuit.

Papa waved a hand as another thought materialized. "Then his inane idea of wanting to meet in Munich because he's afraid the archbishop is going to arrest him because he never officially turned in his resignation. Resignation?" Papa laughed and took a sip of coffee. "Humbug! And Wolfgang's position has long been filled." The cup clattered against the saucer. "Will that boy ever understand the world does not revolve around him?"

I did not mention Papa's part in creating that belief. . . .

He picked up the letter and shook it. "And the writing . . . it is quite clear Wolfgang scribbles something at the last moment, probably as the post waits for him. If he truly cared to communicate out of love rather than duty, he would do as I do and write something of interest each day in an orderly fashion, so when it's post day, a letter is ready to be sent."

"At least he writes."

"Either chicken scratches we can barely read, or letters full of wordplay and fancy dalliances that tell us nothing. I get the distinct feeling your brother loves to receive letters but hates to send them."

I opened my mouth to respond but closed it. In truth, I felt the same way. Papa was the only person I had ever known who enjoyed writing letters, who assumed the task as though he were writing for historians' eyes in some future time.

"So," I said, "does he offer a new date for a visit?"

Papa stood, leaving his coffee and the letter behind. "When it suits him."

⁓

I ran into the house, waving the newest letter from Wolfie. "Papa!"

He was with a pupil and looked at me sternly. "Nannerl, you know better than to inter—"

"You're a grandfather!"

Papa just stood there beside the clavier, frozen in the moment. Then the look on his face changed from peeved to pleasant. Even peaceful.

But then he blinked and the façade was broken. "Let me see."

I brought him the letter, putting a hand on the back of his pupil's head, offering a smile.

Papa read aloud, "Congratulations, you are a grandpapa! Yesterday, the seventeenth of June, in this year of our Lord, 1783, at half past six in the morning, my dear wife was safely delivered of a fine sturdy boy, as round as a ball. I have had the child christened Raimund Leopold." Papa found my eyes. "I am a grandpapa."

I pulled him into a hug. "And I am an aunt. Now there's even more reason to arrange a visit!"

"A grandson." Papa's eyes were distant, then suddenly darted back into the moment. "I wonder if he has the long fingers of a fine musician. . . ."

~

On July twenty-ninth, the day before my thirty-second birthday, my dear brother arrived with Constanze.

"But where is little Raimund?" I asked.

Constanze adjusted her bonnet, poking a stray brown curl beneath its brim. "We left him behind."

I looked to Papa. His jaw dropped. "You didn't bring him?"

Wolfie pulled a satchel from the back of the carriage. "He's only six weeks old, Papa, and we only plan to be gone a month. He's much better off with a family friend."

My disappointment was immense. I'd longed to have a baby in the house. If I wasn't ever going to be in a position to have my own babies, at least I could enjoy my brother's.

Wolfie put the satchel down. "Aren't you glad to see *us,* Papa?"

I realized how glum we were. I didn't wait for Papa to answer but picked up the satchel myself. "Of course we are. Come in, come in."

It was not a good beginning.

~

Constanze was . . . agreeable enough. I tried to like her. I wanted to like her. But there was something missing, something . . . off. She laughed a bit too loudly, chattered rather than spoke, appeared unable to discuss anything of higher magnitude than the weather, and clung to Wolfie's arm as if fearful he would disappear into the mountain mist. Or perhaps she held on fearing Papa would bite.

Not that I blamed her. For though Papa was polite, his level of warmth could also be compared to a facet of our beloved mountains: frosty.

We did our best to entertain them. We showed Constanze the sights around Salzburg and included her in our music making—which *was* spectacular and reminded me of old times. Wolfie had brought along new compositions, and we stayed up until the wee hours performing. I admit Constanze's voice was better than mine, which is to say, socially passable but not professionally sound.

One afternoon in October, Constanze lay abed with a headache. I'd planned to use the free time to catch up on some correspondence that I'd horribly neglected while acting as hostess. But just as I sat at my desk, Wolfie appeared in the doorway.

"Hello, Horseface. Care for a walk?"

I felt an eyebrow rise. "Just the two of us?"

He looked toward the hall and lowered his voice. "She's napping."

I put down my quill. We gathered our cloaks and headed out into the crisp fall air.

Wolfie pulled my hand into the crook of his arm. "So, dear Nan. Isn't she wonderful?"

I patted his hand. "She's very sweet."

He bumped his shoulder against mine. "She's much more than that, sister. She's a wildcat."

I glanced in his direction, not sure what he meant.

Wolfie raised and lowered his eyebrows suggestively. "I have absolutely no complaints. In fact, she continues to surprise—"

"Shh! I don't want to hear this."

He seemed genuinely surprised. But then said, "Oh, I'm sorry. I'd forgotten that you haven't . . ." He stopped walking. "Or have you and your dear captain. . . ?"

"No! And he's not my dear captain anymore. You know that."

In the nearly three months since they'd first come to visit, it was the first question Wolfie had asked about my life. Unfortunately it was not one I cared to answer.

"So there's no hope?" he asked.

There was always hope. And in the past two years I'd held on to the dream that God would grant a miracle and the archbishop would change his mind—or die. I hated to admit that I *had* thought of that as a solution to our problem. Franz and I still saw each other as friends and had tailored our relationship into something that was bearable—though hardly satisfactory. But what else could we do?

"Nan?"

"I've found a rhythm to life here."

He pulled at a stray strand of my hair. "I want you to be happy, Nan. Surely there's some other beau here in Salzburg who can take you away from Papa and give you a life."

I shrugged. "My friends have long ago married."

"Then find someone new. You and Papa are constantly entertaining traveling players, so how about one—?"

I shook my head vehemently. "Papa would never approve of such a life for me. The income would be barely passable, and—"

He tossed his hands in the air. "Papa approve. Papa approve." He sighed extravagantly.

I understood his objections. "I have no choice, Wolfie. You know that."

We resumed our walk. "It's because of me, isn't it? Colloredo's hatred of me, and Papa's disappointment in me, has affected your life."

I took the coward's way out and shrugged.

He dropped my arm. "They are both eccentric, twisted, arrogant—"

"Shh!" I checked the other passersby, offering a smile and a nod. But in spite of my cover, if they'd heard Wolfie's words . . . they would be able to guess whom he was talking about. Salzburg was a small town.

Thankfully, Wolfie lowered his voice. "Why don't you and Franz leave? Go off and start on your own like I did."

"I have thought about it. Many times."

"And Franz?"

I turned down a quieter side street, just in case Wolfie's voice rose a second time. "He's a quiet man. Franz avoids confrontation and complication. Considering the archbishop is his employer . . . he'd need references and—"

"He was my employer too, but now I'm free of him."

"Yet it hasn't been easy for you. Admit that, Wolfie. You *have* struggled."

"Money's not everything, Nan."

It was easy for him to make such a declaration when he had multiple sources of income. As a teacher, Franz's options were far more limited. As were mine. And if Papa would die, his pension . . . I tried not to think of it. If Wolfie knew how we'd scrimped in order to entertain him and Constanze the past three months . . . "God's teaching me patience, brother. Something we all could embrace."

Wolfie shook his head adamantly. "Something I refuse to embrace." He giggled. "Something I don't have time to embrace."

Oh, to live in such a fantasy world.

⁓

Wolfie and Constanze were leaving the next day. I was torn over hating to see them go—longing for life to return to normal, while fearing that life *would* return to normal. Yet working toward their departure, I helped as I could by packing Wolfie's music.

Papa stood at the table by the window. "Did you make a copy of this one?" he asked, holding up Wolfie's newest piano sonata in C.

"Yes, Papa, I got it done this morn—"

"Excuse me?" Constanze stood at the door to the music room, her hands busy with each other.

"Yes?" Papa asked, a bit gruffly.

She took a step into the room. "I was wondering if I . . . if we might take . . . might have . . ."

"Yes?"

She took a fresh breath. "We were wondering if we might take with us a few of the tokens, the souvenirs that Wolfie received on his Grand Tour travels and—"

"Absolutely not!" Papa said.

Constanze took a step back into the arch of the doorway. "Why not?"

I had been shocked by her question *and* Papa's answer, but now, for her to challenge him?

"Because they belong here," he said.

"But we have an apartment," she said. "We have a place for them. And since Wolfie earned—"

Papa took a step toward the locked display cabinet that held the gifts from our Grand Tour. "These items are from the trips of the Mozart *family*."

Her voice grew small. "I'm a Mozart now too."

My heart nearly stopped.

Papa hesitated just a moment, then said, "Perhaps at a later date. When you are better established."

My sister-in-law employed her own moment of hesitation. Then with a quick curtsy, she said, "As you wish" and left the room.

I heard Papa's heavy breathing. "That impudent girl!" he hissed.

"She *is* his wife."

He turned away, back to the music. "But not a Mozart. Never a Mozart."

He muttered something more, but I wisely left the room.

～

My hand dropped and Wolfie's letter floated to the floor.

"Not a Mozart. Never a Mozart."

No chance to ever be a Mozart. Not for dear baby Raimund.

I looked in the direction of the music room, where I could hear Papa giving a lesson. He should know.

But not yet. Not just yet. I needed a moment to absorb that the one baby in the Mozart family was dead: *We are both very sad about our poor, bonny, fat, darling little boy.*

Raimund had died soon after Wolfie and Constanze had come for a visit with us in Salzburg. By the time they returned home their dear baby boy had been dead three months. Of dysentery.

Although I knew of this tragic actuality of life—that the majority of babies died—I'd foolishly assumed Raimund was God's blessing to our heritage. He was a little boy who would take the music into the next generation. Nothing would have made Papa happier.

But now . . . no baby for Wolfie. And certainly no baby for me. Just three Mozarts growing ever older.

Old maid. Old maid Nannerl Mozart.

Feeling a sudden shiver, I hugged myself, then shivered again. If God was not merciful, if the Mozart line wasn't blessed through my brother, there would be no one to hug a needy spinster in her old age.

I could think of no crueler fate.

~

Papa could be as obvious as red paint on a door.

We often had people join us for dinner. That was not unusual. Even the name of the guest that came to sup with us that November evening did not raise any concerns: Johann Baptist Berchtold von Sonnenburg. He'd been a friend of the family for many years and was the town manager of tiny St. Gilgen, thirty kilometers east. Our family was familiar with St. Gilgen because it had been Mama's birthplace. Herr Berchtold had duties that ranged from managerial to pastoral to legal. He was married and had fathered eight or nine children—though I wasn't sure how many were still living. My own dear mama had borne seven with only Wolfie and me left alive. . . .

Which brought back thoughts of baby Raimund.

Setting aside my sadness, and armed with this simple knowledge of our guest, I found no significance when Papa said Herr Berchtold was coming to dinner. But as we sat down to table, with Papa grinning as if this man were the emperor himself, I became suspicious. I hadn't seen Papa so delighted and charming in months.

As usual, I played the good hostess. I passed Herr Berchtold the turnips and innocently asked, "And how is your wife? And the children?"

Papa fumbled his spoon. "Oh. Nannerl. Here we must offer our condolences. For Herr Berchtold has recently lost his wife—his second wife. She died after the stillbirth of their second child."

Herr Berchtold crossed himself. "May God rest their souls."

Condolences mingled with anger as I suddenly saw a haze of conspiracy hanging above the dinner. "I'm so sorry," I managed.

"Thank you," Herr Berchtold said. "Jeanette was a jewel among women." He dabbed his mouth with a napkin. "But in spite of my sorrows, I have been blessed with five living children."

Where there had been many more.

"Do you like children, Fraulein Mozart?"

My heart stopped. I stood and collected the bowl of turnips. "If you'll excuse me, I'll replenish these."

When I entered the kitchen, Therese looked up. She saw the bowl. "I could have done that."

"No," I said, spooning more vegetables from the pot on the fire. "It's fine. I'll do it."

"Are you all right?"

Not at all.

"Are you ill?"

Yes. That was it.

I set the bowl on the table. "Actually, I'm *not* feeling well. Headache. Yes, a headache. I think I'll go to my room. Would you give Papa and Herr Berchtold my regrets?"

But when Therese scampered off to share the news, I did not go to my room. I grabbed my cloak and left the house via the back door. I walked around to the square. I had to talk to someone.

I had to talk to Franz.

~

I removed my hand from Franz's arm, needing to express myself with movement as we walked and talked.

"I cannot believe Papa would do such a thing and be so blatant about it." I took a seat on the stone edge of a fountain. "A man who's been twice widowed. A man who has fathered a gaggle of children. A man who has five children now. A man who is so much old—"

I stopped that objection. Although Berchtold was at least fifteen years older than I, Franz was twenty. That could not be an issue.

"What does he do for a living?" Franz asked.

I didn't see how that mattered but answered. "He's the town administrator at St. Gilgen. He doesn't even live here."

Franz sat beside me. "St. Gilgen is not so far. Your father could visit."

I sprang from my seat to face him. "So you have me married off already? So easily?"

Franz moved a pebble with the toe of his shoe. "He must be financially stable for your father to even consider—"

"I don't care about his money!" A woman filling a pitcher with water looked up. I returned to my place beside Franz. "Five children. Two dead wives. St. Gilgen." I shook my head vehemently. "No. It can never be. I won't allow it."

"But perhaps you must."

"Must?"

He pressed his upper arm against mine and risked taking my hand. We burrowed our hands beneath the folds of my cloak, wedged in the space between his leg and mine. "You want children."

"Of course, but I don't need . . . If God does not will it, then I am prepared to accept His decision on the matter," I whispered under my breath. "I have never wished to have just any children. And to have children by a man who's already fathered so many . . ." I shivered. I was not a prude, and in truth, my objection went beyond his fatherhood to the simple fact of his manhood. I had not shared a bedchamber with my parents most of my life without knowing the essence of such things. Yet to be with a man I did not love . . .

"Then there is the issue of money," he said.

"I deplore the issue of money."

He squeezed my hand. "Your father's original objections to *our* marriage was my lack of good income."

"But he gave his permission—as long as the archbishop said it was all right—so it's not Papa's—"

"Your Berchtold has money."

"He's not *my* Berchtold."

"Didn't you tell me that you and your father have been struggling lately? Even with the student boarders you've taken in?"

"Yes, but—"

"And doesn't your father want to retire?"

"He should retire. Daily, I see a new layer wearing thin."

"His health is also an issue. Yet how can he retire when he knows it will leave the two of you with only a pension—which is less than his salary. If you're having trouble getting by now . . ."

I pulled my hand away. "Why are you talking me into this? I don't want to marry Berchtold. I don't want to marry anyone but you."

He hesitated and cleared his throat. "But you can't have me."

I stood and faced him again, my cloak swinging with my movement. "You're giving me up? Completely? Just like that?"

"It's been two years, liebchen."

"It can be twenty years and I wouldn't care."

"Oh, yes you would. And so would I." He sighed and ran his hands up and down his thighs. "You are still young, but I am old. And meek. And poor. Talk as we might, I am not one to take change easily, which means I am staying in Salzburg the rest of my days. You, who have traveled so much, will find a move to St. Gilgen an adventure."

"A torture."

"A new life, in your own home, with your own family."

"His family, not mine."

"You will have children one day. You will be a good mother. You will survive, Nan. You will thrive."

I shook my head. I would not do either of these things.

Franz stood. "I must go. And so must you." He kissed my cheek and walked away.

Just like that.

I wanted to call after him. I wanted to run after him. But with the square full of people, I could not. Hang propriety! Hang gossip! Hang this horrid town!

Perhaps I *should* leave. It would serve them right.

I walked back to the house and went inside the way I'd left. I would sneak into my room and feign the headache that had set me free of the dinner with—

I started as I saw Papa sitting at the kitchen table. "Sneaking in and out does not become you, Nannerl."

I'd been doing a lot of sneaking lately. Years of sneaking. For ever since Franz had received a no from the archbishop, my excuse for seeing him beyond social occasions had been gone. We'd often met at church. . . . How hard it was not to hold his hand in public. Yet if we'd been seen there would have been repercussions. For we were hiding not only from the wrath of Papa but also from the wrath of Colloredo. If word got back to him that we were ignoring his wishes and still seeing each other . . . both Papa and Franz would have paid dearly.

I removed my cloak, my thoughts reeling. "I thought fresh air would be more advantageous to my headache than lying down."

"A new remedy you've recently adopted?"

I hung my cloak on a peg. "I feel much better."

"You ruined the dinner party, Nannerl. Soon after your departure, respectful of my concern for you, Johann took his leave."

"You should not have been concerned. It was just a headache, and I'm fine now."

"Hmm."

I looked around the kitchen, hoping there was something with which to busy myself, but Therese had already cleaned up. I took down a hanging pan and wiped some water off its back.

"So," Papa said, "did you like him?"

I nearly dropped the pan. I'd expected him to be more discreet, to at least pretend it was just a dinner. For him to blatantly reveal his matchmaking . . .

"Johann's going to be a baron one day. So you would be a baroness."

I hugged the pan to my chest. "I have no desire to be a baroness."

"But if it is offered you. As a gift . . ."

I closed my eyes a moment, hoping this would prove to be a bad dream.

"He's willing to marry you, Nannerl."

Willing to marry me? I thought of another tack. "He just wants a mother for his five children. He needs a housekeeper."

"And you want children and your own house."

I showed him my back as I rehung the pot. "I teach plenty of children. I don't need my own. And I have a house. Here. With you." But my thoughts sped back to Wolfie's dead child and the lingering fear that the Mozart line would die.

"He lives in the house where your dear mother was born," Papa said.

"What?"

"In St. Gilgen. He lives in the house where your mother was born, where she spent the first four years of her life. If that is not a sign that God is behind all this . . ."

I knew the house. It was a nice house. Not the home of a baron, but nicer than our home here. Perhaps it *was* a sign. "You're moving too fast, Papa. Has Herr Berchtold specifically asked—?"

"He has."

I felt my jaw drop. "He barely knows me."

"He's been at the house many times, and at concerts we've attended. Surely you remember?"

Vaguely. He'd been one of a crowd and had not stood out in my mind. For one, he'd been married. For another, he was not a handsome man. His nose was even larger than the generous noses of our own Mozart line; his eyes were even wider set, and his mouth was oddly shaped, especially when he talked. His voice had a slightly nasal tone that made him sound as if he suffered perpetually from congestion. In his favor was the fact that his physique was not repulsive. At least he wasn't fat.

I suddenly realized that my thoughts had entered a place of rationalization, as if I were truly considering . . . I put a hand to my head, feeling the onset of a real headache. "If that's all this evening, I *am* feeling the need to lie down."

He rose from the chair. "No more fresh air?"

I studied his face a moment, wondering how much he knew of my outing. "No. No more fresh air."

With a hand to my arm, he leaned down and kissed my cheek. "You've always been the loyal one, dear girl. The one person who saw the larger picture. Sleep well."

I would not. I could not.

I did not.

~

Johann Berchtold was a persistent man. After the first dinner party, he insinuated himself into our lives, in person when in Salzburg and through letters when he returned to St. Gilgen. He *did* write a wonderful letter. . . .

Johann's determination, along with Franz's subtle withdrawal, wore down my defenses as well as my objections. Just as Papa had mentioned Wolfie's persistence regarding his desire to marry Constanze, the combined efforts of Johann, Franz, and Papa had their desired effect.

A few months later, when Johann proposed, my defenses had long been chipped away and were held together by only the thinnest splinter. My reasons for saying no had shown themselves to be self-centered. If I married Johann, he would gain a wife, his children would gain a mother, I would gain security as well as a chance to bear my own children for the Mozart line, and my father would gain peace of mind, knowing I would be taken care of after he was gone. If I said no simply because I did not love the man . . . It seemed a petty reason, all in all.

If anything, it angered me that I'd even been put in such a position. To be forced into marriage for survival's sake had to be against God's intentions to love one another.

But what if there was no love?

Through our extended travels I'd witnessed countless members of royalty who'd endured arranged marriages for the sake of king and country. Although patently unfair, I could understand that process. It was the price of the crown.

But for us of lesser rank . . . sometimes I wished I were really poor, a farmer's daughter working in the field. A washerwoman at the pump. From my observations these people often managed to marry for love. Their choice of a mate was limited to those of like standing—it was rare for them to marry "up"—but when they did unite, genuine happiness was present. Perhaps because they were more resigned to their lot and not so concerned about attaining any improvement in status, they could capture and hold on to a state of contentment.

As the months passed during Johann's courtship, I too became resigned to the idea that contentment—of some measure—was the ultimate goal. And if one had to achieve that state by giving up a few previously held dreams, or by adjusting one's expectations of bliss and utter happiness, then so be it. I was no longer a child. I knew the world was a pragmatic place. Romance lived in the borderland. Romance was the stuff of fairy tales.

And so, when Johann proposed, I accepted.

May God be with us all.

~

Things moved quickly—at my request. I was fearful I would change my mind, so once the marriage contract was signed (Papa scraped together five hundred florins for me to bring into the marriage, and Johann promised a thousand florins, with an additional five hundred as *Morgengabe*—my monetary reward for being a virgin), Papa made an application with the archbishop to speed everything up. Which he did. We planned to be married on August 23, 1784.

As good a day as any.

I knew I shouldn't feel that way. But as I stood before the mirror in the hall and tied my bonnet I could feel nothing else. Tying that bonnet was likely my last act as a single woman in our home on Hannibalplatz, for I was just moments away from getting into the carriage that would take me to St. Gilgen and the rest of my life. Previously, Franz had said *he* didn't take change well and had intimated that *I* did.

I did not.

I'd lived in Salzburg thirty-three years. I knew how the looming fortress on the hill looked in all four seasons and with every kind of sunlight or cloud cover God could provide. I had watched the ice come and go on the Salzach River and loved the way it crunched and broke to be swept away in the current; I enjoyed the curved plantings of red begonias in the Mirabel Gardens and loved walking around the fountains with my friends. I knew the shortcuts to church, and which coffeehouse served the best cake. There was not a day that went by where I did not stop and chat with someone on the street as if we'd known each other our entire lives.

Which we had.

I was rejuvenated by the smell of fresh grass and greenery when I'd seek solace in the mountains nearby. And while coming back from an errand, I loved hearing music emanating from both our home and from Holy Trinity in the square across the way.

Holy Trinity. Where Franz worked.

I shook my head, willing the thought away. I had to stop thinking of him.

It would be a daily battle.

Papa appeared in the opened front door. "The coach is waiting, Nannerl."

I nodded once and moved to join him. But at the last moment, I hesitated in the arched doorway leading to this home I loved. I would return, but things would never be the same.

Unable to speak, I whispered good-bye to the walls, then hurried away.

A few minutes later Papa held my hands through the window of the carriage. "I will see you tomorrow at the wedding. So many of your friends are coming to join you, Nannerl. You should be very pleased."

"Any word from Wolfie?" I asked.

"He's busy, dear one. You know that."

I knew that. Although my brother's letter writing had deteriorated to a deplorable infrequency, last we'd heard he was working on a string quartet. He had more important things to do than attend a wedding. We'd grown apart through distance, busyness, his marriage, and our different attitudes about life in general. It grieved me.

Papa spoke to the driver. "Carry on." To me he said, "Safe journey."

I withdrew into the compartment. Although I knew I should probably remain at the window in order to take in every detail of Salzburg as I left it for the final time as Nannerl Mozart, I could not.

But suddenly . . . "Whoa!"

The carriage stopped abruptly.

Franz appeared at my window. "Franz? What are you doing?"

He pushed an envelope through the window and into my hands. Then he took a step back and waved the driver on. I leaned out the window, needing to see him. He stood by the side of the square, staring after me. Then he kissed his fingers and raised them in a wave.

I returned the gesture and held my hand erect—as did he—until the carriage pulled us away from each other's sight.

No, no, no, no, no. Go back! I can't do this!

"Are you all right, Fraulein?" asked the woman in the seat across from me.

No, I wasn't. But I managed a nod and sat back in my seat, seeking the shadows.

"Someone obviously cares for you very much," she said, nodding at the letter.

"Yes." It was all I could say.

"Well?" she said. "Aren't you going to read it?"

A part of me wanted to rip open the seal and absorb every word. But the other part sensed what it might say and knew the words would break my heart even further.

"Go on," the woman said. "I have knitting to do. I won't bother you." She pulled out her needles and yarn and averted her eyes.

I broke the seal and unfolded the single page. Franz's lovely cursive graced the paper like artwork on a canvas. His words were just as eloquent: *To my beloved Nannerl. I will always love you. Someday, in God's providence, we will be together once again. Your loving Franz.*

I held the letter to my breast. And began to cry.

What had I done?

When I arrived at the home in St. Gilgen that had once been my mother's, Johann helped me out of the carriage and kissed my cheek. "Welcome," he said. "Welcome to your new home."

It was not my home. It was not my family.

But like it or not, it was now my life.

I willed myself to smile. "Thank you."

He pulled my hand into the crook of his elbow and patted it. "My city offices are on the main floor, but come upstairs to the living quarters and meet my children. Our children."

My body moved up the stairs, but my mind remained on the street, stunned by the finality of this truth. Tomorrow was my wedding day and I would become a mother—*the* mother—of five children.

Then suddenly they were before me in the entrance hall, lined in a row, wiggling and squirming. Their eyes flitted over me, taking me in. Who was this new mama of theirs?

"Hello, children," I said. The oldest, named Maria Anna like me, was a girl of thirteen. Beside her stood four boys aged ten to two. The oldest boy was Wolfgang, Joseph was seven, then Johann Baptist the younger, aged four, and finally little Karl.

They each bowed or curtsied and murmured a greeting, although my husband-to-be's namesake looked me right in the eye and said, "My mother's dead."

I glanced at Johann, expecting him to admonish the child. He did not.

I noticed Maria's face was dirty, there was a distinctly unclean odor in the air, and the boys' clothes were rumpled and torn. Had they been left to run wild since their mother—mothers—had died? There was a certain caged-animal aura to the room. . . .

Joseph raised a hand. "Is the music thing that was delivered yours?"

My heart leaped. As a wedding present Papa had promised me one of those new pianofortes. "It came?"

"Yesterday," Johann said. "Though we really don't have room for—"

"Where is it?" I asked. I immediately realized I'd been rude and offered Johann a smile. "Forgive my excitement. May I see it?"

Maria said, "I'll show you."

She led me into a front parlor, which was bathed in sunshine. The rugs on the floor were worn, the arm on one of the chairs was missing, and the pictures on the wall were cockeyed, but none of that mattered. There, in the corner, sat a new pianoforte. Not an old-fashioned clavichord or harpsichord like those I'd learned upon but a new invention with foot pedals to control the volume, and keys that offered a more pronounced and powerful sound.

"It plays," Joseph said.

I put my hand on the back of his head. "I'm so glad."

"Why don't you play something for us," Johann said.

I sat on the bench and took a moment to lightly stroke the lovely ivory keys. Then, as if they had a mind of their own, my fingers found their place and began. I played one of my brother's pieces, one he'd written long ago for my name day. He'd said the lively movement of the eighth notes was his way of portraying the light in my eyes when I was happy.

I closed my eyes to capture the memory of his words and let the music take over. The sound I received was deeper, more mellow than that of other instruments. And the way the pedals let me sustain a note beyond the pressing of finger to key . . .

Too soon the song came to an end. The notes tried to linger in the air but were doomed to fall away. I opened my eyes and saw a dozen eyes looking back at me.

"That was pretty," Maria said.

Joseph put a hand on top of the instrument. "I want to learn to play like that. You'll teach me, won't you?"

I took my first deep breath of St. Gilgen air. "Yes, children. I will teach you all."

~

I was allowed private time to unpack. Although I would sleep in another room that night—the night before our wedding—Johann had instructed me to unpack the bulk of my possessions in his bedchamber. Which would become our bedchamber.

It was a lovely room, larger than even Papa's room back in Salzburg. But as I ran my hand over the carving on the wardrobe that was to hold my dresses, as I picked up the porcelain figurine of a robin, as I admired the lace edging on a doily, I couldn't help but remember that these things had been used by two other women before me. Johann had been married to Maria for ten years. She had borne him nine children, dying after the birth of the ninth. The four oldest surviving children were her doing. Fifteen months after her death he had married his beloved Jeanette, who had borne him one son, Karl, before dying at the birth of another.

She'd died just sixteen months ago. Now it was my turn.

I shivered. I was doing a lot of shivering lately, as if my body was trying to adapt to this odd combination of expectation and reality. I opened the satchel that had been placed on the bed. I removed a carefully wrapped packet. Three seashells fell onto the mattress.

I picked them up one at a time and placed them in the palm of my hand as if they were precious gems. For they were precious to me. These were the shells I'd plucked from the ocean at Calais on our Grand Tour. I closed my eyes and remembered how the tide had teased my toes, forcing me to run away, only to be drawn back to its edge. In many ways the shells meant more to me than all the golden snuff boxes in the world, for they were symbolic of both my crossing over from one country to the next, and my crossing from childhood to young womanhood.

I'd been on the edge of a new experience then. And now I was at the edge of another.

I carefully placed the shells on the bedside table where I could see them every morning when I woke.

Beside my husband.

Oh my.

~

The wedding ceremony was a blur. The reception afterward was populated by many people I did not know. I feared I would never remember their names.

Only the smiling face of Papa got me through. He was the one constant, the one glue that linked my past, my present, and my future. To see him happy in the day made me seek happiness too.

And I was happy. I was determined to be happy. For what good would come from regrets or could-have-beens? This path I'd chosen, *I'd* chosen. Although the circumstances of life had been instrumental in bringing me to this moment, I could have remained in my father's house forever. I would have gotten by—even after his death. Yet to choose that life of utter loneliness when a life in a teeming home full of husband and children was available to me . . .

It would have been foolhardy to choose the former. This was the better way. For in this choice lived hope and movement and a continuation of more eighth notes portraying the light in my eyes.

I would make this work. I would.

~

The wedding night was . . . difficult. Although I deserved the extra five hundred florins I'd received for being a virgin, I wasn't totally ignorant. My married friends had shared some of their experiences. I knew the basics of how it should work.

And Johann was kind. Very kind.

But as I lay beside him my mind slipped back to Salzburg, back to Franz, back to dreams that had to remain dead and buried. This was my life now. This was my husband.

With God's help it would get better. The Almighty would help me be a good wife.

My life depended on it.

~

I awakened with a start. Lying on my side I saw four-year-old Johann standing by the bed. From my place on the high mattress, our eyes were nearly level. With a glance over my shoulder, I was mindful of my new husband asleep beside me. "What's wrong?" I whispered.

"I'm scared."

As my eyes focused in the moonlight, I saw the glisten of tears on his cheeks. I didn't know the usual procedure in the Berchtold household regarding bad dreams and frightened children, but I did note little Johann had chosen to come to my side of the bed instead of the side of his father.

While I was pondering all this, the boy snuggled his cheek against the mattress just inches away from my head. He smelled a little too much like busy boy. Tomorrow I would give instructions regarding baths and the washing of teeth. But until then . . .

I lifted the covers. He looked at my eyes, asking permission. "Come in," I said.

He climbed onto the bed and I lowered the covers. He scooted toward me, pressing his back into my torso. I wrapped my arm around him, pulling him tight and safe, two spoons fitting one to another.

Once he was settled and still, I whispered into his ear. "Better?"

He nodded.

And it was.

Chapter Sixteen

St. Gilgen was my wilderness, marriage my trap, and the children . . .

I knew it wasn't right that I often thought of my stepchildren as wild beasts, but that's how they acted. Yet could one blame them? From the moment Maria was born until little Karl, death had occupied this house. Eleven children had been born. Six had died. The first mother died in childbirth (no doubt worn out from having nine babies in ten years), and then a few years later, the next passed away. Both women gave their lives in the quest to fulfill their duty to propagate the earth. The children's father was often withdrawn and uninvolved, and I wondered if it was his way of dealing with grief. Or was he simply overwhelmed with the responsibilities of providing for such a troupe?

My first order of business had to do with hygiene. The day after the wedding I made sure the children had baths and knew how to wash their teeth and comb their own hair. I swept through their bedchambers, gathering all their clothes, determining which ones needed mending and which should be assigned to the rag bin.

"But that's my favorite skirt," Maria complained.

"We'll get you a new one," I said.

She shook her head. "Papa won't approve."

Her comment ignited my doubts, for Johann and I had not gone over the household budget. Yet I maintained my resolve. "Don't worry. I will convince him."

She continued to shake her head.

At dinner that night, with five clean faces and fifty clean fingers at the table, I was faced with my next challenge.

After grace was said in a quick murmur that defied translation, after I'd filled each plate with sauerbraten, bread, and potatoes, seven-year-old Joseph scooped some potatoes into his mouth—with his hand. And Wolfgang, aged ten, chewed his bread with his mouth completely open, making the most horrid sight and sound. My patience was sorely tested when Maria slurped her drink noisily and wiped the drip on her chin with the back of her hand.

"Enough!" I said, putting my fork down.

They all froze, including Johann. "There is a problem?" my husband asked.

I covered the racing of my heart by adjusting the napkin in my lap. "There is."

"Can we eat?" little Johann asked.

"No, you may not," I said. "Not until you show some manners."

"Hun-gee!" yelled two-year-old Karl.

"Let them eat, Nannerl," Johann said. "I have work to do."

Identifying their father as their savior, the children all started whining and talking at once. Their cacophony was silenced when I pushed my chair back and stood. I looked at my husband. "May I speak with you in the other room, please?"

Johann had the audacity to swipe his bread through the juice of his meat. "Not now, Nannerl, I—"

"Now."

He looked across the table at me, and it took all my will not to sit back down and accept the piggish condition of my new family—or run from the room in total defeat. I hesitated, but in that hesitation realized that my next action would determine much more than a civil dinner table.

To my surprise, Johann stood. "I find this ridiculous."

He could find it whatever he pleased, as long as I had his ear. As I walked into the parlor, I felt a nervous tingle up my spine. Would he follow?

He did. "I don't have time for this."

I hid my shaking hands in the folds of my skirt. "I know you don't. That's one reason I'm here. Yes?"

"Well, yes, I suppose—"

I took strength in his concession. "As their mother, it is my job to teach the children the basics of life, from bathing to proper ways of addressing one another to being able to eat with table manners that would be acceptable in anyone's home—in the home of the emperor himself."

Johann snickered. "I doubt my children will ever—"

"Our children."

He blinked. And in that blink, I knew I'd won.

"May I have free rein?" I asked.

Johann turned back toward the dining room. "Do what you need to do."

~

The children did not particularly like me those first few months. The poor dears. Yet as we addressed the niceties of life one by one, as we turned chaos into order, they came to respect me. The love would come later.

I hoped.

It was no wonder Johann had wanted to marry me. I could do something of the utmost importance: I could help. Yet any good woman could have done what I attempted to do. At first I wondered why Johann didn't simply hire a governess to help the cook, chambermaid, and undermaid. But as time passed, as I observed the failings and severe limitations of these three servants, as I met the people who populated the work force in the area, I realized that finding a wife was probably easier than finding good help. In their defense, the people of St. Gilgen were salt-of-the-earth people who fished on the lake—the Abersee—or worked in the salt industry or in the glassworks, or catered to the pilgrimage trade that came through on their way to St. Wolfgang's a few kilometers away. But I could also recognize that the main reason they were a coarse people had to do with education, which they sorely lacked—and for which they showed little respect.

St. Gilgen did not even have a real school. Twenty-some children met in the cobbler's home and in the upper floor of the house next door: boys in one location, girls in the other. They were taught only the most elementary level of catechism, reading, writing, and arithmetic.

The biggest hurdle to getting them a decent education was the absence of a full-time teacher. The man who held the job of sexton taught when he had time. Which he didn't have much of because his duties of caring for the devotional vessels of the church and selling religious artifacts took priority. As a result, the classes were unreliable. Often when the teacher was available, the children were scattered. It was a shameful arrangement.

Yet what teacher in their right mind would accept the position? Who would want to live in tiny St. Gilgen with its one church, three inns, public bathhouse (where blood was let and teeth pulled), and a Saturday market that only offered the basic essentials?

I was constantly having to write to Papa, begging him to shop for me in Salzburg. We kept the woman who traveled between our towns selling glassware busy with our weekly letters and trade. And despite what Johann said, I was never extravagant in my requests. I truly needed mustard, vegetables, books, lemons, candles, lard, and various items of clothing. The children's shoes were deplorable, and I traced their feet and had some felt shoes made in Salzburg. Papa did his best to spend our money wisely, but one kreuzer was one too many kreuzers to Johann, and I hated having to question Papa about the costs on my husband's behalf. The entire financial process did nothing to increase Johann's reputation in my father's eyes.

As far as my reputation in the eyes of my children? The littlest one, Karl, was always on my hip. To him, I was instantly Mama. The other three boys were more concerned with wrestling one another and with what was being served for dinner to take much mind of me. The one I best hoped to befriend was the oldest, Maria, who was just thirteen. Perhaps I felt a kinship with her because we shared the same given name; perhaps I felt an empathy for her because I knew she, like myself, had been forced to assume too much responsibility too soon. So it was Maria whom I first invited to partake of keyboard lessons.

One afternoon, after being there four months, I made sure the boys were occupied elsewhere. It was an exceptionally warm winter day, and I told them to go play in the garden near the lake right outside our door. Only then did I call Maria into the front room, to the pianoforte. I closed the doors behind us, turned, and smiled at her. "So," I said.

"Did I do something wrong?" she asked.

I blinked but understood the precedent in her question. "Not at all. I simply wondered if you would like to begin your lessons."

She looked at the piano as if it could reach out and grab her. "On that?"

That was my savior here in the wilderness. If I had not gotten into the habit of playing its lovely keys for a few hours every day, I would surely have jumped into the lake and willingly sunk to its bottom. My hope was that I could teach the children how to play well enough to perform duets. I simply had to create some kind of musical community here. I'd already discovered that most of the local musicians who played at weddings and dances had learned the folk tunes by rote and were incapable of reading a note. They would do me no good whatsoever.

I put my hands on her shoulders and moved her to the bench, pressing her to sit. "This is a very lovely instrument that can open the world to you."

She looked up at me, her brow furrowed. As if she didn't understand the term "world"?

"At your age I was playing in London and Paris for royalty. I played for kings, queens, and emperors, and spoke to them as I am speaking to you now."

"Where's London?"

I tried to contain my shock. "In England."

Her face remained blank.

"Northwest of here." I pointed out the window.

She nodded. "Oh."

We'd tackle geography some other day. . . . I pushed down middle C. "This is where we begin. C. All the keys have a name. The white keys are named A through G, then it starts over again." I began playing a C scale.

"I know some of my alphabet," she said proudly. "I know to R pretty good but get mixed up toward the end."

My hopes for a musical partner crumbled.

The boys ran past the window, and Maria jumped from her seat to see their ruckus. "They're chasing the chickens. They'll get them mad and they won't lay. Can I go?"

I merely nodded. *Go. Leave me alone.*

The front door slammed, and Maria's voice joined those of her brothers. Little Karl screamed and a chicken squawked. I didn't move but remained in the presence of my savior.

Then I silently prayed to my other Savior. *Save me, Lord. Please save me.*

~

I sat down to play Wolfie's newest concerto that Papa had sent me. But with the first chord, I cringed. I checked my fingers. Yes, they were hitting the right notes. The problem was not the pianist but the piano.

Soon after coming to St. Gilgen, I was horrified to realize my pianoforte did not react well to our damp house on the lake. It quickly fell out of tune and the keys often stuck. And worse, there was no one in the area who could fix it. Papa said he'd send someone from Salzburg, but since the archbishop's instruments needed to be tuned three times a week—Tuesday, Thursday, and Sunday for performances—and since the mountain roads to St. Gilgen were impassable most of the year due to rain or snow, and since it took six hours to get to this hamlet by foot *or* carriage (meaning the tuner would have to stay overnight), and since mine was the only piano in the area . . .

It didn't help my mood when Papa seemed to abandon me by going to visit Wolfie in Vienna for months on end. I heard tales of Wolfie having his own pianoforte hand-carried from house to house almost nightly in order to perform. He'd even had it fitted with a special bass pedal. Wolfie was doing quite well and was the toast of the town. Papa went on and on about their lovely apartment with its elaborate furnishings, the lavish dinners, his delight in his new grandchild, Karl, who was nearly eight months old, and of course his high praise of Wolfie's music.

All this while here I sat, a prisoner in St. Gilgen, with my one solace, my one retreat ruined by the idiosyncrasies of my very own home. Yes, I envied Wolfie his instrument, but I also envied his music. When I'd lived in Salzburg, I'd often heard Papa mourn not having the opportunity to hear Wolfie play. Now I felt the even greater loss of not hearing music of *any* sort. I had been banished to a silent oblivion.

Silent of music, that is. There was always plenty of noise assailing my ears. The children did not embrace silence. Ever. And as far as sitting them down to try to work on their education? They had trouble concentrating for more than a few seconds at a time. Perhaps they'd never been required to do so?

How could I—who'd been brought up memorizing intricate compositions from an early age—relate to children far past that age who had trouble remembering the very simplest school lesson they'd been taught the day before?

There was an even bigger issue at stake. How could one love what one did not particularly like?

I closed the lid on the piano's keyboard. I was tired of challenges, of struggles, of being dissatisfied. I wanted to go home.

And I had. Four times Johann and I had returned to Salzburg for a visit. Sometimes Papa had been there, sometimes he hadn't. In fact, two times we'd returned to Salzburg only to find Papa had extended his visit in Vienna. Each time when I locked up the empty house on Hannibalplatz to return to St. Gilgen, I worried that Wolfie was winning Papa over, luring him to stay in Vienna. Why else would Papa risk losing his job at his age? All my pleading for him to return to Salzburg produced little effect. Not that I could blame him.

I heard the glass lady outside and ran to the door hoping for a letter or a parcel from Papa. She stopped, lowered the long handles of the cart, and stood erect, arching her back. "Nothing, Frau Berchtold. He weren't there this week neither. You got something for me to take to him?"

I ignored the package of fish I'd wrapped. There was no reason to send it now. "Nothing," I said.

The woman lifted the handles and started to walk away, shaking her head. "I sure wish your father would get back. This current arrangement ain't doing me a bit o' good."

I agreed with her completely.

~

The post brought better news. A letter from Vienna said that Papa planned to be home in mid-May, which was the following week. Unfortunately, the desire to see me had not been the draw. Apparently the archbishop had given him an ultimatum to return or his salary would be stopped (Papa had received six weeks' leave but had been gone fourteen). Leave it to money to be the propelling force for Papa's actions.

Whatever the reason, my plan was to be there when he returned. But to justify one more trip to Salzburg would be difficult. Johann was a busy man. And once in Salzburg, assured that Papa would be there, I wanted to stay at least a week.

I ventured downstairs into no man's land—or certainly no woman's—my husband's chancellery offices. He'd made it very clear he was never to be disturbed. On Tuesdays he often heard cases regarding breaches of law (he'd had an especially scandalous case of fornication last week where I'd heard the people arguing all the way upstairs). Who knew what he'd been asked to handle this week? Swearing, poaching, working on Sundays? I was just glad the more serious cases were sent to a Salzburg court. I did not want my husband having to deal with murders or witchcraft.

I tentatively made my way into the front office. The clerk, Rolf, looked up. The way his eyebrows rose revealed his surprise and discomfort. "Frau Berchtold?"

"I need to speak to my husband."

Rolf glanced toward the main meeting room beyond the doorway. "He's getting ready for a hearing."

I mustered as much authority as I was owed—which was minimal. "It's important."

After the slightest hesitation, he pushed away from the desk and went into the meeting room, closing the door behind him. I heard their voices. A few moments later, Johann came out, his brow furrowed. "Really, Nannerl. You know this is not appropriate."

I took his hand and led him into an office that archived the paper work of the region. "I am sorry to disturb you, but I have just received word that Papa is returning next week, and I want to be there when he gets back, and—"

"We've already been to Salzburg twice thinking he was going to return. A total waste of time. Your father's rudeness . . ." He shook his head. We'd had arguments about this before. "We were also there in September and at Christmas. I have an important job to do here, Nannerl. I cannot simply leave on a whim to visit your fath—"

"You're going to be a father again yourself," I said.

I had not meant to blurt it out like that and, in fact, had not even considered making it a reason to visit Salzburg now. But once it came out, I immediately saw the advantage.

I waited for Johann to take me in his arms.

He did not.

"Did you hear—?"

"I heard. There will be another mouth to feed."

I felt tears threaten but held them in. Johann did not respond well to tears.

"How far along?"

"About four months," I said. It was my closest determination. Just recently I'd seen a change in my body and had felt the oddest fluttering inside like a butterfly flapping its wings from within. I remembered Mama telling me about such signs. "I want Papa to know as soon as possible. Nothing will make *him* happier."

"He will certainly be pleased. As will the archbishop."

I could have cared a fig about the archbishop, yet indirectly, he *was* Johann's boss.

With a sigh Johann said, "I suppose we can go."

I ventured to bring up an alternative I knew would not be taken easily. "I *could* go alone," I said. "Since you're so busy."

He seemed to consider it a moment, then said, "I cannot have

you traversing those mountain roads in your condition, alone. I will
have to go with you."

"But the children. . . ?" I really did not want the children to go
this time. "I would prefer to tell Papa the news in a more . . . more
tranquil setting."

Johann studied me. Then he said, "We'll have the children go
stay with my brother."

A journey with one husband, no children, and one baby growing inside me. It would have to do.

The point was, I was going home.

~

Going home was easier said than done. The weather had been
rainy and we got stuck on one of the mountain passes, with the
carriage collapsing into the mud four times. Some farmers pulled us
out, but the six-hour trip turned to nine. Yet even with that we got
to Hannibalplatz before Papa. Our shoes and clothes were muddy,
and I had to lay them over chairs so they could dry and be brushed
off in the morning. Dear Therese made us some soup and coffee
before we fell into bed.

Since there was no way for us to know exactly when Papa
would arrive, I didn't want to stray far from the house. Luckily,
Johann did not feel this need and spent our free days out and about
Salzburg doing . . . whatever. I was glad for the solitude. A few
friends heard I was home, and I quickly recaptured a bit of the
camaraderie I'd sorely missed.

Yet there was one particular person I really wanted to see.
Unfortunately, it was not proper for me to go to him. . . .

Blessedly, I didn't have to. On our second day home, an hour
after Johann had disappeared into the streets of Salzburg, Franz
d'Ippold came to visit. It was the first time we'd seen each other
since I'd left in the carriage heading to my wedding day, since he'd
given me the note I would always cherish.

He bowed in the opened door. "Welcome home, Nan. Frau
Berchtold."

"Nan," I said, offering him a curtsy. Our eyes met. "To you,
always Nan."

I felt such a connection with him, as if more than air filled the space between us, as if something tangible swelled and danced and vibrated there.

He looked past me toward the entry hall. "Has your father returned from Vienna?"

"Not yet. We expect him any day."

"Is your husband here?"

"He's gone out."

The boundaries had been set. Franz could not come inside. "Perhaps we could walk?" he suggested.

"That would be lovely."

I found my shawl and joined him outside. He helped me adjust it over my shoulders, and we took up the route we'd taken dozens of times before. He asked about St. Gilgen, and I started to tell him a rosy version of my life there.

The lies didn't last long. They couldn't. Not with Franz. "None of that is true," I finally said. "I'm miserable there. The children run amuck, they are uneducated and show absolutely no penchant for wanting to change that condition, they have not been taught the most basic rules of daily hygiene, the servants are lazy and dirty in their own right, as well as rude, and my new pianoforte is horribly out of tune and I can't get anyone to come fix it."

I hadn't meant to say all this in one breath. I laughed with embarrassment.

Franz did not.

"I'm sorry," I said. "That was quite a list."

He stopped walking and faced me. "Is there no light, Nan?"

I started to answer "Of course there is" but realized if pressed it would be hard . . .

Yet the way his cheeks drooped with concern, the way his eyes peered into mine seeking hope . . . I knew I must come up with something positive to say.

"I am with child."

His face skirted shock, flickered with dismay, then locked on happiness. He took my hands and kissed both my cheeks. "Oh, Nan. I am so happy for you. A child of your own! You will make a wonderful mother."

Not wanting to see his eyes, I took his arm and began to walk again. "But I'm not a good mother, Franz. I have been given the care of five children and am failing miserably."

"They were set in their ways. That's what makes it difficult. Don't blame yourself for a previous lifetime of neglect. And surely, with one of your own . . ."

I wasn't so sure. "Even assuming I am the best mother in the world—which I know I'm not—the conditions at St. Gilgen, the lack of proper help, the ignorance and level of distrust toward any sort of education . . . there is more than mountain and lake holding those people down."

"Perhaps they know nothing else. 'All I know is I know nothing.'"

Let Socrates speak for the past. The present and future were not so pliable. "If only they realized they know nothing. They take no issue with ignorance, for it is their norm."

"And this frustrates you, a woman of education and experience."

I did not want to seem haughty. "I have spoken at length with Johann about this, but he . . ." I shook my head, not wanting to remember Johann's repeated response, nor share it. "I am frustrated, Franz. Frustrated beyond comprehension."

"I can see that."

I put my hand over my belly. "I fear for my child's future."

"As you should."

"If only he or she could be brought up here."

His voice lightened. "Would your husband agree to a move?"

I laughed. "He considers St. Gilgen the gem of the world. His family roots are deep—and stubborn. He will not move."

Franz patted my arm. "Then I will pray for you. For you and the child you carry. Just know that I am here for you. Always."

I knew that. I knew that he was here.

And I was not.

～

I had planned to ease into the news with Papa. I'd welcome him home, have Therese serve a nice dinner, get him comfortable sitting with Johann by the fire, pipe in hand, all warm and content. But as soon as I heard Papa enter the house all plans were forgotten. I ran to him, wrapped my arms around his neck, and pronounced, "I am with child, Papa. I am expecting a child!"

It took him a moment to recover from my exuberant greeting and comprehend my words. But I knew he'd achieved both when he beamed and hugged me close, lifting me off of the floor. "Oh, dear girl. Nothing could make me happier." He let go. "When?"

"Late summer. Perhaps August."

He held me at arm's length and looked at my midsection. "You are not showing yet." Only Papa could get away with such a blatant observation.

"My clothes are tight," I offered.

"And will get tighter!" He put his arm around my shoulders. "And where is your husband so I might congratulate him?"

"On errands."

He handed me his hat and hung his cloak on a hook near the door. "He leaves you alone when you're in this condition?"

"Papa, I don't mind. Really." I hoped the double entendre was evident.

It was. He gave me a pointed look.

I looked away. "Come inside and tell me the news of Vienna. I want to hear everything."

~

I was happy to hear that Wolfie's decision *not* to seek a permanent position had worked out for him and that he was being allowed time to write what he loved most: opera. And yet, this good news also frustrated me. Wolfie had done everything wrong and had gone against all Papa's advice. Yet by doing so he'd broken free of Salzburg and Archbishop Colloredo, lived in one of the cultural centers of the world, spent his days hearing applause for his work, and had married the woman he loved.

I had done everything Papa had told me to. I had been the good child, the obedient child. Yet I had been yanked *from* Salzburg and imprisoned in a town that was devoid of culture. I'd given up the man I loved, married a man I didn't, spent my days dealing with chaos, heard only yells and complaints for all my hard work, and ached in body and soul for the sound of good music and the opportunity to play it.

"You've stopped listening, Nannerl," Papa said.

He was right. "I'm sorry. My mind is elsewhere. I do want to hear. Really I do."

He set his coffee on the table next to his chair and leaned toward me, putting a hand on my knee. "There is something I must talk to you about. A plan I've made."

I cringed, anticipating his permanent defection. "Yes?"

"Wolfgang has asked me—repeatedly—to move to Vienna. To leave my position here."

My heart sank. My fears gained legs. "When do you leave?"

"I'm not going."

It took me a moment. "What?"

He sat back in his chair. "I must admit I was tempted. Very tempted. But I will also admit my concerns about Wolfgang's lifestyle."

"He appears to be living a high life."

"Which cannot last."

"But you said his success grows larger."

Papa shrugged. "Audiences and nobility are notoriously fickle, as is fame and fortune. I fear your brother—and his wife—are spending money they don't have. I fear they are not saving for a time of lesser prosperity."

"Wolfie has never been good at saving for a rainy day."

"To him all days should be sunny or not allowed."

"Being an optimist can be a good thing," I said.

"But being a realist is more prudent."

Neither prudence nor being realistic was my brother's strong point.

Papa tented his fingers and rested them against his lips. "In addition, your brother's word cannot always be trusted."

"How so?"

Papa shook his head. "His ways are boisterous and wild, his hours eccentric, his company is questionable, and his road skirts the path of destruction."

303

"I'm so sorry," I said. And I was.

Suddenly Papa sat forward, his face transformed by a smile. "Besides, I cannot leave Salzburg. I want to be here for you. And be here for the birth of your child."

In seconds I was out of my chair, kneeling beside him, wrapping my arms around his neck. "Oh, Papa! Thank you. Thank you."

"Goodness, child. I never realized it would mean so much to you."

I sat back to see his face. "It does, Papa. I need you. The baby needs you."

He wiped away one of my unexpected tears with his thumb. "There, there, girl. I am not going anywhere. I promise."

I returned to my chair, my heart lighter for his vow.

"In fact . . ." Papa began. "Concerning the birth of your child . . . I want to be present for that blessed event."

"I would love to have you there."

Papa shook his head. "Not there. Here. I want you here in Salzburg for the birth."

I liked the sound of that. But . . . "Johann will never agree."

"He must. He's lost two wives during childbirth in St. Gilgen. I will insist you be here, in this house, where medical help is readily available. How can he argue?"

Indeed.

Papa stood. "In fact, I will talk to him this evening. We must get it settled before you return home." He looked down at me. "Or would *you* rather talk to your husband?"

"No, no, Papa. You do it. I would be greatly relieved if you did."

"Then it's settled."

I breathed easier. Papa would take care of everything.

～

On July 27, 1785, my son Leopold Alois Panteleon was born—on St. Panteleon's Day—at eleven fifty-five in the morning. By five, Papa had taken him to be christened and had become his godfather.

Johann was not present for the birth. He was too busy. But in the five weeks I stayed in my father's house, he and the children did come visit. The oldest four children looked at Leopoldl warily, for they had been through this before: another stepmother having her own child. I could almost see their minds race with questions of how this would change things. As for little Karl . . . I swore I could see a plan brewing as to how he might see if his new little brother would float in the lake. At age three we had already had to fish Karl out several times, once finding him on the point of death. The boy needed constant watching.

"Do we get to keep him?" little Johann asked.

Maria swatted him on the side of the head. "We can't very well put him back, can we?"

"But where will he sleep?" Wolfgang asked. "I don't want to share a—"

"Actually, that's something I need to talk to your father about." I risked a look at Johann.

Papa turned to Therese. "Therese, please take the children out. Perhaps to the square."

I pitied anyone who had gone to the square for a quiet moment because it would soon be shattered by the running, yelling, and hitting presence of my children.

I longed to take Papa's hand, to feel his strong support in what was about to be discussed, but instead took solace in cradling dear Leopoldl.

"What's all this about?" Johann asked.

"It's about our son," I said, stroking the baby's cheek with a finger. "It's about his future."

"It's about his education, his well-being, and the complete fulfillment of his potential."

Johann backed away from both of us, his head shaking no. "You two are plotting something. . . ."

"Not plot—" I said.

"Plotting is too strong a word, son-in-law. Preparing, strategizing, anticipating. These are what need to be done in order for our little Leopoldl to thrive."

Johann looked at Papa, then at me, then at Papa again. "I suppose I have no choice but to listen."

As much as I was glad for Papa's presence, I had to be the one to say it. "I want Leopoldl to stay here with Papa."

Johann stared at me as if he had not heard. Then he blinked. "Stay? Here?"

"Exactly," Papa said. "Nannerl has her hands full in St. Gilgen with the other children and the household. And you yourself must admit that the opportunities for a proper education are very limited there. As a university graduate you share my own love of knowledge."

Johann shared no such love. . . .

"You could visit as often as you'd like, and after the boy gets older, I would come to visit you. Plus . . ." Papa approached the baby and curled the boy's tiny fingers around one of his own. "Do you see these long fingers? These are the fingers of a musician." He kissed his namesake's hand, then stood. "I will fill the boy's life with music, just as I did with my own two children. And with my help and guidance, another prodigy can be molded."

"Maybe he won't like music."

Papa looked shocked. "Of course he'll like music. If a child is exposed to the good earth, he comes to love the good earth. If he is exposed to the process of numbers, he becomes good with numbers. And if he is exposed to music, he loves music." He spread his arms as if there were no argument. "It is a proven fact."

I did not know if Papa spoke the truth but I appreciated his argument. Johann was a man of facts, not emotion.

But then for good measure, Papa added a bit of emotion too. "Besides, you will be doing me a favor. I am alone here. My pupils are few. My job is not as fulfilling as it once was. I need a reason to live and enjoy life again. Little Leopoldl can be that reason." Then he switched back to facts. "I will, of course, cover all his expenses."

Johann looked dumbstruck, as if he had no defense. He finally looked to me. "You agree to all this? You would be willing to leave your baby behind?"

With difficulty I swallowed. "I would. For his own good I would do anything."

"And you think this is for his own good?" Johann asked.

My voice cracked. "I know it."

Johann took a deep breath and let it out slowly. "I cannot believe what I have just heard. Nor can I believe that I am going to agree with it."

We shared the silence, waiting, hoping. . . .

"But you are?" I asked.

"I am."

Papa rushed forward and shook his hand. "You will not be sorry, Johann. This *is* for the best."

I agreed. But I held my baby closer. How could I ever let him go?

～

"Nannerl, you must let go."

Papa stood before me, his arms extended, waiting for me to give up my son.

I knew this was the right decision. I'd thought long and hard about it; I'd prayed about it. But for the time to be now . . . *Too soon, too soon.*

Johann stepped forward, his face a storm cloud. "Nannerl! We have to go. I must be back at work tomorrow. The children are already in the carriage."

I looked at the carriage, which was rocking wildly. I did not want to enter its domain and endure six hours of bedlam. I wished to stay here and lie on my old bed with my baby cooing and kicking beside me. I'd sing him the songs Mama had sung to me. I'd be the one at his side when he pressed his first ivory key on the pianoforte. I'd see his face light up as he realized the cause and effect of his action. *See, my love? That's music. And it can be yours. It will be yours.*

Karl screamed. Maria popped her head out of the carriage. "Mama! Karl bit Wolfgang. Please come help."

Mother. Help. These other children—my other children— needed me. They had never been offered the opportunity of a life full of learning, music, caring friends, and social graces. They were living the consequences of such deficiencies. Perhaps with continued hard work I could break through their pasts and give them some semblance of a good future.

Perhaps.

But in order to do that, and in order to assure this new child received the best the world could offer, I had to give him up. Like the two women arguing over the same baby in front of King

Solomon, I had to prove myself the true mother by being willing to give him up for his own good. I had to love him more than myself.

I squeezed my eyes shut against the tears, kissed his tiny head, and handed him to my father. "Love him for me, Papa."

I hurried to the carriage and climbed inside.

For his own good. For his own good. For his own good.

∼

I read the letter from Papa, then sucked in a breath. "He's sick! Leopoldl is sick!"

Johann looked up from his reading. "Apparently your father's care is not superior to ours after all."

My defenses rose into what had become a familiar position. "He says it's thrush. He has the doctor coming over twice a day. He's sparing no expense."

Johann turned the page.

I brought the letter to him and placed it on top of his book. "Look. See the steps he's taking to make our son well again?"

Johann offered the letter the most cursory glance before handing it back to me. "Then you have no worries."

"Of course I have worries! Leopoldl could die. Papa can only do so much. He is not God."

For the first time my husband offered me his full attention. He removed his reading glasses. "I know that, and you know that. But perhaps it is time he knows that."

"This is not the time to discuss your opinion of my father."

"Who has plenty of his own opinions about himself and everything else."

I was weary of our frequent arguing. "I want to see him," I said. With slow deliberation Johann shook his head and pointed at the window, at the snow blowing outside. I wasn't going anywhere.

I heard a crash from the boys' room. Karl screamed. He always screamed.

Johann put his glasses back on and went back to his reading.

I left the room to attend to some of my children while worrying about the other. I managed a prayer in the process. Only God could help my son.

Only God and Papa.

I was sick to death of sickness.

Only through the tireless efforts of my father was my baby boy treated to the best science had to offer. And the best a grandparent had to offer. Papa, unlike a lot of men I knew, did not shun sick-rooms but availed himself completely of the entire process—from doctor to treatment to prayer. Barring none of the expense. Perhaps this was done because he still harbored regrets about the lack of treatment that had led to Mama's passing.

I received added comfort knowing that dear Franz was paying daily visits to the house, checking on my boy. Papa said he'd taken a large interest in Leopoldl, and the baby knew him and responded to his presence with joy.

Knowing that the two most important men in my life were car-ing for my little man made it possible for me to remain in St. Gilgen. If there would have been any doubt as to the care my dear son was receiving, I would have dug a tunnel through the snow-clogged pass to get to him.

Not that I was well myself. Since Leopoldl's birth, my womanly system had not returned to normal. I felt pressure in my chest and often suffered flashes of heat that overwhelmed my body. I feared getting a feverish illness like that which had killed Mama. And though Johann brushed aside my symptoms as trivial, I knew things weren't right. I also knew that treating any sickness at an early stage was vital.

Only Papa listened to my travails and sent advice from Salzburg doctors. They gave me a detailed regimen of foods that would not increase the heat of my body, self-tests regarding the color of my urine, and prescribed medicines, bloodletting, and exercises to be undertaken at very specific times.

I feared I was pregnant. I prayed for such a blessing—eventu-ally—but also prayed that God would be merciful in His timing. Not now, please. Not now.

And then Papa got sick. Although he'd suffered the usual aches and pains that were the normal accompaniment to a man of sixty-seven years, when one of his good friends died after a short illness that the doctors had proclaimed was "nothing serious," Papa's letters became peppered with complaints of chest pains and pounding in his ears, as well as details regarding his preparations to meet God. His goal was to die well and at peace. In short, he did not want to spend his remaining time worried about debts and Wolfie.

But how could he help it? Doctors and medicines cost money, and the two extra servants he'd hired to help take care of my son cost more money. To top off his worries, Wolfie seemed unconcerned and offered no help whatsoever. Although at Eastertime of the previous year Papa had declared that Wolfie had two thousand florins in his possession, it was apparent by my brother's infrequent letters that he had none of that treasure now. The news from acquaintances was that Wolfie and Constanze were currently moving into more economical accommodations.

Yet he *was* still celebrating some musical success. We'd heard his opera *Le Nozze di Figaro*—*The Marriage of Figaro* had been acclaimed in Prague, and he had another commission for one called *Don Giovanni*. But it was also clear that whatever florins touched my brother's upraised palms were quickly tossed to the wind of past debts. And future ones too.

And then there was talk from Wolfie about leaving Vienna and going to England. The grass was always greener. . . . Papa was totally against it and detailed a dozen reasons why Wolfie should stay put and capitalize on the contacts he'd made in Vienna. Besides, according to Papa, to undertake such a journey, Wolfie should have those two thousand florins in his pocket for expenses.

All this to say, Wolfie had all but forgotten us. Since he'd left us to go to Vienna five years earlier he had not sent a single florin our way—in spite of his lofty words to do otherwise. It was hurtful after all Papa had done for him. I was married now. I was secure—at least financially—but I feared for Papa's worries and how they affected his health. The fact Papa took some money from my husband revealed much about the true state of his affairs.

I offered to take Leopoldl from his care to ease his burden, but he would hear none of it. The boy was the one light in his dim life.

How could I possibly take that away from him?

And then our little Joseph got sick with a falling sickness. He'd suddenly collapse and gyrate horribly. Then the oldest boy, Wolfgang, got sick, and his joints swelled and ached so he could not flex them. The only ray of hope in this aura of dismay was that Maria unexpectedly revealed an aptitude for caring for the sick. Perhaps book learning wasn't everything. . . . I don't know what I would have done without her.

In mid-March she would be sorely tested, because I left her behind in order to make a trip to be with Papa. His health had deteriorated, and I could not in good conscience stay away. So when the sunny spring days led to an opening in the pass, I left St. Gilgen and made my way to Salzburg.

Papa was very ill. He had swollen feet that prevented him from taking care of his namesake, and he had inner pain that the doctor was treating with a plaster. When I first walked in the room, he looked up at me, all thin and pale, and said, "You came."

It was then I knew the pain of his physical illness was only part of the problem.

I immediately set to work helping and comforting as I could. The fact I was also in the presence of my dear baby boy . . . He was twenty months old. Although Papa had kept me abreast of his progress through letters, I had seen him only a few times since his birth. I blame Johann for the dearth in visits. He always had some excuse as to why we couldn't go. Papa had sent me many a scathing letter regarding my husband's overblown sense of worth. As if St. Gilgen couldn't get along without him so he could go visit his son. . . .

Leopoldl was a cheery toddler. A busy toddler. If only he would have let me hold him for more than a few seconds at a time. I hoped his hesitance was due to his age and not the fact he did not know me. He spoke a few words I could understand—and many that I couldn't. He loved playing with his toy horses and would sing to music. Leopoldl often sat on Papa's knee at the keyboard, and Papa would let him explore the keys—but he would not let him pound. Papa was already teaching him to treat the keys with the respect they deserved.

During the evening of the first day I was home I had the most pleasant surprise. Franz stopped by for his daily visit. At the sight of him, Leopoldl raced across the room and Franz scooped him up in his arms, kissing his cheeks and making him giggle. The happy scene made my heart ache for the lack of such scenes in my St. Gilgen household.

Only after the baby was settled onto his hip did Franz look in my direction. He removed his hat and bowed with flourish. "Welcome, Nan. How we have longed for your company."

We exchanged kisses to our cheeks. His were flushed with pleasure and health. I feared for my own appearance. Life had been hard of late. . . .

"Kiss your mother's hand, little Leo."

At Franz's direction, I held out my hand and Leopoldl gave it a slobbery kiss.

"He's going to be a lady's man," Franz said. "A blue-eyed charmer."

"Like his uncle Franz?" I asked.

Franz's eyes met mine, then looked back to the baby. "I'm afraid I have neither the time, the inclination, nor the capability of spirit for such things. A heart once given . . . that's all I have within me."

I didn't know what to say. I'd wanted Franz to find someone to love, but I also reveled in the news he was still single. Oh, the sins of a greedy heart.

The bells for Ave Maria sounded outside, and at their ringing my dear baby closed his eyes, bowed his head, and placed his hands in the position of prayer. Franz did the same, and the momentary sight of their two bowed heads, just inches away from each—

"Amen," Franz said, looking up.

"Am-m," Leopoldl said.

Franz gave him a hug. "You are such a good boy." He let him down, and Leopoldl tried to run out of the room but ended up in the arms of his nursemaid.

"Bedtime, young master."

"No!" Leopoldl's head shook with a vehemence that made his curls bounce and swing.

"He seems to have learned that word well," I said.

"Very well indeed" came Papa's voice from the hall. He stood in his dressing gown and slippers.

"Should you be out of bed?" I asked.

His next words were said to me, but his eyes were locked on my son. As was his smile. "I have no choice. For who else can get this little munchkin into bed but his grandpapa?" With arms extended, he took a step toward the boy, who squealed and ran behind Franz's legs.

"Oh no you don't, little one," Franz said, plucking him up and placing him in Papa's arms. Leopoldl immediately strained for Franz to save him, his eyes and whiny voice doing a good job of melting my defenses. I was all for letting him stay up.

But Papa and Franz obviously had the process perfected. Franz picked up his hat. "I must go or you-know-who will never succumb to b-e-d."

"Uhh-uhh!" Leopoldl said.

Franz kissed his fingers and blew the boy a final kiss. "Tomorrow, little one. I'll come earlier tomorrow and we'll play with your blocks." With a bow Franz said, "I'll see myself out."

When I turned around, Papa had already taken Leopoldl to his room. At the sounds of their laughter, I hung back in the hall and peeked around the doorframe. With the groan of old muscles, Papa climbed into my son's small bed and pretended to curl up to sleep. Leopoldl said, "No, Gampa! Mine!" and pushed at him, easing my father out of the bed while climbing in himself.

"I have you now!" Papa said, tucking the covers around the boy. He pointed to his cheek. "Kiss."

Leopoldl complied, his tiny arms wrapping around my father's neck.

"Good night, dear boy."

"Ni-ni."

Papa came into the hall carrying the candle. He adjusted the door so it would remain ajar.

"He loves you very much," I whispered.

"As I do him." Papa put a hand to his chest, his breathing heavy. "Now help this old boy back to *his* bed, will you, daughter?"

I tucked my father in, checked on my son once more, and made my way to my old bedchamber. The silence that encased me there was like a heavenly cloud. Yet as I got ready for bed, my mind focused on the memory of another sound, just as heavenly.

The sound of loving laughter. Oh, how I'd missed it.

~

I stayed with Papa and Leopoldl two months, and though Papa was ill, I enjoyed my visit immensely. It didn't take but a day for my son to get used to me, and soon he was running into my arms just as he did with Papa and Franz. I even taught him to find middle C on the keyboard by rewarding him with bites of a biscuit. Every time he'd get it right we'd laugh and clap, and he'd snap the bite in his mouth, then grin, revealing two rows of lovely baby teeth.

It nearly killed me leaving him behind. Papa too. But I'd received word that I was needed at home. The children were running wild without me, and by the tone of Johann's letter, I knew my stay in Salzburg had strained him. And a strained Johann was not a pretty sight. Or experience. A crudely written *Come home, Mamma* from Maria at the bottom of Johann's letter was like a plea across the mountains. For certainly in my absence, she was taking the brunt of *my* responsibility. I had to save her. And save them from themselves.

I thought about taking Leopoldl with me. Although the basic conditions in St. Gilgen had not changed, with Maria's slow metamorphosis into a capable helper, I probably could have handled him along with the others. Yet I knew if I removed him from my father's house, Papa would suffer. The joy the baby brought him was immeasurable. Removing that joy—along with my own comforting presence—might cause Papa to give up his fight against the illnesses that plagued him.

The first time I'd left my son, I'd done it for his sake. This second time, I did it for the sake of my father.

Oh, the burdens of conscience.

~

Monica did a quick curtsy. "Ma'am? There's a messenger at the door."

I looked up from my desk. "Is it the post? I'm not done with the letter to my father as yet."

"No, Frau Berchtold. It's not the postman. It's another."

I ran a hand over my hair and rose to greet him in the entrance hall. He was a small man, his clothes dusty.

"I'm Frau Berchtold," I said.

He handed me a letter. "I was told to give this to you, and only you. In person," he said. "Captain d'Ippold sent me."

I let go of the letter as if it were hot. *No. No. No.*

The man retrieved it for me. "Ma'am? He said I should wait for a reply."

I had no choice but to read it right there, right then. But I sensed what it would say. Why else would Franz send a special messenger?

Little Karl ran into the room. "Mama, I'm hun—"

Monica shushed him and pulled him under her arm.

My hands shook as I broke the seal.

> *Your father died this morning at six.*
> *I am so sorry, dear Nan. I am with Leopoldl. Please come.*
> > *Yours,*
> > *Franz*

My legs buckled and I sank to the floor.

"Mama!"

I was helped to a chair, but I knew it would collapse under the weight of my heart.

"Karl, go get your mama some water." Monica's hands fluttered around me like butterflies wanting to light. "What is it, ma'am?"

I shook my head. I could not say the words. I gathered a breath and looked at the messenger. "Tell Captain d'Ippold I'm coming." I stood. "I'm coming."

~

The carriage jostled along the mountain road, and I let the movement take me captive. Left, forward, a jar to the right. Center again. There was no need to try to maintain balance anymore. Not when the core of my balance was gone forever.

"I really wish you'd talk to me, Nannerl," Johann said from his seat across from me.

I made no move to answer through words or even a shake of my head. That this man who rarely had time for any conversation wanted to chat was absurd. You reap what you sow. *Silence you gave me; I give you silence in return.*

In truth, my motives were not so clearly defined. Although in some pocket of my existence I found satisfaction in the fact that I was the one shunning my husband's attempts to connect, it was not the main reason for my refusal to speak.

I did not speak because there were no words. No words in German, French, Italian, English, Latin, or even in prayer that could express the utter ache that gripped my entire being.

Papa . . .

Suddenly, without warning, the grip eased enough for me to grab a breath and let out a wretched wail that enveloped the carriage.

Appalled, Johann sat back against his seat, obviously willing to leave me alone.

Which I was. Completely and utterly.

~

Men.

What did I care about the will, and debts to be paid, and who got Papa's blue satin suit? Papa died on May twenty-eighth, in the year of our Lord 1787, and was buried at St. Sebastian's on May twenty-ninth before Johann and I could even get there. But we had a lovely memorial service for him on May thirty-first at nine o'clock in the morning, and at noon the will was read. During all those days the house was busy with officials taking an inventory, collecting a list of debts, as well as friends expressing their condolences.

I shook hands, accepted hugs, and responded with all the right words, while what I really wanted to do was curl up in my old room and—

I had a better idea. I left the officials, Johann, and Franz arguing over money and possessions, and slipped into my father's room. I cracked the door and stood in the afternoon light. The bed had been stripped of its covers, but there was still an indentation in the mattress indicating my father's favorite place to sleep. On the bedside table were his glasses, a pewter goblet, a pocket watch he'd gotten long ago in London, and a candle. Across the room was the old wardrobe. I pulled open the double doors and ran my hands over the sleeves of the waistcoats. Here was the gray one he'd worn at our wedding. Stuffed toward the back was a red-and-gold suit he'd had made in Paris on our Grand Tour. I pulled it out and noted the smaller size. Papa had gained weight in his old age. I lovingly returned it to its place. The next piece of clothing that gained my attention was his dressing gown. The heavy green brocade was worn at the elbows and cuffs. How many times had I seen him in this gown?

I put it to my face intending to rub its softness against my cheek. But instead I found myself inhaling his scent. I was hesitant to exhale and did so only to inhale again. Musty, spicy, warm . . . it was all I had left of him yet was worth more than anything else listed in the inventory.

I clutched the dressing gown to my chest and stumbled to the chair by the window. I had to move one of Leopoldl's toy horses from the seat, and sank onto the cushion, clutching the toy in my free hand. How could I live without him? How could my son live?

I heard the sound of tiny footsteps, then silence. A few seconds later the door slowly edged open and little Leopoldl peered inside.

"Gampa?"

No. Grandpapa was gone.

I managed a smile and held out my arms to him. He ran to me and, spotting his toy, took it happily. He started to climb into my lap, so I moved the dressing gown to make room. Once settled, he patted the green fabric and said, "Gampa."

I nodded and opened the dressing gown wide. Then I draped it over us both, shrouding us in its meager comfort.

⁓

"Face it, Nannerl," Johann said, back in our home in St. Gilgen. "Your brother does not want any of your father's possessions. He just wants cash."

I shook my head and glanced over at ten-year-old Joseph as he helped Leopoldl build a tower with blocks. Maria, Joseph, and Karl were also accepting their little brother quite well. Unfortunately, our Wolfgang was still ill and had had little chance to spend time with his new brother. His joint sickness caused him much pain.

"But it doesn't make sense," I said, turning my thoughts back to the other Wolfgang in my life. "When he and Constanze visited Salzburg, Constanze made a point of asking Papa for some of Wolfie's childhood souvenirs."

"Did Leopold give her some?"

"No."

"Why not?"

"He didn't think they'd take care of them."

"And perhaps they wouldn't have. Perhaps your brother's disinterest in your father's possessions proves your father right."

"Or perhaps Wolfie's debt is forcing him to override sentiment."

Johann shrugged and sharpened a quill with a knife. "Yet perhaps it would do you well to take fewer of your father's *things* and bring *us* some cash."

I shook my head vehemently. "I can't do that. All his life Papa stressed legacy. Why else would he have urged us to keep the family letters? I have done my best to keep every one."

"Do you really think your brother has done the same?"

I did not. Wolfie lived in the moment and gave little care for the past—or the future.

Johann set the quill down. "Do as you wish, Nannerl. It is not my decision. Our marriage contract specifically states that any monies received from our families will remain our individual property. I will honor that."

I knew he would. For despite my husband's penny-pinching ways, he was an honorable man.

With Papa's passing, and the physical and often emotional distance between Wolfie's life and my own, Johann was all the male family I had left.

Johann and my dear son . . .

Would they be enough?

Chapter Seventeen

Growing older and wiser . . .

Blessings and trials will do that to a person. Age them. And make them wise.

If they are not broken first.

Just weeks after Papa's passing, our boy Wolfgang passed away. He was in his thirteenth year. Dear Maria took it the hardest. She'd tried so hard to make him better.

So once again I had five children in St. Gilgen.

After these deaths, I spent many months veering off course, as if my life had no rudder. How sad that only death makes us see how invaluable we are to one another. Death minimizes faults and petty discord. It mocks us: *Go ahead and complain about one another. I'll get my due soon enough. . . .*

Papa had been my advisor, my encourager, and my organizer. He'd been my greatest supporter yet my harshest critic. I'd trusted him and had known he loved me and would die for me without regret or hesitation. Yet perhaps the greatest lesson I'd learned from Papa was how to approach life. For by watching him adapt, plan, and handle victory as well as defeat, I'd learned that the best way to deal with problems was to attack them one step at a time while trusting in God's providence and care. It became an invaluable process I heartily tried to employ.

A process I wished Wolfie would have learned. My biggest

regret upon Papa's passing was not for myself and Papa but for my brother. I knew Wolfie was busy. I knew he'd often chafed at Papa's advice—even if it did prove wise. And I also knew my brother was different from Papa and me. He dwelt in a place where it was imperative for his mind to be able to roam free and unencumbered. The fact he didn't know how to suspend that abandon in order to deal with the logistics of day-to-day living is what had disturbed Papa the most. And me.

But then something happened that was almost ironic in its timing. Just six months after Papa died, after having freelanced in Vienna for six years, Wolfie was finally offered a permanent position. Christoph Gluck, the Imperial and Royal Chamber Composer for Emperor Joseph, died. And though Gluck had been paid two thousand florins a year and Wolfie was only offered eight hundred, it was still a position. I just hoped Wolfie's debts and spending habits would not swallow the florins before they could land.

Yet Papa would have been proud, and the salaried position gave me hope that Wolfie would be all right. Plus, the timing was excellent because his wife, Constanze, was expecting their fourth child. Unfortunately only one had lived. Risky business, childbearing.

I tried to keep in touch with Wolfie, but his letters were few, yet he *did* usually remember my name day. And though he always sounded genuinely pleased at my effort to reach him and begged for many, many more letters, he also matter-of-factly warned me that his responses would not increase. Whether due to busyness or his lifelong dislike for letter writing, it was a fact I learned to accept.

In truth, we had grown apart because we lived worlds apart. Wolfie lived in a world of his own choosing in Vienna, and I lived in a world of my own choosing in St. Gilgen.

And indeed, it *was* a world of my own choosing.

At the beginning I had voiced many complaints about life in St. Gilgen. Most were valid. I had even gone so far as to resist being happy there. As long as Papa was the tether that held me connected to Salzburg, I never allowed myself to see St. Gilgen as my true home. In short, his death forced me to grow up. Until his passing I had no real reason to discover the real Nannerl Mozart Berchtold. I was always first and foremost Papa's daughter and Wolfie's sister. And though now I was someone's wife and someone's mother, I was also just me. And the odd consequence of this attitude was that the stronger I became in myself, the stronger the children became.

There were more children added to our family. Nearly two years after Papa's death, at midnight between March twenty-second and March twenty-third, 1789, I bore a daughter. My husband named her Johanna after himself, but everyone always called her Jeanette—the name of Johann's second wife. Some thought this odd. Yet somehow I'd always felt a kinship with that woman, for she too had been brought into a family of many children, had added one of her own, only to die in her attempt to bring a second child to life.

No matter what she was called, the other children welcomed Jeanette into the household, especially dear Maria, who said upon her birth, "We needed another girl around here!" It was Maria who took her new sister to be christened on her very first day of life.

Yet amidst our joy was tragedy. Twenty months after Jeanette's birth, in November 1790, I bore another daughter, Babette. But this dear baby did not live past her fifth month and died of the same intestinal complications that had claimed Wolfie's firstborn. We buried her next to her older brother, little Wolfgang.

Birth, death, day, night. Life went on. And I with it.

Yet it seemed that once I allowed myself to *be* in St. Gilgen body and soul, the conditions of our family improved. Eventually, I even got Johann to agree to send the three oldest boys to Salzburg for a proper education. Elated at my triumph, I personally brought them to the school, got them settled, and kissed them good-bye with all my hopes and prayers they would thrive and prosper in the atmosphere of learning.

The next morning, before heading back to St. Gilgen, I capped off the victorious trip by having coffee with Franz. He was still a very good friend.

"You should be very proud of what you've accomplished, Nan," he said as we waited for our rolls.

I knew he meant the boys. My cheeks were still warm with pride from seeing them off. "They have come *so* far. All of them have. You should see how Maria has grown into a fine young woman."

He smiled. "The dirty face is gone?"

"Scrubbed and shining. You know what she told me the other day when I gave her a compliment on how far she'd progressed? She said she'd changed because she'd wanted to become a lady . . ." My throat tightened. "A lady just like me."

"She could have no higher aspiration."

I felt myself blush. "Now she is the one who gets after Jeanette and Leopoldl for *their* dirty faces."

He laughed, then let his smile turn wistful. "How I miss that boy."

I slapped a hand to my forehead. "Of course! I should have brought him with me so you . . . I was just so consumed with making sure the other three had their things and——"

He raised a hand, stopping my defense. "It's fine, Nan. You have more to think about than an old schoolteacher."

He *was* looking rather old of late. "I will always think of you, Franz. You have been a dear friend for ever so long."

He took my hand across the table, squeezed it quickly, then let it go. "For ever so long," he said.

After coffee we parted. Walking in opposite directions, I paused to watch him go. My romantic side would have had him turn so we could exchange a final smile.

But he did not. And so I watched him disappear around the corner and continued on my way. On my way home.

∾

As a child I always thought the milestones of life would come with some notion of premonition—that you would *feel* their presence looming, that on the day of their declaration you would feel differently and suspect that something extraordinary was about to occur.

But without all that many years under my sash, I learned this was not so. The extraordinary events that fill a life—both good and bad—slip in the door unannounced, until you look up from what you were doing, and they introduce themselves.

It happened just this way on a cold December morning, 1791.

Quite unexpectedly—and uncharacteristically—Johann appeared in the living quarters in the middle of the afternoon. I looked up from giving Leopoldl his piano lesson and knew immediately by the pulled look on my husband's face and the letter in his hand that it was bad news making a call.

"What is it?" I asked.

Johann looked at the letter, then at me. "A message from the archbishop. News from Vienna. And . . . and . . ."

Vienna? An inner fist grabbed my heart and squeezed. I shook my head against my biggest fear.

Johann let his arm drop, nodded, and looked directly at me. "Your brother is dead."

An odd laugh escaped. "No, don't be silly. He can't be dead. He's only thirty-five."

"He can be. He is dead. And buried. Yesterday, at St. Marx."

Buried already? My mind moved from denial to acceptance. "What did he die of?"

He presented the letter again. "This doesn't say, but the courier heard a rumor that in your brother's final days he ranted about poison and—"

"Poison!"

"It was discounted. His limbs swelled horribly in the end and he had a fever."

I remembered another time, another sickness—also in Vienna—when a six-year-old Wolfie suffered swollen limbs and a fever. The doctor's diagnosis came back to me. "Rheumatic fever."

"Hmm?" Johann said.

"It sounds similar to the rheumatic fever he had as a boy. The doctor had warned there would be recurrences, and it could weaken his heart."

Johann shrugged. It seemed a cold gesture, and yet, what did it really matter how my brother had died? Dead was dead. Gone was gone.

Johann made up for his shrug by pulling me into a hug. "I am very sorry, Nannerl. Very sorry."

I nodded against his chest.

∼

It took three months for the mountain pass to clear enough to get from St. Gilgen to Vienna, but I was persistent. I had to go and see where my brother was buried. Pay my respects. I would not find resolution until I had played this final chord in our duet.

How disappointed I was that the cemetery contained only communal graves. What a horrid law. I always found much comfort visiting Papa's grave in Salzburg, and little Wolfgang's and Babette's in St. Gilgen.

After my dismal and unsatisfactory visit to St. Marx, my carriage stopped in front of the inn. Before the coachman could open the door, it was opened by my husband. He took my hand and helped me out. "We were worried about you."

I looked behind him and saw all six of our children spilling out from the inn's doorway onto the sidewalk. Their faces mirrored their concern. Two-year-old Jeanette broke away from Maria and ran to my side, wrapping her tiny arms around my damp cloak. "Mama!" she said.

I was about to shoo them inside against the rain when I noticed the rain had stopped. Hints of blue sky peeked through the clouds, promising a beautiful spring day.

"Back inside, children," Johann said. "Let your mother get out of her damp clothes."

They fumbled and stumbled into the inn, and Johann led me upstairs to our room. The children assembled on the beds and window seat while I removed my cloak. They were being unusually quiet.

"Oooh," I shivered. "It was very chilly out there."

"Did you see your brother?" nine-year-old Karl asked.

Joseph smacked him in the arm. "Uncle Wolfgang is dead. She didn't go to *see* him."

Maria sighed heavily and pulled both boys under her arms. "Shush. Both of you. She'll tell us when she's ready."

When Johann pointed at a chair, the younger Johann relinquished it. I sat and the children gathered close. Jeanette climbed onto my lap and I relished her warmth. "I went to the cemetery," I began. "But there was no headstone for my brother."

"Whyever not?" Maria asked.

I explained about Emperor Joseph's law.

"That's ridiculous," Johann said. "We don't do that in St. Gilgen."

"Perhaps that is one advantage to being remote."

I noticed Karl's pout. "So you didn't *see* him? See anything?"

I flicked the tip of his nose, then put my hand to my temple. "I see him in here." Then to my heart. "And in here."

Six-year-old Leopoldl tugged on his father's coat. "Can we get cake now? I'm hungry."

"It's up to your mother," Johann said.

I sighed and released my morning in the cemetery to the past. "I think I'm hungry too."

The children gathered their coats and rushed toward the door in a burst of commotion, then moved out in the hall and loudly clomped down the stairs. My husband was next but paused at the door. "How are you really?"

"I'll be fine. I'm glad I came."

"Good," he said. "Coming?"

"I'll be down in a minute."

He closed the door and the room returned to silence. I let my body relax against the chair and closed my eyes.

Suddenly, unannounced, I heard Franz's words in my ears, his comment made over coffee months before. *"You should be very proud of what you've accomplished."*

And I was.

Seven years previously I'd traveled to St. Gilgen to find a household of wild, unkempt, ignorant hellions. Since then they'd been transformed into good, fine, and vibrant children who were ready to accept the opportunities life had to offer.

Opportunities they had because of me. Opportunities they would *not* have had if I had not become their mother. I let the thought complete itself: the children were better off because of me.

Although my marriage to Johann had been undertaken as a careful, pragmatic decision, I suddenly realized God's hand had not been absent in the match. Perhaps Johann and I weren't the great love of each other's lives, but over the years we'd settled into a good place, a comfortable, compatible place. So what if my own idealistic notion of romance and true love had not been fed? The fact that my decision to marry this twice-widowed man had allowed his children— our children—to receive a chance to prosper and find fulfillment, added meaning to my decision that went far beyond the need for rosy sunsets and soft kisses.

No, I had not become famous like my brother. No, I had not pursued my music as much as I would have liked. And no, I had not married the love of my life. Yet by marrying as I did, I had changed five children's lives for the better. If I accomplished nothing more than that, I could be proud.

How comforting to realize God knows what He's doing.

I stood and gathered my damp cloak. My family was waiting.

CODA

I can't see anymore.

It doesn't matter.

What do I want to see of this life? Whether my eyes are opened or closed, I see what I want to see. My memories are vivid—and perfect. Eyes see flaws that memories can avoid. The advantage of going blind is that with eyes open or shut, I see *them*.

Three men and a woman. Waiting for me. "Don't worry, Nannerl. I've made all the arrangements," Papa says.

"Come join us, Horseface. The music's magnificent here."

I look to Mama, but she doesn't say anything. She's never been much of a talker. Perhaps the rest of us make her talking unnecessary. Or too much work. She just smiles and holds out a hand. I understand her meaning, just as I do the others'.

Then there is the third man. He doesn't need to talk either. Our eyes meet and do the talking for us. His smile makes me smile. And the way he scuffs his toe against the ground indicates intentions far more eloquent and fine than any book of lofty sentences. I realize it is he I long to see the most. For it is he I have waited for the longest.

"Baroness?"

By the tone of the voice it is evident it is not the first time the speaker has called for my attention. Reluctantly I allow myself to be yanked away from the others. I will be with them soon enough. As yet, there *is* one more thing I have to do. . . .

I open my eyes for his benefit, not mine. I recognize his voice. It is Herr Masters—my counselor and attorney. At seeing me alive, I hear his sigh of relief. He rustles papers and I guess their purpose. "Is that it?" I ask.

"It is. It's complete—except for your signature."

I nod. Soon everything will be as it should be—or as good as it can be, considering. "Read it to me."

He does, and I feel myself relax amid the pain. On the cross Jesus had said, "It is finished. . . ."

Soon, it will be.

"Get me a pen," I say. I point toward the desk.

Within a few moments, he returns to the bedside. I feel a tray on my lap. The papers are upon it. "Show me where," I say.

He guides my hand and, once in place, he puts the ink-loaded pen in my fingers. "Here. Sign here," he says.

It is odd to hear my signature, to hear pen scratch against paper without seeing it. How appropriate that in this last important act, I have to rely on my sense of hearing—that sense that has been so inseparable from my innermost being.

I sign my full name in all its ridiculous glory: Baroness Maria Anna Walburga Ignatia Berchtold zu Sonnenburg. But then . . . "May I also sign another name?"

"Another—?"

"I wish the name of Mozart to be on this page."

"Ahh. Certainly." For a second time he positions my hand and I sign *Nannerl Mozart*. I hand him the pen. He takes the paper and tray away. "That should satisfy all involved," I say.

"Including yourself?"

I lean back against the pillows. "Me, most of all."

The papers cease their rustling and I assume he's put them away. "I will leave you, then," he says. I hear him step toward the door, but then his footsteps stop. "Or . . . would you like me to stay?"

Although the question can be answered simply and offhandedly, I realize my reply can have serious ramifications. When one's time is short, letting any person leave the room can mean death might be faced alone.

And yet . . . I decline his invitation and he leaves me. I hear the door click shut.

Come what may, there is no one at my side. Mama, Papa, and Wolfie are gone. Franz, Johann, and even my beloved Jeanette are dead. I am seventy-eight years old. There is not a single friend who's lived as long as I. And though I have an occasional visit from my son, Leopoldl, and Wolfie's son—my nephew, Wolfgang—and they treat me with respect, I do not care to call upon such bonds in these final days.

I have no idea why God has allowed me to live so long—to outlive all whom I have loved. There are a lot of questions I hope to ask the Almighty. . . .

Soon.

I am completely alone.

But then the memories flood back as if to remind me that my last thought is a lie.

I am not alone. And in truth, I have never been alone. Although my life has not worked out as I may have planned, although I have enough regrets to fill a bank, there is one thing that *has* worked out.

I've had people. I've had people who've loved me, cared for me, and did their best for me. I had people then.

And I have them now.

Soon.

Now. All I need to do is take Mama's hand, accept Papa's arrangements, join my brother, and let the love of my life take me in his arms.

I close my eyes and, in this final act, willingly surrender to their invitation.

Fine. Grandioso. Bravissimo.

Alleluia.

Near the end of her life, Nannerl Mozart Berchtold made a change to her will regarding her burial arrangements. Instead of being buried in St. Gilgen near her husband and three children, or next to her father in Salzburg at St. Sebastian's, Nannerl chose to be buried across Salzburg, in the smaller, less grand cemetery of St. Peter's monastery. She had no relatives buried there. But she did join a loved one—*the* loved one. The one man whose love had been denied to her in life would rest near her in death: Captain Franz d'Ippold.

Dear Reader:

Why has no one written about Nannerl before?

It was not something I ever dreamed of doing. For until the idea was dropped into my lap I knew as much (or little) about Nannerl as most people: *Oh yes. Mozart had a sister, didn't he? And didn't they perform together as children?*

The event that opened my eyes to Nannerl's life story happened while I was standing in the Mozart family home in Salzburg in the summer of 2004—that little three-room apartment where both Wolfgang and Nannerl were born. In truth, I was only half listening to the guide, being very close to tourist-information overload. Yet one statement reached into my weary brain and ignited it: *Most people don't know this, but Mozart's sister was just as talented as he was, but because she was a woman, she had little chance to do anything with her talent.* That one statement stayed with me all the way home to the States.

At the time I was putting together a proposal for a contemporary novel (I only wrote novels set in the present day). Because of the tour guide's comment, I got the idea to have one of my characters write a book called *Mozart's Sister.* My agent sent the proposal to publishers.

Within days we got a call from Dave Horton, an editor at Bethany House Publishers. "I don't want the contemporary book; I want the book the character is writing: *Mozart's Sister,* a historical book about the sister's life."

"But I don't write historicals."

"I want *Mozart's Sister.*"

"But I don't write in first person, in one person's point of view throughout an entire book. I write big-cast novels in third person."

"I want *Mozart's Sister.*"

"I hate research."

"I want *Mozart's Sister.*"

Well, then. He seemed so sure, so excited. I could not ignore him—actually, I *could,* but I didn't.

The rest is history. And so, as so often happens when God offers us an opportunity and we say yes, it turned out to be the best experience of my writing life. And, irony of ironies, as I sat in my office with four reference books opened before me, I even found that I enjoyed the research. Imagine that.

Lucky for all of us, the Mozarts were avid letter writers, and as per Papa's instructions, most of the correspondence remains. Because of this I was able to use many of their actual words in this book.

But please note: I am not a historian. Although I made every attempt to keep things as factual as possible, I am a writer of fiction. And during the gaps in the knowledge (alas, when they were all home in Salzburg, there were, of course, no letters!) I filled in the gaps using logic, the facts I had, and my imagination. This was done reluctantly. You should have heard my scream when I read that no one really knows why Nannerl and Franz broke off their relationship! A key point to her life was unknown? And so I once again was forced to take the known elements of life in Salzburg (and the relationship the Mozarts had with the archbishop) and create a logical reason for the breakup. Only God and Nannerl know how right (or wrong) I was. Actually, I have hopes that the Almighty is letting Nannerl know that *someone* is telling her story. . . . I hope she is pleased.

But you must know that the liberties I was forced to take were also flavored by my own feelings—my trying to figure out how *I* would have reacted if all this had happened to me. Even though Nannerl and I were born two hundred years apart, worlds apart, I feel we are contemporaries. Human emotions haven't changed that much. For don't we still struggle to gain our parents' approval and respect? Don't we still battle with jealousy and could-have-beens? And don't we still face the crossroads of life, where we are offered a choice to dwell in the past or move forward to the best of our abilities?

That's what I wish for you, the reader. Take Nannerl's story as an impetus to look at your own life and make it the most it can be. You too have a unique, God-given purpose. The trick is to find out what it is.

I would like to thank three Mozart biographers for their insight: Robert W. Gutman, Maynard Solomon, and especially Ruth Halliwell, who wrote an amazing book about the logistics of the Mozart family. I would also like to thank my agent, Janet Kobobel Grant, for urging me to take this leap; Helen Motter, my editor extraordinaire (who also happens to be an accomplished musician); and editor Dave Horton, who saw something hidden in one idea, sparked a new one, and didn't give up.

Bravissimo!
Nancy Moser